# Praise for
# STEPHEN R. LAWHEAD and
# *AVALON*

# AVALON

## The
## Return
## of King
## Arthur

# STEPHEN R. LAWHEAD

**HarperTorch**
*An Imprint of HarperCollinsPublishers*

HARPERTORCH
*An Imprint of* HarperCollins*Publishers*
10 East 53rd Street
New York, New York 10022-5299

Copyright © 1999 by Stephen R. Lawhead
Cover art by Paul Stinson
ISBN: 0-380-80297-X

First HarperTorch paperback printing: December 2000
First Avon Books hardcover printing: September 1999

HarperCollins®, HarperTorch™, and ♦™ are trademarks of HarperCollins Publishers Inc.

Printed in the United States of America

Visit HarperTorch on the World Wide Web at
www.harpercollins.com

10  9  8  7  6  5  4  3

The Britons believe yet that Arthur is alive, and dwelleth in Avalun with the fairest of all elves; and the Britons ever yet expect when Arthur shall return. Was never the man born, of ever any lady chosen, that knoweth of the sooth, to say more of Arthur. But whilom was a sage hight Merlin; he said with words— his sayings were sooth—that an Arthur should yet come to help the English.
—LAYMON, *BRUT* (CA. 1190)

Yet some men say in many parts of England that King Arthur is not dead, but had by the will of our Lord Jesu into another place; and men say that he shall come again, and he shall win the Holy Cross. I will not say that is shall be so, but rather I will say: here in this world he changed his life. And many men say that there is written upon his tomb this verse: HIC JACET ARTHURUS, REX QUONDAM, REX FUTURUS (Here lies Arthur, king once and king to be).
—MALORY, *LE MORTE D'ARTHUR* (CA. 1469)

The throne of Britain shall become an iniquity to the nation, and a reproach to the people, ere Arthur returns. But, when Avallon shall rise again in Llyonesse, and the Thamesis reverse its course, then also shall Arthur take up the kingship of his nation once more.
—ANEIRIN, *THE BLACK BOOK OF ANEIRIN* (CA. 643)

❋

# Prologue

The low red car skidded to a halt on the dusty driveway outside the whitewashed villa. The driver unfolded himself from behind the wheel, stepped out, and cast a lingering, if bleary, glance down the lush hillside at the red tile rooftops and pale-blue swimming pools of Madeira's elite.

Above the quiet tick of the cooling engine and the warm sea breeze rustling the dry palm fronds, Teddy imagined he could almost make out the clink of ice in crystal glasses and the twittering voices of the buffed-and-polished hostesses below as the evening's social fandango began anew.

Reaching back into the car, he withdrew a nearly empty bottle of Jameson's, unscrewed the cap, drained it, and flung the empty bottle into the overgrown garden surrounding the sprawling house. He then turned and walked to the front door and pushed it open. "Cozu!" he shouted as he stumbled into the cool marble-faced foyer.

There came the quick slap of tennis shoes on the stone, and a small, sallow-faced Portuguese man in an oversized white jacket appeared in the arched doorway leading into the rambling interior of the house.

"Good h'evening, sir," replied the manservant in heavily accented English. "I trust sir has had a pleasant day."

"Tolerable, Cozu. Tolerable." Teddy took a lurching step towards the stairway. The servant quickly closed the door behind him. "The sea was a bit rough beyond the point, so we stayed this side of the headland. Anything come for us today?"

"The package you were h'expecting arrived this morning, sir. I have placed it on the desk in your study."

"Brilliant." He shucked off his pale yellow windbreaker and pushed it at his servant. He looked up at the wrought-iron sconces on the stuccoed walls and the scrollwork balustrade along the upper gallery. Overpriced tack, he thought, not that he'd ever noticed before. Then again, he was seeing a lot of things he'd never really seen before. "Any calls?"

"Two phone calls, sir. As requested, I have allowed the machine to answer. Miss Vierta rang to say that she is staying in the town tonight. You are welcome to join her for a late dinner at her apartment."

"And the other?"

"It was the gentleman from the Foreign Office again— most insistent. I left both messages on the answering machine."

Teddy nodded. "I'm going to take a shower." He belched and took hold of the banister as if to haul himself up the stairs hand over hand.

"Will sir be dining out this h'evening?"

"No, sir will not be dining out. Sir is bloody knackered. Have cook send up a tray. Bring me a bottle of champers— something decent for a change." He started plodding up the stairs. "Oh, and bring the package to my room."

"Certainly, sir."

Teddy dragged himself up the curving stairway and paused at the door of his room, listening. How empty the place seemed when Theresa was out. He shrugged and ambled into the spacious, high-ceilinged room, threw off his clothes, and stalked naked into the bathroom where he took a long, hot shower, emerging twenty minutes later in his favorite old white terry cloth bathrobe.

Relaxed and much revived, he drifted back into his bedroom to see that Cozu had already been and gone. His dirty clothes had been removed, and a clean white shirt and khakis were laid out for the evening. The balcony doors were open, and the glass-and-aluminum table prepared with a gleaming white cloth. There was a sweating bucket beside the table, a crystal champagne flute on a tray in the center, and a large parcel wrapped in brown paper to one side.

Padding barefoot onto the balcony, Teddy seized the dark-green bottle from the ice bucket and glanced approvingly at the pale yellow-gold label as he poured his first glass. He collapsed into his chair, propped his feet on the railing, and, raising his glass to the empty air, said, "Here's to Mister Moët and Mister Chandon!" He threw back his head and drank deeply, savoring the icy bite of the bubbles on his tongue. "Ah! Many thanks, chaps."

Tossing down the rest of the glass, he quickly poured another; this one he nursed, watching the last of the sunset as the colors faded into deepening shades of gray and blue out over the bay. The air was warm and perfumed with the sweetly intoxicating scent of wild gardenia. Below him, among the palms and bougainvillaea, the lights of the stylish villas and verandas of Funchal were beginning to glimmer. The diamond-spangled hostesses were, he imagined, wheeling out the hors d'oeuvres and dishing up the first juicy tidbits of what passed for society gossip.

He poured another glass of champagne, and felt the familiar glow rising from stomach to head. "Where has that blasted Cozu got to?" he murmured.

As if in answer to this question, the servant knocked on the door and backed into the room carrying a covered tray. He stepped silently around the table, placed the tray on the table, and made to remove the parcel. "Leave it," said Teddy, whereupon the manservant busied himself with the dishes. "Don't bother," Teddy told him. "I'll help myself when I'm ready."

"Of course, sir." The butler straightened. "Will sir require anything else?"

"No, Cozu, *sir* does not require anything else but to be left bloody alone."

"Very good, sir." The servant inclined his head, bade his employer good night, and departed, pulling the door shut after him.

When he had gone, Teddy took the cover off the tray and

picked up a slice of cold smoked salmon with his fingers. He dangled it above his mouth, dropped it in, and chewed thoughtfully. He slid another slice of salmon onto a triangle of buttered brown bread, took a bite, and washed it down with icy champagne.

Then, taking up the parcel, he walked back into the bedroom, placed it on the bed, and unwrapped it. Under the plain paper was a simple box of white cardboard. Teddy opened the box to see a handsome facsimile of England's royal crown, and a white envelope. Ignoring the envelope, he took the crown out of the box and studied it more closely. The Star of Africa was zirconium, of course, and the crown itself was gold-plated; but the trimming was real ermine, and the red velvet hand sewn. To the untutored eye, it looked for all the world like the real thing. It ought to, he thought, it had cost enough.

Teddy lifted the crown and balanced it on his head. The weight of the piece made his head slightly wobbly—that, and three glasses of champagne. Steadying himself, he picked up his drink and walked to the mirror in the bathroom; he rubbed the steam from the glass with his sleeve, let his robe drop to the floor, then stood back to regard himself.

Beneath the crown was a ruddy-faced, balding man with a receding chin, a bulbous nose, and a wattled neck running to jowls; but his gray eyes looked out from under low, even brows, his teeth were straight, and his skin nicely tanned from many idle days on his boat. Turning sideways he sucked in his stomach and slapped his belly three times with a satisfied grunt. All in all, not bad for fifty-eight years, he decided.

He took another gulp of champagne and sauntered back into the bedroom, pausing at his desk to tap a button on the answering machine. There was a beep; a woman's voice drifted airily into the room. "Teddy, where are you?" she spoke rapidly, her English lightly spiced with a Portuguese lilt. "I haven't seen you for *days,* darling. I meant to come up, but Amanda is in town and I promised to have a drink with her. But do come down, my sweet. We'll have a late supper, just us two. I've got a bottle of your favorite brandy.

Okay?" There came the sound of a doorbell on the tape. "That's Amanda. Gotta run. Kisses. Bye."

"You mean Armando, don't you, love?" He tapped the button again, and another voice came on—a man's voice this time. It greeted him coolly and identified itself as representing the Foreign Office, whereupon Teddy jabbed a second button to cut it off. "Bastards," he muttered; he had heard it all before.

As the machine rearmed its digital memory, Teddy dropped his hand to the center drawer of his desk, pulled it open, and took out a brown wooden box. He wandered back onto the balcony, set the box on the table, and drained his glass. He stood for a time, clutching the empty glass and staring out into the gathering darkness.

Coming to himself once more, he retrieved the bottle from the bucket and ceremoniously emptied the remains of the bottle into his glass, spilling most of it over the tablecloth. He then turned and heaved the empty bottle over the balcony. From the satisfying crash that followed, he guessed he had hit his new Alpha Romeo Spider in the driveway below.

*"C'est la vie,"* he murmured, and sucked at the rim of his overflowing glass.

He sat down heavily, sloshing champagne onto his bare thighs. Setting his glass carefully on the table, he brushed at the liquid and then took up the wooden box and placed it on his knees. He stared at the box for a moment, then opened it and withdrew the small, silver-plated British service revolver.

He hefted the gun in his hand, turned it, and peered at the cylinder to make sure that each chamber contained a bullet. He transferred the revolver to his left hand and took up his glass with the right.

"To England!" he growled, knocking back the champagne in a single gulp. "Bloody England."

He gazed unhappily at the empty glass, then hurled that, too, over the balcony. Reaching up, he straightened his crown. Then, pressing the muzzle of the revolver tightly against his left temple, he gently squeezed the trigger and blew away the right side of his head.

# Part I

※

# One

Even as a child, James could remember feeling that some mysterious power held his fate in strong, infallible hands. Perhaps a youth spent in the Highlands—where ghosts and Fair Folk still haunt the hidden glens, and the quaint predictions of country sages and seers find enthusiastic reception among the locals—had shaped him more than he imagined. Superstition clings to the ancient hills like the gorse and heather, and it would be unusual indeed if an impressionable youngster did not imbibe something of his surroundings.

He did not ask for second sight; he never sought it, but simply accepted it as a feature of his unique being. In time, he learned that not everyone possessed the power of the *fiosachd*—Gaelic for "the knowing." It covers a range of subtle manifestations—some physical, some mental—which most people view as extraordinary. As a child, however, James did not think himself unusual; he merely considered his gift a sign intended to confirm his special existence. Children are self-absorbed creatures, true enough, yet many was the time he had dreamed of greatness. Many was the time he had awakened in the night to the knowledge that his soul was destined for a higher purpose.

Of course, every child entertains similar thoughts of grandeur. Growing up, however, dulls the secret insistence; life's harsher lessons teach us we are *not* so special after all. Sooner or later, we arrive at the cold realization that we will never be the first astronaut to set foot on Mars; we will not be the doctor whose miracle cure rids the world of cancer; we will not win fame and fortune and the eternal adoration of the masses through the wondrous artistry of our writing, singing, or acting.

Despite this—despite *all* evidence to the contrary— James never outgrew his belief that something amazing would happen to him one day. Although he did come to understand the natural limitations of circumstance, and the extreme randomness of opportunity, deep in his inmost being the belief in his own particular destiny doggedly persisted. Like the *fiosachd,* he was born with it, and it never deserted him. He had always known his life would end in one of two ways: triumph or tragedy. One or the other, but nothing less.

This produced a curious bravado. Once, when as a freshly commissioned officer with the UN peacekeeping force in Afghanistan, Captain Stuart was leading his small company of men down one of the many shattered streets of Kabul, the *fiosachd* began jangling like crazy. He recognized this as its usual manifestation—a sharp tingling or squirming sensation on the back of his neck or down between his shoulder blades—and by it he knew, as the company approached a deserted intersection, that they would be ambushed by snipers. The flesh between his shoulder blades began twitching, and in his mind's eye he saw, as if in the very room with them, six black-turbaned rebels crouching at the windows of a bombed-out apartment block across the street.

He halted the company, chose two men to help him reconnoiter, and the three of them circled around and came into the building from the back. They climbed three floors up a mangled fire escape and crept down a blackened hallway to the room where James knew he would find the rebels. Without the slightest hesitation, he put his hand to the doorknob, pushed open the door, and strode into the room, demanding their surrender.

The six snipers were so surprised, they threw down their rifles and gave themselves up without protest. James' men were likewise amazed; afterwards they made out that he was the fearless hero—a latter-day John Wayne beating back a war party of bloodthirsty Apaches with bare hands and a rifle butt. He won a commendation for saving the lives of a dozen men that day and capturing a valuable rebel cell without firing a shot.

He was also given a citation for valor—a fine gesture but one James felt superfluous. Although, as a career officer, he recognized the tremendous risk—of all the possible outcomes of such an action, the one actually resulting was the least likely—he knew in his bones it was not courage that had sustained him but simple conviction: he knew what lay behind the door and, just as surely, he knew his life would not end in that room.

Even James—who understood better than anyone else the peculiarities of his special gift—accepted the extreme improbability of his childhood intimations of greatness ever coming to fruition. After all, it is one thing to pretend oneself a prince or a pirate; but who, in all sanity, could imagine—much less orchestrate—the extraordinary interplay of incident and accident, chance and serendipity, as well as the immense complexity of enterprise needed to make such a pretense possible in reality?

That this dream should become solid waking reality seemed no less incredible to James than it would have to anyone else. Although he experienced it daily, he did not pretend to fathom it. If pressed for an explanation, he would only shake his head and say that there were forces in this universe which even the most gifted among us apprehend but dimly . . . and the rest of us not at all.

Privately, however, deep in his secret heart, he thought that if there *was* a higher power at work in the world, shaping men to its purpose, then might we not apprehend it in action from time to time? And if so, might not that action look suspiciously like destiny?

                         *     *     *

Like everyone else in Britain, James learned of the King's death from television. It was a cold Thursday night in November, and he was at the Pipe & Drum with Calum and Douglas, watching Hearts in action against Celtic on big-screen TV. Aberdeen was down by one and mounting an attack in the closing seconds of the first half when the picture blanked and a Stand By sign flashed on.

"Hey!" shouted Cal—and half the pub with him. "Bring back the football!"

While the pub crowd was moaning about the interruption, the face of newsreader Jonathan Trent suddenly appeared. "We interrupt this broadcast," he said, "to bring you a special news bulletin."

"Turn it up!" shouted someone from the back.

"Shut up, and you'll hear it!"

"Listen!" hissed the crowd.

"The King is dead," intoned Jonathan Trent. "I repeat: Edward the Ninth, King of England, is dead. Turning to our correspondent, Kevin Clark, on the Portuguese island of Madeira, we bring you this report."

The announcement sent a rumble through the room. "Well, I'll be . . . Did you hear that?" asked Calum.

"I can't hear a thing," James complained.

Instantly, the scene changed to a fresh-faced Kevin Clark, holding a microphone and pressing his left palm against his ear. He was standing in front of a large, modern-looking building in the dark, and he was saying, "I am here outside the Hospital Assunção, the medical facility where the body of the King was taken earlier this evening—about eight o'-clock unofficially—by ambulance from his villa in Funchal. Initial reports, yet to be confirmed, indicate that the King suffered gunshot wounds and was pronounced dead on arrival in the trauma room."

"I'll be . . . " whispered Douglas. "The old bastard really is dead."

"It is not known at this hour," continued the foreign correspondent, "the circumstances surrounding the incident. I am told the Portuguese authorities have mounted a preliminary investigation, and we expect to be issued a report within the hour."

The scene switched back to Jonathan Trent in the London studio. "Thank you, Kevin. Can you tell us the reaction of the British Consul in Madeira?"

"I can indeed, Jonathan," replied Kevin with suitable gravity. "The consulate staff is, of course, well aware of the implications of this tragic event, and are extending their full cooperation to the authorities to aid in the investigation. I have been told that the Consul has been in contact with Number Ten, and that a statement will be issued by the Prime Minister. We have not been privy to the—"

"I'll have to stop you there, Kevin," said Jonathan Trent, breaking in, "but it looks like that statement is about to be made. We go now to Ronald Metcalf at Number Ten Downing Street."

The screen changed to a man in a trench coat with his collar up, standing hunch-shouldered outside a rain-streaked Georgian town house. Television lights lit up the night, glaring off the familiar black-enameled door. Policemen formed a cordon behind the press and television reporters, all of whom were jostling for better position.

"We have just received word that the Prime Minister is about to make a statement," Ronald Metcalf informed the viewers.

"Tell us something we don't bloody know already!" shouted someone from the back of the pub—who was in turn shouted down by those around him.

James found himself leaning forward to hear what was being said.

"It could be any moment. . . . We are waiting for . . . there—it looks as if the Prime Minister is coming out now."

The picture shifted to the front entrance as the shiny black door opened and Prime Minister Thomas Waring emerged, looking distinctly grave and concerned, his compact, athletic form severe in a close-tailored black suit and deep blue tie. Accompanied by a swarm of aides, one of whom held an umbrella over his boss's head, the Prime Minister paused to allow the pressmen a photo opportunity. Then, disdaining the offered umbrella, he braved the drizzle and walked quickly towards the bank of microphones to the staccato click of camera shutters and the strobelike bursts of their flashes.

Stepping before the massed mikes, he looked at the paper in his hand, waiting for the buzz to quiet down. When he sensed the moment was right, he raised his head and, in solemn, subdued tones, said, "I have prepared a brief announcement."

He paused, swallowed, and began reading. "A little over an hour ago, the Home Office confirmed the report that the King of England was found grievously wounded at his villa in Madeira and rushed to hospital where he was pronounced dead at eight twenty-seven Greenwich Mean Time. Official cause of death is yet to be determined, but preliminary reports indicate that Edward succumbed to a head wound caused by gunshots."

The Prime Minister raised his head slowly. "As Prime Minister, I wish, on behalf of the nation, to extend condolences to the members of the monarch's surviving family, his many friends, and well-wishers the world over. Obviously, our thoughts and sympathies are with them in this time of grief. I have nothing more to say." He made to step away from the microphones.

At this, the journalists unleashed a volley of questions at the retreating politician. "Mr. Waring! One question, Prime Minister!" shouted someone over the rest of the pack. "You said *gunshots*—was it murder or suicide?"

The Prime Minister hesitated, then returned to the microphone. "The Portuguese authorities are conducting an investigation. To offer any speculation now would be highly inappropriate. Thank you."

He turned away and started back to Number Ten.

"Where does this leave your Magna Carta scheme?" another journalist shouted.

The Prime Minister turned his face towards the camera but kept walking. "Not now," Waring replied. "I have said all I have to say this evening. I will be making an announcement in Parliament tomorrow. Thank you." He disappeared through the crush of his aides and bodyguards; the door opened before him, and he ducked quickly inside.

A rare silence descended upon the Pipe & Drum—a spontaneous reverence for the passing of the nation's monarch. Not so much the man, James thought, as for the monarchy itself. Ready Teddy had not been a particularly sparkling example of modern sovereignty.

In common with some few of his predecessors, Edward IX was a wastrel and a womanizer, as often as not dragging his reign through the muck with his lascivious shenanigans. Twice he had been named corespondent in scandalous divorces, and he had once come within a hair's breadth of being indicted for embezzling funds from a business venture in which he was a partner. His driving license was in a permanent state of revocation, and he owed huge sums of money to the banks of several countries. He spent far more time at his various properties abroad than he ever did at home—although he still opened Parliament and the racing season, and he was widely quoted as saying he wished he had inherited the crown of Spain because the food was better and weather did not impede one's golf game.

Magna Carta II made all this more or less irrelevant. A misnomer, to be sure, the term was a journalistic tag attached to the movement to dissolve the monarchy of Britain. Whereas the original Great Charter established the rule of law and curtailed the power of the monarch, Magna Carta II aimed to abolish both sovereign and sovereignty altogether.

The scheme featured a series of closely orchestrated phases, each linking a referendum to the necessary legislation. Four times the Government had consulted the people and, four times, passed laws that moved the country ever closer to the final Act of Dissolution.

Introduced by Parliament several years ago, the devolution process had been quietly and systematically working its way through its various stages, beginning with a few slight changes in the British Constitution and a moderate government reorganization which, among other things, abolished the House of Lords. Social reform eliminated all honors, titles, and other lingering vestiges of inherited privilege, while long-anticipated tax reform brought royal lands under the heavy thumb of the Inland Revenue, thereby producing the desired effect of pricing the nobility out of the market.

No government could have pursued such drastic, sweeping measures without the sanction of the British people. Years of wretched excess and royal disgrace had soured public opinion to the point that no one cared anymore. Whatever legacy of loyalty the House of Windsor had built up over the years had been squandered by the latest run of rakish incumbents. Not to put too fine a point on it, the weak-willed, petty-minded monarchs had brought about their own demise. Thus, when Magna Carta II was launched, most people thought it was high time to dump the whole stinking lot.

James never learned who won the football game that night, for the normal schedule of programs was abandoned and there followed a rambling, catch-as-catch-can obituarial documentary on the sad life of the sorry King, interspersed with continuous late-breaking bulletins which added nothing to the fact already evidenced: that the King was dead indeed.

"Oh, come on," growled Cal after a while. "It's not like he's going to be missed. The man was no Mother Teresa."

James had known Calum McKay since the day his family moved onto the Blair Morven estate. Cal's father had been hired as gamekeeper to help James' father, who was managing more and more of the estate, and suddenly James had a new friend. Two wild young bucks, they had gone through school together, skipping classes at every opportunity to ride ponies and go hunting and fishing. Loyal, irritating, diverting, and exasperating—Cal was the brother James' parents never got around to giving him.

Douglas Charmichael was also a long-time friend, and the three of them, bachelors all, often met of an evening at the Pipe & Drum for a pint and a little football. Like everyone else that night, they sat and absorbed the shocking news. For, whatever a person might think of Edward the man, and in spite of the inevitability of Magna Carta II, the nation was confronted that night with the end of a long history of monarchical rule, and that was something that could not be digested in the space of a sound bite.

Quickly bored with the unenlightening coverage of what was already being termed the National Tragedy and since football was not going to return, Gordon, the landlord, switched off the TV, and James braved the crush at the bar to fetch the table another round. "Good day on the moors?" Douglas was asking Cal when he returned with the drinks.

"Oh, aye, good enough. We let one real trophy get away, and two others bolted before we could get close. But the punters seemed happy enough. They each got a kill—that's what matters."

"Who've you got this week?" James asked, handing the drinks around.

"A couple of flash solicitors all the way up from London-town." Calum accepted his pint. "Ta, Jimmy."

"Don't talk to me about solicitors," James grumbled. "I've spent most of the day with them, and I've got a mountain of stuff to plow through tonight."

"These are a right pair, I'll tell you," Cal continued blithely. "Think they're on safari. Matching macs and field glasses, designer sunglasses on little strings around their necks, and silver whisky flasks in their plus fours. They're driving a purple Range Rover, for cryin' out loud, with tinted windows, bull bars, and state-of-the-art audio."

"It's parked outside," Douglas informed him, taking a sip from the foaming pint. "I saw it when I came in."

Cal glanced guiltily around the room. "I don't see 'em— must be in the dining room," he concluded. "You should ha' seen the two of them when the first stag came charging over the hill this morning—almost wet themselves trying to get a shot off." He chuckled. "Oh, they're all right, I suppose. A bit toff, but good tippers. They've been up before." He took a long pull on his pint, and then shook his head. "Man, how about that King, eh? What a sorry end to the whole rotten business."

They drank in silent agreement, each deep in his own thoughts. Then Douglas suggested, "We should go out some weekend. Just the three of us. It would be like old times."

"Sure," allowed Cal diffidently. "Maybe after Christmas."

"After Christmas maybe," James agreed.

Cal and James both knew, if Dougie didn't, that it was far too likely that there would be no more hunting on the estate; by Christmas the Duke's will would be probated, Cal would be out of a job, and James' erstwhile inheritance would be swallowed by an Australian development consortium—the very reason James had spent yet another day in Braemar with the solicitors, trying to hold on to the little piece of the estate his parents thought they had left him.

The pub's atmosphere had become truly grim, and then somebody called for some music, so Gordon fired up his overtaxed stereo with his favorite old Gerry Rafferty tune, loud and thrumming. James put his glass down and stood. "Well, that's me gone. See you, Cal. See you, Dougie."

"Hey, don't go," said Douglas. "It's my turn next."

"Late night tonight and early day tomorrow." He stepped away from the table, said cheerio to Gordon, and started for the door.

"See you, James," called Dougie.

"Give Jenny my love," added Cal; he pursed his lips in a pantomime kiss.

"Try not to let the lawyers shoot you," James answered over the guitars and drums.

Outside, he took a deep breath, tasting the peaty smoke from the hearth fire as it curled on the breeze. The lights from inside gleamed pale and yellow like warm butter, pooling in the puddles on the rain-soaked pavement in front of the pub. The music was almost as loud outside as in, and he walked across the parking lot singing to himself, " 'That's the way it always starts . . .' "

He climbed into his dad's battered old blue Land Rover, frowning at the box of files and documents on the passenger seat, switched on the ignition, and drove from the parking

lot. He passed quickly through Braemar—it was quiet, deserted: the townfolk glued to their TV sets—and turned east
onto the old military road.

The drizzle had lifted and the rain clouds were dispersing
on a quickening west wind. A few stars were shining
through the gaps in the clouds, and a bright slice of moon
was rising in the east. It would be a fine crisp night, he
thought, and his mind drifted naturally to Jenny. Cal's gentle needling put him in the mood, and he suddenly wished
she were there beside him. In the same instant, a pang of
guilt shot through him as he remembered he had not called
her for a week or more. Now that he had the whole of the
Blair Morven estate to look after, he could not see her as
often as he would have liked. He resolved to call her as soon
as he got home.

Crossing the Invercauld Bridge, James headed for Glen
Morven and his cottage above Old Blair. He drove on, eventually coming to the scattering of farmhouses known as Allt-
dourie; it was just after passing the last house before
entering the estate that he saw the spark of light flare from
the top of a hill through the trees.

His first thought was that it was just the moonlight hitting
something—the windscreen of a car maybe. On second
thought, he considered that highly unlikely, and so slowed
down for a better look. By the time he came in sight of the
hill again, the glinting spark had become the glimmering
glow of a fire.

James slowed and cranked down the window. The fire
surmounted the top of broad, bald-topped Weem Hill. He
knew the countryside well; the estate was seamed through
with nature trails—and Weem Hill, a mile more or less from
the road, was one hikers particularly enjoyed. He continued
on slowly until he came upon a plum-colored Range Rover
parked on the mossy shoulder of the road.

"I better go see what the city boys are up to," he muttered,
rolling to a stop behind the expensive vehicle.

Pulling his jacket from the backseat, he shrugged into it,
then reached into the glove box for a flashlight, which he
tapped against his palm a few times before switching it on.

He walked to the other vehicle and shined a beam in the driver's window. The interior was spotless; the doors were locked.

He turned towards the fire. Two lower hills stood between him and the blaze; it would mean a slog over rough wet ground in the dark. James sighed, zipped up his coat, and leaped the ditch. On the other side, he put his hand to the fence post atop the bank, vaulted over the top wire of the fence, and struck off along the rising slope towards the shimmering light on the far hilltop.

Reaching the crest of the first hill, he stopped to survey the situation. The fire still burned as brightly as before, but, try as he might, he could not make out any movement around the perimeter of the blaze. He moved on, descending quickly to the valley floor, jumping the stream at the bottom, and starting up the long slope of the next hill.

It was a good steady climb, and he soon warmed to the exercise; his breath came in gasps that sent puffs of steam rolling on the cold air, and sweat beaded on his forehead to drip down the side of his face. After a day spent in a lengthy, largely pointless meeting with his solicitor in town, it felt good to exert himself a little.

James slowed his pace as he neared the crest of the next hill, and dropped down low. The fire burned hot and bright—a proper Bonfire Night conflagration of heaped scrap wood and shipping pallets—but there seemed to be no one around. He saw no sign of the London lawyers whose car was parked on the road, and wondered where they could have gotten to.

He changed course, moving across the face of the slope so that he would come upon the fire from the side. Just before reaching the crest of the hill, he stopped and crouched down. He listened. The rippling flutter of the bonfire flames, fanned by the gusting wind and punctuated by the gunfire-sharp crack of wet wood, were the only sounds to be heard.

Rising up slowly, he peered over the top of the hill towards the fire. There was no one around. He moved closer—

and had taken no more than half a dozen steps when the hair on the back of his neck prickled.

James halted in midstep, the *fiosachd* jangling; the skin between his shoulder blades quivered. Someone was there, after all.

## ✳

# Two

James moved closer, feeling the heat blast of flames on his face and hands as he mounted the hilltop. He stood for a moment, and then walked slowly around the perimeter of the fire, the flesh between his shoulder blades squirming with the certainty that he was being watched.

"You might as well show yourself," he called loudly to the night. "I know you're hiding here somewhere. Come out."

He waited. The wind rippled the flames ominously, but that was all.

"I'm not leaving until you come out," he said, his voice loud over the sound of the fire. "So you might as well save us both some time and—"

"I am here. No need to shout."

The voice startled him. It came so clear and close, he whirled around—half expecting to see a thug with a high-powered rifle trained on him.

Instead, James saw a white-haired man dressed all in black feathers. He clutched an old-fashioned horn-tipped shepherd's crook of the kind sold in tourist shops north of the border. He stood not a dozen paces away, stock-still, as if he had materialized out of thin air or the hill itself had opened and disgorged him whole.

The stranger made no move, but watched James with an

intense and penetrating gaze, keen eyes glinting strangely in
the shimmering light of the blaze, looking for all the world
like a great bird of prey—a hawk about to take to the skies.

Uncertain what to do, James simply stood and let him get
a good look. After a moment, the old man's lips formed a
thin, ghostly smile, and he stepped nearer. James saw then
that what he had taken for feathers was, in fact, a long, dark
capelike cloak, worn to rags so that it fluttered in the wind.
The man's staff, though, was no tourist tat; it was the real
thing: a stout length of shaped and polished oak topped with
a ram's horn which had been carved with an intricate Celtic
knotwork pattern and inlaid with silver. It looked old as
Moses to James, who thought that it, like its owner, probably belonged in a museum.

"Welcome," said the stranger, coming to stand before
him. "I have been waiting for you, Mr. Stuart."

Until the man spoke, James felt as if he were gazing at an
apparition—and must have appeared mildly alarmed by the
outlandish encounter, for reassurance quickly followed.
"Relax," the man said, his voice almost fatherly. "No harm
will come to you. I only want to talk."

"Did you start this fire?" James asked.

"I did. To summon you."

"Summon me," James repeated flatly. "Why would you
want to do that?"

The man stepped closer, his eyes shining in the light of
the fire. "As I have already said: I wanted to talk to you."

"I have a phone."

"Shall we sit?" He put out his hand, indicating two lumps
of rock a few steps away.

The stranger brushed past, and James caught the scent of
damp moss and peat smoke—an ancient scent, as old as the
hills themselves.

The stranger settled himself onto one of the stones, resting the elaborate crook across his lap. James made no move
to join him.

"Do I know you?" he asked, unable to keep the edgy suspicion out of his voice. For, in spite of the unassailable certainty that he had never laid eyes on the old gent before, a

distinct aura of familiarity clung to him—he seemed to exude it, like heat from a hearth fire.

"Let us say that *I* know *you*."

"Have we ever met?"

The old gentleman hesitated—not as one contemplating a lie but as if he were gauging how much to reveal. "Strictly speaking, no."

"Then who the hell are you?" James demanded, more strongly than he felt. The stranger's manner, though intriguing, was beginning to irritate him. James wanted straight answers. "And why are you skulking around these hills at night?"

"I thought our first meeting should be"—the old gent paused, searching for the right words—"dramatic, let us say. Unforgettable."

"Are you crazy?" James asked.

"Come and sit." The old man again indicated the stone beside him, and James relented.

"Look," he said, moving nearer, "I don't know who you think you are, but—"

"Shh!" The man raised a long finger to his lips and cut him off. "We have much to discuss but little time. It would be best if you would just listen and try very hard not to interrupt. Agreed?" He turned his strange hooded eyes towards James, who dutifully sat down beside him. "That's better."

The old man cocked his head to one side, as if listening to something or someone James could not hear. After a moment, he said, "Uaimh Hill—the Hollow Hill, entrance to the Otherworld. Aptly named, don't you think?"

"Who are you?" James asked again.

"Names can be confusing," the old fellow replied, "and I have so many."

"Pick one."

He gave out a dry chuckle. "You are not afraid of me. Good." He turned his face to the leaping flames and said, "Call me Embries. That will do until we get to know each other better."

"All right, Mr. Embries. Suppose you tell me what you're doing out here setting fire to the hills."

"This is not the first beacon fire this hill has seen—far from it. The estate down there"—he gestured towards the castle grounds lost in the dark distance—"have you ever wondered why they call it *Blair* Morven?"

"Is that important?"

"It is the site of an ancient battlefield," the old man replied. "Many good men hallowed that ground with their blood." The way he said it made James think he was actually remembering the battle as he spoke—all the more since Embries seemed to lose touch with his surroundings for a moment. His eyes lost focus as he gazed into the fire, and his lips moved slightly. The moment passed, and he came to himself again.

"That was a long time ago," Embries said somewhat wistfully, then added, "but the land remembers."

Turning once more to the young man beside him, he said, "I know something that will be of use to you in your fight to save the estate, Captain Stuart."

His use of the old rank sent a quiver of recognition through James, who dismissed it saying, "I'm not in the army anymore."

"No, not anymore. But once a soldier . . . eh?" He smiled his ghostly smile.

"How do you know about my legal problems?" James asked, and then considered that almost everyone hereabouts knew about the trouble he was having holding on to the estate—at least, that part of the estate which had been given to his parents by the late Duke of Morven.

"I know you stand to inherit the gillie's lodge and two hundred acres of good meadow and pine forest if the adjudication upholds your claim."

"You're not a solicitor, are you?"

"I have been many things," the stranger answered. Again James got the distinct impression the man was immensely older than he seemed. "But I think I would remember if I was ever a solicitor." He shook his head slowly, almost wearily. "No, no, I'm not a lawyer of any stripe. I am simply what one might call a student of the land."

"What do you know that could help me?"

The old man's eyes flicked towards him. "Ah"—he smiled quickly—"you are a practical man. I like that. I like that very much. We shall get on well together, I think."

"I'm waiting."

"I think I can convince the proper authorities of the truth of your right to the estate."

James stared at the strange man beside him. As ludicrous as the claim sounded, it was said with such authority he believed Embries completely. "I can't pay you," he told him. "Legal fees are costing me an arm and a leg as it is."

"Then I will make a bargain with you," Embries said. "I will help you with your problem, and you will help me with a little problem of my own."

"But you're not going to tell me what that is, right?"

"Not just yet."

James frowned. "How did I know you were going to say that?"

"It is not a trap, I assure you. A bargain in good faith. It just so happens I cannot tell you any more until you know me better."

"Why?"

"Because I greatly fear you would not believe me."

"I don't believe you anyway, so you might as well tell me now."

Embries laughed, and it seemed to James the old fellow had not laughed in a long, long time. "No, my friend," he remarked, "that would not be bargaining in good faith."

"You've got to give me something to go on."

"Very well," the old man conceded. "I will tell you this much: your affairs and mine are much more closely linked than you might imagine."

"Don't tell me *you* have a claim on the estate, too."

"No." Embries shook his head. "The estate is yours. Never doubt it."

"Thanks."

"All of it, I mean. The entire estate—not just the two hundred acres bequeathed to your father. Blair Morven belongs to you, James Stuart, to you alone. The castle and outbuildings, the timber plantation, all the houses and cottages, the farms, the loch, the church, the family treasures—art, silver, and furniture. Everything. It is all yours."

"In my dreams."

"In reality."

James regarded the old man beside him. What in God's name, he wondered, was he doing sitting out on a windy hilltop in the dead of night talking nonsense with a half-crazy tramp?

Fascinating as it all was, the game, whatever it might be, had worn James' patience thin. He stood. "It's been interesting. Fascinating," he said contemptuously. "Thanks for the information. I'd love to stay and chat; I really would. But I've got chores in the morning, and—gosh, is that the time?—I must be going. Mind you don't trip over your cape on the way home."

"Silence!" hissed the old man. The whole world recoiled at the intensity of the command. Even the beacon fire obeyed; the flames dimmed, as if shrinking inward upon themselves.

Embries stood, rising from the rock as if he were an angry god about to blast an irksome mortal with a thunderbolt. He shook back his tattered cloak, and James could have sworn he heard the ruffled clap of raven's wings. The old man stepped nearer and seemed to grow taller with each step; his narrowed eyes took on a cold, forbidding aspect.

It seemed to James that the years, which had clung so tightly to the old fellow's frame, simply fell away and that he was staring into the face of a man who, while not exactly young, could not be called elderly. Despite the white hair, the eyes that held his were sharp as blades, undimmed by age or time—*beyond* both age and time—wary, worldly, and wise. What is more, they had become an unnatural shade of gold, like a wolf's eyes or those of a hawk.

Raising the crook in his hand, Embries made a swirling gesture in the air. The wind answered the motion with a gust which fluttered the flames and sent smoke billowing over them both. James smelled it—and was once more a soldier, standing on a hilltop with smoke in his nostrils and a weapon clutched tightly in his hand.

"I will not be mocked!" Embries spat.

James stared in dread fascination at the transformed visage before him. In it, he saw the same primitive wildness he had seen once or twice in the faces of the Afghan rebels he had captured and interrogated. Whatever else he was, the man before him was as much a zealot as any of them, James thought, and probably just as deranged.

"Think me a fool. Think me mad. Think what you will, but never mock me."

"I'm sorry," James blurted. The apology was genuine. "But you have to admit this is more than a little crazy. I mean"—he flapped a hand vaguely at their surroundings— "all this."

"If *all this* troubles you, when next we meet it will be in more conventional surroundings," Embries assured him tartly. His voice had lost none of its bitter edge. "Good night, Captain Stuart."

Embries turned and began walking away down the hill, leaving James staring after him.

"Look, let's walk back to the road together," James called. "You can't go wandering around out here at night—it's dangerous. You could fall and break your neck or something, and—"

He closed his mouth. He was talking to himself. Embries had already disappeared.

James legged it back to the highway and found his vehicle as he had left it. The plum-colored Range Rover was gone, however, and there were no lights to be seen on the road in either direction. He looked back at the hilltop. The beacon fire had dwindled to a mere ruddy glow of embers, and even that was quickly fading.

It started to rain as James climbed into his car. He flipped the key in the ignition, gunned the engine to life, and switched on the headlights and windscreen wipers. As he did so, he noticed a small white card stuck under the blade on the driver's side. He opened the door, reached around, and retrieved the card. It read simply M. EMBRIES, and gave a London telephone number.

Shoving the card into his jacket pocket, he executed a

two-point turn in the middle of the road and rattled off into
the night. All the way home he could not help thinking,
*What if the old bird is right? Impossible as it seems, what if
Blair Morven really does belong to me?*

## ✳

# Three

*What a night,* James thought wearily as his vehicle rolled to a stop on the gravel drive behind Glen Slugain Lodge. The old gillie's cottage—which he was desperately trying to keep from being swallowed up along with the rest of the late Duke's much-disputed estate—was his home. As he got out of the vehicle, his eye fell on the cardboard box containing his all-but-forgotten night's work.

"No rest for the weary," he sighed, then retrieved the box and entered the back door of the cottage, passing through the short entryway and into the kitchen. He dumped the case on the kitchen table, and stood for a moment, glaring at it, strongly tempted to forget the whole thing and call it a day.

He could call the solicitor in the morning, he thought, and plead for another day to sort through the files. In light of the National Tragedy and all, Hobbs would probably understand. Then again, since James had begged Hobbs to get him the files in the first place and everyone was doing him a huge favor just to let him have them overnight, he decided he'd better give them a quick glance, at least.

Slipping off his jacket, he made himself a big mug of strong instant coffee, dragged out a chair, and sat down. Drawing the box across the table, he untied the string and lifted off the lid. Inside were assorted files, legal envelopes, official-looking documents bound in black ribbon, a faded green accounts book, and various paper-clipped bundles of papers—all of which he had to examine in the hope of turning up a scrap of evidence which would help establish his claim to the lodge and land.

The problem, as James had come to understand it, was that the Duke of Morven—not the one who had recently died in Australia but the one his father had served: the one who had given the property to James' parents in recognition of his father's service as gamekeeper and factotum—had made application for a transfer of property but had somehow neglected to deed it properly. The old Duke died intestate, and the estate passed to an ailing Aussie cousin who had no interest in it and in fact had never once bothered to come and see the place.

Unfortunately, this elderly cousin had passed away in Sydney, and before clear lines of ownership of the lodge property could be established, James' parents had also died—within a fortnight of each other. To complicate matters further, the Australian cousin's holdings had fallen to a consortium of property speculators who had hired a development firm to press forward their plan for transforming Blair Morven into a retirement spa and golf condominium resort for well-heeled oldsters.

This was a gross oversimplification of the problem, to be sure. Indeed, the whole thing had become so tangled in legal obscurities involving the two countries that even the Aberdeen firm of solicitors which had handled the old Duke's affairs for five generations confessed bafflement. On the off chance that some small but highly significant fact was being overlooked, James had implored them for a last trawl through their archives—the results of which had produced the assortment of documents before him.

He picked up a paper-clipped bundle, slipped off the clip, and unfolded the first page; it was an old grant of fishing rights pertaining to the River Dee which ran through part of the estate. Glancing at the signatures, he recognized his father's tight scrawl. As gillie—that peculiarly Scottish blend of manservant, guide, and gamekeeper which had evolved over time into the position of estate foreman—his father had signed many of these sorts of things: bills, applications, letters, and such, dealing with the day-to-day affairs of Blair Morven.

Tossing the first bundle aside, he picked up another and opened it. After a cursory glance, he took up three or four others and flipped through them. They were a collection of affidavits and warrants, written in obscure legalese, regarding a series of surveys of the property which had been carried out long ago when the old Duke had applied for a permit to grow and export timber.

Next was a brown cardboard file folder full of letters—all of them from various tenants discussing changes in the rent, requesting new machinery or fencing, and similar concerns. Other than the cost of rental property three and four decades ago, James learned nothing to his advantage and quickly added the folder to the stack.

He picked up the accounts book and discovered that it was not, as the printed cover professed, a record of rents and expenses: it was a shooting diary. Every organized hunting trip that had taken place on the estate for twenty years had been documented: not only how many deer were shot but also each hare, fox, and squirrel, each pheasant, quail, grouse, and dove . . . as well as the location, the weather conditions—strong breeze out of the northeast, dry; or, no wind, mist, and light rain—and the names of the people making up the shooting party. Each entry, and there were hundreds, was recorded in the same neat hand—a woman's, he thought—which seemed odd: ordinarily, it would have been the gillie's job to keep such a journal for the laird.

Engrossing as it was, James saw nothing in the book of remote help to him now, so he chucked it onto the growing heap with the hopeless feeling that this was indeed going to take all night and that he might as well get some sleep and call the office in the morning. As he reached to scoop up the pile and put it back in the box, he happened to glimpse the edge of a photograph protruding from the pages of the accounts book he had just discarded.

Opening the book, he slid out the photo. It was a picture

of one of the Duke's shooting parties. In it, six men posed behind four deer and several dozen hare arrayed before them on the ground; three of the men knelt to hold up the heads of the deer, and the remaining three stood behind them with their hunting rifles slung over their arms. One of the men holding a rifle was James' father, the other was the old Duke himself, and between them was the man James knew as Embries.

In his surprise, he almost dropped the book. Gripping the photo as if it might escape, he brought it nearer to his face. There was no doubt whatever—the same tall, almost gaunt physique, the same stark white hair, the same long-fingered hands and pale eyes staring out from the glossy scrap of paper—it was the man he had met on the hilltop little more than an hour ago.

The uncanny coincidence gave James a queer feeling in the pit of his stomach; he reached for his coffee and took another drink, wishing it were whisky instead. The photo was old. Judging from the youthful appearance of the Duke and his father it was twenty-five years old at least, maybe even thirty, yet Embries appeared not to have aged a whit in the intervening years.

James opened the accounts book to the page where he'd found the photo, and saw an entry from 17 October. It informed him that on a warm, partly sunny day with the wind gusting ten to twenty miles per hour out of the northwest, four deer and twenty-seven hare had been killed by six men: Sir Cameron Campbell; Sir Herbert Fitzroy; Dr. Stephen Harms; his father, John Stuart; Duke Robert himself; and one listed only as M. Embries.

Remembering the business card he had retrieved from the windscreen, he reached over and dug it out of the pocket of his jacket. He stared at the name . . . *Embries*. An unusual name—at least, unusual enough for there to be no mistaking that, appearances aside, the man he had met on the hilltop and the man in the photograph were one and the same.

Intrigued now, his senses quickened by an immediate adrenaline rush, he carefully put the accounts book to one side and placed the photo and card atop it. He dug into the box again and brought out another sheaf of bound documents, untied them, and spread them out. It was a jumble of bits and pieces the like of which petty officials everywhere revel in: an old tax notice; a quitclaim for a highway widening scheme; an application for a firearm permit; his father's discharge papers from his old regiment, the King's Own Royal Highlanders. Stapled to this last was a brittle, faded copy of a medical form filled out in John Stuart's name, listing such things as eyesight, vaccinations, and blood type. James glanced quickly at the other documents, which contained equally mundane and uninteresting information, and impatiently swept them aside.

Two hours later, after turning up nothing more helpful than a copy of the Duke's last driving license, James gave up and packed it in. He shoved back from the table in weary disappointment and glanced up at the clock above the stove. Damn! It was past two o'clock—much too late to call Jenny now. She'd have been asleep hours ago.

He stood, retrieved his one genuine find—the shooting party photo—and slipped it carefully back in its place inside the accounts book, put the book inside the box and closed the lid, then stumbled from the kitchen, pausing in the doorway long enough to snap off the light. He shuffled to his room at the back of the house, kicked off his shoes, and collapsed into bed.

The radio alarm roused James at six o'clock to a bleak, sleety morning black as midnight. Four hours of fretful thrashing on his pillow had done nothing to improve his increasingly edgy mood. He was tired and out of sorts; he could feel the nervous energy zinging through him, making him fidgety and anxious. The bizarre meeting on the hilltop had disturbed him more than he imagined. That, combined with the discovery of the photo, made for a restless night as his mind kept turning the thing over and over, revolving like a pinwheel and with as much purposeful resolution.

He lay in bed and listened to ice pellets spattering on the window, and then stirred himself. Entering the kitchen, he saw the untidy heap of documents on the table and, to one side, the box holding the accounts book with the photo and

business card atop it. On a whim, he picked up the card and
stepped to the phone hanging beside th efrigerator and dialed the number below the name.

The phone rang once, twice . . . before it occurred to him
that it was only six in the morning, and Embries would not
have had time to get back to London. He decided to hang up
and try again that evening, but as he made to replace the receiver, a voice said, "Hello?"

Snatching the receiver back to his ear, James replied,
"Hello—who is this?"

"James?" The voice on the other end sounded calm and in
control.

"Is that Embries?"

The speaker did not respond to the question. Instead, he
said, "I am glad you kept my card. Listen carefully; there is not
much time. I want you to come to London. Will you do that?"

"Why?"

"Let us say that all your questions can be answered here
more easily than anywhere else."

"Not good enough," James declared. "I don't know you,
and I don't know what you're up to. Until I start getting
some answers, I'm not going anywhere."

Embries remained unfazed by this blunt refusal. "There is
more to this affair than you know; however, I am not prepared to go into it over the phone." He paused. "There is a
direct train to King's Cross from Pitlochry at 10:21 this
morning. Can you make it?"

"I suppose so," James replied hesitantly. "But I'd have to
hear a better reason than what you've told me so far."

"Come to London, James," countered Embries quietly.
"Two days. That's all I ask. The rest will be up to you. I give
you my word."

For some reason, and against his better judgment, James
believed him. Worn down, his natural resistance low from
fighting the case on his own, perhaps the offer of help, from
whatever quarter, seemed too good to reject out of hand.
After all, he thought, what else did he have going for him?
In that moment, James decided to take Embries at his word.
"All right," he agreed.

"Good. Now then, it would be best if you did not travel alone. You need a companion, someone you can trust. Do you have a friend who could come with you?"

"I don't know. It's pretty short notice. I'll try."

"Yes, do try." Embries paused. "It is important, James. Someone you can trust," he repeated earnestly.

"I understand."

"Tickets will be waiting for you at the station. When you disembark, go to the head of the platform and wait. I will have someone meet you there. Agreed?"

"If you say so."

"Do not worry," Embries reassured him. "You are doing the right thing. Good-bye, James."

Before James could ask about the photo, there came a click and the receiver went dead. He thought of dialing again but decided against it. Clearly, Embries was working some sort of angle, and was not likely to give away anything important over the phone. James busied himself with making coffee, and while the stout dark liquid brewed, he went to the bathroom for a shower and a shave.

He emerged somewhat refreshed, dressed quickly, and headed back to the kitchen for breakfast. While waiting for the antique toaster to spit out two thick pieces of toast, he decided to see if he could catch Calum before he left for the day's shooting. James dialed the number and let it ring, but there was no answer. He hung up, thinking he'd left it too long, and Cal was already out on the moors with his high-tipping lawyers from London.

The toast popped up, and he ate leaning against the counter. Then, pouring another mug of coffee, he sat down at the table for a final perusal of the odds and ends before returning the box to the solicitors. Reaching for the shooting diary, he slipped the photo from between the pages and gazed into the face of M. Embries. How old must he be now? he wondered. Perhaps it was a trick of the light, but he didn't appear to have aged a day since the photo was taken; in fact, he didn't seem to have changed at all: tall, regally slender, his white hair brushed back, pale eyes gazing out with intensity and intelligence.

James' father was standing beside him—how young he looked.

He walked into the living room and took the portrait of his parents from the mantel. It was a good photo—taken on the day James had received his officer's commission. It was May. His father was wearing the same dark suit he always wore at anything requiring formality; his mother, on the other hand, was absolutely radiant in a pale pink dress she had bought especially for the occasion; she wore white gloves and had his dress tunic over her arm, casually displaying the new gold rank insignia on the sleeve. It had been a warm day, he recalled, and he had just taken off his tunic; she had chided him for crumpling it, and took it from him while he snapped the picture. The smile she wore had much of a mother's pride in it, mingled with joy at seeing her son honored.

His father, in contrast, appeared almost sorrowful. There was something diffident and wistful about his expression— as if he were intruding, and knew it, but trying to make the best of an uncomfortable situation. But then, as James recalled, Jack Stuart had never been much for social gatherings of any kind; he found the inanity and superficiality maddening, and endured rather than enjoyed any function he was forced to attend. This, James had always considered, explained his father's woebegone smile.

The phone's chirp broke into his reverie just then. He walked back to the kitchen and picked it up. "Hello?"

"James, man, you're there—"

"Cal?"

"Did you ring me just now?"

"As a matter of fact, I did. How'd you know?"

"You're the only one who ever rings me before seven, actually."

"I figured you were out for the day with your clients."

"They left," Cal told him. "Got a call last night. Urgent business in London, apparently. They paid up for the week and hightailed it back to the city. So I'm free as a bird. I thought we could take the ponies out. It's been a while since I hunted on horseback. What do you say?"

"Funny you should ask. I was going to try to persuade *you* to come with *me.*"

"Where to?"

"London. Your legal friends aren't the only ones with urgent business in the city."

"Is this anything to do with the estate?"

"As it happens, yes."

"Good news or bad?"

"Too early to tell. But I'm going."

Cal hesitated. "Umm . . . I don't know. I should probably give it a miss. There's a lot to do around here. Thanks all the same."

"Look, Cal," James said, "I wouldn't ask only it's kind of important. A couple days is all. And it might make a difference. How about it?"

"Well, the thing is, see . . ."

"I need someone with me," James insisted. "I need you, Cal."

"Since you put it that way, when do we leave?"

After arranging a time and place to meet, James returned to the bedroom, threw some clothes into a duffel bag, along with his dress shoes and a blazer, bunged in his toothbrush and shaving kit, zipped up the lot, and tossed the bag into the back of the Land Rover. He went back inside, secured the house, and scooped up the various documents from the kitchen table and replaced them in the box. Then, tucking the box under his arm, he grabbed his hunting jacket from the back of the chair, turned off the coffee pot, and locked the house. He was halfway to the solicitor's office in Braemar when he remembered that he'd meant to call Jenny.

## Four

The cramped, untidy offices of Gilpin and Hobbs, Solicitors, were open by the time James arrived. Malcolm Hobbs was standing behind his desk, scratching his head. "Morning, James," he said. "Just put it over there in the corner somewhere—anywhere." Indicating the box, he asked, "Any luck?"

"A few interesting items for the family scrapbook. Odds and ends mostly, but no—nothing much," James answered.

"I was afraid you would be disappointed," Malcolm sympathized. "I did try to tell you. They went over everything with a fine-tooth comb. If Old Howard had anything tucked away anywhere, they would have found it."

Old Howard was H. Gilpin, the Duke's solicitor, who had retired a few years ago, and who could still be seen whacking golf balls at the Ballater course of an afternoon.

"Well," James allowed, "I had to see for myself. You know how it is."

"Sure." Malcolm glanced at his watch. "Unfortunately, I have another client coming in any minute"—he smiled apologetically—"so if there is nothing else I can do for you . . . ?" He moved around the side of his desk to lead his visitor out.

"Not at the moment, I guess."

"I'll be in touch as soon as we receive the filing notice from the Aussies."

James thanked him again for his trouble, and returned to his car, slid the key into the ignition, and felt his breakfast surge up into his throat when a hand knocked on the window beside his face. "Malcolm!"

"Sorry to startle you, James," he said, bending his head to see in.

James cranked the window down a few inches. "What's up?"

"I just was thinking, why not go see Old Howard?" Malcolm shivered in the cold. "Just to satisfy yourself we haven't overlooked anything."

"Leave no stone unturned. Yes, I might do that."

"He's got a place in town, you know. If he's not there you can always find him on the town course. Old Howard likes his golf." Malcolm began shuffling in place to keep warm. "Never misses a day."

"I'll keep it in mind. You'd best get inside before you catch pneumonia."

"Right. Ta, James," he said, and scurried back to his office. James glanced at his watch: it was twenty to nine. He had just enough time to find a phone and give Jenny a ring—although, now that he thought about it, he wasn't sure what he'd say to her. He tossed this over in his mind as he drove to the petrol station down the street and dialed her studio from the pay phone on the wall.

"James, it's you!" Jenny's mother always sounded surprised and pleased whenever he rang up.

"How are you, Agnes?" he asked. "Over that cold?"

"Och!" she protested. "It was nothing—a wee chill only, I swear. Some folk around here made far too much of it. I'm right as rain now."

"Glad to hear it. I was hoping to speak to Jenny a moment—is she there?"

"Alas, no, no." She sounded heartbroken. "She just dashed out to make a delivery." Jenny owned a pottery business that shipped pieces all over the world, as well as supplying the local shops and hotels with better-quality tourist items. "I'm sorry," Agnes said. "Could I have her ring you?"

"That won't be necessary. If you could just tell her I've been called away to London on business for a few days. I'll try to ring her when I get back."

"I'll surely tell her," promised Agnes. "Why don't you come to dinner on Sunday? It's Mildred's birthday—eighty-seven, she is. You're more than welcome, James."

He thanked her for the invitation, and said, "I wouldn't miss it for the world, but duty calls. You know how it is."

"That's a shame. Well, take care of yourself in the big city. Come round when you get back."

"You can count on it," James promised, said good-bye and hung up, disappointed.

He filled up with petrol and drove to the Invercauld Arms parking lot where Cal was waiting in his forever muddy green Ford Escort.

" 'Lo, James," he said as he stepped out, pulling a soft-sided black bag from the seat beside him. He locked his car, tossed the bag into the backseat, and climbed in.

Turning onto the highway, James rejoined the sparse morning traffic through town, and headed for Pitlochry. The drive through Glen Shee was one he usually enjoyed. This time, however, he hardly noticed the scenery. Cal slumped down in his seat and closed his eyes, while James, his mind churning, dissected the events of the last few months. He thought about his recent troubles, and how so much turmoil could have been avoided if the old Duke had simply left a proper will. He found himself thinking about his parents, and how worried they had been when the Australians began filling the post box with all their heavy-handed legal letters. James was still in the service at the time, but there was not much he could have done in any case. It took years off their lives, no doubt.

He thought about his mother: bright and enthusiastic, with a wonderfully fanciful sense of humor. She liked nothing more than those newspaper competitions which ask the reader to supply amusing captions for peculiar photos, and routinely had her entries published. She was unfailingly

cheerful, and her manifold kindnesses won her lasting and
loyal friends. In her day, she had been a knockout. James
had seen pictures of her that would have done credit to a
fashion model's portfolio. Indeed, she was still a handsome
woman when she died. The end came so quickly for her that
she did not wither or waste away like so many older women
do when their men go. The doctors said it was her heart, but
James suspected she just couldn't stand to live without her
husband.

He thought about his father. A good, honest man, hard-
working but not ambitious, he had taught James the value of
a job well done and the enjoyment of life's simple pleasures.
Moreover, he instilled in his son a knowledge of his Creator.
It was from his father that James had learned that this life
was inextricably bound with the next. A frustrated vicar,
John Stuart had studied for the ministry, but had left theo-
logical college after only a year or so. Why, James never
learned; his father did not speak of it.

Next, his thoughts turned inexorably to Embries, and the
odd way he had chosen to make his introduction. While it
had seemed mysterious and full of portent at the time, in the
cold light of day, it all seemed slightly silly. Melodramatic.
Much ado about nothing, really. James felt foolish for having been gulled by such obvious flimflam.

Yet, here he was, rushing across country to make a train
to London, and all because of a few whispered words down
a phone line. How, he wondered, did the old boy fit in with
his parents? What did he know that could help save Blair
Morven? Who was he anyway?

Outside Pitlochry, James joined the long, slow queue of
Friday shoppers coming into town. Consequently, they arrived at the station with only minutes to spare and dashed to
collect the tickets. Presenting himself at the ticket booth, the
clerk said, "Middle initial?"

"What? Oh, *A*—James A. Stuart."

"Your destination?"

"London—King's Cross."

"Somebody with you?"

"A friend," he said, jerking a thumb at Cal.

"These are yours then." The clerk slid two tickets under the glass. "Enjoy your trip."

James scooped up the tickets, and the two headed for the platform where the train was waiting. Once they were rolling through the countryside, Cal, propping his feet on the opposite seat, said, "So tell me, what's this all about then?"

"I already told you—it's to do with the estate."

"Yeah, so? Did the solicitor turn up something?"

"Something turned up, but I'm not sure what." Suddenly reluctant to rehearse the scant details leading up to their present situation, James simply told him, "Apparently the answer awaits us in London. I honestly don't know all that much about it myself."

Cal regarded him dubiously for a moment, suspecting there was more James wasn't telling him.

"Um," James said, "it's sort of a long story. I'd really rather not go into it all right now. Can we just leave it at that for the moment?"

"Whatever you say, Sonny Jim. So far as I'm concerned, it's a free weekend in the big city. I even put on a new shirt," he boasted, tugging gently on his cuffs. "Wine, women, and song—here I come."

The train sped through a rain-streaked countryside, and the two occupied themselves talking about the annual village stag hunt; Cal, for the third year running, was to act as gillie as well as organize the prizes. When the lunch hour rolled around, they swayed to the buffet car and bought beer and sandwiches, which they carried back to their seats. Cal took a nap after that, and James soon dozed off, too, sleeping through a minor mechanical hold-up at Crewe, and awaking only when the train pulled in at New Street Station, Birmingham, where four businessmen in smart blue suits got on and started ringing up wives and girlfriends on their mobile phones.

The sky was already growing dark by that time, the short winter day fading quickly into a gray murky half light. James caught a last lingering glimpse of ruddy color low on the horizon as the train came out of the city, and watched it until the twilight closed in. He sat looking out the window and wondering what in heaven's name he was doing. *Have I become so desperate to hold onto my little bit of land,* he wondered, *that I will clutch at any straw?*

*Yes,* he concluded gloomily. *It has come to that.*

The train pulled in at King's Cross. They disembarked with the businessmen, and walked to the head of the platform where James paused.

"What now?" asked Calum, stretching his neck.

"Somebody's supposed to meet us."

"And who might that be?"

"I don't know."

"For a military man, you don't really have this goose chase under control, do you?" Cal shook his head and chuckled.

"Not really, no," James conceded, growing increasingly perturbed for having allowed himself to be so easily led down the garden path. He was just about to suggest they go and try the phone number on the card, when they were approached by a slender, dark-haired youth. His solemn expression made him appear older than he was, and his bearing gave James to know he was a soldier or had been; he had seen the sober look and clipped walk far too many times not to recognize it now.

The young man walked directly to where the two stood waiting. James could have sworn he almost saluted. "Captain Stuart?" It was not so much a question, as a statement of fact.

James acknowledged his terse greeting, and said, "This is my friend, Cal—Calum McKay."

The young man nodded at this information, and said, "This way, sir. I have a car waiting." He reached for James' bag. "Allow me."

"Lead on," he replied, relinquishing his luggage. "My name is James, by the way," he offered, falling into step beside their young guide. "What's yours?"

"Just call me Rhys, sir. I'll be your driver during your stay in London." He glanced around expectantly, and it was all James could do to keep from returning the implied salute.

"Thank you, Rhys," he said, and as he spoke the name aloud, felt an unaccountable familiarity sweep over him. *I know this young man,* he thought. No sooner had the thought formed in his head, however, than it was brushed aside by the realization that, as an army officer, he had known hundreds of earnest young fellows exactly like Rhys; they were a type. And the name—a venerable old Welsh standard—was hardly unique.

They crossed the station, passing the baguette kiosk, burger bar, and Sock Shop, and came to a roped-off area where, parked in the center of three empty spaces, sat a sleek black Jaguar sedan. Cal took one look at the plates and nudged James with an elbow. "Brand-new," he murmured. "I'll take it."

As Rhys merged the car smoothly into the city traffic, his passengers settled back into the cool leather seats and gazed at the lights of the capital through tinted glass. A short drive brought them to the tall Victorian houses of Belgravia, the embassy district, and at last to a long cul-de-sac surrounding a park. Rhys stopped the car outside an enormous white town house with a newly painted black iron fence bearing the sign KENZIE HOUSE. He got out and opened the door. "Go right in. They are expecting you, sir."

"They?"

"Lord and Lady Rothes." The answer brought raised eyebrows from Calum, in whose opinion only the stodgily elitist clung to their titles these days. "They are Embries' associates, you might say," Rhys continued, ignoring Cal's expression. He went on to inform his charges that the Rothes were, from time to time, pleased to offer discreet accommodation. "You are the only guests."

"I see."

"Is something wrong, sir?" He regarded James intently—as if ready to act on his slightest word.

"No, not at all," James assured him quickly. "It's just that I thought we would be seeing Embries tonight."

Rhys relaxed. "Ah, yes, well." He smiled by way of apology. "Mr. Embries' affairs called him away at the last minute. You'll be very comfortable here, sir."

"I'm sure I will," James replied, feeling acutely disappointed for the second time that day.

Rhys stepped to the rear of the car, pressing the key fob as he did so. The boot opened with a sigh as he came around, and he lifted out the luggage.

"You don't have to fetch and carry for us. We can manage," said James, reaching for his bag.

"Certainly, sir," he said. "I will collect you in the morning, and Mr. Embries will see you then. Is eight-thirty convenient?"

"Extremely," replied James.

Rhys wished them both a good night, and drove away. "Who's this Embries chap?" asked Cal as they made their way up the short walk to the steps. "You never told me about him."

"He's the one with all the answers."

Before Cal could ask anything else, the door opened and they were swept into the house by a tall, handsome matron dressed in a trim white cardigan and black-and-white checked slacks. She had well-brushed gray hair, blue eyes, and the kind of fresh, slightly wind-chafed complexion women get from days spent in healthy outdoor pursuits.

"Here you are at last!" she exclaimed, her accent burring gently. "I am so glad you've arrived. Please, come in, come in both of you." She pulled her visitors convivially into a grand foyer, tastefully—and expensively—decorated with polished wood and dark blue wallpaper stamped with tiny gold crests that glittered in the softly flickering light of a dozen candles of various sizes. "I'm Caroline," she said, putting out her hand to James. "You must be Mr. Stuart."

"Yes. James, please. And this is my friend Calum McKay."

"Delighted," replied Caroline Rothes. "This way—I'll show you to your rooms." She led them up a curving stairway to the next floor. "If you're anything like me," she said, pushing open the doors, one next to the other, "you'll be wanting to refresh yourself after a long day's journey. Please, come down for a drink as soon as you're settled. I'll wait for you downstairs."

The rooms were spacious and comfortable. James put his bag on the floor beside the bed, sat down on the edge and bounced up and down a couple times to test the hardness of the mattress, and then went into the blue-tiled bathroom to try out the plumbing.

"I expect you're famished," Lady Rothes said, when they rejoined her downstairs a few minutes later. She led them across the foyer and through a set of wide mahogany doors. "There are drinks and nibbles waiting for you in the living room; they'll tide you over until dinner."

This room was larger than the entire ground floor of Glen Slugain Lodge, and James marveled at the extravagance of space. Two deeply upholstered chairs of dark red leather had been pulled up on either side of a low table that supported a drinks tray and bowls of various sizes containing crisps and crackers and salted nuts. The chairs faced a very large television.

"The news is on shortly," their hostess told them, crossing directly to the TV. She switched it on. "I thought that, what with all that's happened lately, you might like to watch. If not, just chuck a brick at the screen." She beckoned her guests to the chairs. "Come along and make yourselves at home. I have a thing or two to do in the kitchen, but I'll join you in a few minutes."

She swept from the room, leaving Cal and James to fend for themselves. Cal pulled off the top of a bottle of Ruddles County ale, and poured it into two glasses. "Cheers!" he said, handing one to James. His gaze drifted around the room as he drank. "Some place."

"Just like home," James said. He offered the comment as a mildly ironic quip, but Cal's suddenly knowing expression rocked him back on his heels.

"I can see you here," he mused seriously. "I really can."

"I'm not even sure we can afford dinner, to say nothing of staying the night," James replied, trying to lighten the mood again.

"You worry too much, Jimmy. You should be more like me."

"Have a nibble, Cal, and shut up," said James, shoving the bowl of nuts at him.

The news came on and they sat down to watch. It was BBC anchorman Jonathan Trent, looking grave and serious. "Good evening. Tonight's broadcast has been expanded," he informed his audience soberly, "so that we may bring you extended coverage of the National Tragedy, the Death of King Edward." A small golden crown appeared in the lower left-hand corner of the screen; beneath the crown was the royal monogram and above it a black-draped cloth.

"Oh, for the love of God," muttered Cal. "They've given it a logo, for cryin' out loud."

"As promised on our midday report, we have a live update from Kevin Clark in Madeira, but before joining Kevin on location, we take you to the House of Commons for a repeat of this afternoon's announcement in Parliament by Prime Minister Thomas Waring."

Trent, ever the professional presenter, hesitated meaningfully, turned to his on-desk monitor, and intoned, "This was the scene in Parliament this afternoon."

## ✳
# Five

They watched as the television screen flashed up an image of an absolutely packed House of Commons chamber. Every seat on every green leather bench was full, as were the members', press, and strangers' galleries. The aisles were jammed with those without places. Looking both suave and severe, a sober-faced PM rose from the front bench, holding a black portfolio. He nodded to the Speaker of the House, and took his place at the dispatch box.

"Further to my press announcement at Downing Street last evening, Mr. Speaker," he said, "it is my regretful duty to inform this House of the death of our monarch, His Royal Highness Edward the Ninth, King of England, at his winter residence. He was pronounced dead on arrival by the medical staff at the Hospital of the Holy Ascension in Funchal, Madeira, approximately fifteen minutes past eight o'clock local time last night. Preliminary investigations conducted by the police, with full knowledge of and cooperation with our own consular authorities, indicate that the King was found at his home by his personal valet, who, having been alerted by the sound of an explosion, discovered the King suffering from a single gunshot wound to the head.

"It is not known at this time whether the fatal wound was accidental, the result of an action by the King himself, or the tragic outcome of an attack by a person or persons unknown. A ruling on this question has been requested by this government as a matter of utmost priority. We are assured that the relevant authorities are in full sympathy with our concerns."

He paused to take a drink from the glass of water beside the dispatch box, thereby giving members a chance to interrupt with questions. "Mr. Speaker!" they shouted, waving their order papers to be recognized. "Mr. Speaker!"

"Order!" cried Olmstead Carpenter, Speaker of the House, from his elevated chair. "Order, ladies and gentlemen, please! The Prime Minister will continue with his statement." Carpenter glared at the assembled MPs, as if daring them to make another outburst.

"Thank you, Mr. Speaker," continued the Prime Minister when the shouting had abated. "I would merely add that arrangements are being made by this government for the remains of the King to be flown back to London for burial. We have obtained assurances from the Portuguese authorities that the body will be released at the earliest possible moment following the conclusion of their investigations. I hasten to assure the House that even now we are working closely with our foreign colleagues to bring about a swift and satisfactory resolution to what is for all concerned an extremely lamentable and sorrowful affair."

The Prime Minister sat down abruptly, which was the signal for the Opposition benches to have at it. First on his feet and first to be recognized was Huw Griffith, the feisty, wirehaired leader of the Unified Alliance Party, the Government's erstwhile opposition. The UAP was a coalition of five smaller parties which struggled year after year to mount a meaningful, coherent opposition to Waring's British Republic Party juggernaut.

"Are we to understand, Mr. Speaker," roared the amply padded MP, "that the death of our monarch is the subject of a continuing police investigation? Does this indicate foul play? If so, what are the circumstances? If not, what, in heaven's name, does the Prime Minister mean? I would ask the Right Honorable Member for additional clarification, if it is not too much trouble."

Griffith sat down, glaring across the table at his rival. Amid the shouts of friend and foe alike, the PM rose to his feet. "I would most happily provide clarification for the Honorable Gentleman, Mr. Speaker, if that were possible. Unfortunately, I can only say that inasmuch as King Edward was apparently alone in his residence, further details of the tragic event must await the results of the official investigation."

The PM sat down, and the clamor resumed. "Mr. Speaker!" shouted Charles Graham, shadow home secretary, and leader of the New Conservatives, one of the coalition Opposition parties. "I am appalled, Mr. Speaker, that the death of our nation's monarch should be treated in this callous and irreverent manner. Will the Government mount a full and thorough inquiry into this tragic affair immediately?"

The Prime Minister rose and returned to the dispatch box. "Allow me to reassure the Honorable Gentleman, Mr. Speaker, that this government is offering its complete support to those in charge of the investigation. A report is in the offing. If, after receiving that report, we feel further scrutiny is warranted, I can personally assure this House that a government inquiry will be conducted."

The Speaker then recognized a backbencher whose name James didn't catch, but who spoke in a loud voice with an accent that could cut crystal: "Mr. Speaker, will the Prime Minister please confirm that inasmuch as Edward the Ninth was the reigning monarch of Britain at the time of his death, that he will be accorded a State funeral—with all the honor and, may I say, pomp and prestige suitable to such an occasion—and further, will he confirm in unequivocal terms his understanding that insofar as Britain is still a monarchy, he will continue to fulfill his sworn obligation, as the King's Prime Minister, namely, to uphold, defend, and serve the sovereignty of our nation?"

The double-barreled question seemed innocuous enough, but a hushed House waited as Waring slowly rose once more to the dispatch box.

He cleared his throat. "Mr. Speaker, the Honorable and

Gallant Member from Glenrothes has raised an important constitutional point regarding the funeral, and one which is currently being assessed by the Home Office. Their recommendation will form the basis of this government's decision, which will be announced at the earliest opportunity. In the meantime, I most happily reiterate that as Prime Minister, it is not only my obligation, but my very great honor, to defend and serve the sovereignty of this nation."

"Mr. Speaker," the Fife backbencher continued, "should the PM be reminded that he is living in a dreamworld if he thinks he can bamboozle the great British public—"

"Order!" cried Carpenter from his thronelike seat. "The Honorable Gentleman will rephrase the question."

"Thank you, Mr. Speaker," replied the member from Glenrothes, and continued as smoothly unruffled as before, "I would merely ask whether it is the Prime Minister's intention to deprive the nation of the opportunity to mourn their sovereign's tragic death in a manner befitting the long and illustrious tradition of the monarchy of which Edward was the representative, or whether the Right Honorable Gentleman will choose instead to make a cheap political point at the expense of the British people?"

The question was aired before the Speaker could cut it off, and the House shook with the uproar. Speaker Carpenter shouted something, which was lost in the furor. The BBC voice-over announcer pointed out that, as the question had been ruled unparliamentary, the PM was not required to answer—and he didn't. Instead, another question was taken, and a member inquired whether Magna Carta II would be discontinued now that it had achieved its purpose.

This question, which could not have been far from many minds, silenced the House again. As Prime Minister Waring returned once more to his place, every eye was on him, every ear awaiting his explanation.

"This government, Mr. Speaker, has over the last few years endeavored to bring one of our nation's most ancient and revered institutions into step with the realities of a modern democratic nation-state. Magna Carta Two, as it has been termed, was only one of several tools employed for that purpose. But, Mr. Speaker, the plain fact is that the voluntary abdications this government has acquired—"

The House burst into catcalls, whistles, and a blizzard of furiously waved order papers, cheers, and hisses. "Order!" Carpenter roared. "Order! Prime Minister!"

"Voluntary abdications," Waring repeated, "acquired by this government, when combined with the unfortunate circumstance of King Edward's death, however lamentable in itself, does bring to an end what might be mildly termed a 'vexed and troubled reign,' and would therefore seem to vindicate this government's pursuit of disestablishment."

There were whoops and jeers at this, but the Prime Minister coolly reached for his glass of water and waited while the Speaker restored order in the chamber.

"I make no apology, Mr. Speaker," Waring resumed, "for the policy which this government has faithfully pursued for the systematic reduction of privilege for the rich and idle at the expense of the poor and hard-working. I make no apology for removing the burden of an onerously expensive monarchy from the public purse, nor for returning valuable lands and properties to public use, nor, indeed, for releasing royal treasures to the enjoyment of all this nation's people. Further, I would remind this House that these initiatives have enjoyed broad-based support in the country, and cross-party support in this chamber!"

He glared defiantly across the table at the Opposition benches. "I am sure the House will agree with me that, while we may mourn the sad death of a man and the passing of an ancient institution, the actual benefits flowing from this government's policy of royal devolution are incalculable, and must not be sacrificed to softheaded sentimentality."

This drew another raucous flourish of jeers and catcalls which the Speaker of the House, with difficulty, silenced.

"If I may be allowed to finish, Mr. Speaker," resumed the PM, apparently unperturbed by the outcry, "I will conclude by saying that in the absence of any remaining claimants to the throne, and in light of having achieved unqualified successes in accomplishing the goals set before it, this government now considers the work of the Special Committee for

Royal Devolution to have entered its final phase. I will therefore take this opportunity to reaffirm our intention to adhere to the schedule ratified some months ago in this very chamber with regard to the referendum vote for the final Act of Dissolution of the monarchy."

Prime Minister Waring paused and looked up from his notes. "This is an important point. Allow me to underscore it, if you will. In light of recent events, this government will hold the final public referendum on the fifteenth of February, as previously announced, thus securing the will of the nation as regards this timely issue."

With that he stepped back and took his seat on the front bench to the chorused grunts of approval from his supporters and party members, and shouted japes and challenges from the opposition facing him across the room. Speaker Carpenter called the House to order, and passed on to other business, whereupon the PM, the cabinet, most of the visitors, and all of the journalists departed.

The coverage from the Commons ended, but the news broadcast continued; there were live reports from Madeira and outside Parliament, and from pundits gathered in the BBC studio to discuss the implications of the PM's speech and read the tea leaves of political fortunes. James found his attention wandering, and after a few minutes Caroline returned, all apologies over a kitchen disaster of major proportions.

"Did I miss anything important?"

"It's hard to say," James told her. "The question of a State funeral was raised—"

"Excellent! Jolly good!" Caroline clapped her hands once for emphasis. "Oh, that's very encouraging indeed. Well done!"

Baffled by her sudden excitement, James said, "I don't think the matter was settled. Waring seemed to waffle."

"Doesn't matter," Caroline countered. "Thin end of the wedge, eh, Calum?"

"Thin end of the wedge, absolutely," Cal replied, regarding his hostess with a bemused expression.

Lady Rothes switched off the TV, and turned to her guests. "Now then, dinner is served."

James and Cal followed her back through the mahogany doors, across the grand foyer, and into a large formal dining room dominated by a massive crystal chandelier and a floor-to-ceiling gilt mirror covering most of one wall. Cal let out a silent whistle as he took in the elegant sideboard laden with silver tureens and platters; the precious, if slightly threadbare, Persian carpet on the parquet floor; and a heroic Sheraton dining table that could have served as a Thames bridge. A dozen matching chairs surrounded the table, and more stood against the walls at various places around the room.

"Here we are," Caroline said. "I've put you at this end. I hope you won't feel like you're dining in an airplane hangar."

"Not at all," James assured her. "But I see only two places. You're not joining us?"

"I had a light supper earlier. But you two tuck in, and I'll just potter around. I might be persuaded to join you for pudding, if you twisted my arm."

"Consider it twisted," Cal said, pulling out his chair.

"I was hoping you'd say that," she acquiesced nicely. *"Bon appétit!"* She buzzed from the room, disappearing through a door all but hidden behind the sideboard.

"Sterling," murmured Cal, picking up a fork and hefting it in his hand. On the plates before them was a cold prawn salad prepared with freshly made garlic mayonnaise, and no fewer than four stemmed goblets were arranged before each plate. Cal tapped the largest goblet with a tine of his fork, sounding a clear, resonant note. "Lead crystal."

The bell-like tone brought an immediate response, for a door opened across the room, and a young woman entered carrying an ice bucket on a stand. Although she was dressed like a man in black trousers and a long-sleeved white shirt, and her dark, straight hair was cut short as any schoolboy's, her long-limbed figure argued otherwise.

"Hi," she greeted the diners cheerily. "I'm Isobel." Placing the ice bucket beside the table, she withdrew a corkscrew from her pocket and proceeded to open the bottle of white wine in the bucket.

"Hello, Isobel," Cal said appreciatively.

"This," she said, indicating the bottle between her hands, "is a *good* South African Chardonnay." She pulled the cork with a practiced twist of a slender wrist, and poured two glasses. "I think you're going to love it."

"I love it already." Cal smiled, adjusting his collar, obviously pleased he'd worn his new shirt.

She winked at him. "Enjoy!"

Isobel disappeared as abruptly as she'd arrived, leaving a gaping hole in the room. The two men fell silent, eating their prawns and sipping wine which, as promised, was very good. No sooner had they laid the fish forks aside, than Caroline entered with two steaming plates of soup.

"It's plum and parsnip," she informed them. "I know it sounds hideous, but do try it. Donald would have it every day, but we ration him to Christmas."

Like the wine, the soup was exceptional. After a perfunctory sniff and an exploratory taste, Calum tilted his plate and scooped away. It was all James could do to keep him from licking the shallow bowl clean.

Next, it was Isobel's turn to reappear, bringing with her a bottle of red wine, already opened. "I *know* you're going to like this one. It's one of my favorites—not terrifically well known but really solid. It's an eastern Australian Shiraz. And it"—she began pouring—"is"—she filled Cal's glass—"smashing."

She filled James' glass, and then removed the half-empty white wine goblets. "Enjoy!"

"Is this all you do?" Cal asked her.

"I cook as well," she confided. "Starters, salads, and desserts—which are my specialty."

"Will you marry me?" asked Cal.

She gave him a dazzling smile. "Why don't we wait until pudding? In case you change your mind."

With that, she was gone again. Caroline arrived a moment later with a tray of steaming plates. "These are hot," she warned, placing a plate before each of her guests. The air was suddenly filled with a heavenly aroma.

"Lamb and potatoes." Cal sighed happily. "They must be able to read my mind."

"Everyone can read your mind, Cal," James remarked. "Whatever you're thinking is on your face before you open your mouth. Enjoy!" Raising his glass, he took a deliberately large sip. The red, in James' estimation, was even better than the white. Although partial to reds, he knew nothing whatsoever about wine—except to stay far, far away from that nasty Khazak stuff the Afghans served the UN troops. What the soldiers didn't drink, they used to clean their rifles; it stripped away old grease and did not leave a sticky residue.

The two men made short work of the meal, eating in companionable silence.

"*Will* she marry me, do you think?" asked Calum, looking up from his empty plate.

"Isobel? Oh, sure," James told him. "You two can open a wine bar in Aberdeen."

"Stranger things happen, James, my man," he pointed out.

"They do indeed."

A moment later, Isobel came to remove the plates. "Who's for pudding?" she said, refilling James' glass with the luscious red. She moved to refill Cal's glass, and James noticed that she stood much closer to Cal than before.

"You were right," Cal told her, indicating the wine. "This is very good."

"I knew you'd like it." She poured a little extra into his glass. "For pudding we have a really scrummy chocolate torte," she said, replacing the bottle.

"If it's anything like its cook," answered Cal, returning her smile, "I'm sure it's lovely."

"Charmer," she purred and disappeared again.

"I think she likes you," James said when she had gone. "Charmer."

Isobel returned with two plates. Placing one before James, she moved to Cal's side. "Take a bite," she instructed, resting her hand lightly on Cal's shoulder, "and tell me what you think."

Cal dutifully picked up his spoon and took a large bite, rolled it around in his mouth, and grinned. "I was right," he said. "It is terrific. The best chocolate torte I've ever tasted."

Isobel beamed triumphantly. "I'll see to the coffees."

She left them to their desserts, and James dug in. Cal, however, merely stared at his plate. "What's wrong?" James asked.

"You know I can't eat chocolate," Cal sighed. "It always gives me a bruising headache."

"The things we do for love."

Nodding forlornly, Cal took a wary bite. At that moment, the door opened and a lean, lanky man with thinning gray hair stepped quickly in. "Here!" he said, almost bounding across the room. His tie was loosened, his suit coat unbuttoned, and he wore a pair of reading glasses on a cord around his neck, giving him the air of an overworked librarian. "Dreadfully sorry to be so late. Don't let me interrupt. I just wanted to pop in and say hello. I'm Donald." He held out his hand. "You must be James."

"Pleased to meet you," James replied, shaking his hand. "And this is my friend Calum."

They shook hands. The kitchen door opened and Caroline entered with a pitcher of water. "Donald, you're home. Come into the kitchen and we'll get you something to eat."

"Not hungry in the slightest," he said. "But I could do with a slice of that torte—if someone insisted."

"Please, join us," James offered. "Cal says it's terrific."

Lord Rothes did not require urging. Caroline set down the pitcher and went off to fetch him his pudding, while Rothes pulled out a chair and sat down opposite Cal. "I don't mind telling you it's been one of those days," he confided. "Still, we gave as good as we got, I think. Good trip down?"

"A small delay in Crewe, apparently," James answered, "but otherwise tolerable."

"Then you won't have seen the Prime Minister's speech this afternoon, I suppose?"

"As a matter of fact, we caught it on the news a little while ago."

"What did you think?"

"About what you'd expect, I guess," James replied. "No real surprises."

"Ah!" Donald said, jumping on James' assessment.

"There *was* one small victory snatched from the jaws of defeat."

He leaned forward, his expression growing keen and excited. It was only then that James recognized him as the backbencher who had thrown Parliament into a tizzy with his question about the State funeral for Ready Teddy. It suddenly dawned on him why Caroline had been so unaccountably pleased to hear that the issue had been raised in the broadcast. Then, he had been just another pinstriped politico waving an order paper. Now, however, he looked like a schoolboy who has just found out a dirty secret about his teacher. "One small victory. Know what it was?"

# Six

"I wouldn't be surprised if the Save Our Monarchy lunatics put him up to this. Those bastards have been a pain in the ass from the beginning. I want them squeezed until the pips squeak, understand?" Prime Minister Waring thrust himself back in his chair and glared at the unhappy faces huddled around the oval table.

The PM's deputy, a carefully coiffed, Armani-suited redoubtable woman named Angela Telford-Sykes, was first to speak. "Calm down, Tom," she said, trying to smooth her chief's ruffled feathers. "They're just a bunch of blue-haired old dears. They make tea and hand out leaflets in shopping centers. Why, in a day or two, I wouldn't be surprised if—"

Waring's fist struck the table with such force the empty water jug bounced on its silver tray. "We don't have a day or two!" he shouted. "Bloody hell! Is everyone braindead around here?"

Telford-Sykes gazed over the top of her glasses, unmoved. A veteran of many campaigns, she was used to taking much worse from the PM. One or two of the other members of Waring's kitchen cabinet—those few trusted advisors of his inner circle—glanced nervously at the deputy.

"Because of that blasted question," Waring said, lowering his voice, "we're being maneuvered into providing a gala

State funeral for that reprobate winesop. The whole country heard it, for Crissakes! Any hope we had of sending him off with a quiet private ceremony is ruined."

"I don't believe that was ever a realistic option, Tom," Angela said soothingly. "Perhaps they've done us a favor by bringing this out into the open. We can use it."

"Bloody right we'll use it," Waring snapped. "But it will cost an absolute bomb."

Adrian Burton, Chancellor of the Exchequer, spoke up. "As it happens, I've had some figures prepared"—he lifted a sheet of paper from the leather folder before him—"and it looks like something in the region of fifteen million pounds is a reasonable minimum."

Waring stared daggers at the man. "I was thinking more in terms of the *political* cost, Adrian," he enunciated coldly. "I don't give a damn about the money."

"Quite," replied Burton. "Yes, quite."

Waring turned his eyes away from his chancellor. "Hutch has been on the phone all day, doing damage control, but the media smell blood. They are circling. Unless we provide a suitable alternative, gentlemen, this thing could get very painful."

"Hutch" was Martin Hutchens, his press secretary. His slight stature, cheap suits, and prep-school haircut went a long way towards disguising a fiercely calculating, creatively resourceful adversary. When he stumbled across a journalism course at the Poly years ago, the NHS may have lost a proctologist, but the Government gained a top-flight spin doctor. Ever since the televised House announcement, he had been laboring to deflect the increasingly strident insinuations that the Government had something to hide in the matter of the King's death.

"This is where it sits at the moment," Hutchens said. It was time to bring the rest of the inner circle up to speed. "The story is that the King's suicide—yes, we're using the 'S' word now, to desentimentalize the account and to prevent the opposition from whipping up a froth of false sympathy. Anyway, the suicide, unexpected as it was, has surprised us no less than anyone else. Did *The Times* predict it? Did *The*

*Guardian?* Was Ladbrokes taking bets? No. All right. A state funeral takes time to organize—you just can't throw one together overnight. We are sympathetic, of course. We are looking into it—doing all we can. Unfortunately, time is against us—we don't even have the corpse back yet and there's half a week gone. Not to put too fine a point on it, Portuguese embalming practices being what they are"—he made a fluttering motion with his hand before his face as if fanning away noxious fumes—"there are likely to be certain complications."

"For pity's sake, Martin," sighed the Home Secretary, a trim and elegant, dark-haired former Oxford Union president named Patricia Shah. "Might we forgo the histrionics, please?"

"Sorry," he said, moving quickly on. "More important, timing-wise, we host the Pan-European Economic Summit next week. That's true," he hastened to point out. "It's been on the books for months. Everybody knows it. Circumstances may not permit us to do all we would wish for the King's funeral—limited resources . . . available manpower . . . security . . . et cetera, et cetera."

"Are they buying it?" asked Dennis Arnold, Chairman of the Special Committee for Royal Devolution. A long-time party workhorse, he had known the Prime Minister since their days of sharing a flat at university.

"Not entirely," admitted Hutchens. "They'll probably assume we're stalling. But it'll stick until they dig up something else to throw at us."

"This is why we need to find out who is behind this State funeral scheme," Waring reiterated. "I want a thorough and speedy workup on Rothes. What's he up to? What's his agenda? Just as important: does he have a mistress? A fondness for schoolboys? Get something we can use."

"What if we can't find anything?" wondered Burton.

"Invent something, Adrian. Use your head for once."

"There's his title, of course," put in Hutchens. "He's one of the diehards who still uses it. That's what I hear, anyway."

"There," said Waring, throwing out his hand to Hutchens. "He's a greedy, aristo-royalist. We can start with that. We've got to sideline this bigmouthed smart-ass—put the heat on and keep it on. We'll keep him so occupied putting out fires that he won't have time to stir up any more trouble."

"What about the funeral?" asked Dennis Arnold. "What *are* we going to do?"

"I suggest we hold to our original plan," said the Home Secretary. "A simple, tasteful, but extremely low-key affair."

"But, I thought Tom just said—"

"I know what I said," Waring broke in. "But I *will not* be forced into splashing out on a costly public spectacle for that fat bastard—it goes against everything I believe in. I won't do it." He glanced around the table at his five chief advisors.

"On the other hand, we wouldn't want to appear to be unreasonable about this," Arnold suggested. "The people expect a certain amount of decorum at least. If we're seen to be doing Teddy boy down, that could cause a sympathetic backlash. The last thing we want is to have everyone feeling sorry for the old rascal."

Waring bristled, but he knew solid advice when he heard it. He paused, tapping the tips of his fingers together. "All right," he said at last, leaning forward to deliver his decision. "This is how it will be: we stick to the original plan, but allow a few modifications—heaven forbid we should seem *unreasonable*. The cremation goes ahead, but he can lie in state at Buckingham Palace. There will be a small family ceremony—at the crematorium, not at Westminster or St. Paul's. Nothing public, got it? Say the family wants it that way, and we're only respecting their wishes."

The Prime Minister stood up abruptly. "Meeting adjourned. Reconvene lunchtime tomorrow. Thank you, ladies and gentlemen; you are dismissed."

As the first of the inner circle of advisors filed out of the office, Leonard DeVries, the PM's private secretary, put his head around the corner of the door to announce, "Chief Whip is here to see you, sir. Is this a good time?"

"Perfect," Waring replied. "Send him in." To Hutchens and the Deputy Prime Minister, he said, "Both of you stay. I want you to hear this. It'll save repeating it later."

Nigel Sforza, Chief Whip of the British Republic Party,

was a somber man with a pockmarked face and long hands that had a tendency to flap when he became agitated. "I hope I am not intruding, Prime Minister. You did ask me to make my report a first priority."

"Yes, yes, of course, Nigel. Come right in—we're finished here. Hutch and Angela will sit in on this in case they have any questions."

"By all means," said the Chief Whip, taking the seat Waring offered. Placing his briefcase on the floor, he bent to open it and withdrew a handful of papers.

While he rifled through them, Waring explained, "I asked Nigel for a head count so we would know where we stand."

"Right," said Nigel, laying the papers on the table in front of him. "I'd ask you to remember that this was done off the record. If it came to a fight the numbers would probably change—depending on the particular issue in question."

"Point taken," said Waring impatiently. "How does it look?"

Sforza extended his index finger and ran it down the page before him. "We currently have a solid payroll vote of two hundred and ninety, which leaves sixty-one floaters."

Hutchens loosed a low, astonished whistle. "Sixty-one potential renegades."

Sforza glanced up at him. "Depending on the issue," he intoned coolly. "It is highly unlikely we would ever face the desertion of all sixty-one. Highly unlikely."

"But our majority is down to six," Angela pointed out. "It wouldn't take all sixty-one. Only six have to side with the opposition, and we're sunk."

"It won't come to that," said Waring firmly. It irritated him when people pointed out the weakness of their majority. They had come to power twelve years earlier with a comfortable margin of parliamentary seats. The years and bloody battles they had fought as a party had taken their toll, but he nursed fond hopes of building their margin back to its original fighting strength.

"The point is," suggested Hutchens, "it's one thing to abolish the monarchy, but quite another to endorse a full presidential republic. That might be a bridge too far for some of our renegades and fence-sitters. We don't really know how big the potential defection factor might be."

"There won't be any defections," Waring declared firmly.

"Fine. Great." Hutch shrugged. "Fiddle away, Nero. Personally, I smell smoke. This could be the thing the Opposition has been looking for to unite their own wayward ranks. If they were able to get to some of our renegades, we could lose the presidency vote."

He was only stating what Waring had told himself a thousand times since he'd learned of Teddy's suicide. The King's death could not have come at a worse time. It was, in many ways, the worst thing that could have happened to his government. He would have preferred the monarchy to have been dissolved as planned, thus clearing the way for the Act of Presidency. Everyone knew that, as the leader of the party in power, he fancied himself in the role of Britain's first chief executive.

Parliament as a whole was much more doubtful about the benefits of a presidential system than they were about dissolving the monarchy. Even the most ardent republicans disagreed; after all, why throw over one king just to elect another?

The vote on the necessary presidential legislation would be close, and Waring knew he would need every single one of his majority seats to carry the day. For, despite their impressive show of unity and power, the British Republic Party had been running on reputation for some time. Savvy insiders knew already, and the media were beginning to suspect, that their rhetorical bark was far worse than their political bite.

The Prime Minister's great fear was that the occasion of a State funeral would revive the latent royalist sympathy within his party—to say nothing of the nation as a whole—and he would lose even more ground to an increasingly powerful Opposition. Six seats was as slender a majority as he ever cared to see. Years ago, the old Tory party had limped along for a while with a two-seat majority, but they had crashed and burned in the very next general election; and, after a few years in opposition, they had disintegrated completely, ridding the political landscape of their unsightly presence.

Waring had no intention of repeating their mistakes. If necessary, he would lobby every one of the fence-sitters and renegades and promise them whatever it took to secure their loyalty. He ardently hoped it would not come to that.

The Chief Whip put aside his paper and took up the next one. "When questioned about the funeral," he said, "thirty of the floaters were in favor of a full State funeral."

Waring frowned. If half the floaters wanted a slap-up funeral for the old bugger, how many of the rest felt that way, too? Was it worth risking a royalist backlash to appease his wayward backbenchers?

"Poll the payroll," he ordered, making up his mind. "I want the results as soon as possible."

He thanked Sforza then, and dismissed him. When the Chief Whip had gone, the PM turned to his second in command, and said, "It looks like we might have to toss the press a few fish." He drummed his fingers on the table for a moment. "Right. We'll arrange to meet the coffin, and let the newshounds cover it—limousines and a police escort, that sort of thing. I want it tasteful, but low-key—*ultra*-low-key, in fact. This thing will have to be stage-managed to keep it from getting out of hand. Understood?"

"Absolutely."

"Get on it, Angela. Make like it was our intention all along."

"I'll brief Pat and Dennis and we'll pull some options together, and" —she glanced at her slender gold watch— "I should be able to give you a call after dinner."

"Do that."

When the Deputy Prime Minister had gone, Waring turned to Hutchens. "Get the media sorted. A few papers and only one camera crew from each of the major channels. I won't have a circus—got it?"

"Got it."

"Good," Waring said, turning his attention to the leather notebook before him. "Get busy." When his aide made no move, he glanced up. "What?"

"Nothing." The press secretary hesitated. "It's just . . . well, there *is* one last niggling detail."

"For God's sake, spill it, Martin. I don't have all day."

"This Teresa Vierta," said Hutchens, watching the PM's eyes. "Teddy's floozy."

"What about her?"

"I have to know if there is any way she can be traced to us."

The Prime Minister stared at his press secretary for a moment. "I shouldn't think so."

"In other words: yes."

"All right, have it your way. Yes—but only in a most peripheral way."

"Did money change hands?"

Waring glanced away. "Yes."

"Jesus H. Christ!" The young man leaped up. "Why didn't I know about this?"

"You didn't need to know," the Prime Minister told him.

"How much?"

"How much what?"

"How much money did you give her?"

"Not much. Eight, maybe ten thousand—something like that. It was in the way of a one-time payment, ostensibly so she could buy the proper clothes and a better apartment. What does it matter how much?"

"And what was she supposed to do for this? Become his love slave?"

Waring frowned. "Nothing like that. I only wanted information. I had to know if the old sot was going to do the right thing or cause trouble."

"So you set him up with a hooker," Hutch said. "I don't believe this."

"She isn't a prostitute," Waring corrected mildly, unmoved by his aide's dramatics. "She's a socialite."

"I can't believe you gave her money. It's so amateurish. If she goes public with that, it could blow us out of the water big time. No way could I control that."

"Relax, Martin. It's already under control," the Prime Minister said casually.

"Let me tell you, these things have a way of—"

"She won't breathe a word to anyone. Trust me." When he saw that his assurances were failing to persuade his press secretary, Waring added, "Instead of worrying about things that don't concern you, why not try coming up with a way to sideline those Save Our Monarchy demonstrators for a change? They're beginning to get on my nerves."

Hutchens regarded his boss, silently shaking his head.

Waring stood. "That is all, Mr. Hutchens."

"Are you sure there aren't any more hand grenades you care to lob my way?"

"As always, you'll be the first to know." Waring flicked his hand at him. "I'll expect a preliminary report in the morning."

The press secretary made a sour face and departed. Waring sat down and leaned back in his chair for a moment to review the various aspects of the meeting just concluded. When he was satisfied he had covered all the details, he rose and opened the door to the outer office. "Leo," he said to his private secretary, "I'm going upstairs."

"Very good, sir. Good night, Prime Minister."

Waring walked back through the empty meeting room and left by a side door, which opened onto a private lift. Once upstairs, he took off his suit jacket, poured himself a drink from the crystal decanter, picked up the remote control, and settled back to watch the news.

## ✳

# Seven

Caroline arrived with Donald's pudding, one for herself, and a second helping of chocolate torte for Cal. "Isobel insisted," she told him, sliding the plate before him.

Donald, eager to share news of his small victory, remained undeterred by the arrival of his dessert. "I'll tell you what it was, shall I?"

"Please do," James invited.

"The Prime Minister declared in the House of Commons that Britain was still a monarchy." Donald picked up his spoon in triumph. "Didn't you think that was significant?"

"I guess not. Is it?"

"Most certainly, it is—highly significant," Donald remarked, sliding his plate closer. "When the most rabidly antiroyalist Prime Minister ever to occupy Number Ten swears to the House and the nation that he answers to king and crown, I call that significant. Why, for the last eighteen months the devolutionists have had their goons combing the countryside, systematically terrorizing some of Britain's oldest and most respected families, and a host of other decent citizens, coercing everyone into signing away their nobility. Anyone who refused was strong-armed into—"

"Donald," Caroline chided, "don't lecture our guests, dear. Let them eat their pudding in peace."

"Yes, of course," he said, and dug into the thick slab of chocolate with his spoon.

"We don't mind," Cal said, speaking up. "We rarely get to discuss politics with a real, live Member of Parliament."

Donald smiled, spooning up some of the cherry sauce. "Actually, it's rather a new rôle for me—I was one of the so-called 'Horde of Lords' who migrated to the other House when our own club was shut down." Regret flitted across his face, vanishing at once. "Much of the rigmarole is similar, of course. The canteen is worse. The big difference is constituency work, which I enjoy immensely—a happy discovery, that. Didn't think I would. The plum appointments are all committee related, and I've yet to get my oar in." He licked his spoon happily. "Still, it's very satisfying to have one's say in the House and ruffle a few feathers if possible."

"Like today," James pointed out.

"Indeed." Donald chewed thoughtfully for a moment, then resumed, adopting a more philosophical tone. "The King's funeral is important. It is, I believe, fundamental to who we are as Brits. We shouldn't allow ourselves to be robbed of our valuable heritage."

"Is that what they're trying to do?" Cal inquired.

"I'm sure Waring and his minions would like nothing more than for the whole miserable thing to sink quietly out of sight. But we've got our teeth into this one, and we'll give 'em a run for their money they won't forget." It seemed to James that Donald had shifted gears and was now talking about something different. "One has to appreciate the irony of it, really. I mean, the thing that signals the end of the monarchy may be the very thing that will save it."

"Donald," interrupted Caroline, "tell me you're *not* going to go into all that again. It's just too tedious." She looked across the table. "Calum, how are you coming with that pudding? Ready for another?"

"This'll do for me," Cal replied, manfully tucking into the torte, which was even bigger than the first slice. "Thanks all the same."

Lord Rothes took another big bite of his dessert, and then pushed the plate away. "Good pudd," he said, with a slight smack of his lips. "Forgive me, but I can't seem to think or talk about anything else. These are momentous events—absolutely earthshaking. Look at it! We are less than three months away from an Act of Parliament that will bring down the curtain on the world's last genuine monarchy, and what does the world's last genuine monarch do to mark the occasion? He puts a gun to his head and blows his bloody brains—"

"Donald . . ." cautioned his wife, "table talk."

"Let us say that, unable to face the ignominy of being known for all time as the King who presided over the abolition of the monarchy, Edward chose another way out of a particularly unhappy dilemma."

"Suicide, then. Is that certain?" Cal asked.

"No question whatever," Donald affirmed. "Waring only presents the other options—murder and misadventure—because he's afraid some of the blood might spatter on *his* lily-white hands."

"I never liked Edward," Caroline confided, "but I wouldn't have wished this on him. I wouldn't wish that sort of desperation on anyone."

"Rubbish," Donald scolded. "First manly thing he ever did in his life. Teddy knew, as well as everyone else, he'd failed. Had he been a better man he might have made something of his life—he might have made something of his Crown."

"And pigs might fly," Cal observed dryly. "The royals were always a randy bunch of skirt-chasing ne'er-do-wells and adulterers, if you ask me. Self-seeking, self-serving, and self-indulgent stinkers to a man, mean-spirited and stingy as the day is long. Reprobates, rakes, and rascals—you can have the lot of them." He glanced from the ring of faces around the table to his glass and, feeling perhaps he had gone a little over the top, added, "That's only my humble opinion, of course."

"Quite," Donald affirmed. "The final irony"—again, James noticed, he used that word—"is that if he hadn't been the kind of man he was, poor Teddy would never have ended it the way he did and we wouldn't have the chance now to—"

He checked himself abruptly, leaving the distinct impression he realized he had been speaking out of turn. "Well" — he smiled weakly— "let's just say all is not lost. Not by a long chalk."

Lady Rothes changed the subject smoothly. "The coffee must be ready, I expect. Donald, why don't you be a dear and go help Isobel carry in the tray?"

It was Cal who responded to her suggestion. "I'd be happy to go," he said, rising eagerly to his feet. "Donald can finish his dessert."

"I wouldn't hear of it," Lord Rothes protested.

"I'm halfway there already," said Cal, stepping away from the table.

"I expect he wanted to ask about her recipe," James suggested when he had gone.

"He wouldn't be the first," Caroline replied knowingly.

"It's true," Lord Donald observed, placidly spooning cherry sauce from his plate. "That girl is an inspired cook. She could have a job in any of London's top restaurants just like that."

"You're lucky to have her," James said, making conversation. "How long has she been with you?"

"Forever," replied Donald. "She's our daughter."

"Then you're doubly lucky," James told him. "She's a lovely young woman."

"And absolutely indispensable to my work. The average citizen has no idea just how much government goes on behind the scenes. Why, a Member of Parliament is always entertaining someone or other. Isobel takes all the fuss and bother out of it, and allows me to get on with the business at hand. Don't know what I'd do without her."

Talk turned to Scotland then, and mutual acquaintances, whereupon Cal and Isobel emerged from the kitchen—Cal with a tray of cups, and Isobel with a *cafetière* and a pot of cream. "What did you think of the torte, Daddy?" she asked, pausing to give her father a peck on the cheek.

"Delightful, my dear, as ever."

Isobel put down the *cafetière* and relieved Cal of the tray. He resumed his place, and she poured the coffee, distributing the cups around the table. Taking one for herself, she settled beside Cal and announced, "Calum keeps horses for hunting. He's invited all of us to come up over the holidays to go riding."

"You'd be most welcome," Cal told them. "It is a magnificent estate, and there are miles of bridle paths—some of them have never been used by anyone but James and me. It would be a pleasure to show you."

The Rothes declared it a wonderful invitation, and agreed to give it their full consideration. But at the mention of the estate, James felt his heart sink; pleasantly distracted by the company, he'd forgotten that particular burden for a while. He listened dully as Cal recited the splendors of Blair Morven; the Rothes seemed more than mildly interested.

Finally, to James' relief, Caroline called it a day. "You gentlemen must excuse me. I'm bushed, and I'm going to bed." To her husband, she said, "If you have any sense at all, you'll allow our guests to get some sleep. It's been a long day, and I expect they are exhausted."

Donald stood and downed the rest of his coffee in a gulp. "My lovely wife is right, gentlemen. It's late, and I have kept you from your beds long enough. I expect I'll see you at breakfast?"

"I expect so," James said, getting to his feet. "Rhys said he'd call for us at half past eight tomorrow."

Cal rose somewhat reluctantly, and both guests thanked their hosts for a smashing dinner. On the upstairs landing, James wished the lord and lady of Kenzie House a good night, and went into his room. The last thing he heard as he closed the door was Calum asking what time breakfast would be in the morning, and, "Will Isobel be there?"

Cal needn't have worried. Isobel was very much present at breakfast the next morning. A solid night's sleep had put James in a hopeful frame of mind, and he joined a well-scrubbed Cal—already halfway through a plate of kippers and eggs, and a carafe of coffee—at the table in the breakfast room.

"Get here early to beat the crowd, did we?" he asked.

"Morning, James," Cal replied blithely. "Sleep well?"

"Like a stone." Indicating Cal's half-finished plate, he said, "That looks good."

"It's marvelous. Isobel's eggs are like no others—"

"I'll bet." James poured some coffee into his cup and sipped it tentatively.

The young woman herself materialized a moment later, looking delectable in a long blue-green and yellow flower-print skirt, and a green floppy wool jumper with an oversize roll-top neck which slid this way and that to reveal a pretty neck and throat. She greeted James nicely and asked what he would like.

"The kippers look good," he replied, "and Cal tells me the eggs are simply to die for."

"I never said *that!*" Cal shot him a dirty look across the table.

She laughed, and the sound of her voice brightened the early-morning November gray. "Kippers and eggs it is," she said, "and more coffee."

"A man could grow to love it here," sighed Cal when she had gone.

"I think one man already has."

"So, what happens today?" Cal asked, changing the subject.

"Today we find out what all the fuss is about," James replied, and finally revealed to Cal what Embries had said about owning the whole of Blair Morven.

"Get away with you!"

"I'm serious. That's what he said."

"Man, who is this Embries—your fairy godfather?"

"Something like that."

"I thought he was someone your solicitor put you on to. How'd you meet him anyway?"

"I'll tell you, but you have to promise not to hoot."

"I nivver hoot," Cal insisted.

Isobel returned with James' breakfast, and an apology. "Mother sends her regrets that she isn't able to see you two this morning. Daddy likewise. It's complicated." She frowned. "But they both hope to catch up with you before you leave." She poured some more coffee, and left.

"You were telling me how you met your pointy-headed friend," Cal prompted.

James rehashed the details of his curious meeting with the mysterious Embries. Cal listened, growing increasingly incredulous as the story unfolded.

"Let me get this straight," he said when James finished. "Some loony you've met wandering around in the heather in the middle of the night calls you up and says 'Come to London,' and you drop everything and flit off to the city without anything more to go on than 'he seemed to know what he was talking about'—is that right?"

"Crudely, yes."

"Good," concluded Cal, "I was afraid I missed something."

"He was the one who said I should bring a friend with me."

"Figuring, no doubt, that there ought to be at least one brain between us."

"You had to be there," James told him. "It was pretty uncanny."

"I'm sure it was." Cal looked at his friend, shaking his head slowly.

"It hasn't turned out so bad," James said, indicating their surroundings. "You would never have met Isobel if we hadn't come."

"That's beside the point," Cal grumped. "I *knew* this had more than a whiff of snark hunt about it."

"If you knew so much, why'd you agree to come along?"

"And let you go waltzing off to London alone?" He smiled suddenly. "I'm no' as irresponsible as you are, Jimmy. Anyway, you played the I-need-you-Cal card and that trumped the lot."

"I appreciate this."

"I know."

Gulping down the last of his coffee, James pushed back from the table as the doorbell rang. "That'll be Rhys. Ready?"

"Oh, aye," said Cal. "I'll just give Isobel a wee hand with these." He picked up a couple of plates and headed for the kitchen door.

Rhys, punctual to a fault, was standing in the foyer, waiting for his passengers. James greeted him, and said, "Cal's right behind me."

A few moments later they stepped outside to a bright if chilly day. There was water pooled on the pavement and street, and drops of water blistered the mirror-smooth finish of the black Jaguar waiting at the foot of the steps. The sky, however, was brilliant blue, and a watery winter sun streamed through the mostly bare branches. "Where are we going?" Cal asked as Rhys opened the rear door for his passengers.

"St. James's Palace," came the reply. Rhys closed the door, and took his place at the wheel. "Would you mind fastening your seat belts, please?"

It was a friendly safety tip, and one which James and Cal might have done well to heed—psychologically speaking.

## ❋
# Eight

They settled back and watched the city slide silently past the windows as the car sped along Pall Mall towards their destination. The Palace of St. James, like nearly all royal properties, had been appropriated by the Government on behalf of the nation. Under the terms of royal devolution, the former residents had returned the buildings and lands to the public which had, after all, paid for them in one way or another. As if to underscore the point, the Government had turned the palaces and apartments of the royals into offices for civil servants. Only two properties remained outside direct Government control: Buckingham Palace, which had been abandoned by King Edward's predecessors some years before devolution began in earnest; and the Balmoral estate in Scotland.

Buckingham Palace was leased to a private corporation that maintained it as a venue for special State functions but primarily as a tourist attraction, selling tickets for tours. There was still a changing of the guard, but the soldiers and marching band were hired. The contract had a good few years to run, although it was assumed that when the lease expired, Buckingham Palace would go the way of Kensington, Windsor, Sandringham, Hampton Court, St. James's, and the other stately piles already devolved. As for Balmoral, always much the favorite of the royals of yesteryear, the King had been allowed to keep that—as long as he paid taxes on it like any upright citizen. A fellow had to have some place to live, after all.

St. James's, that fine old red-stone monstrosity built by Henry VIII for Anne Boleyn, had received a much-needed general refurbishment; its ruddy façade had been scrubbed until the stonework fairly glowed in the early winter light. Even the giant clock high up in the six-storey gatehouse gleamed a wintry white and gold.

The black Jaguar rolled to a halt at a red-and-white striped barrier, where an armed guard waved the car through. After parking in the courtyard between two wings of the building, Rhys led James and Cal through a second security gate and metal detector, then into a veritable rabbit warren of rooms, corridors, offices, and reception areas large and small, down many flights of steps, and along an underground passageway which delivered them eventually to a tiny vestibule presided over by a steely-eyed woman with bright red lipstick; her hair was scraped tightly to her head, and her stark white blouse was an old-fashioned variety with a high, starched collar.

"Mrs. Garrison," said Rhys, "this is Mr. Stuart." The woman nodded, regarding James narrowly. "And Mr. McKay." Cal beamed placidly at the woman. "Mrs. Garrison," Rhys explained, "is Embries' administrative assistant. I will leave you in her capable hands."

"Good morning." The prim woman rose at once to take their jackets. "He is expecting you." The way she said it made James think she was talking about the Almighty. "He said to bring you in directly." Indicating the door behind her, she said, "This way, gentlemen, please."

Embries' assistant conducted them through a short, book-lined entryway to another door, knocked once, and, without waiting for an answer, pushed it open. They were ushered into a windowless office about the size of a single-car garage. The entire space was wholly occupied with books, books, and more books—overflowing the floor-to-ceiling

shelves that lined every wall. As many as there were, they
shared three traits in common: all without exception were
thick, dark, and old—reeking with age, in fact, giving the
close room the distinct odor of an antiquarian bookshop.
There were no filing cabinets, no credenza, no tables, tele-
phones, keyboards or computers—the universal clutter of
offices the world over.

The man himself was sitting at a great antique wooden
desk, looking officious and efficient in a severe black suit
and waistcoat. His white hair was carefully combed, and his
long hands folded as, head down, he scanned a document
atop the tidy stack before him. His manner, appearance, and
surroundings were so at odds with the way James had last
seen him, he doubted for a moment whether it was the same
person.

Then, as James and Cal moved into the room, Embries
slowly raised his head and regarded them each with his
pale, knowing eyes, and all doubt vanished. This, James
knew, was the same man he had met on the hilltop two
nights ago.

Embries smiled and stood, holding out a slender hand in
greeting. "Welcome, and thank you for coming on such
short notice." Turning to Cal, he said, "And you must
be . . ."

"Calum McKay—Cal, please—at your service." Cal's
massive paw reached out in a handshake that seemed to rock
Embries in his shoes.

"Indeed!" exclaimed Embries with an air of satisfaction that intrigued James instantly. "Indeed," he repeated,
and James decided Embries more than approved of his
friend.

"This is some ritzy office block you have here," James remarked.

"One of the benefits of royal devolution," Embries answered, freeing his hand from Cal's grip. "Even old
warhorses like me get a decent office now. It's small, I know,
but it's private, and I much prefer it that way." He paused, regarding his visitor keenly. "I trust you got on with Lord and
Lady Rothes reasonably well?"

"Very well. Charming people, and most hospitable."

"Good eats," Cal added. "And a fantastic cook."

"Ah, yes" —Embries smiled— "the splendid Isobel. Well, I do apologize for my absence last night. It was unavoidable. But, as it has some slight bearing on the work before us today, I think you'll forgive me."

Eager to get down to business, James said, "And what *is* that work, exactly?"

"You are forthright. I like that. It will allow me to be forthright, too." He drew a straight chair away from the wall for Cal's use, and motioned James to join him on the other side of the desk. "Sit," he directed, indicating his vacated chair. "I have prepared some documents for your perusal."

James moved around the desk, and took the offered seat. Arranged in a neat stack before him were copies of government files—all filled-in blanks, badly typed, and impenetrable jargon. The first one his eye lit upon had a title at the top which read *Registration of Land Use: GA-5C*. Although the title meant nothing to him, he recognized the name Robert Moray, Lord Morven, in one of the typed-in spaces, and realized it must have something to do with the estate.

"We could spend all morning going through this collection piece by piece," Embries said, patting the stack with the flat of his hand. "Or I could simply tell you what I have discovered and work backwards from there."

This more than suited James' mood. "All right, let's cut to the chase. Two nights ago you implied Blair Morven belonged to me. Well? Here I am. Tell me: does it?"

"It does indeed."

"The whole estate?" said Cal, jumping up. "All of it belongs to Jimmy here?"

"All of it," confirmed Embries. "From the heather on the top of Uaimh Hill to the gravel at the end of the driveway— it all belongs to James."

"Man," Cal said, his grin wide with relief and delight, "you don't know how I have hoped someone would say that and mean it." He grew suddenly wary. "You do mean it, Mr. Embries? There's no catch?"

"None whatsoever." Embries moved to the side of the chair and leaned over the table.

"How is that possible?" asked James.

"By reason of the ordinary and ancient right of legal inheritance."

"And what makes you think that?" James asked bluntly. He had not come all the way to London to play games. "If there was even the slightest possibility of direct inheritance, I would have found out about it long ago and I wouldn't be here now."

"You are not listening," Embries replied calmly.

"You're not saying anything worth listening to!" snapped James irritably. "It's all just smoke and mirrors!"

Cal regarded his friend with mystified shock.

"I've already told you a great deal," Embries contended mildly. "Unless there is some special distribution of assets and property to be made in accordance with the last will and testament of the deceased, the legal heirs need not be named. In fact, there need be no will at all, strictly speaking."

"Look, I know all this. What's the point?" demanded James, suddenly angry with Embries for wasting his time.

"Barring any legal impediment—such as a dispute of ownership—under Scottish law the estate would simply fall to the sole surviving heir of the Duke."

In his present state it took James a moment to realize what Embries had just told him. "You're saying *I'm* the Duke's heir?"

"Great God Almighty," croaked Cal, sitting down slowly. "So that's the rub."

"The sole surviving heir to the Duke's estate," corrected Embries, "and therefore entitled to all his worldly goods and possessions."

James stared incredulously at his eccentric benefactor. "And just how do you figure that?"

"By reason of the fact that you are the Duke of Morven's grandson." He said it so matter-of-factly that the full impact did not register on James at once.

"His grandson," James repeated dully. He felt his stomach tighten.

"The son of his only son, to be precise."

*Good Lord,* James thought, mentally taking a deep breath; he looked at Cal, who was shaking his head in astonishment.

Embries settled his long frame on the edge of the desk and regarded his visitors with sympathetic good humor. "I can understand that this is quite a lot to take in, but perhaps I can tell you a story which will explain."

James regarded the old man suspiciously. "Go on then."

"It starts like this," Embries said, smoothing a wrinkle from his smart black suit. "A young nobleman—a marquess, in fact—fell in love with a beautiful young woman named Elizabeth Grant whose family were tenant farmers on his father's estate. The Marquess' father, the Duke, opposed the union hatefully and unreasonably. He was a man of harsh judgments and definite opinions; once he got a notion into his head, it stayed.

"For reasons known only to himself, the Duke took an intense dislike to the lass who had captured his son's heart. I cannot think that it was anything to do with the young woman in question; she was above reproach. It is likely that the Duke nursed a private hope that his son would marry someone of his own station, thereby increasing his fortunes in the world and restoring something of the ancient luster to the family. Then again, perhaps he merely wanted to indulge a show of power.

"However it was, he forbade the marriage. In defiance, the young people eloped, marrying in secret, and then toured the continent for a few months to give the old boy time to cool off and change his mind.

"They returned from the honeymoon to find the Duke more bitter and adamant than ever. He took his son aside and gave him a simple choice: dissolve the marriage at once, or be disowned and forfeit his title, lands, and income, and any possibility of regaining his father's affection for the rest of his life. He left the two young people alone to think about it for an hour or two.

"As it happened, the young Marquess was not at all a materialistic man. I do believe he would gladly have forfeited his inheritance to live in humbler circumstances with the woman he loved. But there was someone else to consider now: his young wife was pregnant. While the Marquess might have been willing to abase himself for the love of his life, he could not bring himself to dishonor the young lady and his unborn child.

"Forced to this dire extremity, the Marquess showed his true mettle. He devised a plan which, although involving a certain amount of sacrifice in the short term, would secure a long-term benefit for himself, his wife, and child. He hit upon the idea of a false annulment. Through a sympathetic solicitor, he fashioned a document convincing enough to fool the Duke into believing his son had finally seen the sense of putting the unacceptable marriage behind him."

As Embries talked, a strange detachment crept over James. Even though the people in the story were intimately known to him, their lives as much a part of him as his own, he could not help blurting, "You're not saying the Duke fell for it?"

Embries rose and began to pace slowly, one hand supporting an elbow, the other fingering his chin. "The Duke wanted to believe his son had acceded to his wishes and, in fact, he had every reason to do so. Still, the old fox was very much a belt-and-braces man. He accepted the annulment but made a further demand. He told his son that he would not be reinstated until the young woman was married off quietly to another. Only then would the young man's future be secure."

"Unbelievable," muttered James.

"Well, the young people were stuck," argued Embries. "They had not anticipated anything like this; what is more, they were quickly running out of time. With each passing day, the unborn child was growing; their secret could not be kept from the world very much longer. What could they do but agree?"

"They caved in to the old bastard," remarked James gloomily.

"Ah, but the Marquess did not surrender without a fight," Embries continued, moving with slow, deliberate steps. "He fought for, and won, a dispensation: the young woman should be properly cared for—in short, she and her new husband, whoever that might be, should receive a house and a position on the estate.

"The Duke—as yet unaware that Elizabeth was with child—reluctantly accepted these terms, whereupon the Marquess played his last desperate card in this whole miserable game. He recruited a long-time friend to pretend to marry the girl."

"John Stuart," James murmured as the final piece of the puzzle dropped into place.

"Yes. The man you knew as your father entered the scene. Now, I do not know if money changed hands, or whether there was some other inducement, but—knowing the people involved—I rather think Stuart acted out of genuine friendship for the Marquess and a sincere regard for Elizabeth.

"These arrangements were swiftly carried out, and soon after the Duke suffered a minor stroke. This encouraged the young people mightily. No one expected the situation to be anything but a short-lived ruse which would be abandoned upon the imminent death of the old tyrant.

"After all, once the Duke was safely in his grave, the Marquess, having inherited his birthright, could do as he wished. His friend John would step aside so he could resume his life with his beloved Elizabeth, and raise his child in a manner appropriate to his station. This was the gist of it. A foolish, fantastic plan beginning to end, but they were young and they were desperate. They had been made aware of the consequences for their child, and willingly accepted the risks. And yet, in spite of all its flaws—in spite of everything—it might have worked.

"The only trouble was that the Duke did not die quickly. He had two more strokes in swift succession; and though each one laid him low, the iron Duke recovered, sending his son into the depths of black despair and depression. You can imagine the Marquess' agony: here, the woman he loves is living with his best friend under the roof that he himself has provided. He can see her, talk to her, adore her from a distance, but he cannot touch her, hold her, make love to her as a husband ought. In due course, Elizabeth gives birth to a son—*his* son—and he can do no more for the lad than is fitting for a laird to offer the child of a tenant. Because the Duke is watching, watching, watching all the time."

James swallowed hard. "Are you saying that my mother—that she became the wife of John Stuart while still married to the Marquess? What's that—bigamy? It's outrageous!"

"Easy, Jimmy," urged Cal. "Hear him out."

Embries shook his head placidly. "Just as there was no real annulment, there was no true marriage, either."

"Adultery, then!"

"No, not adultery. And here we see the beauty of the sacrifice Jack and Elizabeth made. It is, in some ways, the most extraordinary part," Embries said, his voice taking on a note of respect, almost reverence. "In choosing John Stuart, the Marquess chose a true and loyal friend. John lived with his lovely Elizabeth in a completely celibate relationship. He was—and you know this as well as anyone—a deeply religious man, and not to be swayed from any path believed was right. He was a man who placed a high price on his beliefs and did not sell them cheaply."

James nodded. That was the man he knew.

"Also, you must remember, they all expected the Duke to die any day, and this hope gave them tremendous patience." Embries shook his head sadly. "But life is stranger than we can ever know, and far more unpredictable. What we expect to happen and what actually happens very often bear as much resemblance to each other as bright flame to damp ashes."

"What happened?"

"Can't you guess?"

"Ah, can you no' guess what happened, James? Can you no' remember?" cried Cal. "Even *I* remember!"

Instantly, James' memory flitted back to early childhood.

He had a hazy remembrance of the Marquess—talking to his father outside in the yard with three or four dogs running around him. He also remembered the Duke—the formidable dictator with the brass-topped walking stick who seemed determined to make everyone as miserable as himself. Holding the picture in his mind, he recalled what had happened to spoil the plan. "The Marquess died," he intoned softly.

Cal leaned back in his chair, nodding with approval.

"Exactly," confirmed Embries. "The Marquess was injured in an accident—near Glen Shee pass one black winter night his car went off the road—and he died two days later, leaving his father the Duke alive, and his wife and young child in the care of his friend." Embries paused, gazing inwardly at the unhappy scene.

After a moment, he said, "Now then, any of several things might have happened. I know both your mother and John Stuart were all for coming clean and facing the consequences. I counseled against this—"

"You," breathed James aloud. In his mind's eyes, he saw the photo he'd found in the hunting diary. "You knew about this from the beginning?"

"From the beginning? No." He shook his head. "But I knew about it long before it reached this point. I advised against revealing the Marquess' plan for several reasons—the most pertinent and important was that telling the Duke would almost certainly have destroyed the one thing they valued above all else, and for which all three of them had sacrificed so much."

"And that was?"

"Your future."

"*My* future!" James shot up out of the chair. "This is crazy! Fake annulments . . . phony marriages . . . plots and counterplots—it's a soap opera you're selling, and it has nothing to do with the people *I* knew in real life. You make it sound smutty and low. These were my parents, and it wasn't like that. It wasn't like that at all."

"For a fact, Mr. Embries," Cal put in, "James' mum and da' were the finest people I knew. Like second parents to me, and it's an insult to us both if you say a word against them."

Embries stood slowly and looked James up and down. He did not say anything for a moment. He neither defended his story, nor attempted to disperse his listeners' indignation. He merely gazed at James with his pale eyes, and waited until the heat flash of fury had abated.

"You can prove all this, I suppose."

"We would not be here otherwise."

"Show me."

"What do you want to see?"

"Something. Anything. Everything." James gestured towards the stack of papers on the desk. "There must be something in there you can show me to make me believe your story."

"I can show you any number of things," Embries replied quietly. "Proof is easy to come by. Belief is difficult—that is a matter of personal conscience and volition. What could I show you that you would believe? A birth certificate? A will? Documents can be forged, they can be changed. Belief is not here"—he placed his hand on the pile of papers—"it is here"—he tapped his temple with a fingertip—"and here"—he tapped his chest.

"I still want to see it."

"I thought you would," replied Embries. To Cal, he said, "Drag your chair around here so you can see." He drew the stack of documents to him. "Now sit, both of you. We have a long day ahead of us."

Slowly, inexorably, the evidence mounted with every scrap of paper Embries produced. Most of it pertained to the property and the hopelessly tangled settlement of the Duke's estate. James had learned enough about the legal ins and outs of the matter in the last few months to know that what he was being offered was genuine. From time to time, James showed one of the papers to Cal, who leaned over to inspect the document without comment. The clincher came in the form of a wedding certificate. Embries produced this in its turn, and any last resistance James had maintained to this point crumbled away.

Despite what Embries had said about documents being forged and changed, James had merely to glance at the single piece of badly photocopied paper to know it was the genuine article: John James Stuart and Elizabeth Anne Moray, nee Grant, had been married in a magistrate's office in Aberdeen. He stared long at the date. He would have been six years old at the time.

Finally, James had seen enough. Shoving the photocopy across the desk for Cal to see, he pushed back his chair, stood up, and moved quickly to the door.

Embries took a step after him. "James?"

"I have to get out of here. I'm sorry."

Cal stood up quickly. "Where are you going?"

James pulled open the door. "I don't know."

"Here, I'll come with you." Cal started after him.

"No," James told him without looking back. "Stay here."

Cal stepped to the doorway, intent on following. "James, wait—"

Embries called him back. "Let him go, Calum. He will be better off on his own for a while."

Cal hesitated, then returned to the desk. "I guess he got a little overwhelmed by all this"—he frowned at the untidy pile of papers—"all this stuff you're telling him."

"It's a great deal to take in," suggested Embries.

"I'll say," replied Cal. "He's just gone from being a homeless bastard to being a bloody rich bastard—and I use the term in the technical sense."

"An unacknowledged son," corrected Embries. "There is a difference. Still, there may be a few more shocks and surprises to come. He'll need a friend, Calum." Embries grew suddenly serious. "Are you the man to stand beside him?"

Embries allowed the question to hang in the air between them. Cal looked away, gazing out the door through which James had just passed.

"I need to know, Cal," said Embries. "How far are you willing to go?"

Cal swallowed and, dropping back into his chair, began to speak. "James and I used to cut school sometimes," he said, his voice low. "Once we took a couple of ponies without permission, and two rifles. We were, maybe, thirteen—and we were playing the big, brave hunters, setting out to bag the mighty monarch o' the glen.

"We couldn't have picked a worse day—cold, misty, thick fog rolling down the hillsides, couldn't see your hand in front of your face—but we had heard about this stag, and we were determined to bring it down and win the undying admiration of the world. We got out on the moors, and followed this track that James' father had shown him. We rode further and further into the hills—we should have turned back, but we kept going and going. The land got wilder, the hills higher, but we kept going.

"So," he said, becoming part of the event once more, "we stop for a rest, and we're sitting there, and we hear this sound—halfway between a snort and a growl. The mist is heavy and we can't see a thing; we can't even tell which direction the sound is coming from. But we know: *it's the stag!* 'Don't move,' says James. We hold our breath.

"A second later, something big and dark blows past us, and goes straight up the hill. We're on it like a shot. The horses are stumbling on the slick rocks, and it's getting steeper, but we're desperate to keep up. We reach the top of the hill, and all at once the mist clears, and we see it. There it is! God in heaven, it is a magnificent beast—a champion stag with an antler spread out to there"—he opened his arms wide—"and a thick black mane like a lion. The stag stops and turns, and looks right at us. He knows we're there, and he doesn't care.

"Before we can loosen the straps and pull our rifles free, the stag disappears over the hill. Now, it's down and down and down at breakneck speed. To this day, I don't know why one of the horses didn't fall and throw us on our fool heads. But we get to the bottom, splash across the burn, and it's straight up the other side again.

"This time we have to go slower. The hill is higher, the rocks larger, and the footing more treacherous. We get to the top and the stag is waiting for us. Waiting for us!

"There is a tall rock stack behind him, blocking escape that way, and to the other side the hill becomes a ridge that falls away sharp. We have him. James says, 'Go on, Cal. You can have the first shot.' My rifle is in my hands already and I put it up and squeeze off a round.

"The sound is deafening. I'm shaking so bad I can't see if I've hit him or not. The next thing I know the stag is coming at me—head down, those antlers a few inches off the ground. I don't even have time for another shot before it crashes into me.

"The pony rears up and turns, trying to get out of the way. The antlers catch the horse in the belly just under the rear flanks, and I'm thrown from the saddle. The force of the charge pitches the horse clean over onto its back—it's screaming and thrashing, hooves flying everywhere.

"The stag draws back, lowers its head, and makes to charge again—at me this time. Nostrils flaring, blood in the eyes, this beast is coming for me and there's not a doubt in my mind but that I'm looking death in the face. My rifle is gone. I don't know where it is. There's no time to look for it anyway—the hooves are already churning. I see rocks and gravel flying. I see that great head tilt down and the antlers like a dozen spear blades tipped with blood sweeping towards me.

"I'm dead, and I know it. I can't run. I can't shout. All I can do is stand there and wait to be impaled.

"And then . . . and then I feel this hand on my shoulder. And James is there. He pulls me back and steps into my place. The stag is on us. I turn my face away. The shot explodes in the same instant. Smoke fills my nose and mouth and stings my eyes.

"When I look again, I see the stag on its knees—its hind legs are still driving, but the forelegs have collapsed. James shoots again, and the head falls to one side. The antlers catch in the ground, and that thick neck snaps. It sounds like a tree root breaking deep in the earth.

"Silence after that . . ."

Calum paused; the quiet of the book-lined room was complete.

"James saved my life that day," he said at last. "He put himself between me and sure death. There is not the slightest doubt in my mind that he'd do it again. And I'd do the same for him—any time, any place. I'd do whatever it took, and I wouldn't think twice about it." He nodded, a quick downward jerk of his chin to underscore the sentiment. "Does that answer your question?"

Glancing up, Cal saw that Embries' eyes were closed. At first he thought the old man had fallen asleep, but then he saw the thin lips moving rapidly, as if the old gent was reciting a private litany.

"Mr. Embries?" he asked. "Are you all right, Mr. Embries?"

Slowly, the golden eyes opened, and Calum saw in them a strange excitement that both stirred him and chilled him to the marrow. "Forgive me," the white-haired old man breathed softly. "I was remembering another day a long time ago."

Placing his palms together, he sat for a time gazing at Calum over the tips of his fingers, as if toting up the sum of a complex equation. Calum endured the scrutiny, returning the old man's gaze with stoic silence. Finally, Embries lowered his hands and said, "Thank you for telling me that. It means more than you can know."

"I'd do anything for James, Mr. Embries," Calum reiterated stubbornly. "That's my solemn vow."

"Very well, first things first. He will need you to be present and available. Wrap up your affairs. You can leave your work for a while, I believe?"

"I suppose so—seeing it's winter and things are slowing down a bit. I have two or three hunting parties scheduled around Christmas and New Year's."

"Cancel them," Embries ordered.

"Sure. You got something else in mind?"

"Oh, I do indeed. There are one or two other details to explain, but let's just say that it would be best if you remained unencumbered for the near future."

"For James' sake."

"For James, yes," Embries assured him, "and for Britain." His eyes took on the strange excitement once more, and it seemed to Calum as if the man before him was looking through him—or beyond him—to something he found intensely, dazzlingly fascinating. "We will do great things," Embries said, his voice the echo of a whisper. Cal was not even sure if the old man was talking to him.

※

# Nine

Retracing his steps through the hallways and galleries as best he could, James followed one exit sign after another until he emerged into the light of day once more. He hurried across the courtyard parking lot, and headed down the street, not looking, not caring, where he was going. He walked for a time—the brisk, agitated walk of a man with weighty and troublesome matters on his mind.

Time and his surroundings blurred around him. With every step, his mind lurched over the same strange ground—the tangled legal terrain of a score of obscure records. In his mind, James saw them as red arrows on a map, and all of them were pointing towards the same inevitable conclusion: he was not who he thought he was.

*How could it be?* he wondered. *What did it mean?*

He walked on, striking out across a busy street, heedless of the traffic. He came upon the entrance to a park, and swiftly continued in. As the tumult of his thoughts began to calm somewhat, the first questions gradually coalesced into another: why?

*Why is this happening?* he demanded. *Why me?*

Unexpectedly, James received an answer—so clear and loud he first imagined someone had spoken aloud. *Because,* said the voice, which sounded very much like Embries', *you were born for this.*

This so surprised him that he stopped in his tracks and looked around. The pale sunlight had faded into a pewter haze overhead. The wind was colder, and a ground fog was beginning to form. Four or five pathways fanned out before him through the mostly empty park; there were few people around. The path he happened to be standing on was deserted, so he continued on, pushing his hands into his pockets and wishing he had thought to bring his coat.

To warm up, he began to jog.

His leather-soled shoes slapped the pavement hard; he could feel the jolting impact with every step. He passed some people bundled up on park benches; they regarded him with the kind of look reserved for suspicious strangers running in street clothes. James didn't care. It felt good to run, to feel the cold air burning in his lungs. This, at least, was real, he thought. After all that he had heard in Embries' office, he needed something tangible, something physical; he needed sweat and cold and an ache in his side and a blister on his heel to anchor him to reality once more.

The rhythm of running changed the flow of his thoughts; the questions spinning in his head grew sharper, more focused. Instead of asking the vague and amorphous *why?* the question became: *why does this upset me?*

All that Embries had showed him, when added to what he already knew, made perfect sense. And it wasn't as if the news was particularly scandalous—maybe once upon a time, but not now; anyway, everyone even remotely concerned was dead now, except James. If no one else cared about his parentage, why should he?

He thought about the legal wrangle over the estate. *How many times,* he asked himself, *in how many months, have you wished for something amazing to turn up? If once, then a thousand times,* came the reply. A letter, a will, a bolt from the blue—anything to turn the case his way. Now, here it was, the miracle he had secretly hoped would save his home and livelihood. James stood to inherit one of the few great estates left in the entire country. Why be upset about it? Why not embrace it, welcome it, seize it with both hands and shout Hallelujah! like any normal person?

He had no answer. The plain fact was that he *was* upset. He could accept his parents' deception; he could accept his new identity and, insofar as it promised to secure his home and all he held dear, he could even welcome it. Yet there was something about all this that filled him with unspeakable trepidation. He felt sweat trickle down his sides, and it was the cold sweat of pure, undiluted dread.

It seemed to James that the very air swarmed with uncertainty and menace—as if a great weight hung over him on a fast-fraying rope.

It must be fear, he concluded at last. Was he not behaving like a frightened man? Running, desperately trying to escape from the peril he felt closing in around him. *But what was it?* he wondered. What was there about this situation that frightened him so much it had him running like a madman through the park?

When James finally stopped to look around, the sun was already past midday and the shadows were growing long. The sky overhead had a darkly threatening aspect, and a light breeze was kicking up the few dry leaves on the path which had become little more than a muddy track through unmown grass. He was sweating from his run, and was feeling the cold begin to bite. He decided it was time to head back. First, however, he had to figure out where he was.

With quick steps, James returned along the path and reached the place where he had departed from the pavement. Making his way to the nearest street, he left the park and walked quickly towards the closest junction, thinking to find a street sign or two to help orient himself. As he approached the intersection, however, he glimpsed, out of the corner of his eye the motion of a dark shape coming up behind him, and recognized the black Jaguar. The car stopped as he turned around; Rhys jumped out of the driver's seat and opened the back door. Cal and Embries were inside.

"We thought you might be getting cold, sir," Rhys said. "Would you like to come with us?"

James nodded, and slid into the backseat with Embries,

who held out his coat. "Thanks," James said, pushing his arms into the sleeves. The car slid silently into the street traffic. "How did you know where to find me?"

"Oh, I have a nose for these things," Embries answered. James could not tell if he was joking.

"Would you like some lunch or anything?" asked Cal from the front seat. "We brought you some sandwiches." He held up a white paper bag.

"Thanks," said James, accepting the bag and dropping it on the seat beside him. "Maybe later."

The car glided along the streets, and it soon became clear to James that they were not returning to St. James's Palace. "Where are we going?"

"There is a man I would like you to meet," Embries said, "if you have no objection."

"Not at all. Bring him on."

They proceeded smoothly through the city. Nothing was said of James' inheritance, or what they had discussed in Embries' office; each man occupied himself with his own private thoughts. After a while, the Jaguar turned onto Earl's Court Road and headed south, passing one busy high street and then another, and on until they finally passed the Stamford Bridge Stadium where they turned down a side street lined with modest Victorian town houses. Rhys slowed the Jaguar and parked on the street in front of a white-painted double-fronted house at the end of the row. "Here we are," said Embries, as Rhys opened the door.

The small square of lawn was well kept, and the property surrounded on all sides by one of those tall wrought-iron fences that looks like a rank of spears, with the shafts painted glossy black and the spearheads painted gold. A brightly polished brass plaque on the side of the house identified the place as The Royal Heritage Preservation Society.

James read out the inscription as Cal joined him at the iron gate. "Oh, great," sighed Cal. "Aren't these the we-love-our-Teddy nutters?" he asked as Embries came to stand with them.

"They have a quasi-political wing, yes," Embries admitted diplomatically. "The Save Our Monarchy Coalition has

an office here, I believe. However, following the demise of
both Debrett's and Burke's Peerage the RHPS are the best
remaining authority on the nobility," he said, pushing the
gate open. "In fact, the best of Debrett's and Burke's staff
ended up here. I know one of the editors, and I've asked him
to do a little nosing around for us. Shall we go in?"

They opened the door and entered a narrow blue-carpeted
vestibule. A receptionist smiled at them as they came in; she
was talking on the phone, and rang off as they came to stand
before her. "Mr. Collins is expecting us, I believe," Embries
informed her.

"Would you mind waiting? I'll call him. It won't take a
moment." A cheerful black woman with her hair in elaborate
beaded braids, she spoke with the sun-drenched tones of Ja-
maica. She picked up the phone and spoke quietly into the
receiver. "Mr. Collins is just coming down," she informed
them. "He will be with you shortly."

Cal flipped through a souvenir guidebook entitled *Royal
Britain,* and James gazed at the walls, which were decorated
with current covers of the various publications the firm produced: two magazines given to nostalgia for the glory days
of Empire, a clutch of glossy pamphlets extolling various
royal haunts, and an expensive-looking tome entitled *Almanak Royale,* gilt-edged and bound in red leather. He was
beginning to make sense of the operation when they were
joined by a thin man with sparse, sandy-colored hair. His
suit was badly creased and shiny from wear, but his shoes
were polished to perfection. In all, he looked like a rumpled
academic who had won a pair of brogues in the school raf-
fle. "I hope you haven't been waiting long," he said, his
voice youthful, despite the aged stoop.

"Ah, Collins," replied Embries with a smile. "Good to see
you again. I am glad you could find time for us." He introduced James and Cal, and then said, "Mr. Collins has been
working on a special project for me."

"And I am happy to say that it is very nearly complete,"
the little man announced. "Only one or two bits to nail down
firmly, but why don't I show you what I have so far?"
Collins led them through one of the doors lining the

vestibule and into a wide semicircular entry hall half paneled in dark oak. A curved stairway led up to an upper floor and an oval gallery.

He ushered his guests through one of the three doors opening off the landing, and they entered a long, high-ceilinged room lined on both sides with glassed-in bookshelves. Beyond this room was a small conference room with a round table at one end and a great old sideboard on the other. There were six chairs around the table, and a silver coffee service on the sideboard.

"I think we'll be comfortable enough in here," Collins said. "Have a seat, won't you? I'll just get my papers."

He disappeared back the way they had come. Cal strolled the perimeter of the room and let out a soft whistle. "You're definitely moving up in the world, my friend," he said to James.

"What's this special project?" asked James.

"I wouldn't want to spoil the surprise. Let's just say it should be instructive for us all."

Embries crossed to the table and drew out a chair, indicating that James should sit down. Cal took the seat beside him. Sunlight through the window opposite the sideboard filled the room with a wan, wintry light that made James feel as if they were back in school again.

Collins returned and placed a battered Gladstone bag on the table and began pulling out papers by the handful—literally, by the handful, in rumpled bunches, as if they were tissues. He tossed them onto the table and began organizing them into piles. "Peerage law is not my strong suit, I confess," he began, "but I have enough of the rudiments to navigate my way around."

"I'm sure it will be adequate for our purposes," Embries assured him. To James, he said, "Collins is one of the foremost experts on royal succession and title inheritance in the country."

"History," Collins said, smoothing a wrinkled sheet of paper on the table, "is my real passion. Hence most of my work is for the *Almanak*."

"I assume all this has something to do with my inheriting the title and property at Blair Morven?" James said.

The comment was directed more at Embries, but Collins stopped smoothing and looked at him curiously. "I think you'll find it's a bit more than that," he said. "Indeed, it is nothing less than—"

"One thing at a time," Embries said, breaking in. "Let us concentrate on the title and property for now."

"Oh," sniffed Collins, "that is easily done." He pulled a thick brown book from the bag and dropped it on the table with a thump. "This is a record of the Scottish aristocracy dating from 1610. It was drawn up just after James the First acceded to the throne of England." He put a hand reverently on the book and, looking for all the world like a courtroom witness taking his oath on the Bible, said, "Elizabeth the First died without issue. Before her death, she recognized King James the Sixth of Scotland as her lawful heir, thereby uniting both Scotland and England under the rule of a single monarch, a situation which has obtained to the present day. This is why—"

"I had Mr. Collins research the history of the Blair Morven title," Embries interrupted quickly. "He has established a line of ducal succession dating from before the time of King James."

"Oh, it goes back much further, I assure you. We have records here"—his gesture took in the entire building—"tracing the various royal lines back at least two hundred years before *that*." He beamed as if this were in some way a personal triumph. "The Blair Morven title is one of the oldest in Scotland, gentlemen. That much is beyond doubt."

"Is that important?" Cal asked.

Collins regarded him with a puzzled look, then deferred to Embries.

"Let's just say that it is germane to this discussion," Embries replied, "insofar as a clear and continuous line of succession is always desirable when legal problems arise."

Collins shuffled through the pile of papers before him and snatched up a sheet. He clutched it in his fist, careless of the creasing and bunching of the page. "I can authenticate the line of descent." To Embries he said, "If you can establish Mr. Stuart's identity, I can establish his bloodline. It will then be a simple matter of presenting this information to the proper authorities. Faced with the facts, the outcome you predict, Mr. Embries, should swiftly follow."

To James, Collins' matter-of-fact assertion made it sound as if the deeply embroiled legal wrangling of the last nine months were nothing more than a playground tiff between schoolboys. James might have been more hopeful—or, ecstatic, even—if not for the unsettling sensation that the other shoe was about to drop.

"You can show all this in your book?" he asked cautiously.

"Oh, I can demonstrate a good deal more." Collins snatched up another paper with his left hand, crumpling it terribly. The way he grabbed and mauled his documents made his onlookers wince. "This!" Collins said, thrusting the page at James. "This is a summary of my research into the Duke of Morven's title. Peruse it, if you will."

James expected some kind of legal document, and was disappointed to see that it was merely a handwritten list containing eight or ten items which appeared to be titles of some sort, along with a short annotation beside each one. The first one said:

> *Accession of the Comyns,* 1798, (NLS, p. 329). Royal right of ducal title contested. Challenge dismissed. Right upheld.

The second was similar to the first, and made only slightly more sense:

> *Dalhousie Grants & Tithes of Aberdeenshire,* 1924, (ACL, p. 524). Ducal exemption from tithe recognized.

James read a few more, each time pushing them in Cal's direction so his friend could read them. He began to sense the drift of the evidence, but wanted an explanation. "What am I looking at, exactly?" he asked.

"This is a list of references I have used in my preliminary

research," Collins explained. "The titles of the resources I
have used, the earliest date of publication, and the institution
housing the original manuscript or first edition." He stabbed
a finger at the first line. "NLS is the National Library of
Scotland—"

"I see," James murmured, glancing down the list.

"And ACL is the Aberdeen Central Library," Cal observed.

"Precisely. Very good." Collins moved his finger down the
page to the next entry from the end. "*This* is the one which
has brought us here."

James looked where he was pointing, and read:

> *Graham's Peerage,* vol. III, 1844, (BL, p. 67). Primo-
> geniture by official government documentation vs.
> local ecclesiastical record. Gov. doc. precedence es-
> tablished re: unbaptized heir.

"Yes? So?" he asked, unable to keep the wary tone out of
his voice. Outside, the short winter day was fading fast in a
pale pink and violet haze. It seemed to James that if he listened he might hear the howl of circling wolves.

Picking up the book, the disheveled historian turned the
spine towards James, who saw the words *Graham's Peerage*
stamped in faded gold. "This," Collins said, triumphantly,
"clears the way for the state-issued birth certificate to be
used to establish titular succession." He opened the book,
and started thumbing the pages. "At issue here was the inheritance of Lord Alexander Seaforth's son, who—through
negligence, weakness, or his own deliberate fault—was
never baptized." Collins smiled at his little joke. "Or, at
least, his baptism was never properly recorded.

"As it was a large and prosperous estate, there was a coun-
terclaim, of course," he continued, flipping through the
pages, "which was lent some credence by the fact that there
was a documented outbreak of typhoid which swept through
the region at the time; ecclesiastical records from the period
in question are in some disarray. Nevertheless, the case was
undertaken, and a ruling handed down which established the

precedent of inheritance by official government birth certificate." Looking up from the book, he asked, "I assume you have a birth certificate."

"I assume I do," James answered.

"Most people do these days." Collins made it sound as if it were some newfangled invention or a fad he hoped would swiftly pass.

"What Collins is saying," Embries interjected, "is that a valid birth certificate is all we will need to establish your claim to the ducal estate and title."

"Then it's true," Cal blurted, a grin breaking across his face. "James really *is* the Duke of Morven."

"More than that, Mr. McKay." Straightening himself, the thin man made a little bow in James' direction as he said, "Mr. Stuart is the rightful King of Britain."

# Part II

✳

# Ten

The rain spattered like soft bullets on the windscreen, making the road ahead a blur of gray bounded on either side by long streaks of dull, formless green. James felt as if someone had put grains of sand under his eyelids. The train had been late into Pitlochry, and it would be light before they reached Braemar. Cal was slumped in the passenger seat beside him, his head resting against the window, dead to the world.

"You sure you're okay?" Cal had asked for the twenty-fifth time as they climbed into the faded blue vehicle in the train station parking lot.

"I'm fine." James unlocked the door and climbed in.

"Look, why don't you let me drive?" offered Cal. "You can take it easy—sleep if you want. I don't mind."

"I'm fine," James insisted.

"I don't mind." Cal hovered at the driver's-side door.

"Will you get in already? Close the door, it's cold."

"All right, all right, have it your way," Cal agreed reluctantly; he walked around the Land Rover and got in.

"Why this concern all of a sudden?" James asked, switching on the engine. "Much as I might appreciate it, it isn't necessary."

"What concern?" Cal scoffed. He slammed his door, and

James pulled out. They cruised slowly through the sleeping town and out onto the highway. It started raining as they began the long drive home.

Amazingly enough, Cal respected his silence—again, unusually considerate for him—contenting himself with the odd anxious glance, for which James was grateful. He drove through the rain—eyes on the road, hands on the wheel . . . mind stuck in London, endlessly churning over the events of the last two days, trying to make sense of it all.

Even now, with the windscreen wipers smearing the rain across the fogged glass, he heard again the unbelievable words Collins had spoken, and he was once more in that room; he felt again the jolt of alarm.

"More than that, Mr. McKay," Collins was saying, making his comical little bow. "Mr. Stuart is the rightful King of Britain."

James stared at Collins in amazed disbelief. *Either he is mad,* he thought, *or I am.* In that first instant, it never occurred to James to imagine that what Collins said was even remotely true. He glanced at Cal, who was literally agape with wonder. Embries, manifestly unhappy his secret had been revealed this way, glared sourly at the rumpled historian. But Collins had been itching to tell what he knew, and it had just slipped out. He looked suddenly abashed, and came over all apologetic.

"The King," James repeated dully. "Is that what this whole big charade is about?"

Collins shot a worried glance at Embries, who frowned, and then put his hands on the table and rose to stand in his place. "Listen to me carefully, James," he said earnestly. "It has been my intention all along to tell you in a way you would accept."

"You think I'm accepting this?" James demanded.

"I thought," Embries replied, "that if you accepted your identity as Duke, the rest would follow in course. I meant to give you a little time to get used to the idea, however." He darted a quick look of reproach at Collins, who seemed to have shrunk to half his size.

"First Duke, now King," James said, his voice growing

thick with derision. "All in all, not a bad day's work, I'd say. By dinner, I should be Pope."

"It is no joke," Embries said.

"It's well beyond a joke!" James snarled, angry now. "If you had something to say, why didn't you come out and say it—instead of playing all these little games?" He flicked a hand in Collins' direction.

"I, for one, have never been more serious in all my life," Collins put in. "I assure you, Mr. Stuart, my work will stand up in any court of law in this land, the European community . . . the world. I know what I am talking about."

"King of Britain." James shook his head. "This is nuts."

Cal, speechless still, stared at James as if an alien suddenly dropped into their midst.

"King of Britain," Collins repeated, growing enthusiastic again. "I know it has presented something of a shock to you. Yet, it is not so far-fetched as it sounds. The Duke of Morven is, after all, one of several legitimate claimants to the throne. There is not, nor has there ever been, any question about that whatsoever."

"*I* never heard of it." James glared from one to the other, unable to accept what they were telling him.

"Allow me to demonstrate," Collins said, leaping back to his much-abused brown bag. "The problem, from a Scottish point of view, is simply that the Stuart line chose to back the wrong church. They persisted in remaining Catholics when Britain demanded Protestants. Catholic James the Second had been chased to France—unofficially deposed, if you like—and his daughter Mary had taken the throne jointly with her Protestant husband, William the Third. They had the bad luck to die without issue, thereby passing the crown to Mary's sister, Anne." He paused and licked his lips. "Are you getting this?"

"It's mother's milk to a Scotsman," muttered Cal, repossessing his voice at last. "Tell us something we *don't* know."

"Anne was a pleasant enough woman," Collins continued, "what with her card playing and tea parties; unfortunately, she was also a supremely unlucky mother. One would have thought that giving birth to thirteen babies would have secured the hereditary line for generations to come. Poor Anne, however, outlived every one of her children. With no heirs in the offing, so to speak, Parliament became nervous and took matters into its own bungling, incompetent hands."

There followed a lengthy lecture on the more obscure points of peerage law, some of which James followed, most of which he allowed to wash over him. After a while, the words all ran together to form a mucky soup, made all the more incomprehensible by the blizzard of paper which accompanied the lecture.

Collins produced page after page, file after file, one scribbled note after another, citing obscure and recondite references, while James' eyes slowly glazed over. The learned monarchist talked about the Treaty of Union 1706 which joined Scotland and England, and the Act of Settlement which prohibited Catholics from ever taking the throne in Britain again. "You're not a Catholic, are you, Mr. Stuart?" the man from the Royal Heritage Preservation Society asked, and James was sorely tempted to say yes, just to end the deluge of historical facts and oddities of chance and the manifold caprices of Parliament.

They heard about the Old Pretender and the Young Pretender; they heard about Sophia, Electress of Hanover, and her overbearing son George I, who fought Parliament tooth and nail, openly despised the British, refused to learn more than a few words of English, and visited the country only when absolutely necessary. For a time, James imagined he was back in grammar school once more, poring over a turgid textbook in Mrs. Arbuckle's class, reciting the names of long-dead kings and queens, trying to keep them all straight.

Collins told them about papist plots and deathbed confessions—and more than a little about amorous liaisons, and the inevitable proliferation of royal bastards; he spoke of Anglicans and recusants, Royalists and Republicans, Roundheads and Cavaliers, and Hanoverians and Stuarts and Windsors and Tudors and Lancastrians and Yorkists.

Eventually, James grew numb; it was all the stuff of musty old history books, and nothing he heard made him think it had anything to do with him. When he had heard enough, he stood. Weary and hungry, his head ached, his feet hurt, and he wanted to go home.

"Come on, Cal. Let's get out of here," James said, rising abruptly.

Collins, who had been soaring high in seventh heaven, came to a juddering halt. "We haven't covered the unresolved question of female primogeniture yet," he said, blinking at his unwilling audience.

"You'll have to cover it without us, I'm afraid," said James. "We're going home." Cal had his jacket on and was opening the door.

Embries rose, too. "Very well, then. We will leave it there for the time being. It is a tremendous amount of material to get through in one sitting. We can continue our discussions tomorrow."

"*You* continue them tomorrow," James told him. "Cal and I will be on a train heading north."

Embries gazed at James with some dismay. "Don't give up, James. Give it a chance to sink in properly."

"I'm not giving up," James replied sharply. "I'm leaving. I've had enough. I'm going home, that's all. Mr. Collins"—he put out his hand to the historian who was wearing the expression of a puppy unfairly disciplined—"I thank you for a highly entertaining afternoon."

Rhys dropped them off at Kenzie House, and Embries repeated his admonition for James to give himself a chance to let things sink in. "Have a drink and relax. You've had a trying day. We will pick you up tomorrow morning."

James bade them good night, and walked quickly to the door. Once inside, he went straight to his room and dialed Jenny's number from the phone beside the bed.

It rang a few times, and a woman answered; she was laughing and saying something to someone else as she picked up the receiver, so James couldn't tell at first who it might be. "Hello," he said, "could I speak to Jenny, please?"

"James? Is that you?" The warmth of her voice, even over the phone, comforted him. "You sound terrible. What's happened?"

"Nothing. I'm fine. It's just been one of those days." He

took a deep breath, and felt the knots begin to unwind a little. "You wouldn't believe the half of it."

"Where are you?"

"London. Cal is with me. It looks like we're going to be
another day or so, at least."

"I see," she replied; her tone implied she hadn't the slightest idea why he had called. "Well, you two have fun." She
paused. "You sure you're all right?"

"Sure. I'm fine."

"Thanks for calling," she said. "I'd love to talk, but I've
got someone here, so I'd better run. Bye."

After he hung up, James sat staring at the phone for a
time, considering whether to ring her back or not. He picked
up the receiver and dialed the train station instead.

Next, he went downstairs to the lounge where Cal was
fixing drinks with Isobel. "Hi, James," she called, jumping
up, ravishing in a tight red tunic top and black slacks.
"Gosh, you look like a guy who could use one of these." She
handed him a glass of dark red wine.

He accepted the glass, but did not drink.

"Are you okay, James?" Cal asked. "You look all in."

"We're leaving, Cal," James said quietly. "Get your things."

"What about dinner?" Isobel said. "I've got a roast gam-
mon in the oven, and a wonderful chocolate soufflé for
dessert."

"Uh . . . maybe another time," Cal told her reluctantly.
"Something's come up."

James returned to his room, rang for a taxi, threw his few
things into his bag, then went back downstairs to wait. Cal
joined him a few moments later, with Isobel in tow. "Please,
thank your mother and father for us," he said. "Whatever we
owe you for rooms and meals, I'd be much obliged if you'd
send a bill."

"Don't be silly," Isobel scolded nicely. "They'll be sorry
to have missed you." She was disappointed, James could
tell, but was putting a brave face on it. "No doubt we'll see
you next time you're in London."

"Don't forget about the Christmas trip," Cal said. "I'll
call you."

The taxi honked outside; James said good-bye and Isobel kissed Cal on the cheek. "Travel safely," she said as they stepped out the door.

So, now, here they were, driving home early Sunday morning. The sun came up as they came around the Spittal of Glenshee, and it occurred to James that, if Embries was to be believed, somewhere on this stretch of road his father, the Marquess, had met his death. As the highway rose to meet Cairnwell Hill and the ski lifts, James found himself wondering where the crash had taken place.

The road turned sharply and began the steep climb to the pass known as Devil's Elbow—a long, straight haul to the top of the Morven hills. Once through the gap, they passed the Ardblair Ski Centre & Resort, and started down into Glen Clunie where the highway merged with the old military road leading down into Braemar.

Typically, for a Sunday morning, the streets were deserted. James paused before the stoplight at the town's main intersection. Driven by both summer and winter tourism, little Braemar had expanded mightily in the last few years. The town now had a swank, executive apartment complex, a new police station, and a three-way stoplight—not to mention a solicitor's office.

James yawned, and rubbed his eyes, thinking how good it would feel to crawl into bed in a few minutes' time. But even as he sat waiting for the light to change, the clouds parted and a shaft of morning sunlight struck the steeple of the church up the street, causing the painted cross on the pinnacle to gleam and flare with a golden burst of light. It seemed a sign from Heaven. All thoughts of sleep vanished. James glanced at his watch; it was just after nine o'clock. He could still make the service if he hurried.

❋

# Eleven

The cargo jet taxied slowly across the rain-wet tarmac before coming to a halt in front of the waiting vehicles: three limousines and a Rolls-Royce hearse. Prime Minister Thomas Waring stood holding an umbrella over his head, wincing at the sound of the jet engines and squinting in the glare of the overbright lights on a dull, windswept morning. Only five television crews had been allowed to record the arrival of the King's coffin.

Behind the PM stood a small sampling of civil servants, dignitaries, and grandees whose presence had been particularly requested. In a roped-off section a few dozen yards away were a few of Teddy's long-suffering friends and relatives. All were there to observe protocol—that is, to be seen observing protocol so that the Opposition could not manufacture any political ammunition out of the slightest perceived lapse on the part of the Government.

Waring was cold and wanted nothing more than to be done with the play-acting. But he knew the importance of presentation, and here he was presenting the image of a stalwart yet sensitive leader. He could sympathize; he could feel—oh yes, he was not afraid to be seen feeling—but what kind of leader would he be if he allowed personal sentiment to thwart a greater public good? What kind of weak, vacillating pilot would he be if he allowed the ship of state to flounder in the first stiff waves encountered? Rough water or no, he would guide the nation through the storm. Britain was in safe hands.

More and more, he felt he needed to project this very image. After all, Thomas Waring had not risen to the top of the political heap on the strength of personal charisma and ruthless calculation alone; he also had a built-in barometer of such supreme sensitivity that he could detect mood swings, media reactions, and opposition storms while they were still just clouds on the political horizon. Indeed, he had correctly predicted the outcome of no fewer than thirty-nine of the last forty-five public opinion polls on schemes floated by his government.

Waring's early-warning system had allowed him and his government to weather every political cyclone so far, and he trusted it far more than he did any member of his staff. Now, in the wake of the King's suicide, it told him that there was heavy weather on the way, and he was determined to divert it if at all possible.

So he stood with his umbrella, buffeted by the wind and rain, staring stolidly ahead as the great bronze coffin emerged from the hold of the plane. There was no military band, no fanfare to welcome the dead monarch home. Waring wanted as little ceremony as possible.

And then Waring saw the huge, handsome coffin, gleaming in the TV lights. "Good God," he muttered, "where did they get that?"

"The Portuguese would not allow him to be shipped in the military casket we sent," explained Dennis Arnold, known to the media as Waring's stooge, attack dog, nursemaid, or intimate confidant—depending on one's perspective. "The Ambassador was afraid people would think *he* chose the casket. He complained that it made his country look cheap."

"This one makes the dead bastard look like Napoleon, for Chrissakes," fumed Waring under his breath. "Why wasn't I told?"

"There wasn't time. They sprang the substitute at the last minute. President Rulevo personally arranged for something more suitable."

"Remind me to *thank* Rulevo when all this is over," grumbled Waring through his teeth, "personally."

The hydraulic platform lowered the coffin to the ground, where it was met by a phalanx of ten soldiers wearing long black raincoats over their uniforms—another Waring touch. He did not want the sight of a military uniform to awaken any latent sympathy in the populace. They were soldiers, but they looked more like ordinary undertakers' assistants. Protocol observed . . . image carefully manipulated.

The soldiers muscled the heavy coffin from the platform and proceeded slowly towards the waiting hearse. From the open door of the aircraft, the figures of three passengers emerged at the top of the gangway. One was an underling of the British Ambassador, Waring knew, and the other an official of the Portuguese government. The third, however, was a woman dressed in black, her face hidden beneath a black lace veil. The Prime Minister saw her start down the steps and muttered under his breath, "Who the hell is that?"

Dennis Arnold shrugged, and pulled a folded paper from his pocket. "Damned if I know," he said. "She's not on the passenger list. Maybe she's with the Ambassador's party."

"What party?" Waring demanded sourly. "There wasn't supposed to *be* any party."

They watched as the woman reached the bottom of the gangway and stood beside the two officials as the casket was loaded into the back of the hearse. As soon as the rear door closed and the soldiers backed away, the woman turned and started towards the Prime Minister and his colleagues.

"You don't suppose she's Teddy's mistress, do you?"

As she drew closer, Waring recognized the shapely curves ill-concealed beneath the tight black skirt and short jacket. "My God, what's she doing here?"

"Want me to get rid of her?" Arnold started forward.

"I'll handle it," Waring said, pulling him back into line. "Stay here, and act like we expected this."

Waring moved quickly to apprehend the approaching woman before she came within earshot of the others. Although her hair was black beneath the veil, there was no mistaking the green eyes or the full, seductive lips that greeted him with a sly, almost mocking, smile.

"What the hell are you playing at?" demanded Waring.

"Good evening, Mr. Prime Minister," she said, her voice low and beguiling. Despite his anger, Waring felt himself drawn to her.

"You're not supposed to be here," he said. "If anyone finds out we've been—"

"You didn't expect me to stay on that beastly island forever, did you? I couldn't bear it a minute longer." She put her hand on his sleeve.

Waring stiffened. "Stop that," he growled. Removing her hand, he patted it as if consoling her.

Her smile teased. "You couldn't live without me—that's what you said last time."

"I mean it," he said, taking her elbow and turning her around. "If anyone finds out, there'll be hell to pay."

"I need you, Thomas," she said, the ache in her voice weakening his resolve. "I want to be with you."

"All right," he relented, "I'll call you."

"When?"

"In a few days."

"No," she countered, "tonight."

"It's too risky. Now behave, or you'll screw everything up. I'm going to put you into the car," he said, lifting his head in a sad smile of condolence for the cameras across the tarmac, "and I want you to disappear for a few days."

They reached the car, and a soldier opened the rear passenger door. "I'll call you."

She reached out and offered her hand to the Prime Minister in farewell. He took it and she leaned forward. "Tonight," she whispered, and then slid quickly into the back of the limousine.

Waring and his party returned to their limousines and, together with their police escort, led the hearse from the London City Airport.

Everything that *could* be done to minimize the event, *had* been done—and would continue to be done. Both the airfield and the route had been kept secret to the very last minute to discourage any would-be mourners from turning out to watch the procession. Not that anyone would see much, he had made certain of that. But Waring knew down to his socks that public opinion was an unpredictable beast—as likely to bite the manipulating hand as lick it.

Up to now, the renegades and royalists had been kept off balance and out of the way. They had yet to organize themselves into anything remotely resembling a coherent threat. But the King's precipitous death was just the sort of quirky thing that brought factions together and focused objectives. It gave various disparate elements a central cause, created commonality, a rallying point. No one knew better than Waring that all it would take was a sound bite or two with an inappropriate inflection, an unfortunate phrase, the wrong choice of words, and the heretofore carefully managed affair would blow up in their faces.

Already, *The Sun* and the *Daily Star* were making sympathetic noises, talking about the tremendous pressure poor King Edward had faced in his last days. It was no great leap from lukewarm insinuation to a barefaced declaration that the Government had actually hounded poor, misguided, unloved Teddy to death. If left unchecked, Waring knew he could end up bearing the blame for the King's suicide. People were already thinking it, no doubt; it was only a matter of time before some big mouth broadcast it on national TV. He could live with that—his antimonarchy stance had kicked up fierce opposition every step of the way—but if the ensuing outcry cost him any more defections in the House, his all-too-slim majority could vanish overnight. *That* was something he could not accept.

Just last evening, some bright light at Channel 5 had gone on air with the observation that perhaps the perceived climbdown over the King's funeral arrangements indicated a massive failure of nerve on the part of the Waring government.

"Idle speculation, Tom," the Deputy Prime Minister had assured him as recently as this morning. "Nothing but pure, idle, pie-in-the-sky speculation. They have no way of knowing what we originally planned."

Even so, yesterday's idle speculation had a way of becoming today's rampant rumor and, before you knew it, you had a full-scale, Opposition-led media firestorm on your hands. Waring could feel it coming; he could smell it on the wind. Speed, therefore, was his best weapon.

As the limousine and its convoy cruised through nearly empty city streets towards Buckingham Palace, Waring decided it was time to put a little distance between himself and the howling wolf pack.

Waring turned his face from the rain-spotted window and said, "Dennis, I want to move the ceremony to Thursday." The move, he reckoned, would cut down the time the renegades and royalists could use to get a sympathy campaign going. Once the King was safely laid to rest, he would cease to be an effective rallying point.

"You're not serious," the devolution committee chairman said. He took one look at his boss and sighed. "My God, you *are* serious. Look, it can't be done. We're already pedaling as fast as we can. Most of my staff haven't slept in two days as it is. We'll never—"

"Save it," the Prime Minister told him. "We can cite the economic summit meeting—say that we have to take extra security precautions to protect the foreign heads of state. Say we're concerned that terrorists might use the upset caused by the funeral as an excuse to attack the summit. Make it a security issue. No one will argue with that."

"I have no problem *explaining* it," Arnold replied. "Do you have any idea the effort it is taking to organize this thing for Saturday? We're working flat out as it is, and now you want to cut our time by forty-eight hours? Why, there are three thousand policemen alone—"

"Results," Waring said, "not excuses. You're getting to be as bad as Adrian."

"I'll take that as a compliment."

"Don't."

Arnold knew his boss's strengths and weaknesses better than most people. He looked at the tightly drawn face in the dim, shifting light of the car. "What's bothering you, Tom?" he asked quietly.

Waring stared back at him. "You have to ask?"

Arnold thought for a moment. "The presidency?"

"Got it in one," grumbled Waring.

"Look," said Arnold, adopting a conciliatory tone, "it's two months to the referendum—eight weeks, and that's including Christmas and New Years' holidays. The next by-election is more than a year away. The last opinion poll put the public in favor of full devolution by seventy-two percent! Seventy-two! We're in with a comfortable margin."

"Six seats is not what I call a comfortable margin, Dennis. Christ, we came in with over eighty."

"I meant the referendum vote. I know about the seats, Tom. We all know about the seats. How could we forget? You remind us hourly." He paused, exasperated by his boss's obsessive concern over his parliamentary majority. "We'll get them back," he concluded, "and more besides. Let's just get through the next few days without having a stroke, hmm?"

"Your optimism is infectious."

"Eight weeks," Arnold repeated. "The monarchy will be dead, buried, and forgotten by then—along with the monarch." He chuckled, but his boss was not amused.

"The referendum will take care of itself," Waring insisted. "It's the floaters that worry me, Den. If any of them should jump on this royalist bandwagon, we could—"

"What royalist bandwagon?" scoffed Arnold lightly. "There isn't any band; there isn't any wagon."

"Make bloody sure it stays that way," Waring said firmly. "We can't allow any of that bouquet-laying crap. The last thing we need is another Kensington Palace flower show."

"It'll never happen. We're at Buckingham Palace, for one thing."

"You know what I mean, damn it," growled Waring testily. "There are bound to be floral tributes—we can't stop that. But I want them kept to a minimum. If they start piling up, keep them thinned out. And no goddamn teddy bears! Those are to be removed at once—immediately. Got it?"

"Got it. No teddy bears."

"If anyone wants to make an issue out of it, tell them it's by order of the Metropolitan Police—bomb security." Having given vent to his apprehension, the Prime Minister subsided. "We're not having everybody going all teary eyed over stuffed animals. The media eat that stuff up."

"Understood," Arnold said. "Now I want you to understand something, all right?"

"Yes?"

"Everything you say, I'll do it. But it can't be Thursday. You can't plan a state funeral overnight. It can't be done. There simply isn't enough time."

"Very well," Waring agreed. "Friday then."

"God, you don't give up, do you?" Dennis Arnold shook his head slowly. He could see the sleepless nights piling up ahead of him.

"On Friday, Dennis," the Prime Minister stated. "It's got to be Friday."

Arnold puffed his cheeks and exhaled heavily. "All right," he sighed, "if that's what you want, Friday it is."

## ✳

# Twelve

After dropping Cal in front of the hotel so he could retrieve his car, James drove home and quickly showered, shaved, and put on his Sunday best. He made coffee and toast, and collected the newspapers and mail from the last two days to read while he ate. There was nothing of interest in the post, so he scanned the papers—it was all to do with King Edward's death and the minor controversy which had, thanks to Donald Rothes, boiled up over the arrangements for the old boy's funeral.

One faction wanted to see the King quietly cremated in a private ceremony, and another wanted a full State funeral with burial in Westminster and all the trimmings; a third group was agitating for a less expensive yet still tasteful compromise. The debate was made more fraught by reason of the fact that whatever happened, it would all have to be arranged in the next few days because the funeral ceremony had been scheduled for Saturday.

James folded up the newspaper and shoved it away, poured another mug of coffee to keep himself awake and then headed back to town. The small graveled parking lot beside the church was mostly full by the time he got there. The service had already started, so he slipped in quietly and took a seat in a pew at the back. He looked quickly around,

but did not see Jenny or any of her family and was surprised
to find how disappointed he was. St. Margaret's is an old
church, and the only one of which James had ever been a
member. It had been his parents' church, and it was where
he had been baptized. In all the years he had attended, the
church had known but two rectors: Doctor Hillary Oliphant,
and the Reverend Raymond Orr. Both were good solid men
of faith, much, James always thought, like the hills themselves: softly yielding as the mossy, mist-fed turf on the outside, but with spirits as tough as the hard granite inside.

James' father—that is, the man who had raised him as his
son—was such a man, too, and in his better moments, James
hoped he could one day be like them.

One of the wardens—a genial old duffer named Gus—
saw James as he entered and came after him with a news
sheet. "Gude ta see ya', Cap'n James," he said, stretching
out a horny hand. "Ah heered you wast in London."

"Good to see you, too, Gus." They shook hands, and the
organist launched into a rousing hymn, saving James further
explanation. The congregation rose to sing, and Gus crept
away to make his head count.

There were more songs, an offering, prayers, and anthem,
and a lengthy and gently meandering sermon which James
only half listened to until Orr read from the morning's text
in Corinthians: " 'Who makes you, my friend, different from
anyone else? What do you possess that was not given to
you? If, then, you received it all as a gift, why take the credit
to yourself?' "

Although he knew it was only his imagination, James
could not help thinking Reverend Orr looked straight at him
when he read, " 'You have come into your fortune already.
You have come into your kingdom . . .' "

As the service drew on, James tried to lose himself in the
long-familiar rituals, the comforting ebb and flow of ancient
liturgy. Every time he began to relax and let go, however,
some word, some image, would set off a chain reaction, and
the inner turmoil would start all over again.

Why, he wondered, did they have to sing "Crown Him
with Many Crowns" on this of all Sundays? Why was the

anthem "O Worship the King" instead of, say, "Blest Be the Tie that Binds," or some other regularly sung hymn? And why did the good reverend have to keep banging on about the sovereignty of the Lord?

In the end, James gave up trying to fight it and simply prayed, "God, help a drowning man. I'm fighting to keep my head above water, Lord, and I could use a hand just now."

By the time the worship service ended, he was only slightly less anxious and agitated than when it began. Ordinarily, he liked to linger after church to talk to the old-timers and townsfolk—most of whom James had known all his life—but he did not feel up to it today. As soon as the last hymn was sung, he headed for the door. The good rector, always quick on his feet, beat him to the exit.

"James, my boy!" His big booming voice filled the vestibule and spilled out the open door into the churchyard. "Welcome back." He seized James' hand, pumping heartily. "Tell me, how did you get on in London?"

James' heart sank. Of course, everybody in Braemar knew about the trip by now. Jenny's mother had no doubt mentioned it to someone, and the Glen Dee grapevine had taken it from there. In the glens, gossip couldn't travel faster if tinkers took it door to door.

"You know how London is," James replied, "busy, loud, and expensive. I couldn't wait to get back."

The parson smiled and nodded. "Well, no matter how far we roam, it's always good to come back home," he said. "And it's always good to see you of a Sunday, too. Blessings, my boy."

He released James, and turned to talk to the other members of the congregation as the line formed. James hurried to the car, and drove away quickly so he would not have to discuss his trip to London with anyone else.

Patches of high blue sky were showing between the fast-moving clouds. It had all the makings of a glorious afternoon and, suddenly, the last thing James wanted was to be alone with his thoughts in an empty house. He remembered Agnes' invitation to Sunday dinner, and decided he'd accept after all.

He drove through town slowly, considering whether he ought to call ahead first or just show up. He passed the Braemar Parish Church. Services were just getting out, and the little congregation was filing into the churchyard where the older members were making an effort to ignore three teenage golfers carrying their bags down the road to the old golf club. The heathenish youngsters were talking loudly as they went, merrily oblivious of the darkly disapproving Presbyterian glances.

Though in no way an unusual sight on a Sunday in Scotland, the presence of the golf clubs jogged James' memory. On a whim, he proceeded up the road to the town golf course, parked, and went into the tiny clapboard clubhouse. "Is Howard Gilpin here by any chance?" he asked the weedy youth behind the counter.

"Old Howard?" he said. "Oh, sure." He glanced at his clipboard and ran his finger down the list. "He started about half an hour ago."

"Thanks." James headed for the door leading out onto the first tee. "I have to see him. Won't take a minute."

"Sure, whatever," the kid replied. "He's probably on the second green by now."

Walking quickly out onto the course, James made for the second hole. There were two elderly men in bright green, padded shell suits with bobble hats and scarves, heads down over their putters; he recognized one of them as Gilpin. James waited until they had both sunk their shots. "Excuse me," he said, stepping onto the green. "I don't mean to interrupt you, but I was wondering whether I might have a quick word with Mr. Gilpin."

Both men turned from their scorecards and looked him up and down the way old people do when meeting someone they probably know but can't place. They glanced at his street shoes and grimaced as James stepped forward, extending his hand. "It's James Stuart," he said, adding, "from Blair Morven. I think you knew my parents, Mr. Gilpin."

The old man shifted the putter and shook James by the hand. His grasp was cool and strong. "James!" he exclaimed as recognition came to him. He made a stiff half turn to his partner. "Look here, Iain, it's young Stuart—Jack's son." To James, he said, "Well, now. I ask myself, what brings you out on the course? Not the golf, I think. No sticks! So, if you haven't come to join us, what's on your mind?"

The old legal eagle's manner was cordial yet direct. Despite his years, he was trim and wiry, with the short curly hair of a terrier, and James could see he had lost little of his renowned vinegar.

"I'd like a brief moment of your time, Mr. Gilpin. There's something I need to ask you."

"Of course," he agreed. "You shall have it—that is, if you don't mind talking on the hoof. Iain will tee off, and you can ask away. Suit you?"

"Down to the ground."

"Good." He retrieved his golf bag—both men had slender quivers containing only three clubs each—and began striding away.

James fell into step beside him. "Can I take those clubs for you?"

"You want to caddy, too?" he asked, glancing around with a raised eyebrow. "No, sir. I carry my own clubs. The day I have to tip a caddy is the day I lay down my putter."

They arrived at the third tee, and Iain smacked a dribbler down the center of the fairway. There was no height at all, but the ball bounced and carried a surprising distance. "Solid," he said, and walked on.

"I'll catch up with you on the green," Howard called after him. To James, he said, "Now then, this question that could not wait—let's have it."

"It's to do with my parents," James began, suddenly uncertain how to proceed. He hesitated. "Sorry, I'm not sure I know how to ask this."

"Never mind," he replied. "It's moot."

"Pardon?"

"Doesn't matter." Howard gazed after his friend on the fairway. "I knew this day would come sooner or later. I've been expecting it ever since I heard your parents passed away."

"I'm not sure I understand."

"I have something for you. I've been keeping it in my study at home."

"What is it?"

"I'm not at liberty to say. Come see me tomorrow."

"I could come by this afternoon," James offered. "Or, this evening if you prefer."

"Ah, no," he smiled, "that wouldn't do at all. I never work on the Sabbath. It's against my religion." Howard bent down and placed his tee.

"I was taught the Sabbath was from sunset to sunset," James countered.

"You *are* anxious." He steadied the golf ball on the tee, assumed his stance, and took a practice swing. Glancing up at James, he said, "Are you a betting man?"

"Not really, no."

"Pity," replied the old solicitor. "I was going to make a wager with you: if I make it to the green in two, you can come by my office tonight. If I go three, you wait until tomorrow."

"You're on."

He smiled again. "You remind me of your father." He lined up his swing, and struck the ball with a satisfying *thwack*. The ball landed well down the fairway—a good shot, but it would take an even better one to reach the green.

They walked out onto the fairway. Iain had already taken his second shot. Howard alerted him with a shout—which James reckoned was exceedingly optimistic of him—and proceeded to line up his shot, still using the wooden driver. James kept quiet and let him concentrate. The old golfer centered himself over the ball, drew back the club, and swung.

Although he did not appear to have put much into the swing, the ball leapt up as if rocket-charged, arcing out in a high shallow curve—too shallow, James thought, to reach the green. But as the tiny white missile gained altitude, it seemed to grow wings. It sailed on the wind, dropping onto the edge of the green; it bounced once and rolled towards the pin.

James congratulated him on a fine shot, adding, "I guess I'll see you this evening then."

"I guess you will," Howard remarked. James thanked him for his time, and wished him a good game. He stood and watched for a moment as James walked away, then shouted, "Say, you wouldn't want to follow me around the rest of the course, would you? With your luck behind me, I bet I could beat Iain, for a change."

"I'm not really a betting man," James hollered back. "See you tonight."

Returning to his vehicle, James continued along the river road. Glen Dee at Braemar is especially scenic. The river sweeps along in majestic silver swoops bounded by wide green meads beneath brooding dark hills planted in pine. He passed the Birkwood nature reserve below the dour Morrone of Morven, a black, bald-headed crag, and turned off the highway at the Linn of Corriemulzie, proceeding along the granite-chip road to Braemulzie, the farm of Sergeant-Major Owen Evans-Jones, Retired.

"My Jenny," as her father liked to say, "is bi-racial. I'm Welsh, and her mother is a Scot." James thought Jennifer had inherited the best of both, combining the earthly mystical romantic sensitivity of the Welsh and the fiery aggressive visionary ingenuity of the Scots. In Jenny both high passion and inspired practicality were united in the form of a distractingly lovely female. Dark haired and blue eyed, like her father, and smooth skinned and long limbed like her mother, Jennifer was in many ways less a human being than a force of nature.

In school, most of the boys had been afraid of her, and very few of those lads had ever bothered to change that youthful impression. James had seen grown men rendered speechless in her presence and women blanch with envy. When she entered a room, all eyes traveled naturally to her; when a question was asked, everyone turned to see what she would say. She did not join a conversation, she seized it. When you got Jenny's attention, you got *all* of Jenny with it. Some people simply could not handle that.

"Even as a wee girl," her mother once said, "Jenny never walked when she could run, and never ran when she could fly."

There were a few cars in the wide, graveled yard when James pulled up. As with most Scottish farmhouses, one entered through the kitchen. Agnes' kitchen was a large, rambling room with a big, sturdy table of chunky pine in the center, generations old. A dark Welsh dresser dominated one wall and deep cupboards another; a huge old gas-fired black iron stove that looked as if it had seen duty on a WWII troop ship kept the room cozily warm in winter and absolutely tropical the rest of the year. The room was steamy from pots on the boil, and the haunch in the oven filled the house with the delicious aroma of Agnes' patented roast ham in a honey-mustard glaze.

No fewer than fifteen people were standing in the kitchen while Agnes, red-faced and frazzled, hovered about with a wooden spoon in one hand and a pot holder in the other, lifting lids and calling orders to her press-ganged assistants—two of Agnes' young nieces. The rest of the onlookers were drifting in and out of the way, clutching glasses of wine and talking loudly.

"Hello there!" cried a voice as he stepped through the door. "Captain James, isn't it?" He turned to see a thick-necked, stocky man with a bottle of sherry in one hand and three glasses in the other. "You look parched, boyo! Never fear, Gwyn is here." He rattled the glasses.

"How are you, Gwyn?" asked James. Jenny's Cardiff uncle fancied himself the life of any party he happened to join.

"Never better," the ruddy-cheeked man declared. "Here, hold on to this!" He thrust a glass into James' hand and proceeded to fill it to the brim with golden liquid from the bottle. "You're keeping in fighting trim, I see. Young people!" He rolled his eyes dramatically. "There ought to be a law, I say."

"There probably is, Gwyn," James replied, and the Welshman laughed raucously. "Excuse me, will you?" he said, stepping away smartly. "If I want any dinner, I have to kiss the cook."

"Kiss away!" he said, still laughing, and lurched off to refill a few sherry glasses.

Agnes was at the stove, lifting a pot lid, as James came up behind her. "It smells divine," he remarked. "Anything I can do to help?"

"James!" The lid clattered back onto the pot as Jenny's mother greeted him and bussed him lightly on the cheek. "Help? You already have, dear." Nodding towards the overflowing sherry glass in his hand, she said, "Every drop you drink is one less for Gwyn, and that's a help. Now, unless you want to see a grown woman throw a spitting fit, you'll get out of my kitchen at once. There are too many people standing around in here as it is."

"Right," said James. "Call me if you change your mind."

He moved into the living room, which, although not as crowded as the kitchen, contained as many people. There was a tight cluster of folk to one side of the fireplace where the Sergeant-Major was holding forth. "We would never have had the balls to try it on in my day. Makes you wonder what—" He broke off when he saw who had joined the party. "James lad! Good to see you, son! Agnes said you had been called away on business." Turning to the dark-haired, wind-chafed man beside him, "Kenneth, this is Captain James Stuart—caretaker over at Blair Morven." He then explained, "Kenneth is Agnes' brother from over by Balmoral."

James greeted him, and the two shook hands. "We met a year or so ago," Kenneth said, "at the Braemar games."

"James is battling the Australians at the moment," Owen informed Kenneth. He always explained things in military terms. "They're trying to invade Blair Morven."

"Oh, aye," replied Kenneth shrewdly, as if he knew all about the canny stealth of what he called "our kangaroo-kissing cousins." Putting his hand to James' shoulder he wished him a bonny victory. "Do 'em before they do you," he advised somewhat blearily. "They'll have the very turf from under your toes if you don't."

"Any luck in London?" asked Owen. He regarded James with interest. Kenneth, too, gazed up from his glass expectantly.

Obviously, James thought, everyone knew he'd been in

London, and had guessed why he went. Any hope he'd had
of putting it behind him for a few hours vanished. The
thought of having to sift through it all for a suitable morsel
to toss their way made his mouth go dry. "We'll have to see,"
James mumbled vaguely, and excused himself to go find
Jennifer.

He turned and started from the fireplace just as Jenny entered the room from the opposite end. James smiled instinctively when he saw her, took two steps towards her, and
stopped. She was with a tall man with short, dark hair whose
head was bent towards her cheek while he whispered something in her ear. His arm was draped loosely around her
shoulders.

The fellow smiled broadly, and Jenny laughed. Then she
glanced up and saw James standing alone in the center of the
room. She quickly excused herself and came to him. "What
are you doing here?" she said, taking his arm and turning
him around.

"Your mother invited me," he said, and was not pleased
with his suddenly defensive tone. "But I seem to be intruding." He glanced over his shoulder at the young man.
"Who's the bloke?"

"A friend," she said. "You should have let me know you
were coming."

"Obviously," James agreed sourly. "Look, I'll leave if you
want me to. Maybe that would be better."

"Nonsense, you're here now. Stay."

"Thanks," he muttered. "Your welcome is overwhelming."

"What did you expect?" she snapped. "I don't hear from
you for weeks, and then all of a sudden I'm supposed to be
ecstatic that you decide to show up for Gran's birthday dinner. Anyway, I thought you were in London."

The young gentleman joined them just then. "Why don't
you introduce me, Jen?" he said. James heard the possessive
note in the fellow's voice and felt an instant loathing possess
him.

"Of course," she said. "Charles, I'd like you to meet
James, an old friend."

"Delighted," said Charles. "What do you find to do around here, if you don't mind my asking?"

"Oh, this and that. I try to keep busy," replied James. "How about you?"

"Chartered surveyor, for my sins," the fellow replied. "I work for a firm in Aberdeen. I pop over now and again for a little shooting in season. I'm becoming a real sportsman."

"Terrific," said James. "Well, no doubt we'll bump into one another again sometime."

"No doubt. Come along, darling," Charles said, steering Jenny away. "Let's go find the birthday girl."

James, pierced by pangs of guilt and regret, watched them weave through the press of family. He wanted nothing more than to slink away unnoticed, but when he reached the kitchen door, Agnes handed him a platter of ham and directed him to carry it to the table. "Be a dear, James," she said, "and help call people to their places."

Consequently, he endured an interminable meal, made indigestible by the overweening Charles, whose evident designs on Jennifer James found both infuriating and repugnant. It was early evening by the time James found a chance to sneak away. He ducked out the door, paused, and looked thankfully up at the clear night sky. Free at last.

He started across the yard, the cold gravel crunching underfoot. The sound made him feel lonely. He would have gladly given everything he owned, ten times over, just to go back inside and snuggle up to Jenny on the couch, alone, in front of the fire. Instead, he walked to his vehicle, jammed the key in the ignition, threw the gearshift in reverse, and almost collided with someone darting around the back of the vehicle.

## ❊
# Thirteen

"You sure you're okay to drive?" said Jenny, coming around the side of the Land Rover.

"Sorry, I didn't hear you come out." James opened the door partway, and she stepped into the gap.

"You could stay and have a cup of coffee."

"I'm fine. You'd best get back in there or Charles will come looking for you."

She frowned prettily. "You look so unhappy, James. You hardly said two words at dinner. Anything wrong?"

"No, I'm fine. Give your mother and father my apologies for sneaking off like this."

"Don't worry," she snapped. "You were hardly here."

She turned on her heel and swept back into the house. James watched her go, wanting to call her back but lacking the will to do so. He'd have to explain, and he was not ready for that yet.

He headed back to town. The road was deserted, and the town as well. He drove to Gilpin's house, parked out front, hurried up the walk, and rang the doorbell. After a moment, he heard someone rattle the chain on the other side, and a bolt slid back.

"I'd just about given up on you," Howard informed him, "but now that you're here, you might as well come in."

"I know it's an imposition," James replied, stepping over the threshold, "but I really do thank you for seeing me, and I promise I won't keep you."

"Think nothing of it," Howard said. He padded towards a low cabinet on which stood a whisky decanter and an assortment of glasses. "Drink?"

"Thanks, no," James said, following him into the room. The house smelled of cooked cabbage.

Howard poured two glasses from the decanter anyway, and handed one to his visitor. "Just in case," he said. Raising his glass, he wished James good health. They drank, and Howard turned to the white-painted mantel over a gas log fireplace. "You'll be wanting this," he said, and retrieved a square brown packet and handed it across to James. "Maybe you won't think so after you see what's inside."

It was an old-fashioned envelope, handmade out of stiff brown kraft paper—the kind with a big flap that was closed by winding red string around two cardboard disks. In this instance, however, the flap had also been sealed in two places with red sealing wax, which was intact. James turned the envelope over. Written in faded ink were these words:

FOR JAMES A. STUART
TO BE DELIVERED UPON REQUEST

How did Gilpin come to have such a thing? James stared at the envelope and his mind went blank. He was incapable of surprise now—only wonder.

"Are you going to stand there gawping all night? Go on," Howard urged, "open it."

"I've inconvenienced you long enough," James told him. "It can wait until I get home."

"Nonsense. Open it now—you might have questions."

Sliding his finger under the flap, James carefully broke the seals—first one side, then the other—and unwound the red string. Pulling back the flap, he opened the envelope and peered inside.

"Come over here where the light's better," Howard said,

indicating a small desk in the corner of the room. The lamp was switched on. "Sit down there."

James sat as directed, and shook the contents onto the blotter. Several pieces of paper slid out. The first was a short note, written by the same hand that had addressed the outside. It read:

*James, you should find everything you need here to claim your bequest and establish your legacy. Please know that it was never our intention to deceive or deprive you in any way, only to protect you. With much love,*

*Always and forever,*
*Mum and Dad*

Upon unfolding the first piece of paper, James saw a shiny photocopy on slick, brittle paper which had been embossed with a notary's seal—a birth certificate. It was, in fact, his own birth certificate.

His heart beat faster as he looked at the names, knowing already what he would see. Typed in the blank for FATHER was the name Robert Arthur Moray, Marquess of Morven; in the space for MOTHER was written Elizabeth Anne Moray, née Grant. His name was there, too, of course—and yet it *was not* his name, for instead of James Arthur Stuart, the name he'd used all his life, it was James Arthur Moray.

A sudden queasy emptiness spread through his stomach—as if the floor had been yanked from beneath his feet, sending him spinning into free fall. *My God,* he thought, his brain squirming, *it's true! It's all true.*

Pushing the thought firmly aside, he took up the next piece of paper. It was the marriage certificate of Robert Arthur Moray, Marquess of Morven, and Elizabeth Anne Grant. The date on the bottom was a little more than a year before James was born.

He swallowed hard, and lay the paper aside. He could feel Howard watching, but the old lawyer stood quietly aside and said nothing as James reached for the last document, which

was, as he already suspected, the marriage certificate of
John James Stuart and Elizabeth Anne Moray née Grant—
the original from which the copy he had seen in Embries' office had been taken. This one, however, had a paper-clipped
attachment.

Peeling back the certificate, James saw a tidy, legal-looking
form. The heading in block capitals at the top identified it
simply as a *Deed Poll,* and a subhead read: Application for
Change of Name. Skipping over the body of the document,
James' eye fell on the typed-in blanks where the name James
Arthur Moray had been changed to James Arthur Stuart. The
deed was dated the same day as the marriage certificate and,
in addition to the official registrar's signature, likewise carried a notary's seal.

James sat for a moment, staring at the documents—looking, but not seeing. How was it possible, he wondered, for a
few old scraps of paper to so alter the world?

Howard moved a step nearer. "I was hoping it would not
come as a shock, but I see it has." He held out James' glass.
"Here, get some of this inside you. Steady your nerves."

James reached for the glass. "You knew about this," he
said, trying to keep the accusation out of his voice.

"Yes, of course," he admitted. "I've always known. I
helped Robert prepare the fake annulment."

"You knew about my trouble over the estate," James said.
"You knew and never said anything."

"A very wise and powerful man swore me to secrecy,"
Howard answered. "I have never been inclined to betray the
trust that he, and your parents, placed in me." He looked at
James directly, his eyes moving back and forth over his face
as if searching for someone he once knew.

"This morning you said you knew my father," James reminded him, pointing at the papers on the desk. "But it was
Robert you were talking about, not John. You were talking
about the Marquess."

"Yes, I suppose I was."

"Why didn't anyone tell me?" James asked.

Howard swiveled his head slowly. "I can't answer that.
All I know is that I was given instructions, which I put in my

own will, to keep this envelope and give it to you when you asked for it. I made a promise to my friend, and I always keep my promises."

James stared at him and felt a great weakness drawing in upon him, as if all his strength were pouring through the gaping hole in the ground which had just opened beneath his feet. He drew a long, shaky breath and steadied himself. "I understand," he said, not really comprehending anything at all.

"As I say, I know all about your legal tussle," Howard continued. "Hobbs at the office has kept me informed."

"He knows about—" James indicated the documents on the desk, "about all this, too?"

"No," the old solicitor stated firmly. "He knows nothing about any of it. I told you, I kept it secret. No one knew but myself and the people involved. That was the way Robert wanted it—insisted upon it." He paused, looking at James in a kindly way. "With these documents, you now have everything you need to take control of the situation. I'm glad you came to me before it was too late."

James nodded, and the old solicitor raised his glass. "Here's to the new Duke of Morven."

Shock does strange things to people. In Afghanistan James saw a soldier carry a wounded friend through a mine field—never once realizing his own legs had been shredded to bloody ribbons by the same mine that had wounded his friend. He had seen men suffering from shock who went on working, talking, eating, laughing . . . until they simply collapsed into moist, mumbling heaps.

James was in shock as he drove home from Howard Gilpin's that night. So many revelations so quickly, one heaped upon another, had finally tipped him over the edge. He'd fled London to get away from them, only to realize there was no escape. The cumulative effect was, simply, shock. Afterwards, he remembered thanking Gilpin for his help and saying good night, and he remembered climbing into the Land Rover and thinking, *I've been awake for forty-eight hours. I should get some sleep.*

And that was it. Of the seven-mile drive to the estate, he could not recall a single moment. To James, it seemed as if it never happened. Yet, it did—because the next thing he remembered was coming up the drive to the lodge and seeing the place lit up like a beacon. Every single light inside and outside the house was on. That was what registered first. *Someone's broken in.*

The helicopter on the lawn registered next.

"What in blue blazes . . ." He slammed on the brakes and cranked down the window for a better look. It was a small, neat, McDonnell Douglas Tempest, painted black—which was probably why he missed it at first—with gold markings and searchlight array beneath.

Whoever was ransacking the house had certainly arrived in style. James turned off the motor, and got out of the Land Rover slowly. There was no one around. The night was cold and deathly quiet.

Stepping off the gravel path, he walked swiftly to the house, pausing beside a firethorn bush growing at the edge of the drive. He saw no movement inside. The house remained quiet.

The *fiosachd* had given him no prompting, which was curious, in a way, because ordinarily this was just the sort of thing to set it off. Even so, to make certain he was not walking into something unpleasant, James circled the house, keeping well out of the light from the windows.

By the time he reached the back door, he still had no hint about who or what awaited him inside. He paused long enough to pick up one of the walking sticks he kept beside the door, then put his hand to the latch and shoved the door open. It bumped noisily against the inside wall; the last thing he wanted was to surprise someone in the act. James waited and, when nothing happened, he stepped across the threshold.

The two of them were sitting at the kitchen table, mugs in their hands and a teapot between them. Their heads turned as James entered the room.

"I thought I locked the door," he said.

"You did," replied Embries.

"I hope we did not frighten you, sir," Rhys said, jumping quickly to his feet.

"Is that why you turned on all the lights?"

"As you were not here to greet us when we arrived," Embries said, "we thought it might be best to let you know we were here." He stood slowly, looking at James, studying him; the concern in his pale eyes was deep and genuine.

"You left rather abruptly," Embries continued; there was no rebuke in his tone. "I was worried about you, James. I feared we might have overwhelmed you."

"I couldn't stay there anymore," James told him. "London is no place for me."

Unexpectedly, Embries smiled, closing his eyes. "Yes," he sighed, as if this were a long-awaited confirmation. James stared at him, and Rhys stared, too. "Forget London," Embries said after a moment. "There is something I want to show you. Will you come with me?"

"Do I have a choice?"

"Oh, we all have a choice, James. Destiny calls but once in a lifetime, and every person has a choice whether to answer the call or to ignore it. Stay or go, the choice is yours."

"If I stay here," James asked, "what will happen?"

"Nothing too bad." Embries shrugged. "The world will still keep turning. It will no longer be the *same* world, true, but things will go on much as they always have: ignorance, poverty, crime, and vice will increase, as they do. Factionalism, rivalry, greed, and corruption will render all political and social systems impotent—but that is nothing new. Misery will multiply, and this nation will at last fall beneath the shadow. If you stay, you will be well out of it, for a while at least."

He spoke softly, dispassionately—a seasoned doctor relating the symptoms of a common medical condition.

"And if I go with you?"

He smiled and spread his hands. "God alone knows."

"You do make it sound inviting."

"What would you have me say?" Embries asked. "That you will gain eternal fame and fortune, that you will blaze across the skies like a comet and your name will be written in the stars, that you will become the most revered human being in this or any other century—is that what you want me to say?

"It might happen, but the truth is, I do not know. It might be ignominy and disaster; you might be reviled and vilified. You might even be killed."

"Triumph or tragedy," James murmured.

Embries made no move, but his golden eyes darkened with a wild, almost savage excitement. "Come with me, James. I cannot tell you what lies ahead, but I can promise you it will be the adventure of your life. Whatever happens, we will make a noise the world will never forget."

James believed him. His words had the unmistakable ring of truth, and his sincerity was powered by a conviction so pure as to be radiant. Even so, James could not make himself take that first step.

Perhaps it was the fact that he had been roughly two days without sleep. Perhaps it was stupid bullheadedness. He said, "Can I have the night to think it over? I'll tell you in the morning."

"No." Embries shook his head slowly, his golden hawk's eyes narrowing slightly. "Tomorrow will be too late, James. The time has come, and will not come again."

Still, James hesitated. He could feel the strain coming off Embries in waves—as if he were being shaken by a tremendous power which he was struggling to keep under control.

"This is the moment. You must choose now."

❋

# Fourteen

The Tempest swooped low over the smooth, winter-bare hills above Glen Morven, the land rippling beneath the bleached white glare of the searchlights. James' admiration for Rhys' skills had grown as the trip progressed; he handled the fast, sleek helicopter with cool, calm precision in the best tradition of the RAF.

"Here," said Embries, his voice sounding far away in the headset. "This is the place."

It was dead of night when they had left Glen Slugain Lodge. Like a man in a dream, James had stumbled across the black, formless lawn to the waiting aircraft. They had strapped themselves into their seats—Rhys and James in the cockpit, and Embries behind. Rhys handed around the headsets as he warmed up the engine, and then, finishing his preflight check, he opened the throttle and up they went, spinning slowly into an infinite, star-dusted darkness.

They made a long, lazy turn and headed northwest, away from Braemar and out over the wild hills of the Forest of Mar. After a time, Rhys shifted onto a southwesterly course and held it. James settled back and tried to enjoy the ride, but aside from the solitary light from a farmhouse or car on a road, or the distant glow of a town, there was nothing to see. Soon even those small markers dwindled and disappeared.

Darkness above, darkness below, they might have been inside the belly of a whale or down in the deepest cavern. All sense of motion ceased. It seemed to James that they hung suspended between heaven and earth, frozen in time and space. Faces illuminated by the green glow of the instrument panel, they sat in a lightly vibrating cocoon, the universe around cloaked, hidden, unseen and unknown. James listened to the fluttering rumble of the engine—deadened by the headset, it sounded like a continuous low mumbling thunder—and felt himself enter a kind of waking sleep.

Although he remained conscious of himself and his surroundings—Rhys alert and silent beside him, the thrumming whoosh of the blades, the dull wind wash, and all-encompassing darkness—his thoughts cascaded over him in a confused yet compelling jumble of incidental detail from the last two days: the metallic tang of the air in London, light falling on the carpeted stairs at Kenzie House, the slap of his windscreen wipers on the drive home from Pitlochry, the crumpled papers in Collins' hands, the smack of his leather soles on the pavement in the park, the quavery organ at the church service, the slick feel of the old photocopied birth certificate, the boiled-cabbage smell of Howard Gilpin's house, Cal's goofy lovestruck grin as Isobel swayed from the room . . . and on and on.

James remained in this peculiar state for an indeterminate time—an age, an eon—awake but dreaming, his mind turning and turning, thoughts spinning, revolving, images forming in bizarre kaleidoscopic combinations, only to splinter and re-form in yet more strange associations. Time, like the world outside, dwindled away to nothing; it might exist, but it had no substance, no meaning. James, too, simply existed: alive but inert, outwardly immobile but inwardly a flurry of frantic, disjointed activity.

Then, after an eternity, Embries spoke. "Here. This is the place," and James started at the sound of his voice. In the pale globe of light below, he saw the undulating ground coming up fast beneath them. A moment later, the aircraft

touched down. It was still dark. James had no idea how long
they had flown or where they were. Rhys killed the engine
and the lights, and they sat for a moment, waiting for the
blades to stop whirling. They then stepped out onto a silent
landscape. There was not a sound to be heard—no cars, no
farm dog barking in the distance, not even the wind rustling
the coarse, dry grass at their feet.

"We need a fire, I think," Embries announced.

*Good luck finding anything for a fire in the dark,* James
thought. Yet, he felt a sudden warmth and turned around to
see yellow tongues of flame building to a decent blaze.

They stood beside the fire, warming themselves. James,
almost dead on his feet, found himself reflecting on what a
peculiar situation this had become. Step by logical step, he
had progressed from the mundane to the marvelous in the
space of two days. Stranger still, despite the oddness of the
circumstances, it felt perfectly natural to be standing there in
the bleak midnight, feeling the fire on his face and hands—
an activity as old as mankind, he thought.

Then Embries started to sing.

He simply opened his mouth, and an extraordinary voice
poured out—liquid, rich, deep, and wonderful, like fine rare
wine flowing out into the night.

James was so amazed by the unexpectedness of this that
it took him a moment to realize he could not understand a
word Embries was singing. It sounded like Gaelic, but it was
no Gaelic James had ever heard. The melody was at once
piercing and plaintive—achingly bittersweet and soulful in
the way of the best old Scottish and Irish ballads: songs
about dead lovers, lost causes, fallen champions. James
stared entranced as this remarkable man drew breath and
with eyes closed released that splendid voice.

He sang with such authority and understanding, with such
command of tone and inflection, with such presence, it
seemed that he was not merely singing but inhabiting the
song. Or that he was becoming himself *through* the song.
Even as James watched, it seemed as if his normal outward
appearance was peeled away to uncover a much more intriguing, much more mysterious and compelling creature

beneath—as if Embries had lifted a mask he was wearing, only to reveal a yet more fantastic face.

Then again, maybe it was James' peculiar frame of mind—physically close to exhaustion and, thanks to the recent revelations, emotionally fragile—whatever it was, as Embries sang, James felt the *fiosachd* quicken. The skin at the back of his neck tingled, and he began to feel as if he were being pulled in two. It was as if his spirit was a square of cloth snatched up between two monstrous fists determined to tear it in half. He imagined he could actually feel his soul stretching.

At the same time, it seemed to him that the air was hardening around him. He thought, *This is what it feels like to be an insect caught alive in amber.*

The sensation was unnerving: to feel himself stretching, growing ever more tenuous and insubstantial on the inside, yet more concrete and solid on the outside, caused his vision to blur at the edges. He stood before the fire, listening to that magnificent voice and felt himself surrounded by a gentle yet unyielding force; each note of the song seemed to trail a golden silklike thread which encircled James, binding him in shining, luminous whorls.

Then Embries lifted his face to the unseen heavens high above, and the song rose high into the black night. James looked up and saw a glittering spray of red-gold sparks sailing up from the fire. All at once the terrible stretching inside him ceased and he was free. But now it seemed as if he were ascending up through space with the sparks, and that these scintillating flecks of light had somehow gotten inside him. He tingled from head to toe as the *fiosachd* descended upon him with a force he had never experienced. He could feel sparks streaming from his fingertips.

The *fiosachd* enveloped him in a heightened awareness. His senses grew sharp. He could hear the flames rippling over the wood as it hissed and sizzled, releasing the trapped moisture of its cells as steam; each crack and pop of the fire burst upon him like the report of an automatic weapon. He saw not only the flames themselves, pulsing and quivering, but the ultraviolet aura of the flames as well: intertwining coronas surrounding each tongue of flame with a rainbow of multihued crimson. He smelled not only the dusky sharpness of the wood smoke but also the earthy dampness of the moss growing on the bark of the logs.

Slowly, he became aware that Embries' song was not a meaningless jumble of unknown words; there was movement and repetition within a tightly ordered cycle. He could detect a rhythm involving repeated phrases and gradually, as he listened, an intricate rhyme scheme emerged from the blur of unfamiliar sounds. Curiously, even those foreign-sounding syllables were becoming less unfamiliar all the time.

He concentrated and, to his amazement, plucked out a word from the flow: *croidh.* He understood it as "heart." Another word passed by and he snatched it up: *anrheg* . . . "gift." And so on, like a bear swatting fish from a swift-moving stream, he began to seize the sense of the song. The meaning grew gradually clearer. The more words he captured, the more coherent became the meaning, until he understood that Embries was singing about a man, a hero, the defender of his people, who had gone away, leaving his nation without a . . . *roof*? No, leaving his nation open and vulnerable, like a house without a roof.

Away to the east, the sky began to lighten. James noticed that the clouds which had obscured the night sky were breaking up and moving off with the approach of dawn. The darkness dimmed around them to a misty luminescence, and all at once Embries stopped singing. He threw wide his arms and cried, "Behold!"

James understood this as a command, and turned. He saw that they stood at the edge of a treeless plain. Before them rose a low, broad hill—not more than a few dozen feet in elevation, it nevertheless occupied a considerable acreage. On the bank of the hill the ground was broken and uneven, the grassy turf pushed and bunched as if giant fists beneath the surface were trying to break through. The top of the hill was more or less flat, and there were numerous low hillocks scattered haphazardly around, and one sizable mound rising roughly from the center. Several shallow ditches ran at angles across the plain and up the gentle slope of the rise, cutting into the bunched and broken mounds. Everything was overgrown with wiry gorse and thistle and sad clumps of sheep-ravaged heather.

Dour and gray in the thin predawn light, the plain and its low rise seemed as lost and forlorn as any forgotten scrag of land anywhere. Mist hung in damp, wraithlike patches, and water dripped from the low branches of the gorse onto the soggy ground. There was nothing at all distinctive about the place, nothing to catch the eye or spark the memory, much less tease the imagination.

Even so, it was as if James had been struck by a bolt of lightning from a clear blue sky. He saw that God-forsaken plain and thought: *I have been here before.*

But it was impossible. He did not even know where he was—he might have been anywhere north of the border, and there were thousands of places he'd never been. Certainly, this barren landscape with its odd humps and ditches could claim no special place in his memory.

Yet as he turned away from the flames and stepped toward the hill, he knew . . . he recognized, and recognizing, rejoiced with a wild exultation. He felt exhilarated, thrilled, excited, and awed all at once, for it was the recognition a soldier experiences on his homecoming from foreign wars. It was the recognition of a man for his bride when first he sees her on their wedding day. It was the recognition one feels on meeting a close and dear friend after a long absence.

"Behold!" cried Embries. "The time-between-times!"

And the thought came again, with greater insistence and deeper assurance. *I have been here before!*

James gazed out upon the desolate landscape and shuddered, not with cold but with the unanswerable conviction of familiarity. But not—not as he saw it now. He knew it from another time, when it had been a city, when the mounds and humps and hillocks had been buildings and houses and walls, when the ditches had been streets and roads.

"I know this place," he declared, glancing across to Embries, who stood tall and erect, arms outspread, face to the rising sun.

Turning back, James took a single step nearer, and the ground shifted beneath his feet. The covering of turf melted away, revealing shaped stone beneath. Another step and the stones appeared to realign themselves on their ancient footings. *Dear God in Heaven,* he gasped inwardly, *what is happening here?*

Dazed by the surge and whirl of potent emotions, he stumbled forward. The walls rose before him, so that after a dozen steps he was no longer standing on a forlorn plain but moving ever more rapidly towards a wide open gateway set in the high protecting walls of a city, a fortress.

*Caer Lial* . . .

The word appeared of itself, and was met with the same recognition. It was the name of the fortress.

Stiff-legged with wonder, he walked up the long ramp towards the high timber gate. He knew there was no gated entrance, no walls, or streets, and yet all those things *were* there, all around him. He had but to reach out his hands to touch them.

Moving onto the ramp, he glanced back over his shoulder to see that the helicopter was gone. The wood had encroached upon the plain. Rhys and Embries were still there by the fire, silent and motionless, watching him. James moved on quickly, suddenly afraid that the vision would fade before he could discover its meaning.

Once through the gates, he hastened along the narrow, stone-flagged street and made for the center of the fortress, passing an assortment of timber-frame buildings—some round, some oblong—but all with steep-sloping roofs and low doorways, dark beneath the heavy overhang of thatch. It came to him that these were storehouses and workrooms; and, as if in answer to the thought, he heard like a ghostly echo the clang of a hammer on iron and the whinny of a horse. The sound halted him and he turned; there, across a small bare yard, rose a great hall.

Rather, it was simply a large, tall, rectangular building— far larger than any of the others. Four great rough-hewn oak trees formed the corner posts, and another, split in two, supported a lintel of carved stone. The walls were wide laths of

timber below a high-peaked thatched roof. The doorposts
and lintel were painted: red for the wooden posts, blue for
the stone lintel. James saw the painted entrance and knew
the structure was the great hall of a king.

He had no need to look inside. He knew it as he would
have known his own house at Blair Morven. Yet he did walk
to the doorway and peer in. Though dark, James could make
out the immense square hearth in the center of the hall, and
the long boards and bankers of the tables. At one end was a
wicker partition on which hung a huge square banner: a
writhing red dragon on a field of green and white.

The image was primitive and powerful. James filled his
gaze with it, and his pulse quickened at the sight. He marveled at the inexplicable sensation of potency. He had never
seen the flag in his life, yet one glimpse was enough to send
the blood racing in his veins.

*I have lived in this place. I have eaten at those tables, and
slept beneath this roof.*

With this thought came a picture: a great fire in the hearth
and men lining the benches—eating, drinking, talking
loudly of the battle they had won. One man stood out from
the rest: wide of shoulder, he moved with the easy, graceful
power of a war leader; a chieftain in a blood-red cloak, he
carried a whitewashed shield with a crude cross painted in
red. He was speaking to two others—twins, they were, both
tall, with close-cut hair and bands of gold on their bare,
strong arms.

Before James could see more, he felt a weight in his arms,
and another face appeared before him—the face of a woman:
she had markings daubed in blue on her smooth cheeks and
high, noble brow, and wore a warrior's mail shirt; the mail,
however, was made of exquisite tiny silver rings that shimmered like living light as she moved. The slender torc of gold
at her throat identified her as a queen. Her hair was dark—
black as a raven's wing, and her eyes blue as ice under even
black brows. Her lips were warm, and her hands rested with
easy intimacy on his chest. She whispered a name, he felt her
breath warm in his ear, and was overcome by such a powerful longing, his heart rose to his throat.

*I want her. I want to make love to this phantom queen.*

Unable to endure the yearning, James turned and staggered quickly from the hall and back into the yard. Moving away from the hall, he began walking up one of the other streets, and came to a section of the fortress where the buildings were stone—very old; the stone was not simply found slabs, but shaped into blocks, some of which bore the quarry marks. Two of the buildings had upper floors with square windows. Another was a church.

James could not have said how he knew it was a church, for it was a simple, square, rough-stone building roofed in slate. The crude wooden door was open, so he walked over and looked inside. The interior was small, with room enough for only twenty people at most, yet there was nothing inside the single, bare room save a tall candletree and an altar made of three large stones. The edge of the table stone was carved with a small cross at either end, and there were words in Latin etched between them.

Again, even though James did not know Latin, he knew—as if from long familiarity—what they said. "Father of Light, illumine me," he whispered, and felt an irresistible urge to go inside.

He stepped cautiously into the room. It smelled of beeswax and fat—the way it would if someone had just extinguished a candle. He moved towards the altar slab and stood before it, gazing down on the surface where he saw, cut into the top, the long, slender, tapering shape of a sword.

Stretching out his hand, he touched the carving and placed his hand on the hilt of the sword, feeling cold stone beneath his fingertips. It was no dream—solid matter met his touch. James drew back his hand as if he had touched molten metal.

There was a movement at the chapel door, but James did not turn. He knew that Embries had followed him into the fortress. "Memory, they say, can play tricks on a person," he said.

"Is that what this is—a trick of the mind?" James asked, gazing at the sword in the stone, unable to take his eyes from it.

"What do you think?" Embries asked, entering the chapel.

His refusal to answer irritated James. "What am I supposed to think?" he shouted. His voice rang in the bare stone room. Again, Embries made no reply. James demanded, "What's happening to me?"

"I could tell you," the old man replied, "but it would be best if you came to it on your own."

"But why? I don't understand."

"I think you do." He hesitated, and James realized Embries had been about to speak a name—*his* name.

"Why don't you say it?"

Confused and bewildered, James felt himself slipping, a man clinging desperately to a sheer rock face, every handhold turning to clay and crumbling away even as he grasped it. Forcing down the panic churning up inside, he looked Embries in the eye and said, "I *have* been here before, haven't I?"

"Yes." That was all he said, but James needed no other confirmation. His own heart and soul had been telling him nothing else since he set foot on the mounded plain.

"God help me," he gasped, "how is that possible?"

As Embries stepped beside him, James turned his head to confront him. One look, and his strength flowed away like water, for the old man had changed almost beyond recognition.

## ✳
# Fifteen

The man wore Embries' face and possessed his elegant stature, but was far younger than the man James knew, and a virile, wild, restless energy streamed from him like heat from a dancing flame. He had a mane of wild dark hair, and the faint trace of a faded tattoo on his right cheek—a tiny spiral *fhain* mark. The word came naturally into James' mind, but it was a word he had never used in his life.

The man wore a long blue-and-white-checked cloak over his shoulder. The cloak, edged with wolf skin, was fastened by an elaborate silver brooch with the head of a stag; on his neck was a massive torc of beaten gold. His trousers were dark blue with tiny stripes of silver thread, and on his feet were tall boots of soft buckskin. In his right hand he held the same horn-tipped staff James had seen the night of their first meeting atop Weem Hill; when he moved, James caught the scent of peat smoke and fresh winter wind. His eyes were deep gold and gleaming with a keen, fantastic light.

The change was complete, but it was not so much the alterating of his appearance as it was assuming another aspect; Embries had not transformed into someone else, he had simply become more himself. His manner was at once imposing and regal but also welcoming: one king greeting another.

Raising his staff, he stretched out his other hand and held

it palm outward, saying, "The throne of Britain shall become an iniquity to the nation, and a reproach to the people, ere Arthur returns."

His voice, rich and resonant, seemed to come from another world. "When Avalon shall rise again in Llyonesse, and the Thamesis reverse its course, then also shall Arthur take up the kingship of his nation once more."

The words meant little to James, yet he understood the fearful authority behind them, a power that could command and conquer. Who could stand before such mysteries?

Lowering his hand, Embries said, "In you, these ancient prophecies are fulfilled. Let him hear it who will."

James' knees gave way. He sank down before the altar and put his face in his hands. "How is it possible?"

When Embries did not reply, James looked up at him. He continued to gaze down with his intense golden eyes, willing James to make the leap and join him on the other side. But the other side of what?

When James could no longer bear the intensity of that gaze, he looked away. As he did so, he caught sight of the Latin inscription on the altar's edge. " 'Father of Light,' " he whispered, making that prayer his own, " 'illumine me.' "

"You are right to call on God," Embries said. "He is your righteousness and your strength, and you will have need of both in the days to come. Without God there is no king."

James did not raise his head, but he could feel Embries' eyes like hot coals burning into his flesh. Then, lofting his staff over his head, Embries placed the palm of his other hand on James' still-bowed head. Heat and energy flowed from his touch—or perhaps through it—into James. He felt warmth flood through him from head to heel.

"Hear the words of a True Bard," Embries declared, his voice ringing with authority. "I sain thee with a strong saining. By the might of the Swift Sure Hand, I sain thee:

> *"I set the keeping of Christ about thee;*
> *I send the guarding of the Great Light with thee,*
> *To possess thee, to protect thee,*
> *From death, from danger, from loss.*

*"Let the encircling of the Three encompass thee in the
    battle to come.
In the day of strife, let Michael militant be thy
    strong protector.
In the twistings of the fight, let Blessed Jesu stand
    between thee and the hate of the enemy.*

*"I set a cloak of Bright Angels around thee,
To guard thee from thy back,
To preserve thee from thy front,
From the crown of thy head,
To the arch of thy foot,
A cloak of Bright Angels shielding thee always.*

*"The peace of Christ is with thee, and his own loving
    arm is around thee.
The aiding of the True Spirit is with thee, and his fiery
    sword protects thee,
The shield of the Living God is over thee,
Now, and always, wherever thou goest,
Now, and always, wherever thou farest."*

James thrilled to the words; he could feel them striking
deep and quickening in his soul; already they were beginning to shape and change him. It was as if the words themselves were charms of strong enchantment and he was being
transformed from the inside. A strange sensation, yet wholly
natural—it felt to James like waking up after a long nap to
find himself refreshed and ready for a great adventure. His
heart beat faster. His spirit soared.

*This is how it was meant to be!*

He kept thinking, *This is who I am. This is how it was
meant to be. God in heaven, I have come home!*

"Stand up," commanded Embries. "It is not fitting for a
king to kneel before his Wise Counselor."

At his command, James found he could finally rise. He
climbed to his feet and faced him. *Surely,* he thought, *we
have stood this way a thousand times—ten thousand! King
and bard together, now and always.*

"Myrddin," he said. The name appeared of itself. James was not thinking it but, once spoken, he knew it was right. "Myrddin Emrys."

A ghost of a smile played at the bard's lips. "That," he said, "is one of my names."

"And you have so many," James replied. "I remember."

Myrddin's glance was sharp and direct. "You will," he said, his tone at once a challenge and an encouragement. "You *will* remember," he said, "and when you do, all this will make sense. That I promise you."

He turned and started away. "Now, however, we must go. Time is running short, and there is much to do."

James remained before the altar. "Say it," he demanded. "Say my name."

Myrddin turned back and hesitated. James could see him trying to read whether he was ready to hear it.

"I have said yours," James told him. "Now you must say mine."

Myrddin squared his shoulders to face him, his golden eyes prying deep into James' soul, trying to read what he saw there.

"Say it, Myrddin."

"Come away, Arthur," he said softly. "Time flees before us, and we have much to do if we are to save this land."

*Arthur!*

He spoke the name, and James opened his mouth, and laughed out loud.

The name sent a flood of elation cascading through him, and with it a flood tide of remembrance. He saw Cal sitting astride a great horse; he was leaning down, his strong forearm resting on his thigh, a bracelet of heavy gold on his wrist, glinting in the light as he extended his hand to a dark-haired maiden with the offering of a cornflower blossom.

He saw Rhys, arms folded inside his cloak, standing before a crackling fire on the bank of a reed-fringed lake. He was gazing into the flames, his face glowing in the flickering light. His long dark hair was in a thick braid which he wore to the side of his head and over one shoulder. Behind him loomed the massive dark bulk of a cone-shaped hill sur-

mounted by the towering walls of a fortress; overhead the
twilight sky was streaked with stars. His jaw bulged and his
brow wrinkled as he contemplated the thorny problem before him.

"Come away, Arthur," said Myrddin, and once again
James felt a thrill of exquisite delight ripple through him.
"Memories can wait. We must be about our work."

They turned and walked together from the chapel and into
the narrow street. As they moved along the ancient pathway,
the fortress and its buildings began to melt away. The walls
and rooftops glistened, and then slowly faded, growing more
and more transparent, until they could see through them to
the hills beyond. The first rays of sunlight touched the phantom structures, whereupon they dispersed altogether, leaving the two men standing on the grass-covered mound in the
light of a glorious winter morning.

Gone were the walls and buildings, gone the ancient
thatched hall and stout timber gates—everything asleep beneath the thick green turf. Caer Lial was but a scattering of
low, grass-covered mounds and ditches once more. The
walls were toppled, the streets broken and sunk, the fine
kingly hall crumbled, and the handsome banner nothing but
a handful of dust. Grass covered everything, hiding house
and granary, church and hall alike; patches of swiftly dissi-
pating mist hung where warriors had once walked.

The Wise Emrys, too, had resumed his former guise, becoming once more the slender whitehaired man of imperious bearing. Gone was the wolf skin and torc of gold, gone
the dark mane of hair and the checkered Celtic cloak and silver brooch, the tall boots of fine soft leather. But even as
James beheld the change, he saw, faint as a faded line on
parchment, the tiny blue spiral tattoo on Embries' right
cheek just below his eye.

And then that, too, was gone, and James felt a stab of sorrow.

They walked across the mounded ruin of the ancient
fortress and out through the nonexistent gates. On the plain
below, James saw the fire, and Rhys was waiting there. Joining him, James was pleasantly surprised to discover that the

pilot had a breakfast of grilled sausages and porridge ready for them.

At their approach, Rhys took the pot from the fire and poured out the oat porridge into three big bowls sitting on a low aluminum camp table. He dropped a knob of butter into each bowl, splashed cream over the top, and handed them around as they sat before the fire.

Suddenly ravenous, James began to spoon the good hot oatmeal down. Meanwhile, Rhys collected sizzling sausages from a spit beside the flame, put these on plates, to which he added big chunks of fresh chewy bread. He passed them out, and the three settled down to eat. James felt as if it had been years since he'd had a hot meal. He devoured the porridge and scraped the bowl clean, then started on the bread and sausage, tearing the bread with his hands. There was coffee, too, black and hot, and served in thick ceramic mugs.

James finished first and, putting his plate aside, sat holding his mug of coffee, feeling full and happy, and, for the first time in a long time, completely at peace with the world.

Glancing at Embries who was chewing thoughtfully, he asked, "How long have you known?"

"I have always known," replied the bard without looking up.

"Truly?"

He nodded, still staring into the flames. "You cannot imagine how long I have waited for this day."

"You mean you aren't behind all this, orchestrating it, making it happen?"

He turned his face towards James at last. "It is not so simple as that," he replied. "Sometimes, I wish it were."

"But you knew," James insisted, trying to make sense of it. "You knew from the beginning where to look for me, where to find me."

"Knowledge is a slippery thing," Embries replied. "I knew Arthur would return, yes. I have always known that. But I did not know it would be *you*. Let us say, I *hoped*— with a very great and confident hope—that it would be you. Until a few days ago, I was not certain."

"I don't understand. If you knew about me from the beginning, why the lack of certainty?"

Embries paused, considering how to explain. "Suppose," he said after a moment, "that you knew someone in a foreign country had determined to send you a valuable gift—more valuable than anything you can imagine. That much you knew beyond all doubt. The trouble is, you didn't know when they would send it, or how long it would take to arrive. You didn't even know what form it might take. That being the case, what would you do?"

"I don't know. Take up fishing, I suppose—to have something to do while I was waiting for it to show up."

"No," corrected Embries. "What you would do, in fact, is spend every waking moment getting ready. Considering the immense value of the gift, you would make certain that every detail was in place, so that when the gift finally arrived, you could protect it properly."

"So that's what you've been doing? Arranging all the details?"

"I have been toiling away," he agreed, "making preparations so that when the gift finally arrived all would be ready and in good order."

"The photo I found," James said. "It was taken years ago—after a day's hunting on the estate. You were with the Duke's shooting party. You must have been checking up on me even then."

"I have, from time to time, found it necessary to 'check up' on you, as you say." He frowned thoughtfully. "Perhaps you remember the time when you were on a school trip to the Maritime Museum in Aberdeen, and you and two other young chaps got separated from your group down by the docks. You were wandering around the waterfront, lost, frantic, because it was getting late. You knew the bus was supposed to be leaving, and you were growing a little panicky." He smiled at the memory.

"I remember," James told him. That had happened over twenty years ago—he must have been seven or eight at the time and had not given it a thought since.

"Perhaps you remember also the old gentleman who stopped to give you directions."

"He not only gave us directions. He got a policeman

along to take us to the bus in his panda car with the siren going."

"Yes, I believe he did."

"That was you?"

"As I say," he shrugged, "I was making certain everything remained in good order—in case you turned out to be the one I was looking for."

James thought back to other times in his childhood when he felt someone was watching over him . . . probably some-one was. "There have been other times, too."

"Several, in fact. Yes."

James glanced at Rhys who, although he had not said any-thing, appeared to know exactly what they were talking about. "I assume Rhys knows about all this—about who I am."

"Oh, yes, he knows. I could not have managed without his help."

Rhys smiled, and poured more coffee into his mug. "I have only known for a couple years," he said. "I'm glad we don't have to keep it a secret from you any longer."

"I saw you up there," James told him, indicating the fortress mound behind him. "You were one of my warriors."

"The Dragon Flight," said Rhys. He shrugged. "At least that's what Embries tells me. I can't say I remember it my-self."

Glancing around at Embries, James asked, "Who else knows?"

"One or two others: Collins from Royal Heritage, of course, and Donald and Caroline." He made a deprecatory gesture with his hands. "Sherlock Holmes had his Irregulars, and I have mine. Some know more than others, but you need have no fear. They are all tried and true, I can assure you."

Overcome by the complex wonder of it, James shook his head. "Incredible. Absolutely incredible."

"Eventually, I suspect everything will become completely clear," Embries replied. "You will remember more, as I say. Don't try to force it. Just relax and accept what is given in its time."

He held James with his eyes, his expression wise and

compassionate. "Before we came here, I told you that you must choose—whether to accept your destiny or turn aside."

"I followed you, didn't I?"

"You did," he replied. "But now that you have glimpsed something of the shape of that destiny, I must ask you again." He rose to his feet. "Rise, Arthur."

James stood, and Embries put his hands on his shoulders.

"Are you ready to take the throne of Britain?" he asked. "Will you assume your duties as the sovereign King of your country?"

"I will."

Embries smiled. "Here is where it begins." Cupping a hand to James' neck, he embraced him once and then held him at arm's length. "You'll never know how long I have waited for this day."

# ✻
# Sixteen

The flight back to Blair Morven was swift and uneventful. Though exhausted in every nerve and sinew, James could not sleep. The most profound event of his life had occurred—an incident of unrivaled consequence—and he was reeling. It felt as if he had been strapped to a rocket engine and flown to the stars and back. Head, heart, hands—everything: even the soft ground beneath his feet—pulsed and tingled with singular vitality.

Although he did not fully comprehend what it all meant—the deepest significance would elude him yet a little longer—he knew deep in his bones that he had passed beyond some boundary normally closed to human beings and walked awhile in another realm of existence.

As the chopper sped northward, he sat in the thrumming cocoon of sound and watched the green hills and spidery lines of roads far below. Gazing idly at the landscape sliding smoothly by below, his mind was on Caer Lial and the multitude of feelings awakened there.

*How,* he wondered, *could I even begin to explain what has happened to me? Have I lived before? Or has the spirit of a previous age been born in me somehow? Or is there some other even more fantastic explanation?*

James had never set much store in reincarnation—the

endless return of souls to bodies for the tedious expiation of sins committed in previous lives. The human soul was not a glass bottle to be relentlessly recycled time and time again. One chance was all anyone got—that is what he believed. One chance, and one chance only, so you had to do your best, you had to make it count.

But if not reincarnation, then what?

James didn't know. All he could say was that he lost nothing in the transaction, only gained. His perspective on life had changed, and he now viewed the world from a slightly different angle, but his personality—the part of him he knew to be himself—had not altered. Insofar as he could tell, he was still the same person he'd always been. Only now he remembered . . . what?

What, after all, did he really remember?

A few hazy images, brief snatches of faces, the reassuring sound of another name falling on his ear. Not much, in actual fact.

Yet, and yet, the sense that he had at last come home remained strong in him. That, and the perception of recognition filled him with a powerful conviction: he *knew* who he had been and where he had lived. He remembered Caer Lial and the people there because they were in some way part of himself.

He could no more explain how this could be than he could define why a star-dusted sky filled him with such knee-weakening awe, or why the sight of geese flying across the moor sent an arrow of bittersweet longing through his heart, or why the taste of wild raspberries always made him smile.

If not for the strong sense of familiarity, of things remembered, the strangeness of the experience might have overwhelmed him completely. What had happened was strange, passing strange and going a long way towards bizarre; there was no denying that. At the same time, he felt a distinct *rightness* to the experience that reassured him in the face of what could only be logically described as a particularly outlandish hallucination.

There was no logical, rational way to account for this. Even to say he had experienced a vision or hallucination brought on by stress, or sleep deprivation, merely begged the question. A fellow too long without sleep might see pink polka-dotted dragons, but he didn't see the faces of people he knew in another life.

But it wasn't *another* life, James argued with himself, it was this one, this *same* life. This same life, only in another time.

He did not know how to explain it any better than to say that he felt as if an awareness had awakened inside him after a long, long sleep. Whatever it was, this newly wakened consciousness was also part of him—as much a part of himself as his arms and legs or his sense of humor. By some power or powers unknown, an essential part of him had awakened and returned to consciousness. He was not changed. Far from it! He was simply more himself. Like a child who has finally grown enough to wear his father's boots, he was at last big enough to assume his father's throne.

Embries had promised that it would all make sense. James trusted him instinctively. Perhaps Embries' presence gave him the only assurance he had that he was not losing his grip on sanity. Perhaps because he had no other choice if he was going to survive the ordeal ahead, James believed him when Embries said he would remember, and it would all make sense.

Rhys' voice in the headset stirred James from his reverie. "Prepare for landing."

James looked down and saw the white square of Glen Slugain Lodge coming into view beyond the tops of the pines. A moment later, the Tempest floated down, gently bumping to rest on the lawn. As he unstrapped himself and climbed from the helicopter, James wondered what would happen next.

After he and Embries walked clear of the blades, Rhys revved the engine and took off once more. "He'll be back in a little while," Embries remarked. "He's just gone to refuel."

When the Tempest was out of sight, the two of them walked to the house, where they discovered a much-agitated Cal waiting at the kitchen table. The look of relief on his face brought James up short. "I might have known you would be together," Cal said. "I don't mind telling you I was getting worried."

"It's all right, Calum," Embries replied. "I should have left a message for you."

"No harm done," said Cal. "But I was this close to calling out the bloodhounds." He looked from one to the other of them expectantly. "Well, where do we start?"

"First," said Embries, clapping a hand to Calum's shoulder, "I think we must get our friend here married."

Of all the things he might have said, that was the last thing James expected to hear. "Married!"

"You have no objection, do you?"

"Not in principle, but I—" James stumbled, "I mean, a guy likes to plan these things in his own way."

"That opportunity has passed," Embries replied firmly. He sat James down in one of the chairs. "Listen to me," he said, growing solemn. "In two days we must return to London where you will announce your kingship. You will not get an easy ride. To speak plainly, this will be the most difficult and demanding thing you have ever done. The turmoil will be appalling, the outcry horrendous."

"Why am I not surprised?"

"I am serious," he snapped. "This announcement will set in motion a train of events that cannot be stopped once it has begun. You will need companionship, and you will need understanding; you will need the comfort of a woman. In short, you will need a wife and helpmate to share the burden."

"You old romantic," James quipped.

Embries pursed his lips. "I appreciate the fairer sex as much as any man alive," he replied, "but the marriage I contemplate is a union of far greater essence than you comprehend. Listen"—he pulled out a chair and sat facing James—"once you assume the throne your life will no longer be your own. Everything you do, every move you make, every word you speak will be endlessly debated by the watching world.

"Now, suppose that in a few years' time you were to announce your intention to marry. That would make headlines on several continents. The whole nation would become embroiled in the decision. Who is this woman? Is she fit to be queen? Why should we accept her? Is she pretty enough? Has she got what it takes? Do we like her?"

"It would still be my decision," James maintained.

"Of course," granted Embries, "but think of it from the woman's point of view. The media would inevitably get involved, and if, for whatever reason, they didn't approve of your choice, they would propose alternatives. And the people would begin choosing between the candidates on offer. Should you ignore their nominee, your poor queen would forever be reviled and maligned. Her life would become a nightmare."

The way he said it made James think he was speaking from personal, not to say painful, experience. "You have seen this happen before," he said.

"I have indeed seen it happen before," Embries confirmed. "And I do not want it to happen to you. Therefore, I strongly suggest that if you have any thoughts or inclination towards marriage, you must act without delay." He regarded James hopefully. "Would I be wrong in thinking there was a young woman in your life at the moment?"

It was Cal who answered. "There is," he said. "Her name is Jenny—Jennifer Evans-Jones."

James glared at Cal with keen displeasure.

"It's true," Cal insisted. "Everyone says you were made for each other, but you're both too stubborn to admit it."

"I think I know my own—" James began, faltering to a stop as a miraculous change swept over Embries' features.

"Jennifer," he whispered to himself. His serious expression was transformed into one of delight and rapture. He sank back in his chair and closed his eyes. "Of course . . . of course."

Both Calum and James stared at him. After a moment, James asked, "Are you all right?"

"Yes! Yes, it must be," he murmured, and James realized he was talking about something else. Then Embries opened his eyes, leaned forward eagerly, and said, "Will Jennifer marry you?"

James frowned, recalling Sunday's disaster.

"Unfortunately," Embries continued without waiting for an answer, "there will not be time for a gala wedding. We have but two days, remember. Do you think you can talk her into something, shall we say, a little less grand than she might have imagined?"

"At the moment, I'm not sure I could even talk her into going to lunch with me," replied James, and suddenly felt very tired. He stood abruptly. "But I'll give it my undivided attention as soon as I've had some sleep."

"I'll leave it to you," said Embries. "Don't put it off too long."

✳

# Seventeen

Wilfred Collins arrived at the office a good twenty minutes earlier than usual, and was surprised to find the receptionist already at her desk. What is more, she was the wrong one.

"Good morning," he said genially. "I don't think I know you."

"Good morning to you, Mr. Collins," she replied in a low, dusky voice. He could not help noticing that her voice perfectly matched her radiant auburn hair. "My name is Moira. I'm afraid Emerald is ill today. So I'm filling in for her. The agency sent me." She smiled, showing a generous mouth and fine white teeth.

"Emerald sick? Oh, dear . . ." Unaccountably, Collins found himself staring at the young woman, and growing more disconcerted by the moment. "I, um, well . . . I mean, it isn't like her at all. Nothing serious, I hope—with Emerald, I mean."

"I shouldn't think so—probably just the flu. There's a lot of it about just now."

She picked up a pencil and tapped it on the blotter. Her fingernails were long, and her nail polish was dark purple—the color of violets, or a bruise.

He swallowed hard, but found it difficult to take his eyes

off the young woman. He felt his hands growing sweaty, and smiled weakly. Aware that he should say something, his mind went blank as his entire stock of weather observations suddenly evaporated.

"Was there something I could do for you, Mr. Collins?" she asked in her smoke-tinged voice, and he instantly felt himself go weak in the knees with desire. Color rushed to his face and he averted his eyes.

He was on the point of panic when the phone on her desk rang. "Ah, yes . . . indeed, well," he stammered, "duty calls . . . duty calls."

Collins hurried on past the desk to a door at the end of the reception area. He paused to look back at the guest receptionist, and then made his way up the long staircase to his office on the upper floor. As a senior member of the firm, Collins enjoyed a corner room with large sash windows on two sides and a small coal-burning fireplace which he sometimes used.

Owing to his special commission, he had begun taking the precaution of locking his door when he left his office, so he unlocked it now and pushed it open. He then stood on the threshold for a moment, observing his desk and furniture. Only when he had satisfied himself that, yes, everything was exactly as he had left it, did he go in. He closed the door quietly behind him, hung up his coat and hat, and set about unpacking his Gladstone bag.

He worked happily through the morning, nailing down the last remaining details of his special project. From time to time, his colleagues stuck their heads through the door to say good morning or inquire about some arcane detail for articles they were working on, and at 11:30 he attended the monthly editorial meeting. Otherwise, he kept to himself and worked on through to lunch.

At 1:00 precisely, he tidied his desktop, put away the folder containing the official documents he was preparing for his special client, and locked the desk. Picking up the phone, he dialed the number he had been given, spoke briefly to the man who answered, and then hung up. He was reaching into his bag for the small plastic box containing a bacon and cheese sandwich when Philip Hamilton, the sales director, hailed him from his doorway. "I say, Wilfred, fancy a pint and ploughman's?"

"Well, I don't know . . . I brought a sandwich. I thought I might just—"

"Come on, Wilf," Philip urged, "don't tell me you're going to work through lunch again. This special commission of yours is becoming an obsession. Anyway, I need to pick your brain."

"I suppose—"

"I'll buy, how's that?" Philip, a stocky man of middle age, with thick wavy hair and a short brush mustache, approached and took his arm. "The Angel," he said, steering Collins towards the stairs, "or the Frog and Flagon? The choice is yours."

"The Angel's fine," replied Collins.

"The Angel it is."

As they descended the stairs Collins straightened his tie in the mirror on the landing. He pressed a hand to his hair and smoothed it down as best he could, wishing he'd thought to bring a comb. Upon reaching the reception area, he looked for Moira, but she was nowhere to be seen. One of the junior assistants was manning the desk instead, and Collins felt a distinct pang of disappointment as he passed by.

They walked down the street and turned the corner onto a busy street; halfway along was the Angel, a sturdy old local with good ale and a decent lunch. While the pub was not trendy enough to be crowded, the loyal attentions of the neighborhood's secretaries and businessmen kept the kitchen up to scratch.

The two men took the last available table, and Philip went to place their orders, leaving Collins to hold the table. He was idly twirling a pub mat when he saw a pair of long legs in dark stockings emerge from the crowd at the bar. He looked up to see the generous smile and seductive green eyes.

"Moira!" he said, a little too enthusiastically.

"Fancy that," she said, her tone inviting. "We have the same taste in pubs."

Remembering his manners, he jumped up. "Sit down, please. We seem to have taken the last table. Won't you join us?"

"Maybe for a minute," she replied, pulling out a chair.

She folded one splendid leg over the other and Collins felt his heart leap into his throat. "Ho—how are you getting on, then?" he croaked.

"Splendidly. I must say everyone has been very helpful, and I find the work fascinating."

"Do you?" he wondered. "My word, how extraordinary!" He laughed aloud. "Most people think it's boring."

"Not at all!" she replied vigorously. "Royalty, nobility, all that pomp and circumstance . . . the stuff of fantasy, really." She leaned her chin in her palm as she spoke and gazed at him with her deep green eyes as she said, "I'd love to hear more about *your* work on the monarchy."

"*My* work?" He gulped audibly. "I'm not sure you'd find it very interesting. History and what all," he said vaguely.

"Don't be modest," she cooed. "I find history utterly fascinating. Maybe that isn't a fashionable thing to say these days, but I've always been something of an old-fashioned girl." Moira smiled again, knowingly. "Life's too short to be chasing every fad."

Her tone suggested to Collins a woman who had lived a little, who knew her own mind, and was not shy about asking for what she wanted. "Don't you think?" she asked, leaning forward.

"Sorry?" said Collins, tearing his eyes from her breasts. "Oh, yes. Life's too short. I couldn't agree more."

"What are we agreeing about then?" asked Philip as he returned to the table clasping two overflowing pint glasses. "Hello, I'm Philip Hamilton. I think I remember you from this morning."

"Yes, of course," said Collins, speaking up. "This is Moira. She's replacing Emerald for a few days."

"So I hear," said Philip smoothly. "Can I get you anything? We've only just put our order in; I can add to it. What would you like?"

Collins felt a clammy desperation sweep over him. So few

truly worthwhile women like Moira in the world, so many Philip Hamiltons on the make . . . what hope was there for a man like himself?

"Thanks," answered Moira, getting up, "but I've already had my lunch, and I have to dash." She slid the chair back into place, looking at Collins as she spoke. "I guess I'll see you back at the office."

"Yes," he replied, watching her full red lips, "back at the office."

The two men watched her walk away, her short black coat allowing them a good look at her long, shapely legs.

"God," sighed Philip when she had gone, "she's a stunner, and no mistake. What I couldn't do with a bit of that."

"Get your mind out of the gutter, Hamilton," snapped Collins.

"Temper, Wilfred?" wondered Philip, raising his glass to his friend. "You do surprise me."

Feeling he had overstepped himself somewhat, Collins apologized and took a long drink of his ale. "Now then, what was it you wanted to ask me?"

After lunch, Collins once more secluded himself in his office, where he spent several hours correcting copy for the upcoming issue which was due to go to press shortly. Another meeting intervened, and then it was teatime. Consequently, the workday was almost over before he was able to get back to his special project.

Never mind, he told himself, another hour or two would be all he would need to put the project to bed. He worked away happily, putting the final touches on the official report he was preparing. When he finished, he slid the papers into a large cream-colored envelope, sealed it, and walked it down to the mailroom on the first floor; he stayed to watch while the envelope was weighed and stamped and placed in the outgoing bag.

Returning to his office, he gathered up his source materials and placed them in the wall safe where he kept especially valuable papers: client dossiers, the odd priceless document, and precious old books on loan. Next, he turned to tidying his desk, scraping all the loose papers into a heap, which he began to sort for filing.

He heard his colleagues in the corridor as they locked their offices and headed home; one or two of them put their heads through to wish him a good night. Yes, he thought, it *was* a good night.

Feeling rather pleased with himself, he decided to celebrate with a nice hot curry from his neighborhood takeaway. He'd pick it up on the way home. That decided, he pulled a large manila file folder from the drawer, and bunged a stack of archive papers into it. He had just begun to fill out the label when he heard someone in the corridor outside his office.

Glancing up, he saw a shape in the frosted glass door. The figure hesitated. "Come in," he called.

The visitor opened the door and stepped into the room. "I *thought* I didn't see you leave with the others."

"Moira," he said, rising. "I—um, should have thought you'd gone ages ago."

"I like to put in a full day," she replied, looking around the office. "What a lovely room. You must have the best office in the building."

"The managing director might disagree with you," he replied, "but this suits me."

"Your view is nice," she said, walking to the window. She looked out for a moment, and then turned her back to the lights of the city. "They told me you were working on something very hush-hush."

"Me?" asked Collins. "Why, no. Not at all—that is, not very. Who told you?"

"Philip," she replied, leaning against the windowsill. She crossed her long legs and tugged at her skirt. The movement sent an involuntary pang of desire through him, and he decided to throw caution to the wind and ask her out for a drink. "He said you were the most knowledgeable member of the staff when it came to royal succession and such."

"Our Philip has been known to exaggerate," he replied lightly. "Nothing I do is terribly important to anyone, I'm afraid. These days it's little more than a game for intellectuals with a penchant for whimsy."

She gave him a sly, seductive smile. "Oh, I'm sure it is

much more important than that." She stood, running her
hands along her hips to straighten her skirt. "He also said
you had a rather important project on at the moment and that
you were becoming a little paranoid over it."

"He—he did?" Collins grew flustered.

She took a step towards him. "Oh, yes."

He could smell her perfume now; and it filled his head
like a musky, purple mist.

"Well, one mustn't believe everything one hears." He
laughed awkwardly. "Say, would you like to go for a drink?"

"I will," she said, stepping yet closer, "if you promise to
tell me about your special project. I find all this top-secret
work very exciting."

He edged away, backing into the desk. She stepped in
close, almost touching him. He could feel the heat from her
body radiating, enveloping him. Suddenly anxious, his hand
fumbled on the desk behind him as he tried to remember exactly what documents he had left in her view.

"What have you got there?" she asked, bending around
him. Her breasts brushed his arm, and a quiver of desire
coursed through him. Her perfume made him dizzy.

"Nothing," he said, putting his hand atop the file folder.
"It's nothing, really. Just some papers."

He looked at her, and the eyes he had found so seductive
earlier now glimmered with a queer, malevolent light. "Why
are you doing this to me?" he asked, his voice growing small
as fear squeezed him.

"To you?" She smiled, her lips curving away from her
teeth. "It's nothing personal, I assure you."

Seizing the folder, she pulled it from his grasp and
stepped away. "On second thought, I won't be having that
drink," she said and, turning on her heel, she strode quickly
towards the door.

"Wait!" he said weakly.

"Go to hell, Mr. Collins."

A group of Chelsea football fans happened to be passing
below. They had parked in one of the side streets nearby and
were on their way to the stadium, hurrying to make the 7:00

kickoff. Their accounts to police varied slightly, but they all agreed it was the scream that had drawn their attention.

There was an ear-piercing screech, so loud they thought it was a fire alarm. The next thing they heard was the sound of glass shattering, and they looked to the upper floor of the building they were passing to see a body flying through the air.

Did he jump? the police wanted to know.

They shook their heads.

Was he thrown?

The witnesses looked at one another. No, they said, it was more like he was shot from a cannon.

The eldest of the young men described it, saying, "He just came flying out the window, yeah? Glass and everything—it just exploded like. And the geezer was screaming all the way down."

"Until he hit them spears," put in his younger brother, pointing to the wrought-iron railing. "He wasn't screaming no more then."

Did they see anyone leaving the building? Anything suspicious at all?

No, the Chelsea supporters replied, nothing at all.

"Look, can we go now?" asked the eldest of the group, a young man named Darren. "We've already missed the start."

"In a moment," replied the PC. "The Chief Inspector is on his way. He'll want to ask you some questions. Won't take a minute."

"Where is he then? Let's get on with it."

"He's on his way, Sunshine. What's your hurry?"

"These tickets ain't cheap, you know. We'll miss the whole bloody match."

While they waited, the area in front of the Royal Heritage Preservation Society was cordoned off with yellow-and-black-striped plastic tape, portable lights were brought in to illuminate the scene, and a tent was constructed over the body impaled on the railings. A crowd of detectives and scene-of-crimes officers swarmed over the front lawn, combing every blade of grass.

Eventually, the Chief Inspector showed up, and asked to

see the witnesses. He had just begun taking down their names and addresses, when a black, chauffeur-driven Jaguar pulled up, having been allowed through the police barrier at the end of the road. A police constable met the car and, after a brief word with the occupants, opened the rear door and pointed across to Chief Inspector Kirkland.

The witnesses watched as a tall, immaculately dressed white-haired man emerged from the car and strode directly towards them. He greeted the Chief Inspector by name and asked, "May I see the body, please?"

Chief Inspector Kirkland hesitated, then said, "Sure, I suppose it won't hurt anything. I'd appreciate anything you can tell me, Mr. Embries."

The football supporters whined as they watched the two men walk together to the tent which now covered the corpse of the poor wretch who had jumped. The old man was inside only a few seconds, and came out again. They exchanged a few words, shook hands, and then the white-haired gent returned to his car.

As he was driven off, the witnesses caught a glimpse of his face in the police floodlights, and were struck by the fierce, almost fiery intensity of his pale gaze. Then the Chief Inspector hollered for a PC to finish taking down their particulars, and they were at last sent on their way.

## ✴ Eighteen

Hoping to catch Jenny at the studio, James drove up to the pottery to find her. He crossed the bridge and started up the winding road, the steep hillside dark against a brilliant burgundy and orange sunset. The high tops of the hills were wearing a light dusting of snow—so it looked like another good year shaping up for the Braemar ski center. If it proved anything like last year's bumper season, the small businesses of the area—like Jenny's pottery factory—would do a healthy trade.

The JEJ monogram on a piece of pottery was becoming recognized as something special to those in the know. Since starting out in her father's garage, Jenny had steadily built up a sizable business known as Glenderry Pottery, which now occupied the building she designed and built in the so-named glen high above little Derry Burn.

These days, the works employed four other people—two potters, and two dogsbodies to help with making clay, mixing glazes, shipping and so forth—and enjoyed a mostly seasonal trade, with customers traipsing all the way from Scandinavia, France, and Germany to buy bowls and goblets, platters, planters, covered cheese boards, teapots and mugs—all with the distinctive brown-flecked heather, white, and blue glaze of Jenny's devising.

The small car park was empty, and he thought he had missed her; but as he pulled around the side of the building, he saw her car, and a light on at the back. He got out and stretched. He'd slept most of the day, and he was feeling groggy and shell-shocked from all that had gone before. He took a deep breath, drawing the clean, cold air deep into his lungs.

*Nothing ventured, nothing gained,* he thought, and walked to the side door.

"Jenny?" he called, pushing the door open.

Stepping quickly into the darkened studio, he stood for a moment and was about to call again when he heard voices coming from among the drying racks at the rear. He walked towards the sound and met Jenny as she came around the corner with a tray of greenware mugs ready for firing.

"Here," he said, "let me help you with those."

"James!" she said, her smile fading. "You gave me a start."

"I hollered just now," he said, "but you didn't hear me."

"What are you doing here?"

"I came to see you." He reached out to take the tray from her, but she shrugged him aside and hoisted it up onto the rack herself.

"You should have called first."

"Sorry, I didn't think—"

Just then someone called out from the rack behind them. "Hey, Jen, why don't we drive over to Aberdeen for dinner tonight? I know this great little Thai place with fantastic lemon chicken. You'd love—"

James turned as Charles emerged from the racks with a tray of mugs in his hands. "Well, look who's here," he said.

"I didn't know you had company," James said under his breath.

"Here, make yourself useful." Charles handed the tray to James to stack, and placed his hands on Jennifer's shoulders. "Do you like Thai food, Jim? Fragrant rice, and all that?"

"It's James," replied James stiffly. "Uh, no, you two go ahead. Something's come up. I just wanted to talk to Jenny a minute."

"Talk away," said Charles expansively. He made no move but stood looking on benignly, his hands kneading Jenny's shoulders.

"Look, maybe I'd better call you later," said James.

"Yes, maybe that would be best," Jennifer replied crisply.

James stepped towards the door, feeling awkward and unhappy. "Good to see you again—um, James," Charles called as he closed the door behind him.

Outside, James was overcome with jealous resentment. More than that, however, he kicked himself for taking Jenny's affections for granted, assuming she would always be there for him when he wanted her. With a sick feeling in his gut, he glimpsed the possibility—no, the probability—that the train had left the station, and he wasn't on it. He had no one to blame but himself.

He walked to his car and climbed in. Then he sat waiting, wondering, wishing he hadn't been such a blind and selfish idiot. After a few minutes, the light at the back of the studio switched off, and James drove away, lest he be found spying on the couple when they came out. He drove back to Braemar and stopped at the Pipe & Drum for a quick pint before heading home. It was a typical Monday night, however, and the pub was nearly empty. He took a few sips, then reflected that drinking alone was a sad, lonely thing to do, paid up and headed back to the lodge.

Cal was there, cooking bacon and chips. "Where's Embries?" asked James as he came into the kitchen. The helicopter was gone, and there were no other vehicles parked outside.

"How'd it go with Jenny?" Cal grinned as he gave the pan a shake over the flame.

"Progress," replied James. "Is Embries here?"

"They went to London. Collins called and they dashed off—something to do with some documents." He prodded the chips with a fork, and regarded James with such an air of expectation that James grew quickly irritated.

"What?" he demanded. "Why are you looking at me like that?"

Cal smiled and shrugged good-naturedly. "No reason."

"Then stop it."

"Do I have to call you 'Your Highness'?"

"Stop, all right? This isn't funny." James yanked out a chair and sat down at the table.

"Second thoughts?"

"Look," said James sourly, "I hate to pop your balloon, Cal, but an awful lot of details have to fall into place for me to even begin to think about becoming King. The Government's about to abolish the monarchy for one thing. And even if they handed it to me on a silver platter . . ."

Cal nodded understandingly. "You and Jenny had a fight, huh?"

"No, we didn't have a fight," snapped James.

"You're acting like you had a fight."

"Look, we didn't have a fight. There's been a slight misunderstanding. All right?"

Cal went back to prodding the chips. After a while he said, "I couldn't find any beer. You want some toast?"

They ate at the kitchen table in companionable silence, and then decamped to the living room to watch TV. A little after seven o'clock the phone rang, and Cal returned to the kitchen to answer it. "Sure," he nodded, "he's here." He turned in the doorway to look at James. "Not too good, apparently." He paused. "Right, I'll tell him. No problem. G'bye."

He hung up the phone and said, "That was Embries. Something's come up in London."

"And?"

"He'll call back and let us know the situation as soon as he can."

"What kind of situation?"

"He didn't say."

"Anything else?" James inquired, unable to keep the irritation out of his voice.

"He wanted to know how the wedding plans were proceeding."

"He asked that?"

"Not in so many words," allowed Cal, "but that's what he meant."

Fed up with the tenor of the conversation, James stood and tossed the remote control to Cal. "I'm going to bed. I assume you're staying here tonight?"

"I'm no supposed to let you out of my sight, laddie buck," he replied. "Orders from headquarters."

"Fine," replied James. "See you in the morning." He went to his room and got ready for bed. It was early yet, but he was knackered; he shuffled woodenly through his nighttime routine, undressing, brushing his teeth—he felt like a tin robot running on the last dregs of dry-cell energy. Even so, sleep was a long, restless time coming. His mind kept replaying an image of Jenny and Charles holding hands over a candlelit table, plighting their undying love while nibbling fragrant parcels of rice and lemon chicken.

In the end, he succumbed to a fretful dream-filled slumber in which hundreds of horses coursed in wild, swirling herds over empty moorland hills beneath black storm clouds, while men in chain mail shorts ran behind with flaming torches, setting fire to the summer-dry grass.

The Prime Minister switched off the late news and picked up his shoes from beside the leather recliner. He started for his bedroom at the back of the interconnecting suite of rooms which formed his apartment at Number Ten, when a knock came on the heavy, bomb-proof outer door. Thinking it was the duty officer, he turned back, wondering what fresh hell awaited him on the other side.

"Yes, Bailey, what is it?" he said, swinging the door open to reveal not the thick, squared-off form of the Downing Street night duty security officer, but the graceful curves of a flame-haired young woman dressed in a tight-fitting sheath of pale, glimmering platinum-colored material. Her hair was slicked back sleek and wet, as if she had just stepped from the bath. She wore no underclothes, and the clingy, shimmery cloth was so thin it looked like she was wearing water.

"Bailey is taking a coffee break," the young woman informed him.

"Good God!" Waring all but yanked his visitor into the

room, slamming the door behind her. "How the hell did you get in here?"

"Oh, I know my way around most places." She stepped close, pressing her body against him. "Don't tell me you're not glad to see me, Thomas," she said, sliding a hand down between his legs.

He pushed her hand away. "Did anyone see you?"

"Of course not," she said, kissing him on the mouth. Her lips tasted slightly salty, as if she had been swimming in the sea. "I find I can come and go pretty much wherever I want." Winding her arms around his neck, she kissed him again. "Tonight, my darling, I want to be with you."

"Sorry, not tonight."

"Nobody will find out our little secret, Thomas," she said, moving into the living room. She sat down on the leather couch and patted the place beside her. "Now come here like a good boy, and show me how much you've missed me."

Waring remained firmly planted before the door. "I mean it, Moira," he insisted. "I've got meetings first thing tomorrow morning. This is not at all convenient."

"I see." She pouted. "It was convenient for me to spend the last six months on that miserable, dull little island. It was convenient for me to play whore and nursemaid to that bloated old rake of a king. But now that you've got what you wanted out of it, it's not convenient anymore. Is that it?"

He stared at her. "I never asked you to do anything like that."

"You didn't have to ask, lover." She crossed one long leg over the other and let her filmy dress ride up a naked thigh. "We had an understanding."

"You shouldn't have come here. I told you at the airport I couldn't see you. What if someone finds out?"

"You'll get an ulcer, love, worrying like that." She laughed, and her voice changed to a lightly accented Portuguese inflection. "Your Teresa was very discreet, *mia cara*. No one will h'ever find out."

He stared at her. She was ravishing, and the wildness in her—to one who had spent his whole life weighing out the possible consequences of each and every action—was both heady and irresistible. She was as unpredictable as she was lovely, and he valued both qualities equally.

"Come and sit down," she coaxed, leaning forward provocatively. "We have all night to get reacquainted."

Against his better judgment, Waring felt himself drawn to the couch. She reached out a hand, he took it, and she pulled him down beside her, snuggling at once into his embrace. She kissed him long and he tasted again the salty tang of her lips.

"Mmm, I've missed you, Thomas," she breathed, moving his hand to the inside of her thigh. "How are you at making up for lost time? Hmmm?"

# Part III

※

# Nineteen

They put King Edward's coffin in the Picture Gallery at Buckingham Palace: a long, narrow room with high ceilings and walls chock-a-block with priceless paintings. The over-size bronze casket was set up at one end of the room, and a single channel between red velvet ropes provided for those who wished to pay their final respects.

One quick glance confirmed James' strong suspicion that the venue was specifically chosen in order to diminish and embarrass the dead King. There were, after all, far grander halls and larger, more elegant public spaces where Britain's last monarch might lie in something more closely resembling a regal state.

But, no, the image manipulators chose the Picture Gallery—a slyly calculated choice, for it was an undeniably grand room, without being ornate or particularly handsome. The dimensions, despite its size, actually gave it a claustrophobic feel. It was not a room anyone would care to spend much time in, and it certainly was not conducive to emotional or even purposeful reflection—a royal room, certainly, but spiritless and uninspiring.

Although Buckingham Palace was, for many years, the principal residence of Britain's royals, it had always had the unfortunate appearance of a provincial office block which aspired to better things. Workaday and stodgy, there was nothing about the building to lift the eye or stir the heart. The massive slablike blocks that made up the façade were the dismal color of poured concrete; the entrance was meanly functional, the windows squat and small. The visual message the structure sent to viewers was: government institution. For all its statues, Buckingham Palace might as well have been an asylum or prison, for it shared the same grim, utilitarian, relentlessly featureless practicality of any government edifice where notions of grace and glory were rigorously subverted.

This was the drift of James' thought when, on the day before King Edward's funeral, he walked through the great iron gates and followed the nylon rope cordon into the palace. There were many more people than he'd expected, and he joined a sizable queue which shuffled its way towards the entrance. Once inside the palace, visitors were ushered quickly through the entryway and through the Blue Sitting Room—even the names of the rooms were plebeian, indifferent—and into the Picture Gallery.

The moment he stepped into the hall-like room, James sensed the subtle, insidious treachery which was the true aim of the enterprise. The lights were brighter than the occasion warranted, and as the mourners were herded slowly along, single file, to pass before the black-draped coffin, James quickly learned why: the lights burned brightly so everyone could admire the great works of art on the walls.

As the line moved slowly, each visitor had plenty of time to view the various masterpieces. If it had been too dark, no one would have seen them properly and the crowd would not have been suitably impressed. The purpose, it seemed to James, was to distract, to substitute one event—paying final respects to the dead monarch—for another: inspecting a few of the nation's rarely seen art treasures. James had to give the scheming bureaucrats their due. The manipulation was masterfully done; the mourners came to view King Edward lying in state, but left vastly impressed by Rembrandt, Rubens, and Raphael instead.

Poor old Teddy could simply not compete with the glory

of the glowing artworks surrounding him. Dwarfed by towering genius on every side, his boxy coffin with its drab
black coverlet seemed, like the monarch himself, pointless,
pathetic, inappropriate, and out of place . . . and, by the way,
wasn't that Vermeer lovely, such delicacy, such elegance,
such astute observation.

James shuffled along the line, growing more and more
angry by the second. The sheer malicious arrogance of the
attitude made his blood boil, and after only a few minutes he
was ready to storm out of the place. But, on further reflection, he decided to linger awhile and talk to some of the visitors about their feelings. He wanted to know why they had
come, what they thought they were doing, what they hoped
to see.

He began by striking up a conversation with the two people directly behind him in the queue, a young man and his
girlfriend. Dressed in jeans and sneakers, they didn't seem
to be the sentimental kind, but when James asked them what
brought them to the palace, the fellow replied, "I don't
know, mate. Guess I just thought this is the last one, right?
And we should go and see him off."

"We didn't like him or anything," the girl pointed out
quickly. "He was a bit of a rogue."

"We're not sorry he's dead," confirmed the boy. He
shrugged. "We just thought we should do something, you
know?"

Their feelings were echoed by the three middle-aged
ladies behind them. "We've come all the way from Manchester," said the designated speaker for the three. "And
Myrtle, here, is from Burnley." The woman with fluffy blue-
rinsed poodle hair nodded vigorously. "We wanted to pay
our respects. Not so much for *him*" —she indicated the coffin at the far end of the room— "but more for the country.
You know what I mean, love?"

The other two nodded, and the one who wasn't Myrtle
said, "We're doing it for ourselves really. I mean, what kind
of people would we be if we didn't say cheerio to our
King?"

There were more nods all around, and a little man in a

brown raincoat buttoned to his neck leaned forward and said, "He might have been a rum bugger, by jinx, but he was *our* rum bugger! Pardon my French."

This brought laughter, and more people began stepping up to air their views. "I'm glad he's dead," said a matron in a plastic poncho. "I never thought he should have been king in the first place. He wasn't up to it."

"He was a weak vessel," volunteered someone else.

"That's just what he was," confirmed the woman. "He was a weak vessel. It takes a special kind of person, if you catch my drift. Poor Edward should never have been king."

"Why did you come here today?" James asked her.

She glanced around at the people looking on; there were more now, crowding in to hear what the others were saying. "I came because it's the right thing to do," she said proudly. "I don't care what anyone thought of His Majesty hisself; it's the decent thing to do."

This sentiment was greeted with murmurs of approval. One young lady with long brown hair spilling over the collar of her coat spoke up. "There's never been a time when there wasn't a king in Britain—or a queen. I mean, there's always been a monarch—for better or worse someone was always there." She looked to her fellow mourners for support. "I feel kinda sad there isn't going to be one anymore."

"It's a sad day," added the man in the brown raincoat, "a sad day for everyone, whether they know it or not."

"Why do you say that?" James asked.

"Because it's true," he replied adamantly. "Course it is. I had no use for the man." He nodded to those around him. "We all know that. I think he got what he deserved."

"We reap what we sow," offered the Manchester woman, chiming in.

"That's right," agreed the man. "And he's reapin' his wild oats now, I can tell you. I wouldn't give you a fart in a bottle for old Edward over there—pardon my French."

"It's more the institution, like," put in the youngster in the white sneakers.

"That's right," agreed the man, and nearly everyone else with him. "It's because of *what* he was, not *who* he was."

"Mind you," added the woman, "Ready Teddy probably couldn't even park cars at the Naughty King's Ball. He were a right rascal, but there's been quite a few that was far worse. I don't see as it's time for throwing the baby out with the bath water."

James walked slowly back to Kenzie House by a long, circuitous route, trying to distill the common mood of the people in all he'd heard at the palace. Although the day for announcing his succession to the throne was rapidly approaching, he was still not at all certain he wanted to be king. He had not told Embries about his misgivings, however; nor mentioned the fact that things had gone rather sour on the marriage front, too.

Embries was waiting for him when he returned. "Well?" he asked. "How was it?"

"Interesting," replied James.

The old man nodded. "Follow me." Drawn by their voices, Cal entered the foyer just then and Embries said, "Ah, good. You come, too, Cal. I want to show you something."

They went into the room which served as Donald Rothes' office. Embries took a seat behind the desk and, when the two were settled opposite him, he told them the dreadful news about Collins' murder.

"When?" asked James, stunned by the violence of the act.

"Night before last," Embries said, shaking his head sadly. "He was a trusted and valued ally, and I will miss him greatly." He paused and lowered his eyes, as if gazing into a well of sorrow.

"Who would want to do such a thing?" Cal wondered.

"No doubt there are many who would *want* to see the monarchy abolished," Embries replied. "The question is, who would be willing to kill to bring about that end?"

"The Government?" suggested Cal.

"That's only a few thousand elected officials and civil servants," James pointed out sourly. The news of Collins' murder had struck a raw nerve.

"Someone close to the top, I mean," Cal amended. "Waring has been pushing through his devolution scheme like a bulldozer. He's not likely to allow a few bodies to get in his way."

"Think what you're saying, Cal," scolded James irritably. "This isn't Stalinist Russia, you know. The Prime Minister doesn't have hit squads roaming the streets assassinating citizens who happen to disagree with his policies." James frowned, glaring at his friend. "Anyway, who even knew what Collins was working on? Collins' death is probably nothing to do with any of this. It might just be a coincidence."

"I think that unlikely," Embries countered. Producing a thick, cream-colored envelope, he handed it to James. "This is what he was working on."

"What is it?" asked Cal.

"It is James' calling card," Embries replied, tapping the envelope with a long forefinger. "Inside are the credentials needed to satisfy the various organs of State that James *is* who he claims to be. Wilfred finished it shortly before he died."

He then went on to explain the various documents, his plans for them, and how the announcement would be made. "Thanks to Donald's raising the issue in Parliament, the media and public outcry has been such that the Government has backed away from its ill-conceived plan for a hasty cremation. There is now to be a memorial service at Westminster—after which, a procession will conduct the coffin to the train for transport to Balmoral, and burial in the family plot.

"Thus, I can foresee a splendid opportunity for James' announcement to take place outside Westminster following the service. The media will be there in force, and we will make a tremendous splash. I have worked out a special delivery system to make certain the event receives the appropriate notice."

A quiver of trepidation passed through James' gut at the thought. He did not relish the prospect of standing before a thousand hostile cameras and opening himself to cynicism, ridicule, and abuse. He could guess what kind of reception awaited him from a very pro-abolition media. Having just got rid of one rotten monarch, the last thing the nation wanted, according to the press corps, was to welcome another. James knew he would be tried, convicted, hanged, drawn, and quartered before he had even concluded his statement—and he confided as much to Embries. The old man sympathized. "I wish it could be otherwise, but the short, sharp shock is best if we are to bring the nation to its senses."

They began talking about how to stage-manage the announcement. James listened and tried to imagine that the discussion was in some way relevant to him, but he could not make the connection. The subject kept eluding him, and he found the casual assumptions and tacit understandings surrounding him increasingly irritating. When he could stand it no longer, he stood and announced that he was going out for a walk to clear his head and think about what he wanted to say.

"Good idea," said Embries. "Enjoy your anonymity a while longer."

The thought depressed James. He strolled with a restless, desperate aimlessness, while his emotions churned away inside him. It was his own fault, he knew, for allowing the thing to get so far down the road without calling a halt to it. Despite what he had said to Embries at Caer Lial, he had not truly believed he would actually take the throne. While he was happy enough to play along up to this point, now the game was turning serious. What if Embries was right? What if Collins' death was directly connected to the work he had done to establish James' claim to the throne? If so, the stakes were high, and growing higher: one man had already given his life for the cause, and it was not even a cause James was certain he was willing to pursue.

But if James did not do his part, then poor, hapless Collins had gotten himself killed for nothing. This made James angry. Collins' death was a needless sacrifice. What is more, it was a sacrifice that demanded a response from him, a response he was not willing to match.

He had not asked for this; none of it was his idea. It was all happening way too fast. He needed time to think things through, but who could think while events flashed past with such blinding speed?

Well, James decided, it was time to call a halt to the giddy, headlong rush to the throne—before anyone else got hurt. He would tell Embries that he had decided not to pursue his right to succeed to the throne. Tonight, he would tell him that, however worthy and noble the idea, it was just not going to work out.

That decided, James turned around and retraced his steps, thinking how best to break the news to Embries.

At dinner, he was preoccupied, only half aware of what was being said around him. The others noticed it, James could tell, but Caroline and Donald kept the table talk light and did not intrude on his thoughts. Cal made one small attempt to draw him out. "Cheer up, man," he said from his place beside Isobel. "Day after tomorrow you'll be King, and the naysayers will just have to lump it."

The evening passed, and James failed to find either the words or the time to speak up and tell Embries he wanted out. He remained awake most of the night, and rose very early. Throwing on his robe, he went downstairs to the kitchen to make some coffee. He saw the phone on the wall and decided to call Embries.

He dialed the number and it rang. "Hello?" Embries said, picking up the receiver on the second ring. *Didn't he ever sleep?* James wondered.

"I have to talk to you right away," James told him. "How quickly can you get here?"

"James," he said, his voice taking on concern, "is something wrong?"

"How long will it take you?"

"About fifteen minutes," Embries said. "Why? What has happened?"

"Nothing's happened," James told him. "We have to talk."

"I'll be right there."

James hung up, and busied himself searching for coffee. Isobel appeared—tousle-haired and yawning in a tartan flannel robe—to stare at him sleepily.

"G'morning, James," she said, switching on the lights. "I heard someone creeping around down here. I thought we had burglars."

"I'm sorry. Did I wake you?"

"No, I wanted to get up anyway. I know today is red-letter important, so I thought I'd make everyone my famous breakfast buffet. You can all stoke up. God knows, it'll probably be days before you have another chance to eat a proper meal."

"You could be right about that," James granted. "I'd settle for a cup of coffee right now."

"I *never* do anything in the morning without coffee," she told him, pulling cups the size of cereal bowls out of a cupboard. Embries arrived as Isobel was pouring out the first pot of coffee. "G'morning, Mr. E.," she said sunnily. "Come to check up on your blue-eyed boy here, to make sure he doesn't do a runner like last time?"

Embries regarded her shrewdly. "That is exactly why I have come."

"Coffee?"

"Thank you, yes, Izzy," he said, accepting a steaming cup from her. "Now then, James, what is on your mind this morning?"

"I can't do it," James replied bluntly. He no longer cared who heard it or what they thought of him. He had lost enough sleep over it, and wanted only to get it off his chest. "I can't play the king for you. You'll have to get yourself another boy. I quit."

## Twenty

Embries leaned back in his chair and sat for a moment, drumming his long fingers on the breakfast table. When he spoke, his voice was measured and calm. "Well, let's have some breakfast and then I want to show you something. I want you to come with me."

"Where?" asked James, suspicion creeping into his voice.

"It's here in London. Close by, in fact."

Embries fastened his golden eyes on James with an intensity that made him squirm; he could feel them boring into his flesh, and stiffened with resistance. "I don't know. . . ."

"An hour or two is all I ask. You can spare me that much, I think."

"My mind is made up," James insisted. "If you're thinking of trying to talk me out of it, don't bother. You'd only be wasting your time."

"It's my time. Let me worry about that."

"All right," James agreed, "but if I go with you, that's the end of it."

"The decision, as I promised you, will be yours alone."

"Okay," said James, "so where are you taking me?"

"First, we eat," replied Embries, the intensity relaxing somewhat. "Then, we go."

Cal appeared for breakfast just as they were getting ready to leave. "What's up?"

"James and I are going out for a little while," Embries told him. "I would very much appreciate it if you would remain here and keep Isobel company."

"Sure, whatever," replied Cal, glancing to James for confirmation. "If you don't need me."

"Have some breakfast, and help Isobel with the dishes," James told him. "We won't be gone long."

Leaving the house, they turned left at the gate and walked quickly up the street. "Rhys is away on a few errands," Embries said, "but this is better. I want you to rub shoulders with your people."

"I see what you're trying to do," James said.

"Do you?"

"It won't work."

"We'll see."

They walked to the corner and headed off in the direction of the nearest Underground station, where they joined the morning commuter crush on the platform—working men and women of the usual types: businessmen and -women, junior executives, secretaries, shop assistants, students of various nationalities—everything from City moguls to cleaning women. The rush hour was in full swing, so they had to wait for two trains before they could find a place in one of the overpacked carriages.

Once aboard, they rode a few stops and disembarked at St. James Park so, as Embries put it, they might witness the passing spectacle in all its transient glory. What he meant, James discovered, was that he wanted to see the rush-hour flow of traffic whizzing around the London streets. Shoulder to shoulder with serious men in pinstriped suits and women in drop-dead skirts and smart jackets, they walked up the street towards Big Ben and the Houses of Parliament.

The streets were slick with mist from the river and awash with city buses, black cabs, and luxury executive cars; bicycle daredevils took their chances along the curbs, and phalanxes of pedestrians moved through the high-octane exhaust fumes in synchronized lockstep along the broad pavements as far as the eye could see. James, who thought he was growing used to the big city, found the mad rush disturbing; he felt himself growing more and more annoyed by the careless, headlong race and the heedless discourtesy of the participants. He watched with mounting irritation as, stony faced, his fellow pedestrians pushed and shoved their way to their destinations.

"How can people live like this?" he wondered aloud at one point.

"Good question," Embries replied. "That is a very good question."

They came onto Parliament Square, which was gridlocked in three directions with the fourth inching along at the speed of cold treacle. He despaired of having to make his way through the honking maelstrom, and just as he was about to abandon the chase, Embries said, "Follow me, and look lively."

With the grace of a gazelle, the old man darted sideways through the crush and was off. James pounded after him and, with the help of traffic police in yellow Day-Glo macs, managed to reach the far side of the square unscathed. They continued on quickly to the entrance of Westminster Abbey. The traffic here was only slightly less fraught, the frenzy more subdued. There were scores of people milling around— bevies of foreign students with matching green backpacks, several school groups in blazers and ties, tourists in sensible shoes—and all of them waiting to visit the abbey. It was forty-five minutes to opening time, and already the winding queue covered the forecourt. James looked dismally at the line of people, and resigned himself to a lengthy wait on the damp pavement.

"This way," Embries said, moving off in the opposite direction. They passed the gift shop and entered the street that ran alongside the great church, passing tour groups of old-age pensioners from Leeds and Cardiff and a gaggle of French students sitting on the lawn smoking cigarettes and drinking Coca-Cola. They paused at the entrance to Church House where Embries was greeted by an elderly verger who, after a brief word, led them down a corridor, unlocked a door, and conducted them out across the tranquil abbey garden to another, much older, heavier door.

"This is the entrance to the cloisters," the verger explained, taking up a huge ring. Selecting one of the large iron keys, he unlocked the door, and they stepped into the columned walkway.

The abbey was silent and still. James had only been inside the great church once before, and that was when, as a young soldier, he had taken part in a service for the Unknown Warrior. Closing the door behind them, the verger turned at once to an ancient double door set low in the wall, chose another key, and placed it in the first of six keyholes. A moment later they were standing in a low, vaulted room which seemed to be dug down into the foundations of the church.

"This is the Pyx Chamber," the man announced, snapping on the lights at a switch beside the door. "Very special room, this." He gazed up at the elaborate stone vaulting with evident pride, and then said, "You won't be long, will you, Mr. Embries? The doors open at nine o'clock sharp. You'll have to be out by then."

"Don't worry, Joseph, we will be gone by then." Embries thanked the verger, who left, closing the door behind him.

"Pyx?" said James.

"This was once the storehouse for the national treasury. Every year the gold- and silversmiths of London met here to test their metal against the absolute standard in the Trial of the Pyx, named for the box in which the test plates were kept," Embries explained. "Before that, it was a chapel for the builders who were constructing the abbey, and before that, a pilgrim chapel. This"—Embries spread his hands—"is nearly all that remains of the great monastery created by King Edward the Confessor."

James looked around the room; save for the elaborate vaulting work, the chamber was utterly lacking in decoration. The stonework was simple and basic, the stones themselves chipped and rough—as if the chapel had been constructed entirely of rejected materials. Taken altogether, this bare, humble room, crouching beneath the feet of its magnificent sister edifice, seemed as far removed from its surrounding finery as a rat catcher's daughter from a queen. "I suppose," he ventured, "you had some reason for bringing me here—besides the history lesson."

"The history *is* the reason," Embries replied. Pointing to a window long ago blocked up with red bricks, he said, "That window once opened onto the Thames. Hard to imagine now."

"If stones could speak," murmured James.

"But they do," Embries assured him. "They tell their secrets to those who know how to hear." He closed his eyes and stood motionless in the chamber as if he were listening at that moment.

James watched him, feeling more and more as if he had made a big mistake in coming here, in coming to London— in ever listening to Embries in the first place. "So what are they telling you?" he asked, his small pool of enthusiasm evaporating rapidly. He wanted nothing more than to get it over with and go home.

"They tell me that in a former age, men believed in a kind of sympathetic magic. If someone wanted to build a chapel, for example, he would try to find the most holy stones possible."

"Okay . . ." James looked around the bare room. There was little to distinguish one block from another.

"Stones which had been consecrated, let us say, by virtue of having come from a holy site or having been used in a holy structure."

"They took stones from other churches," James said indifferently. "So?"

"Edward the Confessor was determined to build a great monastery, so he put out a call to all the holiest places in Britain and gathered stones from far and wide—including Iona and St. David's. He found some a little closer to home, as well," Embries said, stepping towards a crude altar set in an arched niche. The altar was made of unshaped stones, many of which were in very poor condition.

"See here," he said, squatting down at the base of the altar. "Look at the shape of that stone and tell me what you think it is." He pointed to a large, squarish block on the right-hand side which formed a sort of cornerstone for the rest of the altar.

James looked as directed. "Fairly unremarkable," he replied. "More or less like all the others."

"The shape," Embries said. "Think."

James knelt down beside Embries for a closer look. "It's more or less wedge-shaped," he said, "other than that, I don't see anything out of the ordinary."

"Does that suggest anything to you?"

James shrugged; he felt like a slow-witted schoolboy trying to guess the answer to a dauntingly obvious mathematics problem. Embries turned his eyes to the arch above the altar. "A keystone?" said James.

"A keystone," confirmed Embries. "By including this particular stone in this position, it is as if the master mason was saying that this chapel, which was to be the keystone of the English church, was itself founded on the keystone of an earlier church."

James nodded. It was mildly interesting, but he did not see what it had to do with him.

"That stone," Embries continued, "came from the doorway of London's first genuine cathedral, founded inside the original city walls no great distance from here."

As Embries spoke, James saw in his mind's eye a narrow, cobblestoned street close crowded by buildings of Roman brick. The end of the street opened out into a small courtyard filled with heaps of quarried stone, where workmen wearing little more than dusty rags dragged sledges of rock towards a veritable forest of timber scaffolding.

"Well, Uther Pendragon had died, and Britain was rapidly descending into chaos. Each year the Saecsen, Picti, and Scoti grew increasingly bold and ruthless, and if that weren't bad enough, the petty kings were at one another's throats, laying waste the land. Bishop Urbanus called a council of kings to decide once and for all who should replace Uther and lead the war host of Britain against the barbarian invaders."

At these words, James saw the torch-lit interior of the church and a room full of angry men wrapped in their long cloaks against a cold winter wind that gusted through the unfinished building. Each, with his own noblemen for support, faced another belligerently across the ring, while the Bishop stood in the center, hands out-thrust in supplication, ardently beseeching them to put aside their animosity.

The small kings paid him no attention; frustration was mounting, and tempers were boiling over; there were shouts and threats of violence. And then, there was Myrddin in their midst. Quiet, triumphant, towering in his confidence, hand upraised, clutching a sword—the great battle sword of Emperor Maximus, the Sword of Britain.

With the end of their shouts ringing in his ears, James looked at the keystone, and he saw the deep-cut cleft. It might have been made by the blow of a chisel, only this cut struck into the heart of the stone, far deeper than any mason's tool. He saw the narrow crevice and knew what had caused it.

"The Sword of Macsen Wledig," murmured James. "Myrddin did that."

"He did indeed," Embries replied with satisfaction. "I told you these old stones could talk."

All at once the image shifted to another winter's day, years later. As before, the kings were gathered in the church to debate who among them might ascend to the High King's throne. As before, it was the evening before the Christ Mass; this time, however, a stranger had come to join the proceedings. A young man approached the altar uncertainly while Bishop Urbanus read out his long-winded prayer in a desperate attempt to forestall the acrimony and bitterness to which this council would soon descend. For years, the insane arrogance and absurd posturing had made a mockery of his good intentions. Still, he hoped, and so he prayed, and praying heard the soft footfall approaching. Urbanus glanced across the backs of the kneeling kings, first in annoyance at the interruption and then in amazement: the youth carried the Sword of Britain in his hands!

James felt his own hands grow tight with the clenched weight of cold steel, and suddenly he was there: he sees the bowed heads lift as the Bishop's prayer falters. The sword!

Astonishment on the faces around him quickly gives way to bristling anger. They are on their feet, their prayers forgotten. There is only the dry rustle of shoe leather on stone. No one speaks. It is the false calm before the storm.

Instantly, the violence breaks like thunder after the lightning's sharp flash. Voices: irate, outraged, demanding, questioning. Hands: straining, grasping, making fists, reaching for weapons. Bodies: thrusting forward, crowding in. But he does not flinch. He grimly holds his ground as all hell breaks loose around him. The lords of Britain surround him now. They are shouting. *Usurper! Upstart!* Like scalded pigs they scream.

The holy sanctuary has become a bear pit. He stands bold and silent in the center, unmoved by the violent reaction his presence has provoked. He has become an effigy carved in stone, and the noblemen are savages writhing around him, rage and fear twisting their faces into masks of hatred.

Weapons glint in upraised fists. *Kill him! Kill the usurper!*

Urbanus struggles forward. Arms above his head, hands waving, face as white as death, he calls for peace and order. No one hears him; the Bishop's words are lost in the whirling maelstrom of hatred. A hand snakes out and the Bishop falls to the floor, blood spurting from his broken nose.

*Kill him! Kill the usurper!*

The din is deafening. The crowd crushes nearer.

*Kill him! . . . Kill him! . . . Kill him!* they cry. It is a death chant.

Arthur lowers his head and tightens his grip on the sword.

And then, above the clamor, there is heard the sound of a tempest, the blast of a mighty gale. The petty kings fall back. They cover their heads and their eyes strain upward into the darkness above. Is the roof falling? The sky?

When they look again, the Wise Emrys is with him, standing beside him. They cry trickery, sorcery, and demand to see the proof that even now their eyes will not accept. Shoving, jostling, they push their way out of the church and into the yard where the forlorn keystone stands in the snow. Their torches flicker over the naked stone; the sword is not there. . . .

James, rapt in his strange, vivid reverie, leaned towards the stone. He reached out a hand and, like Doubting Thomas putting his fingers into the sacrificial wound, touched the cleft in the stone and believed. What he had seen was true.

"You said for me to get myself another boy," Embries said. "There *is* no other boy, James. There wasn't then, and there isn't now. You are the only one."

"That's why you brought me here. You knew I would remember."

"I hoped you would recall something of what had to be faced long ago, and find it within you to shoulder the burden once more."

James gazed at the keystone and tried to imagine the awful span of years between that winter's day long, long ago and this one. Although he could remember it in a curious, dreamlike way, he could not make the required leap. Yet, as solid as the stone before him, and as certain as the cleft striking deep into its heart, he had faced the enraged nobility of Britain as they shouted for his blood. He remembered, and felt the weight of conviction settle upon him. Very well. He had done it once, he could do it again.

Rising slowly, James turned to the man beside him. Myrddin Emrys, faithful through all things; he had stood with him on that fateful day, and would stand with him now. "Bring it on," James said softly. "I'm ready."

Embries smiled. "Then let us begin. There is much to be done before your announcement." He made to turn away, but James put out his hand and stopped him.

"Not so fast," James said. "If there's going to be a battle, I want to fight it on my own turf—at Blair Morven. That's where we make the announcement."

※

# Twenty-one

At the same moment the contingent of Coldstream Guards were removing Edward's casket from the Picture Gallery and placing it in the back of an undertaker's hearse, a young man in a dark green blazer, black trousers, white shirt, and blue-and-yellow-striped tie, was arriving at the Whitehall offices of the Chairman for the Special Committee for Royal Devolution. He carried a thin black-leather briefcase and an appointment card.

After presenting himself in the lobby, he passed through a metal detector, and an armed guard searched his briefcase; he was then admitted, signed in, and conducted along the corridor to a red door and ushered into a suite of offices decorated with very modern, very expensive, Italian titanium-and-leather furniture, handmade Swedish wallpaper, and French abstract paintings. The young man was greeted by the office administrator, who took his appointment card and waved him to one of the low, polished-leather seats.

He had just settled himself comfortably when the administrator, replacing her phone, announced, "Mr. Arnold's assistant can see you now." She indicated a door marked with the name D. Toley, and said, "It's right through there, if you'd like to go in."

The fellow in the green blazer thanked the woman but declined, saying that he preferred to wait until the appointed time. The woman drew his attention to the clock on the wall and observed that it was an hour and fifteen minutes until twelve o'clock.

"You are very kind," the young man replied politely. "But I have my instructions. I would prefer to wait."

This same scene, with numerous variations, was enacted at the offices of every major newspaper, radio, and television station in the city of London, as well as the metropolitan areas of Wales and Scotland. In all, 277 couriers—young men and women dressed in identical dark green blazers and striped ties—arrived at their various destinations carrying identical black-leather briefcases.

Each declined to see or speak to those with whom they had made their appointments until twelve o'clock. All waited patiently, the briefcases on their knees. Several of them, because employees of the offices they were visiting were also watching, were able to view the televised coverage of King Edward's funeral.

What they, and anyone else tuning in, saw was a small convoy of black vehicles—a hearse and three limousines—making its way slowly along empty streets through a drab, drizzly November morning. No horse-drawn caisson or carriage decked in royal livery, no floral tributes heaped high on the coffin, no teary-eyed, mournful masses. In fact, very few people lined the streets, and most of these had not braved the damp weather to watch the procession with their grieving fellows, but were unwary pedestrians united only in the misfortune of having their progress arrested by the police cordon. Unable to continue with their errands, they had no choice but to wait until the cortège passed and the barriers were cleared.

When the hearse arrived at Westminster Abbey, the casket was carried in and placed on a low stand before the outer quire screen. The massive nave was brightly lit by the lights of the TV crews, and the turnout was decidedly more respectful. The few friends and relatives of the deceased, augmented by ranks of government and ex-royal functionaries, filled the limited seating, presenting a suitably somber yet tidy contingent of mourners. Prime Minister Waring and his deputy, the Home Secretary, and the Chancellor of the Exchequer, along with spouses and various family members, held the front rank of seats; opposition party MPs, led by Huw Griffith, filled two rows behind them.

After a brief voice-over description of the ancient chapel, the ceremony commenced. A single large candle at the head of the black-draped coffin was lit by the Dean of Westminster, signaling the organ to play a dutifully solemn hymn. Ladbrokes, the betting agents, received several phone calls during the piece from people willing to wager good money on whether or not the last hymn Teddy ever heard was also the first. The bet was declined, not because it was unlikely but only because insofar as the King was dead the result could not be authenticated.

After the hymn, the Dean read out a passage from Psalms, and led the congregation in a prayer—in which the Almighty's clemency and mercy were invoked in large measure, and the deceased's worthiness glossed over entirely. Following the prayer, a soprano with the English National Opera sang Cantaloube's *Baïlèro* which was widely and erroneously reported to have been one of Edward's life-long favorites.

There followed a lengthy homily by the Canon of St. Paul's, the Right Reverend Perceval Preston-Giles, who seemed quite concerned that a tone of harmonious equanimity should be struck. While, by earthly standards, Edward, by any account, was not a particularly godly man, he said, by heavenly standards he was really no worse than any other unregenerate sinner. Suspecting that he may have overtipped the balance somewhat, he tried to correct himself by asking the congregation to look deep within themselves and see how well they measured up against God's yardstick. The proof of a life, he said, was not how well it was lived, but how well it was loved. The Canon surmised—nay, was fairly certain—that Edward had been loved. Wisely declining to name names, he let it go at that, and quickly moved on to his closing point which was that death, the Great Leveler, was no respecter of persons, and that it would therefore behoove

every person in the land to look long and hard into his soul
and determine to put his house in order, because no one,
whether prince or pauper, knew when he might be called before the throne of God and the Final Accounting demanded.

The service then concluded with another prayer and a
hymn, whereupon the organ played while the Coldstream
Guards removed the coffin to the hearse for its slow drive to
King's Cross where a special train was waiting to convey the
coffin to Scotland for its burial in the family cemetery at
Balmoral Castle. As the funeral procession left the chapel,
the bells began to ring and, simultaneously, in 277 offices
across the British Isles, couriers in dark green blazers stood
and presented themselves and delivered their packets to their
designated recipients.

Each packet was labeled with the words TIME-SENSITIVE
DOCUMENTS, OPEN IMMEDIATELY. Below the label was a
small, unmistakable royal insignia, but one which had not
been seen in England for over a thousand years: a blood-red
dragon, similar to that adorning the flag of Wales. The
dragon was emblazoned on a shield surmounted by a cross,
over which floated a crown.

Instantly intrigued, most of the recipients opened their
packets on the spot. What they found inside was a collection of photocopied documents pertaining to the noble lineage of one James Arthur Stuart. Each individual copy was
itself duly witnessed and notarized to establish its authen-
ticity, and two glossy color photos of young Mr. Stuart included; one showed him in full dress military uniform, the
other in a more informal pose. Lastly, the packet contained
a rather stiffly worded declaration by an officer of the
Royal Heritage Preservation Society confirming the legitimacy of Stuart's claim to the sovereignty of Britain. Taken
altogether, the items led inexorably to the startling conclusion that, whether anyone knew it or not, the country had a
new king.

In the unlikely event that anyone missed the significance
of the packet they had been given, a press release was also
included, which spelled out precisely what the documents
and declaration meant. Further, the release stated that a for-

mal announcement would be made by the new monarch from his home, Blair Morven Castle, at six o'clock GMT.

The quick-witted among the news-gathering fraternity were instantly aware of the tremendous scoop which had been placed in their hands. Their slower, more cautious brethren, however, asked the couriers who had sent the packet, and was it genuine?

The couriers refused to say any more—other than to direct their questioners' attention to various aspects of the packet: the notary's seal, the gentleman's service record, the Royal Heritage Society's letterhead and stamp, and the photos. The green-blazer brigade then departed, leaving behind them the chaos of editors, publishers, and broadcasters in pursuit of a major story.

This quest quickly took the form of hasty telephone calls to the several primary institutions. Although the switchboards of the firms involved quickly jammed, those who were able to get through had their queries confirmed. They were assured that the information issued was accurate and authentic. Having ascertained the integrity of the documents, the chase moved to a more physical phase.

Where is this guy? they demanded.

The press release specifically mentioned an announcement to be made by the new monarch. Where was this Blair Morven Castle?

Within an hour of the close of King Edward's funeral service, reporters and camera crews for the major news agencies were on the way to Scotland—most by way of private plane, several by helicopter. A considerable number were dispatched by rail, causing a shortage of seats on several services as camera crews, sound men, grips, and production supervisors jumped on any train heading to Scotland.

For a few lucky Northerners, the distance to be traveled was not great, and they arrived in plenty of time to set up their equipment in the best spots. The rest, however, had to make do with whatever they could find once they got there.

They quickly discovered that the new King was not in residence, but an agreeable chap who identified himself as the monarch's representative—a stout, soft-spoken young man called Douglas Charmichael—was ready and waiting for the onslaught. He held an impromptu press conference on the castle lawn in which he disclosed the fact that the King was even now en route to his home, and was expected to arrive promptly at six o'clock that evening. This development was greeted with relief and dismay in equal parts by the newsmen and their crews. On the one hand, they were happy not to have missed out on the scoop, and had time now to establish a proper beachhead; on the other hand, the moment of revelation would not take place for several hours, during which time they had to wait outside in the cold.

With time to kill—and nothing but negative reports from the trains, planes, and coaches—the intrepid media mavens launched a search. Stringers were hurriedly pressed into service to cover all the smaller regional airports, coach stations, and train depots. Promised a sizable bounty for an early sighting, they eagerly worked the crowds, faxed photos in hand. Despite their diligence, all they managed to turn up was a handful of near misses. As the day wore on, the manhunters began to despair of sighting their quarry. Local roads were combed outward to the major highways, which were followed from Braemar. Reporters on the road used mobile phones to call in the registration numbers of the suspect vehicles—a task made much more difficult by the wintry darkness descending over the north. The number plates were swiftly checked against the police register of names and addresses for possible live candidates.

Thus, of the many vehicles that instantly fell prey to the media pack, almost all were just as rapidly eliminated from further investigation. Three however, were not so easily dismissed; because of reportorial "hunches" or the inability to obtain a number-plate match, these were singled out for special consideration. The first, a red Rolls-Royce near Banchory on the Aberdeen road, drew the greatest attention; but two others, a late-model brown Lexus, and a black Jaguar sedan—both sighted on the A93 north of Perth and the Spittal of Glenshee respectively—were also live possibilities.

When the Roller stopped for petrol in Aboyne, and the oc-

cupants were revealed as a retired banker by the name of
Figgis and his wife and mother-in-law, the chase concentrated on the two remaining suspects.

Meanwhile, in the news studios of the major networks,
newsreaders and commentators, who had been breaking into
regularly scheduled programs almost hourly since noon to
announce the latest wrinkle in the swiftly evolving story,
now joined their colleagues in the field and asked them to
describe what was happening at Blair Morven. They were
told about the two automobiles even now making their way
towards Braemar, and airborne cameras provided murky infrared images of cars on the highway.

As the clock ticked down to six o'clock the BBC went on
the air with live pictures in split screen of the two vehicles,
and asked the question: could one of these cars contain the
next King of Great Britain? If so, which one?

News presenter, the "highly respected Jonathan Trent,"
informed an intensely fascinated nation that any moment
they would be bringing live coverage of the historic announcement as it happened by way of their crews on location. He then went directly to Kevin Clark, who had been
flown back from Madeira some days earlier, asking him to
describe the situation at Blair Morven.

"Thank you, Jonathan," said a frozen Kevin, his breath
puffing in the cold northern air. "The atmosphere here could
not be more keenly anticipatory. As you can see behind me,
the television and radio crews of every major news organization in the country are here, and we are eagerly awaiting
the arrival of the new King.

"What a truly amazing day this has been! This revelation
could not have been better timed or organized to garner
maximum attention. Our own crew has been instrumental
in—"

The screen switched back to the studio, and Jonathan
Trent said, "We'll come back to you in a moment, Kevin, but
it has just been confirmed that one of the two vehicles currently under investigation—the brown Lexus . . . yes, that is
confirmed—the Lexus has turned off the road at Bridge of
Cally and is currently heading towards Pitlochry. That

leaves the Jaguar, which is now just outside Braemar." The screen showed the fuzzy grayish infrared picture of the top of a dark car moving along a dark road. "It would appear that the next King of Britain is nearing his destination."

Jonathan came back onscreen then, and said, "While we are waiting, we will go now to Gina Thompson for this special report."

The screen switched to an office, and the camera zoomed in on a desk on which had been spread several pieces of paper. The silky voice of Gina Thompson announced, "At twelve o'clock sharp this afternoon, an envelope containing these documents was delivered to the office of the King of Arms, at the College of Arms in London. Identical parcels were simultaneously delivered to, at last count, two hundred and fifty-four other news agencies and offices in the capital and throughout Great Britain. Each parcel contained documents identifying this man"—the screen shifted to a close-up photograph of a young officer in military uniform—"by the name of James Stuart, as the next reigning King of Britain."

Dark-haired Gina then appeared on screen. "Fantastic as it might seem to some," she announced solemnly, "that claim is being regarded as genuine. Our own investigation has so far corroborated the evidence contained in the mysterious parcel. It is not known at this hour who is responsible for disseminating this information, or how this remarkable claim was uncovered. But, as these documents suggest, although a king may have been buried today, the monarchy is far from dead." She smiled grimly at her witticism, and then said, "Back to you in the studio, Jonathan."

"Thank you, Gina." The newsreader turned to an owlish man sitting nervously across the desk from him. "With me in the studio now is Thurgood Pilling, the Norroy and Ulster King of Arms at the College of Arms. Tell us, Mr. Pilling, is this claim likely to stand up in a court of law, or wherever these cases are heard?"

The round-faced man smiled timidly, and cleared his throat. "Please, allow me to clear up a few misconceptions. While it is true the College of Arms is the final authority on all matters pertaining to nobility in this country, we do not deal with questions of Scottish royalty. Neither do we adjudicate such matters."

Jonathan looked surprised. "No? But I thought the Norroy and Ulster King oversaw *all* of the north, including Northern Ireland."

"Yes," allowed Pilling, "that is correct."

Now the news presenter appeared bewildered. "I'm afraid I don't understand."

"All of the north," said Pilling, "of *England.* I'm afraid you must have the wrong impression. Scotland has its own college of arms, if you will—the Lyon King of Arms. This body, roughly analogous to our own, is responsible for all matters arising in and pertaining to Scotland."

"I see." Trent appeared deflated by this pronouncement.

"However," the owlish Pilling continued, and Jonathan Trent's hopes revived, "I can tell you that from what I have seen, the claim—were it to be made in our jurisdiction, so to speak—would have no difficulty being proved. In other words, while I cannot speak for my Scottish colleagues, I will venture the opinion that, where their criteria and requirements are similar to ours, the documents I have seen are more than adequate to the task at hand."

"For our viewers," put in Trent quickly, "by documents you mean, of course, the birth certificate, the Royal Heritage Society affidavit, and so forth."

"Indeed."

"Thank you, Mr. Pilling," he said, dismissing his guest and turning to face the camera once more. "There you have it: were the claim to be mooted in England, it could be proved." He glanced at a sheet of paper on the desk before him, and said, "There has been no official statement from Downing Street as yet. We are hoping to have a word with the Prime Minister following the official announcement, which we are, like the rest of the nation, awaiting with bated breath."

He paused and arranged his papers. "This is the BBC, bringing you special coverage on our Six O'Clock Report."

Trent's face was replaced by a graphic of the dragon symbol adapted from the one found on the press packet. Beneath the dragon were the words *"Monarchy: End of an Era . . . Beginning of a Reign?"*

When he came back on, Trent said, "Now let us take you to Westminster Abbey, the scene earlier today of King Edward's funeral, Ronald Metcalf reporting."

The image shifted to Westminster, garish yellow-orange in the floodlights, and Ronald Metcalf standing before the closed chapel door with a microphone in his hand. "Dour, grim, almost brutal in its brevity—these are words which would seem to sum up the funeral service for the last reigning monarch of our country. Certainly, no expense appeared too small for what may—or may *not*—be the last royal funeral in Britain. For the select few gathered here, as well as those who viewed at home—"

"Thank you, Ronald," interrupted Trent. "We'll have to come back to you on that story. We have just received confirmation that the self-proclaimed King has been sighted—that is, the car containing what looks to be the next King of Britain has been sighted in Braemar. What can you tell us, Kevin Clark?"

Kevin, his voice quivering with cold and excitement, announced, "That's right, Jonathan. The car has left Braemar and is proceeding towards Blair Morven. I can hear the helicopters—they seem to be just beyond those trees to the south of us here—which would indicate that the vehicle is very near, perhaps—yes, it must be—on the estate even as we speak.

"The mood here has intensified in the last few minutes. We are, as anyone can imagine, keenly interested to get our first look at this man. Is he a poser, an imposter? Or is he the genuine article? We hope to have those questions answered before long."

The windblown reporter paused, pressed his fingertips to his right ear, and then said, "The car is on the estate. Stuart is expected to arrive shortly, and now . . ."

There came the thrumming of helicopter engines, and the camera shifted to a view of the expansive castle lawn. There were so many television crews encamped on the grass, the scene resembled a carnival all lit up for business. Lights large and small, many with reflector umbrellas attached, bathed the lawn and drive in a wash of brilliant white, while journalists and their crews huddled around their heaps of gear—cameras, boom mikes, parabolic sound reflectors, battery packs, and coils of cord and wire. There was a surge of bodies around Clark as reporters and their cameramen went after the shot of the arriving car.

"Yes, I can see the vehicle now," Kevin Clark continued, trying to remain calmly objective. "Yes, it is a late-model black Jaguar . . . I cannot see inside it at the moment . . . It is now coming up the drive towards the house where I am now standing. There is only the single vehicle—no parades, no processions, no entourage . . ."

The screen showed the car as it rolled slowly to a halt on the gravel yard in front of the house. The lights glittered on the paintwork and tinted glass. Instantly, the car was surrounded, inundated by the waiting crowd as they jostled for prime position. And then everything went still.

The driver's door opened and a young man in a smart black suit stepped out to the chorused click and whir of the cameras. Ignoring the media attention, he turned and opened the rear passenger door. For an instant, the entire television world held its collective breath. There was a movement at the open door, and the next King of Britain emerged.

From one end of the country to the other, a television audience numbering close to thirty million saw a sandy-haired young man with the physique and easy grace of an athlete, standing straight and tall in a severe dark suit. They saw him take in the ranks of media folk gathered around him and smile. The smile went a long way towards earning him the right to be heard, for it was a confident yet genuinely appreciative smile, not the practiced grimace of the professional politician or the plastic rictus of the Hollywood huckster. It was the friendly, unaffected grin of one who is truly pleased and honored by the occasion.

The King smiled, and the flashes blazed. And then, in a purely spontaneous moment of welcome, the assembled media army began to applaud. Most peculiarly, especially for hardened media pros, the applause did not die away in an embarrassed ripple, but grew more enthusiastic as James, smiling, genuinely moved and appreciative of his reception, offered an impromptu bow in acknowledgment of the honor paid him. And when he stepped into their midst to shake their hands, the press pack actually began cheering.

This spontaneous act of welcome proved infectious, for it was widely reported in the next day's papers that in pubs, homes, and offices, all over the country, viewers applauded and cheered, too.

Later, skeptics would say that it was only the release of tension after the mad scramble to capture the first glimpse of the man who would be king. Others said that it was merely a way of breaking the ice of what was after all a very awkward moment. Still others said it typified and was a physical expression of the confused emotional state of the country following King Edward's death.

Perhaps it was all those things. Even so, the image of the young man of regal bearing, receiving the adulation of those who had waited many hours in the winter cold to see him, was the perfect portrait of the new King—a fact not lost on the photo editors of the national press. Most newspapers in Britain carried the photo—the rest ran some variation of it— on the front page; it also made the papers across Europe, the United States, Australia, and Canada, as well as the rest of the world.

When the acclaim finally slackened, James Arthur Stuart raised his hand for silence, and tens of millions leaned forward to hear what he would say.

## ✳
# Twenty-two

James stepped out to confront a gathering of men and women almost faint with expectation. Having waited through the day in a state of heightened anticipation, the crowd surged forward to meet this new upstart of a king.

He looked at the faces of all those strangers, so eager, so hopeful, and it seemed to him that in that moment—if for *only* that moment—they needed him and genuinely wanted him to succeed. *Here,* James thought, *I have been bracing myself for an angry confrontation, but they only want to welcome me.*

Indeed, the enthusiasm of the crowd lifted him high, and he was swept away on waves of optimism and goodwill. He found himself so overwhelmed, it was some moments before he could find his voice to speak. So he just stood there and grinned. Then, he bowed in acknowledgment of their homage, and the camera flashes went off, and the applause started.

In the same instant, James felt the *fiosachd* quicken. The skin on the back of his neck tingled, and he felt a queasy sensation in the pit of his stomach as if the earth were dropping away from beneath his feet. The scene before him abruptly changed.

All the photographic and video gear disappeared, as did

the castle and car and drive. It seemed as if the crowd were standing at the upper end of a gently sloping meadow, with thick forest pressing in all around. James did not need to turn around to know that if he looked behind him he would see the leather campaign tent which had once belonged to Uther Pendragon and, behind it, row upon row of picketed horses. Spread out on the wide meadow before him a number of bonfires had been lit to take the chill off the night; but there was a ring around the rising moon, and he knew there would be snow before another day was done.

*The people have come to me,* he thought. *They expect something. What is it?* He looked at their hopeful faces, the way they leaned towards him in their yearning. What did they want? What did they need?

James reached out to them with the *fiosachd,* and suddenly he understood. *There is a battle coming,* he thought. *The enemy is approaching and will soon close upon us. The people are looking to me for reassurance. They want to know that I will not fail them, that my courage is sufficient to the day. They want to hear me tell them how it will be, so that when the fight begins in earnest they can trust me to lead them to victory.*

He looked out at the close-grouped crowd and heard the fluttering hiss of the torches and the crack and ripple of the bonfires; he gathered his people to his heart and began to stoke the flame of their valor. For the British are a remarkable race, quick to rally, slow to fear, quietly determined and able to endure the worst with patience and fortitude. They possess a natural nobility staunchly resistant to oppression and injustice. Although uniquely tolerant, and therefore difficult to rouse, once roused, even the least among them is capable of great heroism.

*The battle begins here. As always, the battle begins here and now. Before the first blade is drawn, before the foe is sighted, we begin by putting fear to flight.*

They were waiting for him to awaken their courage for the battle to come, so he said, "You honor me with your presence here tonight, and I welcome you, one and all." A rippling flare of light met this first utterance, and the torches and campfires of another time became camera flashes and TV spotlights once more.

"A few miles from here a king was buried today," James told them, looking away to the east. "With the ending of his reign, another begins. This is the way it has always been in this land, and it is right that it should be so now. I know there are forces at work in our country which would make it otherwise. Yet, God willing, a monarch shall always reign in Britain.

"I say this, not from selfishness or ambition—unless it is the ambition to restore Britain to her rightful place in the world. As I look around me now, I see the hope in your faces, and I, too, take hope. For I see in you the yearning for a better way, a higher purpose, a more meaningful existence than any offered by our materialistic, narcissistic, fatalistic age. I tell you the truth: this longing is not misplaced. Rather, it is our heritage, and it is borne in the blood and bone of Britain's true daughters and sons.

"Indeed, it is part of the very character of our island race to ever and always look beyond the narrow horizons of time and place and circumstance to the paradise we have seen shimmering in the west. Listen, my friends, and I will tell you a wonder."

Raising his hands, palms outward in the age-old gesture of declamation, James knew deep in his inmost heart that he had stood this way before and spoken the words he was about to speak. He had no need to plan them, or even to think about them. The words were written on his very soul.

He gazed out upon the expectant faces of the crowd, and loosed the words to do their work once more. "There is a land," he said, "a land shining with goodness where each man protects his brother's dignity as readily as his own, where war and want have ceased and all tribes live under the same law of love and honor. It is a land bright with truth, where a man's word is his pledge and falsehood is banished, where children sleep safe in their mothers' arms and never know fear or pain.

"It is a land where kings extend their hands in justice rather than reach for the sword; where mercy, kindness, and

compassion flow like deep water, and men revere virtue, revere truth, revere beauty above comfort, pleasure, or selfish
gain. A land where peace reigns in the hearts of men, where
faith blazes like a beacon from every hill and love like a fire
from every hearth; where the True God is worshipped and
his ways acclaimed by all.

"This is the Dream of Taliesin, Chief Bard of Britain. If
you would know this land, know this: it is the Kingdom of
Summer, and its name is Avalon. Fortunate are those who
stand before me this day. Countless generations have lived
and died longing to see what you now behold: the appearing
of a king who can lead his people to Avalon.

"I tell you the truth, the Kingdom of Summer is close at
hand. Taliesin's dream can become reality; it only awaits our
good pleasure."

Lowering his hands, James was aware of an embarrassed,
uncomfortable silence. He realized his mistake then—people were no longer accustomed to being addressed this way
by those who led them. He could almost hear them thinking:
is this man a charlatan? is he insane?

"I want you to know, all of you, that we stand on holy
ground," he continued. "Many years ago, in this very place
fewer than two hundred warriors led by Arthur, *Dux Bello-
rum* of Britain, met the massed warbands of Saecsen, Jute,
and Picti under the leadership of the wily marauder Baldulf.
Though greatly outnumbered, the valiant British not only
stood against the foemen, but also put a far superior enemy
to flight. The cost was fearful. When the battle was over
fewer than eighty Britons remained standing.

"The blood of the defenders hallowed this ground, and
out of recognition for the sacrifice of those brave dead,
Arthur gave this land to one of his battlechiefs with the expressed stipulation that it should be held in perpetuity for the
defense and support of the sovereignty of Britain. The link
forged that day long ago has held fast; the chain remains unbroken—to this day and to this hour. Through the many
storms and gales of adversity, the ducal fiefdom of Morven
has remained steadfast and loyal—not to the temporal
monarchy, which is all too often invested in weak and falli-

ble men—but to something higher and purer: the True Sovereignty of Britain.

"Today, two ancient and powerful forces are united once more: the kingship of Britain and true sovereign power. Kingship, as everyone knows, is a simple matter of birth into a noble house. True Sovereignty, however, is only ever a gift from Almighty God, who alone raises up and establishes those who will wield power in his name. As a wise man once told me, 'Without God there is no king.'

"But today, my friends, I tell you there *is* a king in Britain. A new reign begins from this moment, and with the help of the Almighty's Swift Sure Hand, we will live to see this nation flourish and return to its paramount purpose in creation: to be a beacon of hope and grace to a world lost and languishing in the darkness. This has ever been Britain's true calling, and as your King, I intend to restore the glory of our nation, and lead it to its rightful place—for the good of all people everywhere, for the good of those who live beneath my rule as well as those who stand watching from a distance."

James could sense the battle forming in the hearts and minds of his listeners. Once, these words would have kindled bright fire in the soul. Now, however, it was like stirring damp ashes with a stick. How to make the dead embers live?

"A moment ago," he continued, "I told you about a battle that had been fought on this holy ground. The revival of Britain will be a fight no less fierce, no less costly than the one Arthur fought long ago, the enemy no less terrible. I tell you now, that battle has begun.

"Already, doubt and fear are creeping into your thoughts. Already the joy with which you first welcomed me is fading. Very soon, the crass cynicism of this age will rear its hideous head and roar its paralyzing cry. These are the first of the enemies we will face, and there are many more. How swiftly is the battle joined!

"Even so, there is worse to come. The declaration of my reign will provoke the rulers and powers of darkness. I warn you now, the conflict to come will be great. But when the enemy appears with weapons drawn, and when the thunder of their drums and battle horns drives the strength from your hands, I ask you to remember that we do not go into the fight alone. The Swift Sure Hand goes before us, and will not forsake us.

"As Arthur told his scant few soldiers here in this place on that fateful day so long ago, I tell you now: Whether tomorrow finds us in triumph or defeat, I leave to God. I do not ask you to defeat an enemy, I ask only that you stand with me to the end, that our courage may be the spark that kindles the flame of hope in our kinsmen's hearts. Once kindled, that flame will grow, and it will become a consuming fire that drives every enemy before it.

"Listen! This is where the battle to restore Britain begins. I, James Arthur Stuart, call you to arms. Join me! Fill your hands with strong steel, bind courage to your hearts, and take your place beside me. Together, we will make of this island realm a blessing to all the nations of the earth. Together, we will bring about the wonder that is Avalon."

# ✳

# Twenty-three

The day's fishing had been moderately successful, and the crew of *Godolphin Girl* were looking forward to their evening pint at the Smugglers' Arms. The short winter day had left them over two hours ago, but the moon was bright, throwing a tracery of silver netting over the sea. The wind was light out of the south and unseasonably warm. They were seven miles off the Cornish coast, making for their home port of Penzance when they noticed the sea begin to bubble.

"Trevor! Pete!" shouted the boat's skipper, George Kernan. "Look'ee aft!"

Trevor Qualk, the boat's first mate, put his head around the small wheelhouse and looked over the rail. He saw nothing but the scattered reflection of the moon over the calm sea. "What was it?" he called back.

"T'sea is aboil!" came the skipper's reply.

"Where?" he shouted. "There's ne'er a ripple all the way to St. Mary's."

Peter Kernan—the skipper's son, and one of the two other fishermen aboard—was sluicing down the aft deck and happened to be dipping water when he saw a great bubble rise like a dome to burst on the surface. "I see it!" he shouted.

"Where?" hollered Trevor, leaning out over the rail.

Andy Gullicks, the fourth deckhand, was tying up nets when Peter shouted. He looked back just in time to see the ripple caused by the disturbance. "Away to the southwest!" he confirmed, and joined Peter at the stern.

Trevor walked back and took his place beside them. He was about to ask if they were having him on, when a third great blister, almost twice as large as the first two, bulged up and burst on the surface. At almost the same instant, further away, several more huge bubbles surfaced. The sea rippled in outward-racing rings that overtook the ship and set it rolling in the water.

"Holy God," said Trevor. "Ain't never seen anythin' like that."

"Did ya see those ones?" called George from the wheelhouse.

The three fishermen replied that they had indeed seen them. Peter ran to the wheelhouse and grabbed the binoculars. Steadying himself on the rail, he put the binoculars to his eyes and scanned the moon-bright sea. He saw the water heaving and boiling with great belly-shaped domes. Passing the glasses to Trevor, he turned and called to his dad that he thought he could see land two or three miles away to the southwest.

This caused the sea-wise George to cut the engine and join his crew on deck. They passed the binoculars from one to another, and tried to determine exactly what it was they were seeing. Even with the brightness of the moon, the dark shapes were still so far away that they could not decide if they were there at all. They debated whether to turn around and go for a closer look, but George ruled it out; a cautious sailor, he felt charging off into the unknown too risky a venture.

"Maybe we should get on the radio," suggested Peter, "and see if anyone is out tonight."

"We could call Samstead's in Hugh Town," put in Trevor. "Maybe they heerd some'at o' this."

Just then another enormous boil burst not twenty meters away to starboard, throwing a shower of seawater up with a hearty belch. A few seconds later they all smelled a stench like rotten eggs, and the sea fizzed and roiled as the wave swept towards them. "That's it," said George, making up his mind at once. "We're gunnin' for home."

He went straight back to the wheelhouse and brought the engine up full. A few minutes later, they sighted the light on Gwennap Head, and a short while after that, they could see the scattered lights along the coast. They made for the brightest cluster, and within the hour were gliding into port.

As they came into the harbor, Trevor called their attention to the unusual number of people gathered on the quayside. "Don't say nothing about what we seen," George warned them. "Best let me do the talking, until we know how the thing sits."

The boat slid into its berth. "You didn't have to throw a welcoming party," he said, tossing the mooring rope to one of his mates standing by on the pier.

"Good day?" the man called back.

"Fair to middlin'," reported George. "It were worth the trouble at least." He directed Peter and Andy to make the boat fast and get the boxes of fish onto the quay for the van to pick up.

"You haven't heard, then," said one of the men, a fisherman known as Germoe. "There's a new king appeared in Scotland."

"Scotland is it!" said Trevor. "I'll be damned."

"No, we haven't heard anythin' at all," said George, climbing up the ladder to the pier. "Been out all day—good day, too, the sea was calm as May morning. Warm. You should'a come out with us."

"I would'a," said Germoe, "but I'm still waiting for that blasted shaft coupling. It's a damned shame to lose a day's fishing, but you missed a whale of a show on the news. This bloke pops up in Scotland, claiming to be the new King. They had him all over the six o'clock news. Captain in the army, they say. Decent bloke, to look at him. What'd you catch?"

"Mackerel, mostly, but we got a fair few John Dory and a dozen dab, two lemon sole, and some pollack," said George.

"You didn't hear about anythin' going on between here and Scilly, did ya?"

Germoe indicated the crowd. "That's why we've all come out. Samstead called up about an hour ago—said they were having some shakes out there."

George and Trevor glanced at one another. "What kinda shakes?"

Germoe shrugged. "Just shakes. Pictures jumping off the wall and such. He thought they'd ride it out, but if it got any worse maybe we'd stand by to come rescue them if they needed rescuing." He gave a nod to the rest of the men, boat owners most of them, standing around on the pier. "That's what we're all doing—we're standing by."

"What about sendin' a Sea King to check it out?" asked Pete, climbing onto the pier. "One o' them could be out there in fifteen minutes."

"Why? You see something?"

"We did," said Trevor. "Damnedest thing it was, too: sea bubbles big as a house, twenty or thirty of 'em."

"Where was this?" wondered one of the nearby fishermen.

"Hi ya, Eric," said George. "C'mere and listen t'this."

George then went on to explain about looking out the wheelhouse window and catching sight of something on the sea. "Mebbe two, mebbe three hundred meters away. It's gone again in a blink, so I keep the place in sight case it comes again, and by golly, next thing you know, there it is again—a little further south this time. I calls out t' Trev and asks does he see anythin', and he says no."

"I didn't see nothin' until Andrew up and hollers it's off to port, and then I see this whopper like so." He made a balloon shape with his fingers and set it expanding until it burst. "Sploosh! Like that. The waves catch us two minutes later."

"But it weren't much," said Andy, wiping his hands on his jeans as he stepped in beside Peter. "Rocked us about a bit is all."

"It got a little choppy in harbor a while ago," confirmed Eric. Lifting his eyes to the harbor beyond the seawall, he said, "Looks quiet enough now, though."

"Pete got hold of the glasses," Trevor said. "What we spied out there was some black shapes out Scilly way, but we couldn't make nothing of 't."

"We thought as how we ought t' go check it out," put in Peter. "But then one o' them eruptions goes off right off port bow and we hightailed it home instead."

"Did Samstead say anythin' about that?" asked George.

"What kind of eruptions?" another boatman wanted to know.

"Big ones," replied Trevor.

"Who's got big ones?" called someone else.

"Pipe down, Macky," said Germoe. "We're discussin'."

"They just belched up," Peter informed them. "Threw off a stink, too."

Andy nodded. "Rotten eggs."

"Brimstone," surmised Germoe.

"That's what we was thinkin' all right," confirmed George. "Brimstone."

"D'ye see any flashes o' light with it like?" asked Eric. "The ol'-timers said as how they sometimes seen flashes o' light with them big bubbles."

"What ol'-timers you talking about?" demanded George. "I been fishin' these waters for near twenty years, and I ain't never heard o' no brimstone bubbles and no flashes o' light."

"Oh, sure," replied Eric. "My da' used to tell us all the time. Granda'—he was on a boat once that near capsized when one went off dead under it."

"You don't say," said Germoe. "How far back was this?"

"Oh, sixty—maybe eighty year ago," replied Eric.

A man in a cashmere flat cap and blue boiler suit joined them. He was smoking the stub of a panatela. "Evenin', gents," he said.

"Evenin', Noel," they all replied.

"I been on the radio with Samstead. Everything's settled down now. Haven't been any more shakes since the last one, maybe an hour ago. I think we can all go home. I got your numbers and I'll call if we need you."

Most of the boatmen and fishermen began drifting off in

the direction of the Smugglers' Arms. "Right," replied Eric. "I'm off t' pub. You fellas coming?"

"In a minute," said George. "I'm goin' to speak to Noel first."

Noel Gant, the harbormaster, stubbed out his cigar and lit another one as George described what they had seen out on the water. "You ever hear tell o' anythin' like that? I never did."

"No," answered the harbormaster, "can't say as I ever have. I had a quick call around earlier, and it looks like you were the only ship out tonight. Tony and Bill were out early this morning, but they were back before dark. Tommy went up to Falmouth, and I checked with them up there, but they had no boats out."

"Thank the Lord for that," said George. He looked around at his crew. "Well, we better get on over t' pub before they run out of beer. Right, lads," he said, turning to Peter and Andy, "get those fish over t' quay and I'll see ya there." To the harbormaster, he said, "Buy you a pint, Noel?"

"Thanks all the same, George, but I've got to go back and listen for Samstead. I told him to give it another thirty minutes and call me again just in case."

"All right then. See ya." George started off, adding, "You call us if you need us, now."

"Yeah, sure enough." He sent them on with a wave, and wandered back to his office on the quay.

At the Smugglers' Arms further down the quayside, the television was on behind the bar, and in the lounge, too, and both rooms were full as people watched the nine o'clock news recap of the new King's speech. Already, the fellow had been branded the Young Pretender—in recognition of the last Scottish nobleman who had tried to restore the monarchy to its rightful heritage.

The boatmen were skeptical but tolerant in their views of the new King. Several—George included—went so far as to voice the opinion that if they had had a king as well-spoken as this young fellow, the royals might not have run aground so badly as they had in recent years. "They might still be afloat," he said, and many agreed with him.

After the news, talk turned to the sea and the strange events near the Scilly Isles which they'd heard about and which the crew of *Godolphin Girl* had experienced. When the bar crowd learned that George and his crewmen had witnessed the phenomena firsthand, none of them had to pay for another pint the rest of the night.

# ✳

# Twenty-four

$A$voiding the reporters encamped outside his door, Prime Minister Thomas Waring left Downing Street via the back entrance to Number 11 next door. He had called for a car, and was picked up and quickly driven away. He slumped back in the cool darkness, and felt himself relax for the first time that day.

It had begun well enough; a drab, dreary morning, the weather had cooperated admirably. The funeral, he thought, had been a success. They had struck just the right note: formal but not sentimental, and with enough ceremonial pomp to satisfy the wetboys who were always bleating on about protocol and tradition but not enough to create any lasting impression on those who saw it. Not that many *did* see it; early viewing figures suggested that fewer than one household in fifteen had tuned in. Despite any latent interest, the number was kept low thanks largely to his insistence on holding the funeral on Friday when most of the nation was on the job, finishing the working week.

That was a coup, and he could rightly be proud of it. He scarcely had time to pop the cork on the self-congratulatory champagne, however, when Dennis Arnold rang to deliver the unexpected news that, according to a press kit which had been delivered nationwide just a few minutes ago, the country had a new king.

Upon querying the veracity of this claim, Arnold had insisted, "No, it's true. I've got one of the packets myself. It's all on the up-and-up, all very official. I think we will have to treat the claim as legitimate and act accordingly. All the news agencies are taking it seriously."

"Bollocks!"

"My sentiments exactly."

"How did this happen?"

"What do you mean?"

"I mean how in hell did you let this guy slip through the net?"

"You can't think there was any way to foresee anything like this. I mean it's—"

"That's what you're paid for, dammit!"

"Be reasonable, Tom."

"Don't give me that *reasonable* crap. You've had six years and all the manpower you needed; we've had *laws* passed, for Chrissakes! I gave you everything you needed to make sure this *couldn't* happen, and now you call me and tell me it just did."

There was a pause on the other end of the line. "I don't think it's anything to get worked up about."

"Then you're a bloody idiot, Dennis. I'm telling you it's a disaster."

"You're upset. Perhaps we should continue this discussion when you've had a chance to cool off."

"Of course I'm upset. I've just been told that everything I've worked for has come unglued. What the hell am I supposed to say?"

"I'll call you, later. We'll talk this over."

"You're damn right we'll talk this over."

He slammed the phone down so hard his private secretary came in to see what was the matter.

"I'm surrounded by idiots and assholes," the Prime Minister shouted. "Other than that, everything is splendid—jolly damned splendid!"

He then poured himself a glass of that champagne and

switched on the television in his office to see what the damage might be. At first, he was inclined to think he had overreacted somewhat. Perhaps Arnold was right after all. The broadcasters were treating the item as a curiosity—little more than yet another fascinating example of English eccentricity.

But as the afternoon wore on, and more information was gleaned from various sources, the tone began to shift dramatically. What had been greeted with mildly amused derision was now being regarded with increasing respect. To Prime Minister Waring's growing dismay, the story began to eclipse the carefully contrived and orchestrated coverage of the nonevent that was King Edward's funeral.

By four o'clock every television channel was doing twenty-minute updates. By five o'clock most had suspended their regular broadcasts in favor of background stories and endlessly looped commentary on the state of the search for the mysterious new King. By six o'clock every TV and radio station had gone to live on-the-spot coverage of the extraordinary event.

As the BBC Six O'clock Report began, Waring, surrounded by his staff and advisors, watched in slack-jawed horror as a tall, good-looking young man emerged from the back of the black Jaguar sedan to the obvious delight of the eager newshounds. Far from being a kook or crackpot, he appeared intelligent and fully self-possessed. What is more, he exuded a commanding presence Waring would have killed for. The young man smiled and the media pack actually applauded.

Before Stuart had even opened his mouth, the Prime Minister knew he was in trouble. Oh, but then the young King began to speak, and Waring realized trouble was not a strong enough word; he was staring bleak disaster in the face. Instead of the usual royal flummery—filled with oblique references to "oneself" and bland archaisms to do with duty and privilege—this young pretender spoke with uninhibited passion about a rich, heroic past and a glorious, attainable future. And as if that weren't enough, he laid out his vision in simple, heartfelt terms which could not fail to reach their mark.

Waring had shaken his head in utter disbelief as the
would-be King had gone on to speak of the Britain he
wanted to lead. Rather than steer clear of inflaming nation-
alist sentiments, the man reveled in it, fanning the spark of
British pride with a simple but persuasive honesty.

To make matters worse, he accomplished all this without
awkwardness, without arrogance, without even the slightest
hint of pomposity. There was no whiff of the latent conde-
scension, conceit, or deference always present in the royals.
*My God,* thought Waring, *the bugger is as humble as he is
handsome.*

All in all, it was a tremendous performance, and one
which managed to appear both spontaneous and unscripted,
but which Waring was certain was neither. Impressive as it
was, as far as Waring was concerned it was only that: a con-
summately polished performance enacted for the cameras
by a shrewd and calculating upstart for purposes unknown.

The Prime Minister did not wait for the press conference
to finish, but switched off the broadcast following the young
King's speech. Then, turning to his staff, he said in quiet,
measured tones, "This man is a threat."

Some of the younger advisors opened their mouths to object, but Waring halted them with a raised hand and a dark
glance. "I do not know what he thinks he can gain from this
stunt," he continued, "but I want him to know that his moment in the spotlight is over. Finished."

Turning to the Deputy PM, he said, "Angela, I want to
know who is behind this. I want to know what game they
think they're playing. I want to know what they want."

Telford-Sykes, through her long association with Waring,
knew the danger signals; she knew when to shut up and do
what she was told. "I'll get on it," she said. "Right away."

Waring turned next to his press secretary. "Hutch, this
media circus has to be shut down. If he's campaigning for
something, I want him to know his campaign is dead in the
water. It is going nowhere. I want it stopped before he gets
any more airtime."

"Done," replied Hutchens.

"The rest of you," the PM said, "get busy and assemble

everything you can on him. I want a full dossier first thing tomorrow morning."

"Do you want to make a statement?" asked Angela Telford-Sykes.

"God, no," sneered Waring disdainfully. He gestured at the blank television screen. "Dignify that crap with a comment? Are you joking? Let them have their fun. When we make a response, it will be to blast him to kingdom come."

He dismissed them all to their work, and sat for a while staring at the blank television, thinking about what he had seen. The more he thought, the more agitated he became. He got up and stalked to the next room, the private secretary's office. DeVries was nowhere to be seen, but two of his assistants—young single women whose names he had never bothered to learn—were sitting on the edge of one of the desks, watching the press coverage of the King's announcement.

"He's gorgeous," one of the assistants was saying. "Ooh, that delicious Scottish accent. He's a total dish."

"Mmm," agreed her co-worker enthusiastically. "I could eat him up with a spoon."

The reaction of the two young women caused the Prime Minister's scalp to tingle as cold dread descended full upon him. Where only a moment ago he had been alarmed, now he was panic-stricken. The sight of the two young females almost hugging the television screen, and their idle banter as they drooled over the newcomer, frightened him more than anything he had seen or heard so far. For in them he saw the shape of the battle to come.

Waring stepped into the room. "Where's Mr. DeVries?"

Both women leaped up as if scalded. "Sorry, Prime Minister, we were just—"

He held up his hand. "I don't care." He offered a small, deprecating smile and glanced at the TV. "I agree, he's very sharp. I'm rather taken with him myself." He turned his smile on the young women.

"Mr. DeVries stepped out for a moment," the senior of the two volunteered. "He said he'd be right back. I'll tell him you want to see him as soon as he returns."

"Please," replied Waring, moving back into his own office.

He crossed to his desk and sat down, but could not concentrate on any of the items waiting for his attention. He kept seeing this man Stuart, standing there God and everybody, pouring out his heart and soul. It was unheard of. Extraordinary. And, if the reaction of the two females in the next room was a reliable indication, the world was eating it up—with a spoon.

There came a knock on the door and Leonard DeVries opened the door a bit, and stuck his head in. "You wished to see me, sir?"

"Smoking is a filthy habit, Leo," he said. "It'll kill you one day."

"Of course, sir," agreed his private secretary affably. They had this conversation from time to time. "Was there anything else?"

"Send my car around to Number Eleven. Back door, please."

"Right away. Shall I note your destination?"

"I'll inform the driver when I see him," replied the PM. "If anything comes up I can be reached on the mobile."

"Very good."

As soon as DeVries disappeared, Waring rose from his desk, moved to the small coat closet, and retrieved his dark blue cashmere topcoat and gloves. He then made his way along the connecting corridors at the back of Number Ten through to the house next door. He considered having a word with the Chancellor, but decided anything Adrian Burton had to say on the matter wouldn't bear thinking about. The man was a buffoon.

So he pushed through the heavy, bomb-proof doors and went out into the garden to wait. The back gardens were always manicured to perfection, even in winter, and now the rosebushes were done up with tiny white fairy lights. *Happy bloody Christmas,* he thought when he saw them. With Christmas on the way, the whole country would be feeling all warm and squidgy and sentimental—something else he could do without. The Great Unwashed were suckers for cheap sentiment, and indulging it was always something of a bouncing Betty, politically speaking, as there was no telling where it might explode, or how often.

He shook his head wearily as he paced slowly down the path. Teddy's funeral had gone off without a hitch; they had foreseen and countered every contingency—except this one. How could he have imagined something like this would happen? He had just rid himself of the last King, and now he had another on his hands. Black emptiness welled up within him at the thought.

Well, he resolved, taking a deep breath, if it came to it, he'd bury this one, too.

The car arrived just then, and he opened the garden gate and went out into the narrow, bollard-lined drive. The security man jumped out and opened the door for him. "Good evening, sir," he said.

"Good evening, Robert," Waring replied, climbing into the back of the car.

"Where to this evening, sir?" asked the security man.

"Nowhere in particular," Waring replied. "I just want to drive around, get some fresh air."

"Very good, sir." Robert closed the door and climbed in. He punched the central locking switch and the door locks clicked shut. He then spoke quickly into a tiny microphone under his lapel, rattling off a string of syllables and numbers that meant nothing to Waring. There came a chimed beep from a box on the dashboard in front of him, and he turned to the driver. "We're clear. Go."

The car moved out and passed the blue security box. The duty officer lowered the spiked chain at their approach and waved them through. The emerald-green saloon rolled smoothly onto Horse Guards Road and joined the sparse traffic on The Mall. The driver worked his way through the streets north to the Embankment, and then drove along the river.

As the car approached New Bridge Street, Waring leaned forward and said, "Let's go by St. Paul's; I want to find a phone."

"You can use this one, sir," the security man reminded

him. He picked up the car's mobile phone, and started to pass it back.

"Thank you, Robert," the PM replied. "But I'd rather use a pay phone if you don't mind. It can be done, I believe."

"Of course, sir," he answered, giving the driver a sideways glance. The driver shrugged.

They cruised along slowly, and came to a rank of phone booths near the Old Bailey. "This will do," said Waring, and both he and his minder got out of the car and walked to the phones. There was no one else in any of the booths, so the PM selected the first one that accepted coins, opened the door, and stepped in. Robert, speaking into his lapel, planted himself outside, his back to the door while his boss made his call.

After slipping a number of coins into the slot, Waring tapped in the number. The phone rang several times, and his heart sank lower with each unanswered ring. He was on the point of hanging up, when a low, silky woman's voice said, "Yes?"

Waring sighed. "I have to see you."

"Thomas! What a pleasant surprise." The voice sounded far from surprised. "How did I know you would be calling?"

"Tonight."

"My, you *are* the anxious boy," she purred. "I don't know whether I should see you or not. I think you made your feelings perfectly clear last time."

"This isn't like the last time," Waring said, trying his best not to sound as desperate as he felt.

She laughed—a full, throaty laugh which teased and taunted even as it seduced. "That's what they all say, my darling."

"Please," he said. *God,* he thought, *it is almost worse talking to her than* not *talking to her. Ten seconds on the phone and she already has me begging.*

"Very well," she relented.

"I've got a car; we can pick you up."

"No," she replied crisply. "That would not be wise. Thank you, but I'll make my own way."

"When?"

"I shall have to consult my diary, I think."

"Tonight."

"Ah." She paused as if considering the suggestion. "No, I think not tonight. You'd best sit tight for a little while longer."

"Soon then."

"Say it, darling."

"What?" Waring's stomach tightened.

"You know," she insinuated. "You won't see me unless you say it."

Waring swallowed, and glanced over his shoulder. His bodyguard did not appear to be listening.

"I'm waiting, Thomas. You know how it upsets me to be kept waiting."

Clutching the phone tightly to his cheek, he whispered, "I . . . I worship you, Moira."

"Lovely, my sweet." She laughed again, and whispered, "See you soon. . . ."

He slammed the receiver back into the cradle and pushed open the glass door of the booth, almost knocking Robert the minder off his feet.

"Where to now, sir?" asked the security man.

"Home."

They walked to the waiting car and, just as the minder opened the door for the Prime Minister, the first shock wave struck London. The ground trembled—but only for an instant—and the tremor was accompanied by a sound not unlike that of an Underground train passing beneath the street. Waring thought nothing more about it.

# ✳

# Twenty-five

Contacting the Prime Minister had been the new King's first priority. There were conventions to observe, mutual obligations to fulfill, a new reign to inaugurate; free and open lines of communication would be immediately and continually necessary. So, following his broadcast announcement, James called Downing Street to arrange a meeting with Thomas Waring. But the switchboard would not put him through. He sent a fax. No reply. He wrote a letter and had it in the post that same night. Three days later, he was still awaiting a reply from Number Ten.

Despite the PM's silence, Embries assured James that the organs of state were conscious of his presence, and were actively engaged in dealing with his claim. "Your announcement caught them unaware," he said. "Do not imagine that they will treat it as anything less than a declaration of war."

If the Government was incommunicado, the rest of the world was eager and anxious to talk. Embries had warned James that the declaration of his kingship would cause a considerable stir. Even so, he seriously underestimated the size of the uproar. James was thinking countrywide, when global would have been closer to the mark. The commotion was extraordinary.

Within minutes of the declaration broadcast, every media

organization in the United Kingdom—and most of the rest
of the world—was beavering away, intent on either proving
or disproving his kingship. The Court of Claims, a traditional body charged with examining all assertions of royalty,
had been hastily convened by the Earl Marshall—recalled
from retirement—to investigate the new development.
While James was fully prepared for his claim to be subjected to rigorous and meticulous scrutiny—indeed, he welcomed the challenge—many of the stories emerging from
the resulting media feeding frenzy were factually wrong,
some were pretty far-fetched, and a few were unbelievably
fantastic.

Of this latter type, one story featured an interview with a
psychic from California who said the spirit of the deceased
King Edward had appeared to her in a séance and revealed
to her that this new King was not only a fraud, but had actually been Adolf Hitler in a former life, and was once more
embarking on the path of world domination. This assertion
was staunchly refuted by two other psychics. One in Glastonbury insisted the new claimant had instead been Alfred
the Great. Another, in Cardiff, maintained that the new
claimant was actually James Teach, cutthroat brother of Edward "Blackbeard" Teach, which by miraculous coincidence
had been the deceased King Edward's identity in a former
life.

The lunatic fringe aside, it bothered James that the serious
press had cooled to him, adopting an aggressively skeptical
stance which they put across in the most jaded, cynical, and
factually irresponsible terms. Judging by the tenor of their
investigative reports, the press corps seemed angry that he
had come forward and that his claim might indeed prove
true. They called him "The Man Who Would Be King,"
"Lord Jim," and "Monarch O' the Glens."

On Tuesday following the declaration, one paper suggested in veiled terms that James had paid for his lordship
out of money given him by radicals from the Save Our
Monarchy organization. On Wednesday, a scandal sheet al-
leged that he had hired hit men to bump off the old Duke so
he could inherit his title.

It was all James could do to keep from calling a press conference every few hours to correct the latest inaccuracies. Embries cautioned against this, and instead advised that they simply ride out the storm. "The more they convince themselves of your integrity," Embries told him, "the less convincing we will have to do along the way."

"I hope you're right," James replied, gloomily eyeing the day's stack of newspapers.

"Hope," snapped Embries, "is a precious commodity—save it for situations where it can help sway the outcome. Your kingship is a fact, and one which will be amply demonstrated to be true."

He was, James suspected, thinking about Collins' death. One man had given his life for this truth and, regardless of what Embries said, James honestly hoped he had not died in vain.

As the days went by, the evidence was shredded, ground, and sifted fine; nevertheless, the various experts at the College of Arms failed to uncover any impediments to James' kingship. None of the serious media organizations managed to scrape together any sign of skullduggery, or flimflam, and no cogent objections appeared forthcoming. Thus, the end of the first week of his reign approached, and no genuine opposition had emerged to undermine the legitimacy of his claim to the throne of Britain.

Collins had done his work well, and it stood up to the most severe analysis and investigation possible. He had foreseen and disarmed every potential objection. In this, he had struck the first blow for Britain before the enemy had even been aware of the battle.

Meanwhile, James did his best to ignore the media storm and instead busied himself with organizing his household. For the first time he was resident in the castle in whose shadow he had lived most of his life. There were numerous adjustments to be made on the domestic side, as well as mountains of material to digest pertaining to his kingship. The latter was accomplished under Embries' exacting tutelage; for hours each day, James was instructed and quizzed by his mentor on royal protocol, the British constitution, economics, European social history, statecraft, and diplomacy.

Meanwhile, the press had set up camp in the forecourt of Blair Morven and, like a besieging army, had virtually occupied little Braemar. A prisoner in his own house, James could not take so much as a single breath of fresh air outside without creating an instant stampede of cameramen and reporters. He did so once, and four journalists were injured in the resulting mêlée. Embries decided it was time to call in a professional.

"This is Shona McCrery," he said, introducing a short, somewhat plump young woman the next day. "She is from St. Andrews, and has been living in London for the past four years, working for Page One, the media consultancy firm."

"Good morning, everyone," she said pleasantly. "Your Majesty." She favored the King with a small bob of her head. "I hear you have paparazzi problems." She smiled wickedly, and James detected a pugnacious soul who relished a good brawl. "Not anymore you don't. From this moment, your media hassles are a thing of the past."

"Welcome aboard," said Cal, who had labored under the strain of having to deal with the reporters' continual pestering presence.

"Call me a personal representative, call me a royal spokesperson—call me anything you like, but as of right now, today, all statements to journalists—print, radio, or television—go through me. It will greatly enhance our credibility, not to mention our quality of life, if we are heard to speak with a single, distinct voice. That voice will be mine."

She served the same affable, no-nonsense notice to the newshounds huddled outside—many of whom she knew on a first-name basis. Reassured by her controlling presence, the press accepted the new regime without a grumble. She negotiated the boundaries, both geographical and professional, beyond which the media could not stray; she fixed the ground rules for press conferences and interviews, and instituted a rota system for controlling how many reporters were allowed on the estate at any one time.

Blair Morven proved itself a worthy base of operations

for the fledgling sovereign and his staff. The traditional seat
of the Morven dynasty was a huge, rambling pile of whitewashed stone, constructed in the grand old Highland style
around a central hall with clusters of various rooms scattered
on three floors, and four circular turrets, each of which had
been converted into comfortable, self-contained apartments.
In years past, the old Duke had spent a great deal of time and
money upgrading the plumbing and fixtures, and had made
the place, despite its size, quite livable and homey. The top
floor contained mostly bedrooms, the middle floor was offices and workrooms, and the ground floor had seven reception rooms for guests. A 1950s addition housed an
industrial-grade kitchen and storerooms. The ancient edifice
was large enough to guarantee some privacy and at the same
time enable the new King to keep his support staff handy—
if not in the castle itself then in the nearby cottages surrounding the old stable yard, and elsewhere around the
estate.

Uninhabited for the last few years—the staff having been
pensioned off by the Aussies—the castle needed attention.
At James' direction, Cal undertook to persuade a half dozen
of the old Duke's former retainers—including the cook, a
vast, smiling, red-faced woman known only as Priddy; and
her husband, Mr. Baxter, the head gardener—to return to
their previous employment.

Furniture was taken out of storage, and rooms long abandoned, cleaned and rearranged for use. Everything from
linen pillowcases to Edinburgh crystal decanters were un-
packed, inventoried, and returned to use. Paint and wallpaper were chosen and ordered; and every square inch of the
castle was dusted and vacuumed, and then dusted again.
Arrangements were made with a firm in Aberdeen to up-
grade security using the latest unobtrusive high-tech equipment. Priddy laid in a kitchenful of staples and contracted
with local butchers, greengrocers, and bakers to supply the
royal table. Mr. Baxter pored over garden catalogs and ordered his stock for the coming spring.

Blair Morven, which had been mostly a dusty museum,
began to reassume the nature and function of a noble house-

hold. To James, it was as if a fine garment, which had long lain forgotten and neglected in mothballs, had been aired out and brought into the light of day once more. As more rooms were opened, Cal took up residence in the castle, and Shona had an apartment of her own—as did Embries, Rhys, and Priddy and Mr. Baxter. Within days, the estate began to vibrate with a level of activity that rivaled its earliest years as the seat of a ducal dynasty.

And still no word from the Waring government. James' attempts to contact the Prime Minister were persistent, and all were ignored. His intention was to resume the traditional weekly meeting between the monarch and his PM—as he suggested in one unanswered fax, e-mail, telegram, and registered letter after another. Shona had also attempted to contact Waring's personal private secretary to arrange a phone call, but to no avail.

"He can't play hide 'n' seek forever," James observed one day. "I'm not going away. I'm like death and taxes. He's going to have to face me sooner or later."

Recognition of James' declaration arrived in the form of three men in dark suits, who appeared without warning one bright December morning. Presenting themselves at the door, they identified themselves as officials working for the Committee for Royal Devolution, and they asked if they could have a word with Mr. James Stuart. At Embries' direction, they were invited into the Duke's library, and kept waiting for fifteen minutes while Embries briefed James on what to expect. "They have come unannounced, hoping to take you by surprise. Just remember what we've talked about, and you have nothing to worry about."

"We'll meet them together, right?"

"Cal will be with you," he said. "It would be best if they did not see me just yet."

When they joined their visitors in the library, James greeted them and asked the nature of their business. The spokesman of the group, a tidy middle-aged man of average height and impeccable grooming, smiled condescendingly as if he were a bailiff and James a quarrelsome tenant he had come to evict on behalf of the absentee landlord.

"I am Mr. Thompson," he said, extending a well-manicured hand. Indicating the two with him—one bald-headed company man like himself, the other a younger fellow with light brown hair and the open guileless countenance of a chap who has yet to discover who his true enemies are—he said, "This is my assistant, Mr. Reuley, and"—he nodded to the youngster—"this is Mr. Gilchrist."

James acknowledged them in turn, and then said, "Gentlemen, this is my chief of staff, Mr. McKay." Cal, a frown of disapproval firmly in place, nodded.

"We would prefer to discuss our business in private," Thompson sniffed disdainfully. "When you hear what we have to say, I think you will agree that it is the wisest course."

"Your visit has been anticipated," James told him, sitting down on the edge of the desk. He offered chairs to no one, so his visitors remained standing. "As you have neglected the common courtesy of arranging an appointment, I can only assume you must be either extremely busy or extremely rude."

"As you might imagine," Thompson said, ignoring the reproof, "your claim to the throne has caused a considerable flap." He made it sound as if the sole purpose of James' declaration had been to cause him trouble. "I am certain you can understand also that, in light of the proposed dissolution of the monarchy, your claim cannot be allowed to stand."

"Go on," James said. "I'm listening."

"Allow me to come directly to the point," the man said, gesturing to his accomplice, who opened a briefcase and brought out a thick square of parchment. It was wrapped in a wide red satin ribbon, which he proceeded to untie. "May I?" he asked, indicating the library table.

"By all means," James said.

He placed the parchment on the table and unfolded it. James stepped to the table and found himself looking at the infamous Magna Carta II. It was interesting, he thought, that they had actually drawn the thing up roughly on the order of the original Magna Carta—red ink on a great square of sheepskin. Clearly, they meant this second document to be fully as historical as the first, and were striving for some sense of inevitability through symmetry.

Beneath the block of text headed *"Declaration of Abdication,"* were lines for no fewer than fifty-eight signatures. Every member of the royal succession had signed—dukes and duchesses, princes and princesses—and now only the top signature was missing. This was the space poor old Teddy was meant to have filled in.

"As you can see," Thompson said, "only one remains." He produced a fountain pen, which he handed to James. "If you would be so kind as to sign here"—he pointed to the top line—"we will gladly be on our way."

James placed the pen on the table. "I have no intention of signing this document."

"It is merely a formality," Thompson replied smoothly. "Your refusal will not change anything. The Act of Dissolution will proceed—with or without your signature."

"In that case," James observed placidly, "it makes no difference whether I sign or not. Does it?"

A sly smirk appeared on young Gilchrist's face. He suppressed a chuckle, and James knew he had an ally.

"Oh dear, oh dear," Thompson tutted. "I had hoped we would be able to reason together. You see, the devolution will go ahead as planned. The necessary legislation is already in place, and the last referendum is—as you *must* be aware—only a matter of weeks away." Taking up the pen, he extended it towards James once more.

"I fail to see why that should influence my decision."

Thompson gave a disappointed shake of his head, and turned to Cal, as if he might be the cause of James' reluctance. The grimly silent Mr. Reuley spoke up. "Perhaps Mr. McKay might persuade His Majesty to avoid the unnecessary unpleasantness which is certain to derive from a too-hasty decision."

By way of reply, Cal reached out and snatched the pen from Thompson's hand. "You heard the King. He's not going to sign your piddling paper."

This was too much for Gilchrist; he gave a little snort of laughter and swiftly clamped his mouth shut. Thompson glared at his underling with murderous intent.

"Forgive me," said Reuley with icy insolence. "I intended no disrespect."

"No doubt this was the sort of unnecessary unpleasantness you were alluding to just now," Cal replied.

Gilchrist could not stifle his laugh this time; he burst out with a hearty guffaw which caused his boss to glare daggers at him.

"You must excuse my young colleague," Thompson said, his voice dripping with poisonous derision. "He seems to be having difficulty keeping his mind on his work today."

"Or perhaps," James suggested lightly, "he simply finds flogging this dead horse a waste of his valuable time and talents."

"I am indeed sorry you have chosen to take this attitude," Thompson tutted. "I had hoped I might prevail upon you to do the honorable thing." He fished another pen from his coat pocket, and made a show of unscrewing the cap and offering it to James. "I will ask you one last time. Your signature, if you please."

"Don't sign it, Your Majesty," said Gilchrist, speaking up at last. "You don't have to, and they can't make you."

"Leave us," Thompson said through clenched teeth. "That is an order." He nodded to Reuley, who took a step towards the young man.

James raised his hand and stopped him. "As I have already said, I have no intention of signing this document, and I will not be harassed or otherwise intimidated into doing so. If obtaining my signature was the sole item on your agenda, then our business is concluded."

"That is your decision, unwise as it may be," Thompson replied with elaborate disdain. He turned stiffly and began refolding the parchment. "We can do nothing more," he sniffed. "Mr. Stuart's refusal is duly noted and will be reported. The matter is out of our hands." Handing the parchment back to Reuley, he said, "Come along, gentlemen."

"No." It was Gilchrist.

Thompson stared at him. "We are leaving now. Go to the car at once."

Again, Gilchrist refused. "No," he said quietly. "I'm not going back."

With great effort, Thompson, almost shaking with rage at

having his authority so blatantly challenged, gave the young man an icy smile. "This is neither the time nor the place for one of your schoolboy tantrums," he said, forcing the words out with exaggerated precision.

Ignoring his superior, the young man turned instead to James. He took a step nearer and went down on one knee before him. "Your Majesty," he said, "it would be a very great honor to serve you in any way I can."

Thompson, almost goggle-eyed with apoplexy, stared at the earnest young man on his knee before his king.

"Please, sir," Gilchrist said, his voice steady and low. "If you accept me, I will do anything you ask. I swear it."

Extending his hand to the young man, James laughed and said, "Rise, Sir Knight. I accept your pledge of fealty."

Thompson gave his former associate one last withering glance, turned on his heel, and strode imperiously to the door, leaving Reuley to scuttle after him with the parchment and briefcase. No one bothered to see them out.

Gilchrist shifted uncertainly from one foot to the other, looking both humble and relieved; now that his act of defiance was over, he appeared less confident than before. "I'm sorry if I embarrassed you, Your Majesty. I'll leave if you want me to."

"You didn't embarrass me," James assured him. "As it happens, I have room for quick-thinking, able-bodied people like yourself. If you don't mind pitching in on whatever job needs doing."

"Anything," the young man replied. "I don't care. I'll work for nothing." He drew himself up, squared his shoulders, and declared, "I heard your speech that night, and it connected with me. You spoke of the Kingdom of Summer, and from that moment all I wanted was to serve you, and to serve Britain. I was never meant to work for a snake like Thompson. I'm glad someone finally stood up to him. He's had it coming for a long time."

"It would take more than him and his fancy paper to put the wind up James' kilt," Cal remarked. "Don't give it a second thought."

"You saw all those signatures?" the young fellow contin-

ued. "Some of those people were really very nice—true no-
bles, through and through—but he treated them like scum.
He didn't need to do that; it was pure meanness." Gratitude
and admiration mingled in his quick, infectious smile. "I've
been waiting all my life for something like this. And I have
friends, sir—men just like me who would give their right
arm to be part of something worthy of their time and energy."

"I'll bear that in mind," replied James. "For now though,
why don't you go upstairs to the press office and ask for
Shona. Tell her I said to put you to work. We'll arrange pay
and such later."

"Gilchrist is a Scottish name," Cal said. "Where are you
from originally?"

"My family is from Inverness," he explained, "and there's
a load of aunts and uncles up there still. But my dad worked
for the Foreign Office, and we moved around a lot. I was
born in France, but never felt it was home." He smiled, and
the color rose to his cheeks. "Now I feel as if I *have* come
home."

"What's your first name?" James asked.

"Gavin, sir," he replied, "a family name, apparently."

"Welcome aboard, Gavin." James grasped the young
man's hand, and a tingling sensation traveled up his arm and
down his neck. The *fiosachd* came upon him, and he felt as
if he were welcoming back a friend who had been absent for
many years. "I'm glad you're here," he added.

Eager to begin, Gavin went off to find Shona and secure
his place in the new regime. James and Cal went next door
where Embries was waiting. He had his notebook open on
the desk before him, and was writing furiously.

"Our boy was fantastic," crowed Cal. "You would have
enjoyed it."

"Thompson looked a little too familiar," Embries answered. "It is entirely possible our paths have crossed in the
past, and he might have remembered me. So far, my presence has eluded detection. I would like to keep it that way a
little longer." He looked up from his notebook. "That aside,
you are to be congratulated."

"Why?"

"The simple fact of their showing up means that the Government has accepted the legitimacy of your claim. If they had any hope of discrediting or dismissing you outright, they certainly wouldn't have bothered trying to get your signature."

"I managed to squeeze a 'Your Majesty' out of him in the end."

"Plus, we got a new recruit out of it," put in Cal. "You should have seen them, Embries. I thought Thompson was going to bust a gusset."

"What did they expect, coming here like that?" said James. "We can't even get Downing Street to return our phone calls—did they really think I would sign that thing?"

"They had to find out how serious you are," Embries suggested. "They have to know what they're up against."

"I'll show them how serious I am," said James. He turned and walked to the door. "Care to come along, Cal?"

"Sure. Where are you going?"

"Suddenly, I feel like taking a walk in the garden."

"James, wait," said Embries, calling him back. "What are you going to do?"

"Things being the way they are," came the reply, "you can probably see it on Newsnight."

✳

# Twenty-six

Stepping out onto the graveled yard, James was instantly besieged by cameramen and journalists. They clustered so tightly around him that Shona threatened several with expulsion if they did not give the King room to breathe. "Back off!" she warned. "There is plenty of room for everyone. Let's all behave."

"You are here at the King's pleasure," Cal reminded them sternly. "Don't blow it."

When they had established rough order among themselves, Shona announced, "The King has prepared a statement which he would like to share with you now. There will be time for questions immediately after." Turning to James, she said, "His Majesty, the King of Britain."

"Thank you, Shona," he said, stepping forward. There was a last jostling for position among the assembled news people, as James began. "A few minutes ago I received a visit from representatives of the Special Committee for Royal Devolution—the so-called Magna Carta Two. I was invited to affix my signature to the document which has caused such anguish and controversy in our nation." He paused, looking out at the eager faces of the reporters, enjoying the effect his appearance was having. "I declined."

"Did they say what would happen if you didn't sign?" shouted a woman a few rows back.

"Questions later, Gillian, please," Shona reminded the journalist. "Thank you."

"I refused to resign the sovereignty of Britain," James continued, "and I want everyone to know that I will continue to resist any and all efforts to make me relinquish the crown. Further, it is my intention to reinstate the traditional weekly royal prime ministerial audience at once. From today, I will be expecting to receive the Prime Minister, and I urge his office to contact me at once to make arrangements."

This, as James suspected, caused an instant uproar among the gathered media folk. They leaned in anxiously, thrusting their arms into the air to be recognized; those at the back shoved forward to get a better vantage point.

"Thank you," James said. "I'd be happy to take your questions now."

It took a few moments to quell the uproar and for Shona to introduce a modicum of order. "We'll do it my way or not at all," she said. "Today, the last shall be first." Pointing to a tall cadaverous-looking man straining in the back row. "Gordon Granger, you're on."

"Gosh, thanks," said Gordon, so delighted at his unprecedented good fortune that he promptly forgot why he'd been called upon.

"Could we have your question, Gordon?" asked Shona.

"Your Majesty," said the journalist, "you used the word 'urge' a moment ago. Are we to take that to mean you are not now in contact with Downing Street?"

"That is correct," replied the King. "We are not in contact with Downing Street at present. The truth is, the Government has thus far ignored all our attempts at communication. We've sent letters, faxes, telegrams—you name it. They won't even return my phone calls."

Some of the journalists snickered at this. "Is this why you chose to make the announcement just now?" a woman in the front row asked. Shona gave her a dirty look, but the rest of the pack seemed content to listen to the answer.

"I would have preferred to proceed through the proper

channels," James replied, "but one way or another, I will be heard. Once, not all that long ago, a subject would have lost his head for ignoring his monarch."

"Are you going to ask for Prime Minister Waring's head?" someone shouted.

James smiled. "Don't tempt me."

"Will you meet here at Blair Morven," asked someone else, "or in London?"

"If memory serves," James answered, "the meeting traditionally takes place at the monarch's principal residence. Since this is the only place I've got, I guess the audience will have to be here."

"What will you talk about," called another journalist, "when, or maybe I should say, *if* the PM agrees to meet with you?"

"The conversation has traditionally been privileged," the King replied. "I see no reason why that should change. I can tell you, however, that I have no hidden agenda. We will talk about the governing of our nation, and how to do what is best for Britain."

This statement was instantly taken up. "Many people believe that what is best for Britain," said the woman named Gillian, "is the abolition of the monarchy—an opinion Prime Minister Waring obviously shares. What do you say to that?"

"Ladies and gentlemen," said James, "forgive me if I have not made myself clear on this point. I mean to reign as King of Britain. I believe the monarchy can be restored, and I hope that I will be given a chance to prove myself not only a worthy monarch but also to demonstrate the value of having a king on the throne."

There were more questions after that, and James found himself growing more at ease as his command of the situation increased. When Shona finally called for the last question, he was actually sorry to break it off. "What did you think of that?" he asked after rejoining Embries in the library. "You'd have been proud."

"You should have seen him," Cal crowed. "Our boy was impressive. He had them eating out of his hand."

"I did see him," remarked Embries tartly. "That was broadcast live. Very impressive." He frowned. "Oh, well, the damage is done."

"What damage?" James demanded. "I told the truth and meant every word."

"The Prime Minister may not forgive you for calling him to account. You've forced his hand in a most public manner. He will resent being made to look foolish. He is certain to retaliate."

"Let him," James declared. "I can handle it."

"Can you?" Embries regarded him with sharp disapproval. "We shall see."

The evening news broadcasts featured the King's impromptu press conference in unstinting detail, showing his announcement in its entirety, replaying many of the questions he had answered and summarizing the rest, and then following the report with an expert analysis of what some commentators called an extraordinary development.

"Extraordinary, my ass," growled the Prime Minister. "A dog eats its own vomit, and they call it extraordinary."

"I hate to say it, Tom," remarked Dennis Arnold, the Devolution Chairman, "but I think it was a mistake not to return his calls. He is the King, after all."

"I don't care who the hell he is," Waring fumed. He and his two top aides were having a drink and watching the news in the Prime Minister's Downing Street apartment. "I will *not* be dictated to by some jumped-up pretty boy who fancies himself a latter-day Laird of the Isles."

"Sure," said Arnold, "I can sympathize. But look where it's got us. We're going to have to talk to him. I'm not saying you have to like it."

Waring glared at his advisor, then turned his attention to his press secretary. "What do you think, Hutch?"

"Dennis is right," said Hutchens. "We should talk to the guy at least."

"And if we don't?"

"Worst case? The press will say we fear a confrontation. They'll say we're running away from a showdown."

"So what?"

"If we're seen to be running away," Hutchens continued, lacing his hands behind his head as he leaned back in his chair, imagining the ramifications of his worst-case scenario, "the press will smell fear. They'll be on us just like that."

"We've weathered media storms before. We can ride this one out—*if* it comes to that."

"Oh, it *will* come to that all right," the spin doctor warned. "They'll hound us day and night. They'll take it up as a cause, and worry us with it until we give in."

The Prime Minister rose from his place on the sofa and began pacing in front of the TV. "So this clown calls the tune and I'm supposed to dance—is that it? He whistles and I have to come running. To hell with that, and to hell with him!"

Dennis shook his head. "We can't simply ignore him. Look—" He put out his hand to the TV. "We tried that and it didn't work."

Waring collapsed heavily into his chair. He knew his advisors were right, but it galled him to have to admit he'd underestimated this new King. It galled him more to have to meet with the conniving bastard. Still, even with defeat staring him in the face, he wasn't ready to give in. "It's getting late. We'll take this up at the staff meeting tomorrow morning. Dennis, get on to Cecil Blackmoor and get a legal opinion. There may be a way out of this yet."

Dismissing his aides, the Prime Minister spent an unhappy evening with the remote control stuck in his fist. He slept poorly and rose early to survey the first of the day's newspapers over breakfast—which put him off eating altogether—and arranged with the kitchen for rolls and coffee to be laid on for the staff meeting. At eight o'clock on the dot, the Prime Minister took his private lift down to the ground floor, greeted the day shift, and made his way to the conference room.

Adrian Burton, Chancellor of the Exchequer, arrived first. "Good morning, Thomas. Touch of frost in the air. Winter could be early this year. We just might get that white Christmas everyone is so unaccountably fond of. I don't suppose you've made any plans yet? You're always welcome to share the festivities with Mildred and myself."

*Typical,* thought Waring; *the man hasn't a clue.* "When I get around to making my plans, you'll be the first to know," he replied.

Oblivious of his chief's sour mood, Burton took his seat and helped himself to coffee and a croissant. "By the way, there's a TV crew at the gates."

The Prime Minister looked pityingly at his minion. "There's *always* a TV crew outside the gates, Adrian. They live there."

"Quite a large one." Burton broke his croissant and dipped one end into his coffee. "Larger than usual, I should have thought. I say, is this going to be a long meeting, PM?"

"Who wants to know?" said Waring.

"Well," replied Burton, "as it happens, I'm meeting Mildred and the directors of the Children in Need campaign for lunch. We've been asked to give out the CIN awards for distinguished service."

"Oh," remarked Waring, "we'll be finished by lunchtime—wouldn't want to ruin your photo op."

"Quite," agreed Burton, munching away happily.

The Deputy Prime Minister arrived next, with a groggy Martin Hutchens in tow. "Good morning, Tom," said Angela Telford-Sykes, throwing her briefcase onto the long table. "Saw Leonard outside. There's bad news."

"What?" said Waring dully.

"Alfred Norris had a heart attack yesterday," Angela reported. "He's in the IC unit at St. George's. It doesn't look good."

"Christ almighty," muttered Waring darkly.

"Excuse me," said Burton, "who is Alfred Norris when he's at home?"

"For God's sake, Adrian," Waring growled. "He's one of our loyal backbenchers."

"Bristol North," put in Angela.

"If he kicks it," Waring said, "our majority is down to five."

"I see," intoned Burton solemnly. "One would think you cared more about the majority than you did about poor old Norris."

Waring rolled his eyes. He was already at the end of his tether, and the meeting had not yet begun. "Keep me posted," he said to Angela, then asked: "Anybody seen Dennis?"

"Spoke to him ten minutes ago," Telford-Sykes replied. "He may be late, but he's on his way. Shah likewise."

Waring glanced at his watch, then looked down the table at his inner circle of advisors. He fastened on his press secretary. "Heavy date last night, Martin?"

"Heavy enough," replied Hutchens, already pouring his second cup of coffee. "Someone remind me never to go to Stringfellows again."

Dispensing with the small talk, Waring said, "I'm going to assume everyone saw the broadcast."

"The whole world saw the broadcast." Hutchens sat back, sipped his coffee, and looked at his boss with red eyes. "I think George Bush said it best: 'We're in deep doo-doo, guys.'"

"Excuse me," said Burton. "I feel I'm missing something here. Which broadcast are we talking about exactly?"

Waring glanced at the Deputy PM, who replied, "The King's press conference. Don't tell me you didn't see it, Adrian."

"The King's thingy? Course I saw it," Burton said. "Most of it, anyway."

"Jesus, Adrian," Hutchens said, "didn't it strike you as essential viewing?"

"Actually, no. It didn't. Don't watch telly during mealtimes as a rule," declared Burton indignantly. He glanced around, looking for support for his domestic policy. "I did, however, videotape it for later consumption. Bit of a flap, what?"

At Waring's behest, Telford-Sykes began a summary description of the broadcast's salient points, during which the absent Patricia Shah and Leonard DeVries appeared and took their places, followed by Dennis Arnold, carrying a manila folder bursting with bits of scribbled paper.

"Thank you, Angela," said Waring when his deputy finished. Turning to the latecomers, he said, "Welcome, comrades, glad you could favor us with a few moments of your precious time. The subject of this morning's tête-à-tête, as you will no doubt have guessed, is last evening's royal press conference. We're here to decide what to do about it. Any questions?"

"Can he really do it?" wondered Patricia Shah, fingering the rim of her coffee cup. "That is the pertinent question, certainly."

"It's part of the royal prerogative," replied Dennis Arnold, Royal Devolution Committee Chairman. "And, yes, he can do it." Addressing the PM, he said, "I rang Cecil Blackmoor as you requested." Glancing at the others, he said, "Cecil's the Royal Branch Subcommittee legal eagle. I've been working quite closely with him on the legislation for royal devolution—"

"Yes, yes," snapped Waring impatiently. "We all know who he is. Get on with it, Dennis, for God's sake. What did he say?"

"Basically," Arnold announced grimly, "we're screwed."

"Damn!"

"There goes damage control," remarked Hutchens. "Shot to bloody hell." Taking the top page from his folder, he crumpled it into a ball and tossed it across the room.

"Are you saying," inquired Patricia Shah, "we have no constitutional recourse?"

"We ain't got recourse. We ain't got squat, Jack," quipped Hutchens. "The King's got us by the short and curlies, and he knows it. Who is advising this guy anyway?"

"The problem seems to be," Arnold continued, ignoring the press secretary's outburst, "that, despite having lapsed under the previous monarch, the ministerial meetings remain entirely—"

"I *know* what the problem seems to be," growled Waring. "Bloody Christ! I have to meet with the King, and *be seen* to meet with the King. He's got the fawning attention of the whole world, and the next thing they're going to see is me, hat in hand, bowing and scraping at his front door."

He glared furiously at the ceiling. "I won't do it, by God. I won't."

"He seems likely to make an issue of it, Tom," pointed out the Deputy Prime Minister, "if you fail to honor his request."

"Let him," replied Waring. "Let him try, the bastard. We'll fight him every inch of the way." The PM glanced at the faces around the table, gauging his support for the fight. He saw Dennis Arnold's frown, and said, "What now?"

"At the very least it might provoke a constitutional crisis."

Before Waring could reply, the Deputy PM jumped in, "Think about it, Tom. We could easily end up winning the battle and losing the war. I say, why risk it?"

"Who is advising this guy?" wondered Hutchens again.

"I don't see we have any choice," Arnold said, "but to comply."

"We comply," continued his deputy, "and bide our time. In a few weeks it'll be over and forgotten."

"I won't forget," muttered Waring. He hated losing. He hated grinning for the cameras and making lame excuses when things went wrong. Most of all, he hated the monarchy—now more than ever.

"The King found a loophole," Angela suggested. "Big deal. It gains him nothing in the end. He's on his way out."

"Then *you* go shake hands with the son of a bitch," said Waring. "Damn it!" He slapped the table with the flat of his hand. "Why didn't we revoke royal prerogative first?"

"In hindsight," agreed Arnold, "perhaps we should have. At the time, you will recall, it wasn't remotely an issue. Bit of bad luck, is all—hardly fatal."

"Don't be too sure," murmured the Prime Minister.

"We'll just have to make the best of a bad situation," observed Chancellor Burton. "Take it on the chin. Roll with the punches. I'm sure it will all work out for the best."

Unable to stomach any more of Burton's blithe clichés, Waring stood abruptly. "Meeting adjourned."

The Government's best and brightest rose slowly, closing their notebooks and talking among themselves. "Hutch," ordered the PM as the Press Secretary shoved back his chair,

"I want a draft response to the King's demand on my desk before lunch. Get on it."

"Just a thought," said Hutchens, moving towards his boss, "on how we go about this." He slid into the chair next to the PM's. "What if we don't say anything—just do as he wants, and not make any fuss. These meetings are supposed to be confidential, right? Well, we just go along—no fanfare, no statements, no photos or film, right? We just turn up, fulfill our obligation, and, wham, it's over and done. Like Angela said, no big deal."

Waring considered the idea. "Downplay it, you mean."

"I mean," said Hutchens, warming to his own plan, "if we go crying and carrying on like it's the end of the world, everybody's bound to sit up and take notice. On the other hand, if we keep mum, act like it's just business as usual, they'll soon lose interest. No smoke, no fire."

"He could be right," said Arnold, joining them. "If we don't issue a statement, the papers have nothing to print."

Hutchens shrugged. "I figure it's worth a shot. Either way, we're no worse off than before."

"All right," agreed the Prime Minister, making up his mind at once. "That's how we'll play it. No statement. And"—he pointed his index finger at his Press Secretary—"when the media phone up to ask what response we're going to make, you tell them quite simply that of course we are planning to comply. We're His Majesty's loyal subjects; we wouldn't dream of doing anything else."

"You got it, PM," replied Martin Hutchens, smiling at the wonderful duplicity of it. "Anything else?"

"Yes," said Waring. "On your way out, tell DeVries to set up the meeting for the day after tomorrow."

"So soon?" asked Angela. "Is that wise?"

"I want to keep the bastard on the hop. He's going to learn very quickly who's calling the shots."

## ❋

# Twenty-seven

"Call her," urged Cal. "What good is it being King of Britain if you can't call up a girl when you feel like it?"

"Thanks, Cal," muttered James. "You've certainly put the problem into proper perspective."

"Go on. Talk to her."

"Did it ever occur to you that it's *because* I'm King that I *can't* talk to her? It wouldn't be the same now."

Cal stared at him as if he had begun speaking gibberish. "The same as what? It's Jenny we're talking about, not Alice in Wonderland. Jenny! Remember?" He shook his head at James' stubborn reluctance. "Look, if you don't call her, I will—and I'll tell her how you've got your knickers in a twist over this."

"All right," James conceded. "Point made." He glanced at his watch. "It's too late now—I'll call her in the morning."

"In the morning is too late. Call her now."

"Look, I appreciate what you're trying to do. But I'm meeting with the Prime Minister the day after tomorrow. I've got preparations to make. I can't—"

"That's not until the evening." Cal walked to the phone on the table in the corner of the room, and started dialing. He listened for a moment, and extended the receiver to James. "It's ringing."

James crossed the room in two strides and snatched the phone out of Cal's hand as a voice answered on the other end. "Hello?"

"Ah, hello. Is that Agnes?" James said, glaring furiously at Cal, who was moving towards the door.

"Oh, my heavens!" came the reply. "James—I mean, Your Majesty—how good of you to call."

"I know it's late, Agnes, and I'm sorry for disturbing you like this—"

"Not at all! We've just been watching you on the telly. Just think, you King, and the Prime Minister—coming all the way up here to little Braemar. Whatever next?"

"Yes, we're definitely living in strange times," James replied. "I was wondering if I might speak to Jenny for a moment."

Cal smiled. "You can thank me later," he whispered, closing the door behind him.

"Is she there, Agnes?" James said.

"She's here," Agnes told him, "and I know she'd love to speak to you. I'll get her."

There was a clunk as Agnes put the phone down, and James heard her calling for Jenny as she moved from the room. He flopped down in a nearby chair, shoving his feet out in front of him.

"Yes?" The voice on the other end startled him. He sat up.

"Jenny? Listen, I'm sorry for calling you like this," he blurted, "but I want to see you. I think we should talk."

"All right," she said.

"I mean," he rushed on, "whenever's convenient. It doesn't have to be right away. I just thought—the way things are . . . I mean, I was hoping we could—"

"I already said okay," Jenny broke in. "If you think we have something to talk about."

He caught the dark undercurrent of her tone, but sailed on. "How about tomorrow? Lunch, say? Thing is, you'll have to come here. I can't actually go anywhere just now without causing an international incident."

"Tomorrow lunch is fine," she said, registering neither enthusiasm nor interest at the prospect.

James hesitated. "Good . . . um, well, I guess I'll see you tomorrow then. . . ." He knew there was something more he should say, but could not think what it might be. "Good night, Jenny."

She rang off without saying good-bye, and James sat looking at the phone for a while, wondering why that had gone so badly. What could he have said that would have made a difference?

She arrived the next day and was conducted straightaway to James' apartment. He had taken over the old Duke's rooms on the upper floor—a sitting room, small dining room, and a massive bedroom. The table in the dining room was set for two, and there was chilled white wine on the sideboard.

"Good to see you, Jenny," he said, welcoming her in with a circumspect kiss on the cheek. "Thanks for coming." He helped her from her coat. "I thought we'd eat up here—the dining room is so big and formal and all. Would you like something to drink? I've got—" He started towards the sideboard.

"Why didn't you tell me you were going to be King?" She stood in the center of the room facing him.

"Well, it all happened pretty fast," he said lightly. "It wasn't anything I planned, exactly."

"You could have told me at least."

"I suppose I should have said something. But, truth is, I didn't believe it myself at first."

He looked at her, uncertain what to say next. *God, how I've missed her,* he thought, drinking in the sight of her.

"What?" she asked, growing suspicious. "Have I got mud on me?"

He grinned. Mud was the occupational hazard of a potter, and she was always asking that. But her long brown sleeveless knitted tunic, deep burgundy skirt, and creamy silk blouse were spotless for a change. Fresh from the winter cold outside, she looked radiant.

"No," he told her. "You're perfect." Her long dark hair was pulled back into a thick braid; a few loose strands at the sides and forehead fell forward, framing her face like the feathers of a raven's wing. "Better than perfect."

He poured two glasses of wine, and handed her one. She took it and sipped, watching him over the rim. He took a sip of wine to steady himself. "Marry me, Jenny," he said, and watched the fire flare up in her eyes.

"Marry you!" she snapped. She put her wineglass down with a thump. "Oh, that's just great! Is this why you wanted to see me?"

"Really, it just came to me. I wasn't plan—" he began, but she wasn't listening.

"What am I supposed to do?" Jenny demanded. "Am I supposed to go all aflutter and melt into a pool of warm goo because you want to marry me? Oh, yes, Your Royal Highness, of course I'll marry you! Is that what you think?"

Her anger took him aback. "Well, I hadn't actually—"

"Forgive me if I seem slightly underwhelmed," she continued. "But I waited *years* for you, James Stuart. And now this—just when I've made up my mind to get on with my life."

"You mean the pottery business? I'm not asking you to give up anything. You can still—"

"You don't get it, do you? It's not just the pottery, it's you, it's Charles and me—it's everything!"

"Do you love this Charles?"

Livid, she faced him, eyes blazing. "That's beside the point."

"I thought it *was* the point. Do you love him?"

"Don't start," she warned. Glaring at him, she crossed her arms over her breasts. He could feel the heat of her anger at ten paces.

"You know, I always thought we would be together. I always thought we were meant for each other, and I thought you felt that way, too. But you decided to be a soldier, and went off and did your soldier bit. Meanwhile, I sat around and waited. I waited for you to come home and do the honorable thing, and when at last you *did* come home, I watched you get all wrapped up in this damned estate of yours."

He stared at her as if at a stranger. "I couldn't ask you before. I had nothing. Everything depended on saving what I could of the estate—it was all I had to offer you. Don't you see? If I'd lost that I'd have had nothing."

"You think I cared about that?" she said. "I didn't give a damn about what you had to offer me. It was *you* I cared about, you idiot! I could have cared less if we lived in a cardboard box beside the highway. I didn't want your miserable old cottage. I wanted you."

"Well," James said, taking a step closer; he spread his hands towards her. "Now you can have it all."

"I don't want it all!" Unable to look at him any longer, she turned away.

"Listen to me," he said, stepping behind her, "I'm sorry. It's true, I don't understand what you're feeling right now. But can't we sit down and at least try to figure it out?" He put his hands on her shoulders. "I love you, Jenny. I always have. And I need you—now more than ever. I think I have it in me to be a good king; at least I want to try. But I can't do it without you, Jenny. I need you beside me."

He felt her shoulders stiffen under his touch. "Is that why you want to get married all of a sudden?" she demanded, whirling around to face him. "Because you need a queen to help you pull off this pantomime of yours?"

"No," James replied quietly, as understanding began to dawn in him at last, "I want you to marry me because you are the most wonderful woman I have ever met, and I would be lost without you."

Taking her hand in his, he said, "I want you to marry me because from the first moment I ever laid eyes on you, I knew we were meant to be together forever. I want you to marry me because I am a better person when you are with me. I want you to marry me because I love you, Jenny, and I cannot imagine a future without you in it."

Raising her hand to his lips, he kissed it, and said, "I have always loved you, Jenny, and I always will."

She regarded him doubtfully.

He kissed her hand again, and sensed her softening towards him. "Will you marry me?"

"No, not like this," she replied, withdrawing her hand. "I'll have to think about it."

"That's not what I was hoping to hear."

"No? Tough, because that's what you get." She turned and picked up her coat. "And that's a whole lot more than you've got coming." She walked quickly to the door.

"Don't go, Jenny. Stay and have lunch at least."

She looked back as she stepped through the door. "I can't."

## �֍ Twenty-eight

Prime Minister Waring was not at all the grayish, bland drudge so often portrayed by satirists and comedians—a fact which surprised James. He had prepared himself to meet a colorless bureaucrat, and instead found himself face-to-face with a man who had the charismatic presence of a stage celebrity. His compact, spare form was trim, and his manner sharp as the cut of his expensive Savile Row suit. For someone who reputedly did not get out much, the PM appeared extremely fit.

Waring arrived in a convoy of three large black cars—two of them full of security men—and was accompanied by two aides, one of whom carried the official red dispatch box. He stepped from the car in a glare of camera flashes and TV spotlights.

As Shona had promised, the assembled media were ready and waiting to capture the historic moment; she even allowed the crews to set up their cameras right outside the front door. James made a show of greeting the Prime Minister on the steps, and welcoming him and his small entourage. They paused for photos and TV footage, and James took a few questions from the assembled journalists before going inside.

As soon as they were beyond range of the microphones,

Waring dropped his neighborly politician mask, becoming businesslike to the point of brusqueness. "Your Highness," he said, grinding the words out between his teeth as if they were chips of flint. "I would very much appreciate it if we could cut the crap and get this charade over with."

"We thought you might be tired from your journey," James responded. "Would you care for a drink?"

Waring's smile was as stiff and nasty as his reply. "No, thank you. I have no wish to prolong this farce a moment longer than necessary. I am needed back in London—I have a country to run."

"No rest for the wicked—eh, Prime Minister?" said Cal.

The skin around Waring's eyes tightened with intense animosity. "May we begin?"

"Of course," James replied, trying to maintain his good humor. "Please, come this way."

He led the PM, his two aides, and a handful of security men to the throne room—the old Duke's trophy room next to the main hall—where Waring promptly commandeered the carved wooden chair at the head of the table, placing his aides on either side. James allowed them to get settled, and then said, "As this is a highly significant occasion, I thought we would invite a few photographers in to capture the moment."

Waring opened his mouth to overrule this suggestion, but Shona had already cued the photographers, who trooped in and began snapping away at the PM and his minions sitting alone at the head of the table, like reluctant, dyspeptic honorees at a much-loathed feast.

"Why don't we pose before the fireplace?" James suggested, taking his place at the hearth.

The photographers immediately began snapping away, saying things like, "Brilliant, Your Majesty," and, "Very tasty, Your Highness."

Stone-faced, the PM rose and joined his host, keeping his hands firmly clasped before him so he would not have to be photographed shaking hands with the King. After a few dozen more pictures for the press, Gavin moved the photographers on, and Waring returned to the table.

"I have asked my personal advisor to join us," James announced, walking past the table to a grouping of more comfortable chairs. "Perhaps you would like to take a seat, Prime Minister Waring, while I summon him."

"It was expected," Waring said, "that these meetings should be strictly private and confidential."

"Confidential, certainly," James affirmed. "But as you have brought your aides, I see no reason to exclude mine. It won't take a moment."

He stepped to the door and signaled Gavin, who was shooing the press out the castle door. Returning to the comfy chairs, the King chose a chair opposite the PM. Embries, who had been waiting outside, entered and, after a brief encounter with the security men at the door, walked quickly to join the others.

"Prime Minister," he said, holding out his hand in welcome, "it is a pleasure to meet you. I have been looking forward to this for a very long time. My name is Embries."

The PM shook hands diffidently; something about the tall gentleman seemed familiar. "Enchanted," he muttered. Then, turning his attention to the business at hand, he said, "If there are no more photo opportunities, or advisors to summon, might we get on with it?" He glanced at his watch.

"Duty does weigh more heavily on some than others," Embries replied ambiguously.

The PM looked at him again—as if trying to decide if this was someone he ought to recognize. Unable to place the face, he turned to James. "You may as well know up front that I deeply resent your intrusion into the affairs of my government. I cannot imagine what you hope to accomplish with whatever game you're playing at. But you are sadly mistaken if you actually think it will get you anywhere."

"You seem to be laboring under a misapprehension, Mr. Waring," James replied amiably. "It is no game. As I am the King, it is my right to concern myself with matters of State—a right, I might add, which is older than Parliament itself."

Waring drew breath to challenge this statement, but James was not finished. "Furthermore," he said, "you exceed yourself, Prime Minister. Certainly, it is *my* government which you direct, not your own. In spite of the considerable constitutional changes you have advanced, I would remind you that you serve at the monarch's behest. When you sit in your cabinet meetings, it is the King you represent. In fact, Mr. Waring, you are my Prime Minister, and hold your office at my pleasure. Therefore, I will meddle with *my* government to my heart's content."

Waring glared with cold-eyed hatred. "What do you want?" he asked after a moment.

"Since you ask, I'll tell you," James replied. "I want to discuss with you, weekly, your programs, policies, and progress on social reforms which I mean to propose. I want to remain apprised of the legislation you intend to introduce, and which I will be asked to pass into law beneath my signature and seal. I want to know of all ministerial appointments, resignations, and reshuffles *before* they happen. In short, I want to know precisely how my government is functioning in all its many parts."

"Finished?" Waring sneered. "I will tell you what *I* want, shall I?" His voice was tight and thick with loathing. "I want to see you exposed for the scheming little turd you are. I want to see you, and all the clapped-out aristocrats like you, consigned to a well-deserved oblivion, and your self-serving system of inherited privilege eradicated forever. In short, I want to see you, and everything you stand for, destroyed utterly and completely."

James eyed his visitor dispassionately—resisting the powerful urge to smack Waring's smug face with his fist. "Inherited privilege, did you say? Since you raise the issue, let us see what I have inherited, shall we?"

"Must we?" Animosity streamed from Waring like a volatile vapor.

Ignoring the gibe, James said, "On his succession a king in an earlier time would have become the head of the Church of England, but not anymore. Under the Acts of Dissolution, the first referendum not only separated the Church from the State but from the monarchy as well, so I inherit nothing of ecclesiastical authority.

"The second referendum dissolved the Commonwealth, thereby removing the monarch as titular head of Britain's former colonies and protectorates. In short, I do not even get my picture on so much as a two-penny stamp. The third referendum dissolved the House of Lords, and revoked all hereditary titles, replacing them with a life-peerage system which will ensure that no one beyond the present generation passes on the legacy of nobility."

Waring listened to the account of his multipart scheme to dismantle and abolish the monarchy as if mentally ticking off items on a checklist to see if James left out anything.

"Referendum number four licensed the government appropriation of all royal lands, nationalized the royal residences, and extended punitive back-tax liability to the royal family. The royal art collections, libraries, and furnishings of the stately homes and palaces have been nationalized and all items of value placed in trust for the British people."

"And not before time, too," Waring said. "It should have been done long ago, but no one had the guts to do it."

"As sovereign of Britain," James continued, "I inherited no residences, no art collections, no priceless treasures of any description, no limousines, no cars or carriages, no horses, no royal yacht. I have no royal retinue—no chamberlains, no equerries, stewards, dressers, yeomen, footmen, coachmen, pages, gentlemen-at-arms, or lords-in-waiting. I have received nothing from the public purse, or at the public's expense.

"In fact, if you care to look around you, Mr. Waring, you will see the total of my inheritance. I have this house, this estate, and that is all. After the death duties have been paid, it is doubtful I shall even have this. In the meantime, I pay for the upkeep of the house and staff myself. There is no civil list, and no British taxpayer has been asked to stump up a penny for me. I am not complaining—indeed, I prefer it this way. I don't think anyone should be owned by his possessions, Mr. Waring, not even monarchs.

"As for privilege—well, let us say I had the privilege of attending the woefully underfunded local comprehensive school; nevertheless, I had the privilege of encountering some dedicated and overworked teachers and was fortunate to go on to university at Dundee—not Oxford or Cambridge. After graduation, I had the privilege of serving my country in the armed forces—where I was further accorded the privilege of two tours of duty in Afghanistan, one in Kazakhstan, and one in the Sudan. For the past several years I have been privileged to scrape a living as foreman of this estate. In a very good year, I might realistically hope to clear sixteen thousand pounds, out of which I could expect to pay five thousand or so in taxes of various sorts. While becoming King has multiplied my expenses astronomically, it has not increased my income appreciably.

"So now, I ask you, Mr. Waring: which part of my upbringing speaks of privilege to you?"

The Prime Minister stared dully ahead, but offered no reply.

"Put another way, Mr. Waring," James said, "if my life is in any way an example of the inherited privilege you hope to stamp out, then God help us all.

"If, on the other hand, you are simply mouthing emotionally charged phrases designed to elicit a knee-jerk response in the voting public regardless of any actuality, veracity, or meaning, then you are a liar and a hypocrite in thrall to the politics of envy."

Waring, smiling the thin, vicious smile of an assassin, drew himself up to answer the challenge. "Say what you like, Your Highness." The words were a curse in his mouth. "In six weeks the nation votes on the final referendum, and then you—and everything you stand for—will be history." He rose quickly, and nodded to his entourage to prepare his exit. "Now, if you will excuse me, I have put up with this ludicrous distraction long enough."

"Yet you will put up with it a little longer, I think," James stated firmly. "Sit down, Mr. Waring. We are not finished here."

Waring sat down again, hands on knees, looking like a fugitive ready to bolt at the first sign of trouble. "What is the point?" he demanded. "Why are you doing this?"

"You astonish me, Prime Minister," James answered. "Twice I have stood before the nation and explained the reasons for my actions. Perhaps you missed my televised speeches, or perhaps you were not paying attention." Waring glowered at the King with dull hatred in his eyes. "Let me put it to you as simply as I can: I intend to see the monarchy of this nation restored. I intend to make Britain great again, and I intend to do so with your help, or without it."

"Was there anything else?" Waring said, his voice dripping scorn.

"It doesn't have to be like this, you know," James told him. "We could put aside our differences and work together. We might even come to like one another—who knows? At the very least, it would be better for Britain." James guessed what he would say, but he had to make the offer. "How about it, Mr. Waring?" he asked, extending his hand towards the Prime Minister. "Peace?"

"In six weeks this little game of yours will be over, finished forever," Waring said. He regarded the offered hand, but made no move to take it. "Enjoy your reign, Your Majesty."

"Good-bye, Prime Minister. I look forward to continuing our discussion next week." Turning to Cal, who had entered and was standing with his back to the door, he said, "Calum, please show these gentlemen out."

The Prime Minister turned and stalked from the room without looking back. The photographers and TV crews were waiting as he emerged from the castle. Under a hail of shouted questions, he dived into the back of his waiting car; as soon as the security men gave the ready sign, the three black sedans drove away.

When they had gone, everyone decamped to the second-floor conference room. "Well? What do you think?" James asked as they settled in for their debriefing. "Any observations?"

"I didn't hear all of it, of course," replied Cal. "But from what little I *did* hear, I think it safe to say you're off his Christmas card list."

"The hate," said Embries, shaking his head. "I expected

him to be difficult, but he didn't even make an effort to disguise it."

"It is well known in Whitehall," Gavin replied, "that our Prime Minister is a man whose life begins and ends with power—its accumulation and preservation. No wife or family, and few real friends, if any. He has devoted every aspect of his existence to obtaining the highest political office. Long ago, he set his sights on becoming the first president of the British republic, and the prize is almost in his grasp. You stand in his way and he hates you for it."

"Waring? The first president of Britain?" Cal wondered. "Bloody marvelous."

"Waring's obsession fuels his attempt to eradicate the monarchy," Embries said pointedly. "Once the old system is out of the way, there's nothing to stop him. He'll go down in history as the greatest reformer since Oliver Cromwell—or so he thinks."

"It's true," Gavin agreed. "The final referendum is his ticket to immortality. The British presidency was a common topic of lunchtime debate among freshman civil servants—whether the American form of presidency was the best system, or whether we should adopt the European model. We got into some heated arguments over executive accountability."

"Do tell," remarked Cal. "And here was I thinking civil servants were all dull as ditchwater."

After a lengthy analysis of the meeting, they went down for some of Priddy's famous fish pie, then spent the rest of the evening watching the coverage of the PM's visit on the various news broadcasts. Gavin, James noticed, grew increasingly reflective as the night wore on. Seeing the PM on TV saying over and over again how this meaningless charade was just the sort of nonsense the referendum would bring to an end had, James suspected, begun to have an adverse effect on the former civil servant.

At one point, he looked so forlorn, James said, "Cheer up, Gavin. We knew the job was dangerous when we took it."

"Sure," he said, forcing a smile. "I know." Then, unable to

sustain even that much enthusiasm, his face fell. "Waring is right: it's less than six weeks to the referendum."

"You know what they say: six weeks is a lifetime in politics," James told him. "I'm not dead yet."

# ✳

# Twenty-nine

"**I**f I didn't know better," said Dennis Arnold, "I'd say the man was a ghost."

"You couldn't find anything?" asked Waring, pulling the coffee cup away from his lips. "Hell, Dennis, you've been working on this for the better part of a week. What's going on?"

"Don't get excited," the Devolution Chairman said, sliding into a chair beside the Prime Minister's desk. "I didn't say we haven't found anything." He opened the folder in his lap.

"Well, then?"

"It's just that there's nothing much to it," Arnold replied. "And what there is appears very insubstantial." He withdrew a photograph from the file and passed it to the Prime Minister.

Waring picked it up. "That's him. That's the man I saw."

"When would you say that photograph was taken?"

"How the hell should I know?" Waring shrugged. "Any time in the last year or so, I guess. What difference does it make?"

"Not much," replied Dennis Arnold. "But what if I told you that picture was taken in 1978?" He withdrew another photograph and placed it on the desk. "This one was taken by one of our agents on the grounds at Blair Morven a few days ago."

"My God!" remarked Waring. Snatching up the picture, he placed the two photos side by side. "He hasn't aged a day." Holding up the first photo, he asked, "Where did you get this?"

"It was taken at a departmental dinner given in his honor," Arnold informed him, "the day he retired."

"Retired? From what?"

"The Scottish Office, apparently. Something to do with the registry department—although that's largely hearsay. I haven't been able to trace him back any further."

"If he worked for the Government, there's a record."

"Don't be too sure. The departmental branch he worked for was phased out in the late eighties, and the employment records were taken over by another agency and subsequently destroyed."

"Convenient."

"Yeah, but it doesn't end there," declared Arnold. "On a hunch, I mentioned Embries' name to some of the elder Whitehall mandarins, and one of them came up with a lead. He said to check out St. James's Palace, as he remembered someone of that name once had an office there."

"And?" asked Waring, becoming absorbed in spite of himself.

"Bingo!" answered Arnold, allowing himself a satisfied smile. "It turns out that someone named Embries has been acting as a consultant for various organs of State for as long as anyone can remember—undertaking special projects for task forces, quangos, government focus groups, that sort of thing. Part of the arrangement was the use of an office *in perpetuity*."

"You mean he's on the payroll? He's one of ours?"

"Not exactly. He isn't on the payroll, because he doesn't get paid. It's strictly service in exchange for the office and parking privileges, and so on."

"Jesus."

"I know. That used to be standard practice, apparently. Who knew the guy would live so long?"

"You're telling me that for the last thirty-odd years this Embries has been poking around inside the corridors of government and nobody knew it?" Waring shook his head. "Unbelievable."

Arnold looked down into his file and pulled out a sheet of mostly blank paper. "Here's what I was able to find out."

"Name and national insurance number—that's it?"

"That's it. And the national insurance trail is cold, too. According to their records, he is missing, presumed dead. All they have is a seventy-five-year-old address in Wales somewhere, and no indication that he ever collected a penny in benefit."

"It's a shambles, Dennis," said Waring, tossing the paper onto the meager pile. "Even the name isn't complete: M. Embries? What's the 'M' stand for?"

"Your guess is as good as mine."

"My God," sighed Waring. "Nobody knows who he is or what he does, and he's been around since Moses."

"Actually," Arnold pointed out, "plenty of people know him—that is, know *of* him. They just don't know much *about* him. He sort of comes and goes as he pleases, and no one's the wiser."

"A bloody ghost."

"Exactly."

"What about this office at St. James's Palace?"

"I went over and checked it out. But there's nothing there."

"No office, you mean?"

"Oh, I found it. No difficulty there. Like I said, plenty of people seem to know about him. The office itself wasn't much—a single room and an alcove; little more than a broom closet. There wasn't even a phone—hence, no phone records. The place was empty. Apparently, everything was cleared out as of ten days ago. According to the building supervisor, Embries handed in his keys, and the space is soon to be taken over by a copying machine."

Waring stared at his aide in frustrated wonder. What was he dealing with here?

"There are one or two other scraps of information." The

Chairman of the Special Committee for Royal Devolution tossed the file folder onto the desk. "But that's it, mostly."

Waring picked up the folder. "You said he retired from the registry office in 1978. What was he doing before that?"

"Before that is anybody's guess. The name pops up a few times in various computer files—it's distinctive, but not unusual, especially in Wales. We can't tell if it's the same person or not. Beyond that, we haven't been able to turn up anything substantial."

"Maybe you're just not trying hard enough, Dennis," said the Prime Minister, growing irritated by the lack of information.

"You're welcome to let someone else have a go," Arnold replied. "Be my guest. Just don't forget that an awful lot of records were lost when files were transferred to computer. Rather than waste taxpayers' money transcribing every last scrap of paper, the government at the time simply tossed out anything that wasn't absolutely vital to the continuity of service or national security."

"So that's that," said Waring. "Dead end."

"Afraid so." Arnold rose. "Then again, maybe it doesn't matter who he is or where he comes from. I mean, we could spend all our time and energy trying to discover his pedigree, or we could just accept that he's on the scene and deal with it. At the end of the day, what difference does it make? You said you met this fellow, talked to him. He's one of the King's advisors, right?"

"That's what they told me."

"Then he should be pretty easy to get a hold of—if someone really wanted to, that is." He hesitated, then added, "You know, if push came to shove."

"It just might come to that," Waring mused. "Someone like Stuart doesn't just appear out of nowhere. There's a machine behind him, a force driving him. From where I sit, this Embries chap is the one calling the shots. If we can get to him, our worries may be over."

"Then I don't think we really have anything to worry about, do you?"

Waring leaned back in his chair, regarding his friend; he

kept few secrets from Dennis Arnold. "If you put it that way, I guess not. Politics can be a rough business. One day soon he may wish he'd never come out of retirement."

"The referendum clock is ticking," James announced. "We should get out and do something."

"What do you want to do?" asked Cal. "Campaign for king?"

"Would that be such a bad idea?" James challenged. They were sitting together in the conference room in what was quickly becoming a daily ritual—the morning staff meeting. Nearly a week had gone by since his meeting with the Prime Minister; there had been no change in the state of play where Downing Street was concerned, and he was growing impatient.

Also, Jenny was taking an awfully long time to think about his proposal. He'd called her twice and sent flowers—with a card asking her to forgive him and let him make up for lost time—but word came back that she had gone to Wales to think things over. James felt this was a bad sign, and uncertainty, along with enforced inactivity, was making him anxious.

"You want to be seen doing something kingly," observed Embries. "Well and good. I agree, it would be wise to let people see what manner of king they will be asked to support."

"Slaying dragons, rescuing damsels, things like that?" remarked Cal. "What's a king supposed to do these days?"

"Maybe Waring and his lot are right," conceded James. "Maybe the country doesn't need a monarch anymore."

"Never say it," Embries replied sharply. "Never think it."

Addressing the others gathered around the table, he said, "If anyone here doubts the seriousness of our enterprise, or the dire necessity which makes the survival of the crown an absolute imperative, then be gone." His eyes shifted towards Cal as he said this last.

"Sorry," muttered Cal. Feeling the need to redeem himself, he said, "What about making a donation to a charity? Christmas is coming. 'Tis the season for giving. Make a speech, and get your picture in all the papers."

"How about reviving the Christmas Day address?" said Rhys.

"That's it!" Cal seconded the idea at once. "You'd get a lot of mileage out of something like that."

"People still remember the Queen's Christmas speech," Rhys continued. "It was a big deal back when I was a kid. The whole country stopped to listen to it." He glanced around the table, gauging support for the notion.

"It's true," Gavin agreed. "My family always did. Something like that would make it seem like old times."

"A king's Christmas speech—I don't know . . ."

"How about an interview instead?" Shona suggested. "We could get one of the big guns in here for a cozy fireside chat: Christmas Day with the King. Jonathan Trent would jump at the chance to do it. You haven't given a real interview since your declaration. Maybe it's time you did."

"A speech is all very well," said Embries. "It may even prove worthwhile. Still, no matter how well it is received, it will not answer the fundamental question of your kingship."

"And that is?"

"What does it all mean? If you are to win the hearts and minds of the people, you must decide the nature of your kingship. What is your reign to be *about*?" At James' expectant glance, he said, "I cannot do it for you. No one can. You must discover it within yourself. Only when you know what your role is can you count on anyone else to understand, much less to follow."

James frowned. "I'm not sure *I* understand."

"A wise man once told me, 'It is difficult for people to follow a dream,' " Embries explained, " 'but they will follow a *man* with a dream.' Think about it.' "

A thoughtful silence descended over the group for a moment, broken by Cal, who wanted to know, "What about the speech?"

James reluctantly gave his assent, and Shona began making phone calls. By the time negotiations were completed, James had agreed to an hour-long interview with Jonathan Trent—at Blair Morven—on Christmas Day.

No one, but no one, had any interest in making it easy for

James. For a start, the BBC refused to establish subject parameters, nor would they let him see the questions ahead of time. Instead, they insisted that Trent—a professional, highly regarded, award-winning journalist—would conduct himself with all the tact and respect appropriate to the occasion. End of discussion.

The machinery of presaged failure ground into operation as soon as the terms of the interview were agreed. Once notified of the event, the newspapers began running features on what they called—for reasons known only to themselves—the "Christmas Confession," while their resident pundits began guessing, and then second-guessing, what the King would say. Several daily papers proposed lists of topics he might wish to include, such as the location of the Holy Grail or whether he might reinstate the Round Table. One tabloid ran a competition in which readers were asked to supply a question for Jonathan Trent to ask James. The winner would, apparently, have his or her question included in Trent's interview.

James couldn't decide which he found more disagreeable—the inundating cascade of calls from aggressive, impudent journalists which Shona was forced to take or the not-so-hidden expectation in the press that he would be shown a fool and a failure. The easy assumption was that lightning would not, could not, strike twice.

The media, James decided, was a very cynical beast.

# Part IV

# ✳

# Thirty

"Are you sure you want to be doin' this, miss?" asked George Kernan, not for the first time since leaving Penzance harbor.

The young woman rose from arranging her equipment, turned, and faced the ship's skipper. "Asked and answered, Mr. Kernan. For the third time: yes, I know what I am doing." Her green eyes, almost turquoise against the deep blue of her new overalls, skewered him with angry intensity. "The sea is calm; the weather fine. Don't tell me there is a problem with the boat, or I shall become quite cross."

"No," George hastened to assure her, "she's in first-class condition, is *Godolphin Girl*. You won't find a better boat this side of Falmouth."

"Then why do you keep pestering me with your ridiculous concerns?"

"It's dangerous, miss, is all. Now, I know we agreed, but I thought you was only—"

"Dangerous!" She spat the word with a force that made the seaman wince. "For the amount of money I'm paying you, Captain Kernan, you can well afford to keep your qualms to yourself, don't you think?"

Kernan had faced difficult charters before; he drew himself up and gave it one last try. "But diving alone, miss—

that's the crux. We'd got no idea that you was attempting anything like that. We thought you only wanted to see the commotion like."

"But I most certainly *do* wish to see the commotion. I wish to see it close up, Mr. Kernan. As for diving alone, if the site has become as busy as you say, then I shall hardly be alone, shall I? In any case, I take sole and entire responsibility for myself. Is that clear?"

"Of course, miss."

"Now then, if you and your idiot son will simply do as you are told, there is no reason anyone should get hurt." Her green eyes narrowed. "Do we understand one another?"

"Yes, miss." George swallowed. "I understand."

"Good," she said, dismissing him with an imperious flick of her hand. "I do not expect to be interrupted again. You may inform me when we are within a mile of our destination."

"Very good, miss."

Captain Kernan stood for a moment, watching the belligerent young woman at her preparations. That day on the quayside she had been all sweetness and light, her low, throaty laugh enchanting as he told her how he and his crew had discovered the boiling, sulfurous sea, and recounted tales of various inexplicable doings in those queer waters. Why, she had even made him feel gallant and obliging when he accepted her money for the upcoming charter.

Still, he had tried to dissuade her. "Two thousand pounds is a lot of money, miss—ah—" He fished for a name.

"You're right," she had agreed, counting the bills into his hand. "And you deserve every penny, Captain Kernan. You've been so helpful—agreeing to take me out on short notice—it's the least I can do."

*Well,* thought George, scratching his head ruefully, *there was no 'you deserve every penny' today. Women!* He should have figured something was up when they arrived on the quayside to find her already waiting for them with her knapsack and diving bag. "You're late," she had informed him with a snarl. Throwing a map at him, she had pointed to a red circle drawn on the water north of St. Mary's. "That's where we're going," she had said.

*I should have given her back her money then and there,* he thought. *It's Christmas Day, after all.* He returned to the wheelhouse where his son, Peter, was at the helm.

"Any luck?" asked Peter.

"I tried." George sighed. "She won't have it any other way but that we take her out so she can dive the site."

"She'll get herself killed," Peter replied. "It ain't safe. Did you tell her that?"

"I told her right enough. She's pretty determined." He looked out at the smooth, glassy sea. "It's a good day. It'll probably be all right. Anyway, seems she paid enough for the privilege."

"All the same, if anything happens to her out here," observed Peter, "it'll be our butts in a sling, and two thousand pounds won't seem like so much then. We shoulda refused to leave the harbor."

"She paid in advance," George reminded his son. "What are we supposed to do? You see how she won't hear a word yer sayin'."

"Here, take the wheel," said Peter, moving around his father. "I'm going to talk to her."

His father grabbed him by the arm. " 'T'won't do no good, son. Leave her be. Best thing we can do now is pray she don't get into trouble and we can be home and dry for dinner." Peter, unconvinced, reached for the door. "I mean it, boy," his father said, gripping him tighter. "I done what I could. Now just leave her be. It's her skin."

Accepting his father's caution at last, Peter returned to the helm. "I don't like it," he muttered, casting a glance through the window behind him to the aft deck where their strange, auburn-haired passenger had an expensive wet suit arrayed. "Diving all alone an' on a holy day an' all. It ain't right. Look at her. She ain't no oceanographer, if you ask me. We should never have taken the money."

"Mark me, it won't happen again," his father vowed, shaking his head slowly.

The sturdy little boat sped easily towards its destination— a point twelve miles off the southernmost tip of the Cornish coast. They had set off early—at their passenger's request—

and now they knew the reason why: she intended to spend the short winter day underwater.

The unusual nature of the charter had initially failed to arouse their suspicions, for the simple reason that, because of the curious goings-on around the Scilly Isles, the whole coast had been in something of a mild uproar from St. Austell to Land's End. Nearly every seaworthy boat had been approached for lucrative charter services since that night when the eruptions first began—mostly by geologists, marine biologists, and other sorts of sea scientists, although there were a fair number of adventurers and well-heeled tourists as well. *Godolphin Girl*'s uncomplaining skipper had taken his share of sight-seers out to watch the queer, stinking bubbles erupting from the seabed, too; and most of the boat owners he knew were eagerly augmenting their meager winter incomes ferrying thrill seekers back and forth to the mysteriously boiling sea.

Although the initial flash of media interest in the phenomenon had largely faded, the sulfurous belches continued unabated. Some sailors maintained they were even increasing in frequency, size, and duration. George found it difficult to say whether this was true or not, despite assurances from several long-time seamen that it was. What is more, Germoe and some of the other sailors who had taken a sudden and intense interest in things scientific—seeing that oceanographers seemed to have very deep, grant-funded pockets—maintained that it could be scientifically demonstrated that the little clutch of islands constituting the Scilly Isles was actually rising, albeit very slowly.

Life at Penzance harbor, as elsewhere along the coast, had definitely become more interesting—especially following the *Sun* newspaper's feature article of a week or so ago. George had saved the front-page headline which read LLYONESSE RISES AGAIN!

As proof of the headline's somewhat exaggerated claim, the story included a none-too-convincing photo of some boats in the harbor at Hugh Town, and William Taylor, the harbormaster, pointing to a scum line on the seawall indicating the drop in the water level. The scant scientific evi-

dence was little more persuasive, but did support the is-
landers' contention that their homes were gaining altitude at
the rate of a centimeter or two a day. Citing the almost continual tremors accompanying the ascendance, geologic experts warned that a quake of major destructive proportions
might be imminent. Urgent plans, the paper said, were being
made to evacuate the islands' three thousand inhabitants as
soon as possible.

George knew a good many of the islands' boatmen, and
none of them had heard a single word about any urgent plans
to evacuate—which just went to show that a body could not
believe everything he read in the papers.

"There's *Saint Keverne*," announced Peter after a while,
"half a mile off the port bow."

The captain turned to where his son was pointing. The site
was relatively deserted—there were only two other boats
that he could see; two days ago there had been at least
twenty. "An' who's that out beyond her?"

"Don't know," answered his son, taking up the binoculars
with one hand and raising them to his eyes. "Could be
*Trafalgar*," he decided.

"I thought Macky said he was going up Falmouth for an
engine bearing."

"Maybe it's someone else then." Peter jerked his thumb
over his shoulder. "You'd better tell our tourist lady to start
getting ready. We'll be on zone soon."

George left the wheelhouse, shaking his head. "On zone"
was one of the many terms his son had picked up from the
scientists; he didn't use such words himself, and he was a little surprised that his son—and most of the rest of the Penzance population—seemed to adopt the jargon so easily.

" 'Scuse me, miss," he said, affably enough, considering
his brusque dismissal earlier. "We're coming up to the site.
Do you need any help with your gear?"

"When I require something from you, I will ask for it," the
young woman informed him. With that, she unzipped her
blue overall and stepped out of it, revealing a dazzling figure in a brilliant red one-piece swimming suit. Handing the
captain the overall, she sat down on the bait box and began

drawing on the lower half of a brand-new, insulated wet suit of dolphin gray.

She was suited and zipped in moments—donning her headpiece, strapping on her small, neat doughnut-shaped air cylinder, and slipping into flippers of garish green fluorescent plastic. As the boat's engine slowed and began juddering in neutral, Peter called, "This is where you wanted to be, miss."

She stepped to the rail, tested the mouthpiece, and then said, "Put out the buoy, Mr. Kernan."

The skipper did as he was told, and threw out the bright orange diving marker and flag. "You sure you got enough air in that thing, miss?" he asked, eyeing the newfangled apparatus skeptically.

"Plenty," replied the woman, tying a bag of nylon netting to her diving belt. From what the captain could see, the bag contained a few small bits of underwater gear.

She turned and sat down on the rail, her flippered feet splayed out in front of her. She drew on a pair of diving gloves. Next, she spat into the mask, rinsed it out, and drew it over her face with both hands. Then, adjusting the mouthpiece, she leaned back, tipping herself effortlessly into the sea.

Once beneath the smooth surface of the water, Moira rolled over and, with a fluorescent flutter of her acid-green flippers, swam gracefully away from the boat. Free of the annoying fishermen and their stinking boat, the keen abhorrence she felt for the human species began to dissipate in the cold, silent waters. Owing to a mild autumn, the winter water off the coast was clear as glass, allowing her a perfect view of the undulating landmass as it rose from the ice-blue depths far below.

Somewhere down there, undisturbed for centuries, lay a prize worth all the world. Only two people alive knew its existence. Embries, that fatuous meddler, was the other one, and he did not know where to begin the search. But she knew, and this was her advantage.

Three times she had faced the self-righteous old fool, and three times he had escaped the fate he so richly deserved.

This time, however, she would not fail, because this time she would not strike at him until the Lia Fail was in her grasp. Meanwhile, she would content herself with making Embries suffer by tormenting his precious puppet of a king. She would enjoy that almost as much as destroying the old fusspot himself.

Directly ahead, she could see the leading ridge of an upward-jutting plateau—a flat expanse, tilted like a table on wildly uneven legs. One glimpse of that distinctive shape rising from the sea's dark heart and her own heart beat a little faster in recognition. "Llyonesse" . . . the word fairly resonated in her soul . . . *home*.

It was this area that had been causing the most excitement in the oceanographic community. The water here was shallower than anywhere else between Land's End and the Scilly Isles, allowing scientists a reliable means of measuring the daily alteration in the depth of the seabed.

The region was well known in Cornish folklore. Legend had it that bells were sometimes heard beneath the waves; in more superstitious times, the sound was widely believed to presage violent storms or to herald the loss of a ship. There were tales of phantom lights luring the unwary to watery graves and men who were dragged to their deaths in the arms of beautiful maidens. Stories abounded of fishermen glimpsing fair cities under the billows: high walls, towers, paved roads, bridges, and splendid palaces.

Although no one could ever manage to locate these many-towered palaces once they had been seen, the tales nevertheless gained credence because, in times past, fisherfolk were known to have brought up many curious objects in their nets: small jars and shards of Greek-style amphorae, bits of shaped stone incised with odd markings, beads of black glass and pink coral, metal ingots shaped like twigs melted into clumps.

It was not melted ingots or amphorae which thrilled the marine scientists now, however; it was that the seabed did appear to be rising at a slow but significant rate. Should the trend continue, they estimated, the leading edge of the plateau would be high and dry in a little over six weeks.

Geologically speaking, upheavals and inundations off the Cornish coast were so commonplace as to hardly rate a mention. In fact, the whole southern half of the British mainland had been in and out of the sea several times in the ancient past. The famous white cliffs of Dover may tower three hundred feet above the waves at the moment, but schools of fish once swam over those same chalk cliffs, and doubtless would again.

All the same, the appearance of a new landmass in British waters had not happened in recorded history; thus, the scientific boffins were understandably excited. They were trying by all possible means to keep their excitement to themselves, however. Already the zone was getting too crowded with tourists; the British Oceanographic Trust did not need dozens of international research teams on site as well. So, for the time being, they were keeping their findings secret, allowing the sight-seers to content themselves watching the gaseous bubbles which erupted at unexpected intervals in various places around the area. Meanwhile, they were accumulating data and building a profile of the entire underwater region.

Moira's own interests could not have been further from surveying or bubble spotting. For her, the resurgence of Llyonesse meant her long vigil was coming to an end. Soon she would possess again the power that had once made her name a byword for fear in five languages. When she took up that power, she would resume the name. Until then, it must sleep a little longer among the legends of an older time.

She gained the ridge, and continued on over the plateau, swimming with smooth, rhythmic strokes of her long legs. The upland rising beneath her appeared an ordinary example of the typical sea floor: a murky expanse of muddy sand supporting scattered bits of oceanic vegetation. Here and there, rocky outcrops broke the green-gray monotony, providing shelter for the fish and interest for the searching eye.

One such outcropping appealed to Moira more than the others, and it was to this one that she was instantly drawn. She swam down towards it, descending further into the silent blue-green half light. The rocks in this particular grouping were oddly uniform in size and shape and, on closer inspection, did seem to be slightly out of place with their aquatic surroundings. They were large—boulder sized—and roughly cubic, the edges blunted but still traceable, like great, shattered building blocks.

Reaching the stones, Moira swam around and over the heap, looking at the shapes; she put out her hands and touched the pockmarked surfaces of the nearest blocks. Rough and pitted though they were, the stones stirred her in unanticipated ways.

Resuming her search, she swam in a wide circle around the heap of stone, examining the seabed. On her second pass, she found what she was looking for: a slight, yet still identifiable, wrinkle in the mud of the seafloor. Little more than a pucker rising a few centimeters from the muck, it would not have been noticed by anyone who did not know it was there.

Once seen, however, the discoverer would have been struck by the unusually straight line of the thing. At this point, the casual explorer would have concluded that he had happened upon a man-made feature of some kind and, indeed, it looked more than anything like a cable, or pipeline, had been laid down; silt and mire had covered it in the intervening years, reducing it to a mere bump on the ocean floor.

However, had they followed the line of the supposed cable, as Moira did, the curious diver would have learned that it ran unswervingly east to west and that it gradually grew larger. As it grew—widening and thickening—the straight line became less coherent. Gaps appeared and blocky protrusions jutted up at angles.

Moira pursued the increasingly rough line across the plane of the tilting plateau, following its descent into deeper water until . . . all at once, the line ended in a cairnlike heap of jumbled stone. Directly ahead, she could see the darker blue of the void where the landmass shelved away as if carved off by the blow of an axe.

Her heart writhed in frustration. So close, so very close . . . but not yet.

She swam nearer and looked at the sloping edge of the plateau disappearing down and down into the inky blue darkness. She would have to wait until the uneasy seabed lifted the island higher before she could get her hands on the prize. *Patience,* she told herself. *You have waited so long already; you can wait a little while longer. What is time to you?*

Still, she could not bear to go back without at least touching one of the stones, making contact with the home she had lost so long ago. Glancing at her diving watch, she noted the time remaining on her air tank, and dove towards the heap.

She reached the top of the mound, thrilled by the uniform size and shape of the massive stones. Looking back the way she had come, she followed the straight and unbroken line. From her vantage point, it was clear what that line represented: the remnant of an enormous wall. And the mound of tumbled stone had once been a high tower on a corner of that wall.

An image of that wall and tower came into her mind's eye, and she saw it as it once had been. The wall was not high, but it was broad and wider at the bottom than the top so that the wall face slanted inward as it rose. The breastwork at the top was a single solid rim of stone; there were no crenellations, only pyramidlike projections, roughly man-sized, at regular intervals along the top.

In all, there had been five towers—one at each of the four corners and one over the wide, iron-clad timber gate at the entrance. The towers were taller than the walls, rising above the squat solidity of the ramparts like long, tapering fingers. Slender windows, twelve in all, pierced each tower near the sharp-peaked roof, allowing light into the round upper rooms any time of the day.

Moving carefully over the cluttered heap of stone, Moira began searching among the individual blocks. She found a place where several larger stones had fallen together in such a way as to form a shallow cave. After first trying her weight against the massive blocks, she reached into the nylon bag at her belt, removed a small diving torch, and switched it on. She shined the torch into the hollow to make sure there were no nasty surprises inside, and then went in.

The floor of this hollow cavity was littered with broken stone. Holding the torch with one hand, she began turning the smaller pieces over, examining them and setting them aside. In this way, she dug down into the heap, exposing fresh stone to the light. After shifting a dozen or so broken pieces out of the way, the torch beam fell upon an altogether different shape: long and slender, and flared outward at either end.

She knew, even before the light found it, what she would see: a long serpentine rib, running the length of the fragment—like an artist's representation of water as a stylized series of waves, each crest and trough exactly the same.

Moira stared at the simple design, her heart thudding with the shock of recognition. She reached out a gloved finger to trace the pattern, and saw the fragment restored: it was a piece of stone tracery which had formed the inner frame of one of the tower's twelve windows. She saw this, and into her mind flashed the image of a golden-haired young woman gazing out to sea, her face illumined by the fiery brilliance of the westering sun. High above, the keening cry of seabirds filled the cloudless sky, circling, circling and diving; far below the wave-figured window, the fretful sea, red as blood in the dying light, dashed itself upon the rocks.

There in the underwater cavern, Moira crouched, cradling the fragment of shaped stone to her cold breast, remembering.

She heard again the sound that had filled her with such piercing longing: a young man singing; he was sitting on the cliff top in the flame-colored twilight, singing a song of love to an unknown lover. She held her breath as the shimmering notes of the harp quivered on the air, and Taliesin's matchless voice rose like a graceful and effortless prayer towards the heavens.

Oh, the desire awakened by that voice was more powerful than anything she had ever known. She wanted to possess the object of that yearning, to own it, to worship it. But even as she felt her heart lifted on the first waves of desire, she knew it would forever remain beyond her. It belonged to a world she could not inhabit. Even as she listened, transfixed at her window, the first seeds of envy were sown. In time envy would turn to bitterness, and bitterness to hate. What Moira could not possess, she would destroy.

When at last she stirred, she placed the carved stone fragment into the net bag, secured it, and began her long swim back to the waiting boat.

## ✳

# Thirty-one

It snowed on Christmas Eve, and the press pack, with homes and families of their own to go to, decamped quietly following the evening news so that when James pulled back the curtains in the morning it was to a brilliant field of pure, spotless, glittering white—and not a single journalist in sight.

He enjoyed a leisurely breakfast for a change—tea and toast by the fire in his sitting room, looking out on the snowy hills. He called Jenny to wish her a happy Christmas, but her aunt said she had gone to early chapel with her cousins. Accompanied by Rhys and Embries, he drove into town for the Christmas Day communion service at St. Margaret's; Reverend Orr was in good form, his sermon pithy and mercifully succinct. The congregation, agog at the King's unexpected appearance—even though James had been attending the church for over twenty years—sang all the carols, and enjoyed mulled wine and mince pies with him following the service. Then it was back to the castle for a quick lunch, after which he and Rhys dressed for hiking and took a long walk up into the forest rising behind Blair Morven.

After days indoors, James found the silence amid the snow-covered pines refreshing and the sharp, nipping cold a

293

genuine treat. Cal, Shona, Gavin, and the rest of the castle staff had been given as much of the holiday off as possible. By five o'clock, however, almost everyone had returned, with assorted relatives and sweethearts in tow.

James called them together and handed out a few small gifts, and raised a toast or two with Priddy's eggnog—in anticipation of a sumptuous Christmas supper following the interview, should he live through it, whereupon he had to abandon the festivities to prepare for the ordeal. Embries, Rhys, and Cal departed with him, leaving the rest of the guests to fend for themselves. Lest anyone be tempted to sneak away, Shona had brought a television from her room and set it on a tea trolley so she could wheel out the TV and switch it on for everyone.

The sixteenth century great hall had been given over to the TV crew, where it was decided the interview would take place. While James received a light dusting of make-up in the anteroom next to the hall, Cal followed up on arrangements with the production crew; Rhys, ever watchful, quietly made the security rounds, checking everything twice; and Embries undertook to encourage James. "Just relax and be yourself. Let people get to know you, and you'll be fine," he said.

"I don't know why I let everyone talk me into this. I'd rather wrestle alligators."

"You have nothing to worry about. Jonathan Trent is as scrupulous as they come."

"Why do I find that somewhat less than comforting, I wonder?"

"Don't worry, James," he coaxed. "You can trust him to be fair. I'd be very surprised if he took any cheap shots."

"Great. You'll be surprised, and I'll look like an ass."

"You've done your homework well," Embries assured James. "Your mastery of the details is nothing less than remarkable. We've covered every contingency five times over. You're going to be splendid. Really."

James nodded glumly. A criminal going to the gallows, he felt, had more to be happy about; at least the condemned man didn't have to endure endless postmortem discussions of his performance.

There were people everywhere, clomping through the anteroom and swarming the hall, each intent and busy. No one actually took any notice of James, until—as the seconds ticked down towards the evil hour—a blue-jeaned young woman with a clipboard and a stopwatch approached. With a gesture that almost looked like a curtsey, she said, "Your Royal Highness, five minutes, please." She held out a small, bulbous object with a long pigtail of stiff black wire. "Could we mike you now, sir?"

Once the tiny microphone was duly attached and hidden, the young woman with the clipboard led him away. "I'll take you in now. By the way, I'm Julie. Mind the cables underfoot."

She opened the door and ushered James into the great hall, now awash in brilliant white light. It was a great deal quieter here, the activity less fraught if no less intent. Four men were standing beside a portable sound desk, drinking something pale out of clear plastic cups. James, his mouth suddenly dry and his throat parched, wished he had a shot of whatever they were having.

Julie threaded her way carefully among the lighting trees, aluminum flight cases, and various other bits of electronic gadgetry and onto the cleared space which formed the set. Three large video cameras on wheeled carriages stood at the ready. A small sofa had been plucked from one of the rooms and brought to sit at an angle to the fireplace in which a roaring blaze had been prepared. On a low table before the sofa sat a crystal carafe of water and two crystal goblets; a large, overstuffed armchair faced the sofa.

"Is it going to be this *hot* the whole time?" James asked, taking his place on the sofa. Julie expertly straightened his jacket and tugged his collar into place.

"You'll get used to it, Your Majesty," Julie said, taking up her clipboard and stopwatch from the coffee table. "One minute!" she shouted. The men gathered at the sound desk snapped to attention—one on the desk, the others to the cameras. "Where is Jonathan?"

When no one replied, the production assistant shouted again, "Has anyone seen Jonathan?"

A call went out for Jonathan, and Julie asked the King to test his microphone. She consulted her clipboard and stopwatch once more. "Thirty seconds!" she cried. "Where are you, Jonathan? The whole world is waiting."

"Here's Jonathan!" someone called, and a tall, distinguished man in a dark suit stepped swiftly onto the set. James recognized him at once as the fellow he had seen countless times, sitting behind his desk at BBC studios, reporting the day's events and interviewing guests. Taller than he imagined, a little younger, and better looking, he carried a leather notebook in one hand and his lapel mike in the other.

With practiced efficiency, he clipped the mike to his tie and, smiling warmly, put out his hand. "Your Majesty," he said with a slight bow. "Very pleased to meet you. Allow me to introduce myself. I am Jonathan Trent."

Before James could reply, Julie shouted, "Ten seconds!"

"Quiet now, everyone!" called the director from somewhere near the sound desk. "We're live in five . . . four . . . three. . . ."

The assistant producer, holding two fingers in the air, backed away from the set. She pointed directly at Trent, mouthing the word *"Go!"*

James felt a rush of nervous excitement jolt through him, and they were on the air.

Smiling warmly into camera one, the suave presenter leaned forward casually over his notebook and said, "Good afternoon, this is Jonathan Trent, and we are broadcasting live from Castle Morven near Braemar in Scotland, the home of our nation's new monarch who, for the next sixty minutes, will be allowing us a rare and exclusive insight into his life, his aims, and his hopes for Britain on this festive day."

He paused, arranging his posture in the chair, as if readying himself for serious business. "We hope the next hour will prove stimulating, thought-provoking, and enlightening as we attempt to gain the measure of the individual whom some have termed 'The Man Who Would Be King.' "

Turning to James, he smiled again, saying, "Your Royal

Highness, best wishes and happy Christmas. First of all, let me thank you for graciously allowing us into your home on Christmas Day, and for agreeing to this interview."

"You are most welcome, Jonathan," James replied, fighting the urge to clear his throat. "It is my pleasure."

Trent glanced at his notebook, folded his hands, then looked at the King and said, "One month ago, no one had the slightest inkling Britain would have a new monarch. Yet here we are: your claim to the throne has been recognized and, against all the odds, your reign has begun. How does that make you feel?"

Trent smiled, encouraging James to take the plunge.

"Quite honestly, it has been something of a shock," James told him, trying, in the most unnatural of circumstances, to sound natural and spontaneous. "Unlike virtually every one of my predecessors, I did not grow up in a royal household; I was not raised with any notion, however remote, that I might be king one day. I am the first to admit that if not for a rather singular chain of events, no one would ever have heard of me and, of course, I would not be speaking to you now."

"It reminds me of the old adage, 'Some aspire to greatness, some achieve greatness, and some have greatness thrust upon them.' You have certainly had greatness thrust upon you. But tell me, did you also aspire to greatness?"

"My aspirations have always been very simple," James replied. "To be a good man, a good husband, and a good friend. My father was such a man, and I have always tried to be like him."

Trent swooped. "You mention your father. May we talk about your family for a moment? Even by today's fairly relaxed standards, your early life must have been, shall we say, somewhat confused?"

"Nothing could be further from the truth," James protested mildly. "You are referring to the recent discovery of my true parentage. The man I knew as my father, John Stuart, raised me and loved me as a son, and—"

"Yet," interrupted Trent, "although your mother was legally married to the Marquess of Morven, she was living with John Stuart at the time of your birth—a relationship which was to continue for many years. Isn't this so?"

"Yes, that is true."

"Then if, by your own admission," he continued quickly, "your parents were living an elaborate lie, how can your childhood be considered 'normal' in any sense of the word?"

"Simply because it was," James insisted gently. "You see, my parents loved each other very much, and they loved me. It was out of that love that sacrifices were made which people today may not understand. One of those sacrifices was to give me a solid, normal upbringing in a stable, happy home. In this, they succeeded admirably, and I have always been grateful—all the more, now that I know the truth."

"I see," replied Trent, adopting a tone which implied that he was far from convinced. "Moving on, let us turn to the upbringing you mentioned just now. You grew up here, in a small Scottish town, an uncomplicated rural town, a town that depends almost totally on tourism for its continued survival. It is in many ways as far from cosmopolitan life as possible—very far from the world of politics and government, diplomacy, trade and commerce, and the complex affairs of the great nation-states which make up the world we inhabit today. How, I am wondering, could your upbringing have possibly prepared you for the rôle you are about to play?"

Out of the corner of his eye, James saw Cal standing behind camera two, face ashen, shaking his head in misery. He realized, too late, that it was going to be a hatchet job—blood and butchery transmitted worldwide, the new King of Britain cut down to size by the BBC's most trusted and admired interviewer.

Steeling himself for the onslaught, James looked Trent in the eye, and replied, "Your question appears designed to imply that I somehow lack the proper qualifications to be King of Britain because I did not grow up insulated from life by a cloak of royal privilege."

Trent waved aside the observation. "Not at all," he said genially. "I was merely trying to determine how it is that you see yourself fulfilling a very demanding rôle on the international stage when, by your own admission, you have had no proper training or upbringing?"

"Mr. Trent," James countered, "did *you* know at the age of five, or twenty-five, that we would be having this conversation today?"

James paused so Trent could murmur, "Of course not." Then he continued, "None of us ever knows what life will throw in our path. There is no way to be completely prepared for every possibility. That being the case, it is my belief that people do best in life when given a good, solid base on which to build. So, the question becomes: What makes for the best base, the best foundation?

"Now, then, I would have thought that children raised in stable, safe communities, surrounded by caring and competent adults, and granted the freedom of their environment— not forgetting plenty of fresh air and exercise, and time to think and learn their own hearts, and develop their own particular skills—I would have thought that children raised like this are best equipped to meet the challenges of life in an unpredictable world."

Trent made as if to break in, but James had begun to find his rhythm, and wasn't to be put off his stride.

"Further, I think that the world you speak of, this world of high finance, global trade, international politics—in short, the world of money and power—is only part of a larger reality, and most likely not even the most important part. After all, the various activities and occupations of government, trade, and diplomacy can be mastered by almost anyone who has the least inclination to do so—indeed, we see it happening all the time. Then again, I've always wondered, if the world of money and power is so overwhelmingly important, why are all the stockbrokers and politicians buying up country retreats and moving their families to small, rural communities far away from the heady affairs of the great nation-states on the international stage?

"The point is, give a child a good, solid foundation on which to build—that is, a mind that can think, a heart that can feel, a conscience that knows right from wrong—and there is no limit to what that individual can do in life."

James leaned back, trying to control his breathing. Wrapped up in his argument, he was in danger of hyperventilating. Trent reacted by adopting a patronizing smile, augmented by the slightest shake of his head in dismissal. "You make it sound almost utopian," he said, as if the word were self-evidently damning.

"Perhaps," James allowed, feeling his blood warm to the cut and thrust of argument, "someone deprived of the simple benefits I have described might seek to discount them out of ignorance, envy, or spite. Nevertheless, this great country of ours has worked very hard for a very long time to make precisely these things possible for its citizens. Call it utopian if you like, but there are millions of people who, like myself, were raised in just this way and have moved on to lives as secure, happy, productive citizens."

"All the same," refuted Trent, "these millions of otherwise well-adjusted citizens are not asking anyone to accept them as reigning monarchs."

"I believe it comes down to leadership in the end," James replied. "Leadership, as my old sergeant used to say, is not so much where you come from but where you're going. Character, in other words, not circumstance. As King, I ask no one to accept me by the circumstances of my birth. I ask only to be judged by the quality and integrity of my character."

Jonathan Trent pursed his lips and glanced down at the notebook in his lap. James could not tell whether he had scored any direct hits with that answer, but the adrenaline was flowing now; he could feel the buzz of conflict, and was eager to meet it. *Bring it on, Trent,* he thought. *Show me what you've got.*

"Setting questions of integrity aside for the moment," Trent said, nicely parrying James' attack, "you must read the papers. You must realize that in less than five weeks' time this nation will go to the ballot box in a referendum vote to abolish Britain's monarchy forever. That is to say, in a few weeks you will be out of a job. What are your feelings about this?"

James smiled; this question had been foreseen. "As an

army officer, one of my first assignments was to the British contingent of the UN Peacekeeping Force in Afghanistan, where I led a company of young soldiers just like myself. One night, after patrol, about eight of us were sitting around the fire, talking. Several of the men had reached the end of their tour of duty and were due to head home in a few days' time; they were telling us all the things they were going to do the minute they got back.

"One of these soldiers, a Glaswegian called Gus, announced, 'I'm going to buy my girl an engagement ring and ask her to marry me.' The words were scarcely out of his mouth when there came a whir in the air. Someone shouted, 'Mortar!' and we all hit the dirt. The shell exploded right where we were standing.

"When the smoke cleared there were only three of us left. Five young men were blown to bloody bits, and I found myself lying next to Gus, who had lost his right arm and most of his chest."

Trent regarded James with sympathetic dispassion, his professional cool very much in place; he gave away nothing.

"That night I learned the true nature of existence," James explained. "Life is fragile, and it is short. None of us knows what the next moment will bring—let alone the next five weeks. I could go under a bus tomorrow, and that would be that.

"The point is, I can't say whether I will be King after the referendum. All I know is that I am King now, at this moment. And while I have this moment, I intend to be the very best monarch I can. I intend to reign to the best of my ability—whether that reign is five hours, five weeks, or fifty years."

Trent pressed his lips together and nodded appreciatively. "Clearly, you seem to believe there is a place for a king in a modern democracy. But, truthfully, isn't the monarchy a dead institution—an outmoded throwback to an era best forgotten?"

"I used to think so," James confessed. "Like most people in this country, I heard that opinion expressed so often that I swallowed it without ever thinking about it. But recently I have been forced to come to grips with what sovereignty means—and, more important, what it must mean for our country."

"In other words," Trent broke in, "you have discovered some benefits for yourself in what is a uniquely lucrative and prestigious position."

"That is a glib assumption—which, I might add, the media work very hard to promote for their own purposes," James stated. "The truth is, when one begins to understand it properly, the first thing one realizes is that kingship is very costly."

"Come now," goaded Trent, smiling smugly, "you have to admit the perks aren't so bad. I mean, here you are, plucked from obscurity and presented with a millionaire lifestyle overnight. You're fêted by the nation at the taxpayers' expense, and given the best of everything wherever you go. How can you call any of that costly?"

"Again, you assume too much," James told him. "While it is true I was plucked from obscurity, as you say, I have gained nothing at the taxpayers' expense—not so much as a bus pass, in fact. Nor am I presented with the *best* of everything; wherever I go, I pay my own way. But that is not the cost I had in mind. I was thinking more of the personal cost—the physical, emotional, and spiritual cost, if you will."

"Very well, let's talk about that then," Trent agreed, implying James had somehow fallen into his trap. "For decades, the throne of Britain has been sunk in decadence and moral decay. For decades, a lengthy succession of uninterested, if not dissolute, monarchs have presided over a period in our nation's history in which our international standing has steadily diminished, our social problems have increased, and our country flounders from crisis to crisis without purpose.

"All the while, the party in power has labored to run this country in the guise of His or Her Majesty's Government, subjected to royal oversight, seeking the sovereign's wisdom in dealing with the problems besetting the country. Prime ministers have come and gone, governments likewise; the one constant in the equation is the monarchy—often said to provide a valuable continuity which protects the nation from the violent swings in political trends other countries must endure."

He stared at James as if daring him to disagree, then said, "I would suggest, however, that whatever encouragement, advice, or opinions the monarch has shared with his governmental servants, the nation's problems have not diminished but have, in fact, grown steadily worse. It appears that the much heralded 'continuity' supplied by this insanely conceited institution is, when all is said and done, merely the continuity of British decline.

"The very best that can be said about the modern monarchy is that it is, and has been for a very long time, ineffectual and irrelevant to the difficulties this nation faces in the modern world. As an institution, it is intractable to change, secretive, and self-serving." Trent, in full sail now, delivered his well-prepared salvo. "You may accuse me of glib assumptions, but the royal establishment has consistently provided the nation its worst examples of idle privilege and neglected responsibility. In fact, you could say it is remarkable the nation has put up with the vile, extravagant waste for so long. For generations, the royals have squandered not only the wealth and substance of the nation but also the goodwill of their subjects.

"In short, the monarchy has become a gross and offensive anachronism—a costly fossil of medieval feudalism— which will no longer be supported by a much-deceived and deluded population. Britain demands accountability and competence of its leaders. There is simply no room in a modern democracy for a system based on unmerited privilege and false class distinction."

"Mr. Trent," James replied, "was there a question in that diatribe?"

Not waiting for an answer, James continued, "You have made some serious indictments, and I am sure many viewers will agree with your sentiments. Once, I might have even said such things myself. But your logic is flawed and your conclusions are false."

Trent made no reply, merely inclined his head in an invitation to elaborate.

"You call the monarchy ineffectual," James began, feeling the clarity sharpen. He felt unassailable. Invincible. "You write it off as an irrelevancy—yet, you still wish to hold it to blame for the ills of the nation. Tell me, then, which is it?"

"I'm not sure I follow." Trent's attempt to deflect the blow he sensed coming was misjudged.

"It is perfectly simple," James replied. "If the monarchy is irrelevant, then by definition it can have no real influence on the affairs of the day. It seems to me, you condemn the reigning monarch for his lack of influence, while at the same time refusing to allow him any relevant rôle by which he could conceivably effect meaningful change. Thus, you make the monarchy the cause of the problem, yet deny it any part in the solution."

Trent tried to blunt the counterattack with an objection, but James cut him off.

"I'm not finished," James said. "You contend that the monarch has watched a lengthy succession of prime ministers and governments come and go while the nation's difficulties have worsened. I would like to point out that each successive government has steadily, relentlessly stripped the monarchy of its powers, at the same time removing itself from any sort of meaningful accountability to the sovereign and gathering more authority unto itself.

"If, as you suggest, the nation's troubles have drifted from bad to worse, should not some liability lie with the government ministers—men and women whose *sole responsibility* it is to deal with the nation's problems?

"Yet, of the two parties mentioned, you heap the blame for our problems on those powerless to act—monarchs past and present—while absolving from all guilt those who possess not only the power but also the obligation, duty, responsibility, and wherewithal to heal our land.

"Now, I ask you, Mr. Trent, is this fair? Is it even logical? I mean, you hold to public ridicule the monarch, whose sole approach to matters of state is advisory and ceremonial, and exonerate the Prime Minister and his government. Who, I ask you, is running Britain? Who is in charge? Is it not the democratically elected members of Parliament and the Prime Minister—the very people who, with the entire machinery of government at their command, are uniquely placed to find and offer solutions to the problems besetting the nation?"

James was in full command now; the words seemed to come of themselves. Each singing stroke was effortless and precise. He regarded his adversary across the divide and said, "Let's not relegate the monarchy to the sidelines, deny it any vital part in the ongoing battle, and then fault it for losing the war. Not only is that manifestly unfair, it is willfully prejudiced."

Trent was ruffling the pages of his notebook, hoping to break James' concentration so he could jump in. But James saw the trick for what it was, and swept it aside.

"You say the monarchy is self-serving. Then what, I wonder, do you call a government which is comprehensively seen to be devoting more and more of its vital energies to sabotaging its opponents and getting itself re-elected, rather than finding a way out of the morass of our common plight?

"You say the monarchy is secretive. When, I wonder, was the last time the Prime Minister allowed a camera crew into Number Ten on Christmas Day, or any other day? When did the Government *ever* allow a journalist to report on the proceedings of a cabinet meeting? Is it not also the case that the rivalry and jealousy between the various departments of government have reached such proportions that leaking documents is no longer a cause for scandal, but instead has become a practical and useful means of communicating information which allows the source to undermine opponents while remaining anonymous? What is that, if not self-serving secrecy in action?

"You berate Britain's monarchy for its incompetence, but where, in all fairness, is its sphere of influence to be found? The monarch is everywhere circumscribed by convention, his powers curtailed, his voice silenced. Denied a worthwhile public rôle—and a voice—is it any wonder the monarchy is deemed anachronistic? It seems to me you confuse incompetence on the part of the monarchy with simple indifference on the part of the public.

"Despite the hopelessness of his condition, the monarch must never complain. He must at all times display a humility which can only be described as servile. He must at all times uphold the traditional functions of his position, but he is never allowed a say in the shaping of the country of which he is the titular head. He must at all times provide an impeccable example to the nation, exemplifying all virtues, yet he is never allowed to make the slightest moral demand on those who wield authority in his name. He must at all times receive the opinions of his subjects, but heaven forbid he should express an original view of his own!"

"We seem to have struck a nerve, Your Highness," Trent remarked, smiling weakly. The blood on the carpet was his.

"I have given these things a great deal of thought in the last few weeks," James replied evenly. Having beaten his erstwhile adversary, it was time to begin the reconciliation. "As I say, there was a time, not too long ago, when I would have articulated the same accusations you have made today. Since assuming the crown, however, I have been forced to look at kingship in a completely new way."

"Any conclusions you'd like to share with us?" For the first time since the interview began, Trent appeared genuinely interested in what James might say.

"I think it is true that Britain has been disappointed in the monarchy for a long time. I have been asking myself why. Why have we been so disappointed?

"For, if the King is merely a remnant of a vanished time— a medieval fossil"—James acknowledged Trent's assertion—"who serves no worthwhile function or purpose, a living relic whose usefulness ceased many centuries ago, then why do we still care?"

He allowed the question to hang for a moment. "In my experience, we human beings care only about those things that matter to us, the things we value. And when something or someone we care about lets us down, it is only natural to feel disappointed.

"In thinking about this, I have come to the conclusion that

we are disappointed in our monarchy, because we still care
very much about it. And because we care, we expect something of it. But why? If it is true that the King is only a self-
serving and incompetent figurehead, where does this
expectation of something better arise? It makes no sense—
neither the disappointment nor the expectation make any
sense at all—unless . . ." He leaned towards Trent slightly to
draw him to his side. Out of the corner of his eye, James saw
the camera glide in closer, too.

"*Unless,*" he repeated, lowering his voice slightly, "unless
all the allegations and accusations are a tissue of lies."

"Lies?" wondered Trent, intrigued.

"Damned lies," James confirmed. "Our discouragement,
our dissatisfaction, our disillusionment make no sense unless there is in reality something at work behind the
scenes—a truth, if you will, which has been too long denied."

"And what might that truth be?" asked Trent, now the dutiful straight man.

"The truth is, despite all evidence to the contrary, the
monarchy does matter, the monarchy has a valuable service
to perform for the nation; there are forces at work in the
world which are ordained by God and which people may
thwart, or disregard for a time, but which will not be denied
forever. True sovereignty is just such a force, and when the
monarchy is conjoined in a True King, then Britain will be
exalted once again.

"You see, Mr. Trent, I believe that Britain has always had
a special part to play in the world. For far too long we have
been unable, for one reason or another, to play our part, and
that has been deeply discouraging to us. But today, here and
now on this Christmas Day, we begin to recover our heritage, to resume our rightful place. To do that, we need a
king—a prime minister cannot do it, a president cannot do
it. We need someone who is not only above but also *beyond*
the mundane concerns of party politics, yet who embodies in
his person the best hopes and aspirations of the nation and
its people, someone before whom all the citizens are deemed
equal and equally accountable. In short, we need a monarch.

"Not just any monarch," James hastened to add. "We do not need another Ready Teddy or another smiling, aloof, and ineffectual figurehead. We need a True Sovereign—a king who will sacrifice and serve, and wield power on behalf of his people."

Julie, the assistant producer, moved to the fore; waving her hands for attention, she held up three fingers.

"That is why," James continued, "I am determined that the monarchy of this nation will not be allowed to disappear without a fight. First thing after the New Year's holiday, I am taking my message directly to the people."

Trent appeared delighted to have received this scoop. "A campaign for King, Your Highness?"

"Call it what you will," replied James.

"No doubt we will be hearing more about this in the days to come. Unfortunately, our time is up," said Trent reluctantly, and managed to convey genuine regret in his tone. "We must leave it there for now." He hesitated. "However, I cannot conclude this interview without asking you just one more question."

Julie, waving two fingers, began frantically shaking her head.

Ignoring her, Jonathan Trent shifted his notebook and turned a page. "A personal question, this time, if you don't mind." His glance was almost apologetic.

"Your Royal Highness," he said, his manner that of an amiable intimate, "on the day you declared your kingship, if you will recall, you recited a story which you called the Dream of Taliesin. I don't mind telling you I was moved by that at the time, and I made it my business to discover the source of that quote. Now, the BBC has a tremendous research department, absolutely world-class, but try as we might, we could not discover your source. In fact, our chief researcher insists that speech isn't recorded anywhere. Surely, you didn't make it up. So, I'm wondering, where did you find it?"

James swallowed, thinking fast. He couldn't very well tell the world that he simply *remembered* it, that it had come to him at that precise moment in a vision.

"I learned that from a friend of mine a long time ago," James replied, hoping Trent would not pursue it further. "It has always inspired me. I suppose I thought it appropriate to the occasion, so I used it."

"Also in that speech," remarked Trent, "you mentioned the Kingdom of Summer, and you called it Avalon. As we all know, Avalon is closely linked to King Arthur. What did you intend by invoking that connection?"

"I was speaking from the heart," James answered. "That speech was, in many ways, the inspiration of the moment."

"And yet," insisted Trent, "you spoke so eloquently, so forcefully, for your vision of Britain, I can hardly believe it was merely happenchance." Regarding James frankly, he asked, "Do you see yourself as something of a latter-day King Arthur—returned to lead us into Avalon?"

"Let me explain it this way," James replied slowly, weighing his words carefully. "As someone who has been critical of modern monarchy's failure to live up to its high calling, I have been compelled to find examples of good kingship. I went back to history, you might say, to see if I could discover a sovereign worthy of the name on which to base my kingship. In King Arthur, I found very much what I was looking for."

"A rôle model," remarked Trent. "Is that all King Arthur is to you, a sixth-century rôle model? Surely, there must be more to it than that."

"Never underestimate the power of a positive example, Mr. Trent."

"Some of my more, let us say, romantic media colleagues have suggested that the underwater disturbances around the coast of Cornwall are the fulfillment of an ancient Arthurian prophecy—to do with Llyonesse and so forth. Would you care to comment?"

"I've read those stories, too"—James smiled diffidently—"and some of them are highly entertaining. I suppose you could say I am as intrigued as anyone else. But I'm afraid earthquakes and hurricanes and so on are a little out of my line."

And then, mercifully, the interview was over.

Jonathan Trent closed his notebook and folded his hands. "Your Highness," he said, smiling cordially, "on behalf of the many millions of people all over this great nation who have tuned in to this interview, I thank you for opening your home to us, and for allowing us a fascinating glimpse into your life. Once again, may I wish you a happy Christmas."

Turning to camera one, he said, "To all of our viewing audience, this is Jonathan Trent, at Castle Morven with the King of Britain, saying good night."

He smiled optimistically, and held his smile until Julie, her hand pressed to her earpiece, shouted, "We're clear!"

Trent's shoulders slumped. James felt the tightness in his stomach relax; suddenly he felt as if he'd run ten miles in combat gear.

Tossing aside his notebook, Trent stood and solemnly intoned, "Your Majesty, I am deeply grateful for your willing participation. It has been an honor. As I said a moment ago, your declaration touched me deeply. I wanted very much to believe you; I was on your side—"

"You have a most peculiar way of expressing goodwill," said Cal, stepping forward quickly to join them.

"I apologize if I seemed over the top. Perhaps I felt obliged to present the strongest opposition I could find." Turning to James he said, "The fact is, though, I really was on your side from that moment. I suppose, like most people in this country, I had pretty much given up on the monarchy. The last thing I wanted was for some good-looking, smooth-talking, hooray-Henry aristocrat to come along and bamboozle the nation with a sparkly speech and a lot of cheap razzmatazz."

Trent regarded James as if he might be the long-lost brother he had been searching for all his life. "When the opportunity for this interview came up, I decided it would probably be my one and only chance to put you to the test. I had to know if you were for real."

"I hope he passed," Cal said, stepping forward. He had by no means forgiven Trent for ambushing his friend.

"Let me put it this way: I threw my best punches today, and he came through unscathed. I've interviewed enough politicians, celebrities, and professional con artists of one kind or another to know when I'm being lied to. A fraud would have cracked under the strain."

Shona appeared just then, her plump face glowing with pride. "Well done, Your Majesty," she said.

"Was I okay?" asked James.

"You were brilliant, sir," she answered. "And I'm not the only one who thinks so." Producing a mobile phone, she held it up to her ear and spoke into it, saying, "Yes, I have him now. Here he is."

With that, she handed the phone to James. "Hello?"

The voice on the other end said, "The answer is yes."

"Jenny?"

She laughed. "Of course, Jenny! How many other women have you proposed to lately?"

# ✳

# Thirty-two

"I'll boil the bastard's balls for breakfast!" muttered Thomas Waring. He clicked the remote control ineffectually at the television screen before giving up and throwing the blasted thing at the TV. Reaching for the phone on the nearby stand, he jabbed a button. "Waring here," he barked. "I want Hutch right away."

There was a pause at the other end of the line, and then a woman's voice said, "I am terribly sorry, Prime Minister, but Mr. Hutchens is in New York City for the Christmas holiday." It was Geraldine Joseph, staff secretary, who had obviously drawn the short straw on the holiday rota. "He is not due back in London until late tomorrow evening. Do you wish me to ring him for you?"

Bloody Christmas, thought Waring. In his anger and agitation, he'd overlooked the fact that his staff was off for the day. He glanced at his watch—five hours earlier in New York; they'd just be sitting down to dinner. "No," he grumbled, "don't call him. Just tell me who is in town."

There was another pause, longer this time. "It seems that Mr. Burton is at his constituency residence in Dulwich," answered Geraldine. "Hmm . . . Oh, I see that Mr. Arnold is with his family at Gravesend, and . . . Mrs. Shah is at her estate in Kent." She paused once more, and Waring could hear pages turning. "I'm afraid those are the nearest," she said at last. "All the rest seem to be further afield, Prime Minister."

"Call Dennis Arnold. Tell him I want to see him as soon as he can sneak away." He started to hang up, and added, "Thank you, Gerry, and happy Christmas."

"You're very welcome, Prime Minister. Happy Christmas to you."

He replaced the receiver and walked to the sideboard, and poured a hefty splash of brandy into a crystal snifter. From a new box on the coffee table, he selected a hand-rolled Cuban cigar—his one celebration of the day—and sat down in his armchair. The TV was still going: Claymation reindeer dancing across the screen. Waring stared at the set dully, wondering how much damage this latest bombshell would do.

Taking a sip of his brandy, he considered ringing Shah and Burton as well, but decided there was nothing to be gained by spoiling their celebration. Let them have their holiday; he and Dennis would decide what should be done. Having made that decision, he got up and went in search of a match.

He was halfway through his cigar and onto his second brandy when the duty officer rang to say that Mr. Arnold had arrived.

"You look like hell," said Waring as the devolution mastermind entered the room. "Here, have a brandy." He extended a cut-crystal snifter, which his old friend accepted gratefully. "Didn't take you long."

"I was already on my way when Gerry caught up with me," Dennis Arnold explained. He took a healthy slug of the brandy.

"Sorry to interrupt your festivities," Waring said.

"You didn't," Arnold replied. "It was the fool King who did that. Who the hell does he think he is anyway?"

"If you were already on your way," Waring said, "then you couldn't have seen the end."

"No. I heard him say he was going out on the road to fight for the monarchy, and that's when I left. I got the tail end of it on the car radio. Why—what else did he say?"

"There was some crap about King Arthur, and Trent went all loopy and sentimental. God, it made me sick."

"What?" Arnold tossed back a bolt of brandy. "Our yobo thinks he's King Arthur now?"

"He doesn't say that—but, by God, I wish he would." Waring turned and retrieved the bottle from the sideboard. He felt better knowing he was not the only one upset. "You know, Dennis," he said, refilling the glasses, "that gives me an idea. We might just be able to dig a hole for our Arthurian friend to fall into."

"He's certainly due for a fall," the devolution chairman agreed.

"It goes without saying that anything we discussed would have to remain just between us."

Dennis Arnold peered around the room. "I don't see anyone else here, PM."

Waring waved his aide to a seat on the couch. "The speed with which the media can turn against someone is truly astonishing, wouldn't you agree? Riding high one moment, shot down the next. Shocking when you think about it."

"No one knows that better than I do, Tom. You can't survive in government this long without participating in a few media dogfights. God knows we've had our share."

"It may be that our King's honeymoon with the media is coming to a swift and ignominious end," Waring said. "In fact, I think he might quickly discover what a fickle friend the great British media can be."

"It's a harsh lesson," replied the devolution secretary thoughtfully. "Some people never recover."

Waring recharged the glasses then, and proposed a toast: "To King James," he said. "May his inglorious reign commence."

They raised a glass of Christmas cheer and drank to the ill health of the King, then spent a happy hour dreaming up various dirty tricks. When at last Arnold rose to go, Waring inquired how the Embries investigation was coming along.

"Nothing but dead ends there, I'm afraid," he replied. "We've got a few stones left to look under, but I don't think we'll find anything useful. Still," he smiled suddenly, "maybe all this new media scrutiny will turn up some dirt."

"You know, Dennis, it wouldn't surprise me in the least," Waring agreed.

"I'd better go before they send out the dogs," James said.

"No one knows you're here?" wondered Jenny. "Is that wise?"

He shrugged off her concern. "What could happen to me? Besides, I didn't think you'd want our secret beamed out to the nation for tomorrow's breakfast."

"No," she allowed, "I suppose not. But you should at least tell Cal or someone where you're going."

"I'll be fine," he said, opening the door and stepping out into the cold, dark night. The air was crisp, and heavy with the scent of snow. "Don't come out; it's freezing."

"So keep me warm." Jenny stepped into the circle of brightness beneath the back door light.

James gathered her into his arms and kissed her lightly. "I love you, Jen. I know I should have asked you to marry me years ago, but I'll make it up to you. Our engagement party will be spectacular, I promise."

"So you said." She kissed him again. "But you don't have to do anything extravagant to keep me happy. Are you sure you want to go through with it?"

"The wedding?"

"Announcing the engagement," she corrected. "We could just have a few friends around and pop a cork, or something. Hogmanay is less than a week away."

"I've got a staff now to take care of such details," James said, gathering her close. "Leave everything to me. I want this New Year's to be special. You're going to be a queen, after all."

"Don't remind me."

They kissed again, and the first flakes of snow began falling. Several snowflakes settled on Jenny's hair and eyelashes and clung there, glittering in the light like tiny clusters of diamonds. "I love you," James murmured, holding her close, feeling her warmth against him. "But I do have to go."

"Sleep well, my love," Jennifer whispered, releasing him with a full and passionate kiss. "Something to dream about."

James started for his old blue Land Rover, resisting the strong temptation to scoop her up and carry her off to bed. Opening the vehicle door, he turned back to see that Jenny was watching him from the doorway, silhouetted in the light.

"I'll call you in the morning," he told her. "Now, go inside or you'll freeze."

She didn't say anything, but blew him a kiss in farewell. She was still watching as he drove from the yard.

Next morning, after the King's staff assembled for their daily meeting, James announced his intention to host a slap-up Hogmanay celebration. "I want it to be a New Year's Eve bash to end all bashes—sit-down dinner and entertainment laid on. Spare no expense. I've drawn up a guest list." He slid sheets of paper across the table to Shona and Cal. "I want everyone on the list to get an invitation."

"Mind if we invite a wee friend or two as well?" asked Cal.

"Got someone special in mind?"

"If you remember," replied Cal, "I invited Izzy and her family up to the estate to go riding." At James' blank look, he said, "Isobel Rothes, remember?"

"Isobel, sure. Why not? Let's cast the net wide," said James. "The more the merrier."

"Would I be right in thinking you had an ulterior motive for hosting this party?" asked Embries. He held his head to one side, regarding James shrewdly.

"All will be revealed on the night," James told him. Eager to end the scrutiny, he rose abruptly. "Right! Everyone get busy. We've got a party to plan."

James, like many Scots, considered Hogmanay the great event of the calendar, and the only fitting and proper way to usher in the New Year. Throwing open Castle Morven for a royal gala celebration—the first since Scotland reclaimed the throne—would, he thought, provide the perfect opportunity for the future royal couple to announce their engagement.

Cal and Gavin undertook the cleaning and furnishing of the great hall; Shona spent hours closeted with Priddy in the cook's pantry, poring over the old Duke's favorite recipes and drawing up a menu. Rhys, along with Mr. Baxter and anyone else who happened along, was press-ganged onto foraging and decorating crews.

A truck was driven up into the forest, and a load of fresh greenery cut and brought back to deck the hall. The Duke's fine bone china—which hadn't seen the light of day for thirty years at least—was uncrated, washed, and sorted into place settings; likewise the silver and crystal. Assorted salvers, bowls, tureens, and decanters were removed from display cases, polished, and brought back into service. Some of the pieces, so old and eccentric their uses could only be guessed at, provided a few good laughs and were swiftly snatched up for decorative purposes.

As the short winter days moved swiftly on, arrangements steamed ahead; everyone became caught up in the fizzing spirit of the occasion, and a harried conviviality set in. The night before the party, James went to bed exhausted, and with a mountain of chores left to do, but feeling that if this *was* to be the last royal Hogmanay ever to be celebrated, at least it would be one to remember.

On December 31, Jenny and her cousins, Roslyn and Cara, arrived in the morning to help with the final preparations. The Rotheses appeared just after lunch; Caroline and Isobel came bearing gifts, and Donald a briefcase full of unfinished business. "An MP's work is never done," he explained. "But I promised the ladies I would not keep my nose buried the whole time we're here."

Introductions were made all around, and Jenny, Caroline, and Isobel settled down to making one another's acquaintance. Meanwhile, Calum and James were discussing the Prime Minister's recent visit with Donald, who was keenly intent on getting them to reveal all that had taken place.

"I saw it on the telly, of course," he said enthusiastically. "The arrival and departure, I mean. Beyond that,

Downing Street is strangely silent. They normally leak information like a rusty bucket, but for some reason everybody over there is incommunicado. But I can tell you the Christmas interview is still the talk of the town. There isn't a soul in all Whitehall who wouldn't kill to have been a fly on the wall of Number Ten. Are you really going through with it?"

"With what—the campaign? Yes."

"You're serious about that?"

"Entirely," James replied.

"He's already got us organizing the venues," Cal put in. "It's going to be a genuine roadshow."

"Jolly good," enthused Donald, and professed himself delighted by the prospect. He leaned forward and seemed about to impart something important.

Caroline saw her husband in a posture of intrigue, and raised a mild protest. "Donald, darling," she called from across the room, "you promised to wait until Embries gave you the all clear. Or am I mistaken?"

Donald puffed his cheeks. "Oh, very well. I did say something like that." He smiled apologetically. "I suppose it'll have to wait."

"We've got all night ahead of us."

"Speaking of which . . ." Cal said, glancing at his watch. "You'll have to excuse me—I've a few last-minute chores." He grinned suddenly and confided, "Actually, I was thinking of maybe getting Isobel to help me raid the Duke's cellar. How about it, Your Highness? Fancy a posh tipple for tonight's revel?"

"I expect nothing less," James replied with regal aplomb. "Those bottles have been gathering dust long enough. Bring 'em out, I say. High time they did some good for King and Country."

The two left, and Donald and James joined Caroline and Jenny. "Donald has got me all curious about this secret of his," James told Caroline. "Can't he give us a hint?"

"It isn't anything to do with me," she protested. "This is something Donald has cooked up all on his own."

"You flatter me, my dear," said Donald suavely. "I am

merely the happy second fiddle, content to play his small part in the great symphony of our eventful times."

"Pull the other one," Caroline told him. "He's been behaving like a spy for the last two days or so. People coming and going at all hours of the day and night, strange cars parked outside, murmured phone calls, obscure messages, notes passed under doors. All very hush-hush. Honestly, I expect a police raid any moment."

"We have had to be rather discreet, darling," Donald reminded her gently. "It wouldn't do in the present political climate to tip one's hand too early."

"Now *I'm* intrigued," said Jenny.

"I'm afraid I seem to have promised not to say anything until I've spoken to Embries."

Talk turned to other things then; tea arrived, the afternoon fled, and before long it was time to get dressed for the party. Jenny, aided by her cousins, arrayed herself in a long, low-cut, blue satin gown with long blue gloves; with a length of Ferguson tartan over one shoulder, and her long dark hair tied in a blue velvet bow, she looked every inch a Celtic queen. James dressed in his best kilt and jacket—complete with the Duke's old belt with an enormous silver buckle, and his father's *sgian dubh* tucked into the top of one wool sock.

As the clock struck seven, James took his place in the castle foyer to greet his guests. Besides Jenny's immediate family and relations, numerous local friends had been invited: drinking buddy Douglas; the Reverend and Mrs. Orr and their daughter Janet; Malcolm Hobbs, James' long-suffering solicitor, and his wife and children; Calum's parents; Shona's boyfriend; Gavin's girlfriend; along with the rest of the castle staff and their families. It must have amounted to nearly half the town and surrounding countryside. They all came dressed in their finest: the men in kilts, for the most part; the women in ball gowns, many with gloves, and most with traditional tartan shawls secured at their shoulders with jeweled brooches.

James stood for over an hour greeting them all, and watching the foyer and corridors fill up. He had given instructions that the great hall was to be locked and no one allowed in until the dinner bell had been rung. The delay served to heighten the anticipation; unable to help themselves, the children took turns trying the door handles every few minutes to make sure the doors were still locked.

When the last guest had arrived, James signaled Rhys to sound the bell, whereupon the King announced that it was his very great pleasure to extend the hospitality of Castle Morven to all his friends. "Embries," he called across the crowd, "open the doors and let the festivities begin!"

# ✳
# Thirty-three

The two huge doors were opened to reveal a room fragrant with the scent of peat and pine, and glowing with candlelight and hearth fire.

Artificial light had been banished. Massive iron candletrees—rousted out of the stables and reblacked—were stationed in every corner, each bearing a score of candles; there were candles all along the center line of the tables and also in the high, deep window wells all around; huge cathedral candles and slender tapers. A log and peat fire burned lustily in the enormous fireplace, taking the chill off the vast, high-roofed room.

The old oaken floor had been washed and waxed, and the two long medieval banqueting tables as well; every surface gleamed with a dull, ruddy luster. Every knife, fork, and spoon, every salt-cellar and sugar caster had been polished; every plate, goblet, cruet, and bowl gleamed in the soft lustrous light. Ivy trailed in long garlands from the stag heads and ancestral portraits on the walls. Boughs of spruce were piled heavily over the mantel. A low stage had been set up at the far end of the room, and this was all but covered in ivy and spruce.

To step across the threshold was to step back in time. Sim-

321

ple, elegant, and inviting, the hall looked very much as it would have looked during the High Middle Ages.

*The old Duke's armor-wearing ancestors,* my *ancestors, would have seen the hall just this way,* James thought.

A trivial thing, perhaps—the modest festive decoration of an old room—yet James did feel that in some way he was connected with his ancestry and lineage; he felt rooted. No longer a usurper playing laird o' the manor, he *was* the laird. He was the King and, for the first time since assuming the throne, he actually felt regal.

This realization produced in him a peculiarly intense longing; the *fiosachd* tingled, and he glimpsed, like the ghosts of Christmas past, the images of all those lords who had preceded him. They filled the hall, welcoming him with satisfaction and approval, raising their bowls to drink his health. The phantom image faded as quickly as it had arisen, but the effect lingered long, lending the festivities a mellow, golden glow.

Calum and Isobel had masterfully plundered the old Duke's wine cellar, and the resulting treasures were lined up like soldiers the length of the two great tables; reinforcements stood at the ready on improvised sideboards around the room. There were other choices as well, from heather ale to sparkling apple juice, and as they entered each guest was offered a glass of whatever they fancied. Cal and Izzy drafted Gavin and his girlfriend, Emma, to help with the drinks, and all four worked the crowd with bottles in both hands, priming the celebration pump.

Children flitted around the room like fairies. Dazzled by the candlelight and medieval ambience, they darted among the tall folk, their eyes wide with delight. The girls in their satin and tartan dresses and velvet hair bows and the boys in their diminutive kilts and high socks looked like miniature, less-restrained versions of their elders, racing from one end of the hall to the other, hooting and giggling.

When everyone was assembled, the bell sounded again and the guests were invited to find their places at the table. Shona and Cal had worked hard on the seating arrangement, and their ingenuity took some capricious turns. Embries, for example, was paired with Malcolm Hobbs' nine-year-old daughter, and Mr. Baxter was placed between Caroline Rothes and Gavin's girlfriend. James could not help notice that although he had not been allowed to sit with Jenny, Shona had managed to save a place for herself next to Rhys, and Cal was pleased to find himself next to Isobel.

No sooner had the last guest taken his seat than the first course appeared: Priddy's champion oak-grilled salmon with peppercorns and cream. A smallish sample only, James was resisting the temptation to lick the plate when someone at the end of the table set his crystal goblet ringing with a spoon.

The guests looked up to see Sergeant-Major Evans-Jones standing at his place. "There is an old custom in the valleys where I was born," he announced, "that on gala occasions such as this, the chaps help out with the serving so the dear ladies are not left with all the chores." He paused, and added with a wink, "It's a long, long night, after all."

Looking up and down the room, he called, "Are ye wi' me, lads? Say aye!"

There came a chorused Aye!, and the Sergeant-Major cried in his best parade-ground bellow, "On yer feet, men! Let's show 'em how it's done!"

The menfolk rose and began clearing the first course plates and carrying them to the kitchen, where a very surprised Priddy protested that she didn't want a lot of clumsy men tromping through her kitchen—but Owen wouldn't hear of it. In no time, the two of them had the next course dished up and served: haunch of venison, roasted with fennel and herbs.

Among the castle's tableware, Priddy had found a half dozen silver platters large enough to hold an entire haunch, and these were carried out, with great ceremony, three to each table. Bowls of steaming vegetables followed: potatoes roasted in dripping, braised carrots and parsnips with coriander, and apples baked with cloves, brown sugar, and rum—all filling the hall with a magnificent aroma.

Six stout and trustworthy men were given the task of carving the haunches. The bowls were taken place to place, and plates were filled. The next hour was presided over by the clink of cutlery and the happy murmuring hubbub of conversation punctuated by bursts of laughter and much passing of bottles. Could the Duke of Morven's worthy claret ever have been put to such a noble purpose, James wondered, or enjoyed half so much?

Cal and Izzy had plucked the best vintages from the cellar, and made sure the glasses were generously and regularly supplied. Once during the meal, Isobel appeared at James' side with a bottle in her hand. *"This,"* she promised reverently, "is going to be *magic*."

Gathering the attention of all the nearby guests, she proceeded to uncork the bottle. "Now, you'll have to drink this right away," she said, pouring a small amount into each glass. "It won't last long, but it will be amazing."

As soon as she finished pouring, she raised her glass. *"Slainte!"* She tossed it back in a single gulp, rolled the wine around in her mouth, and swallowed. "Oh, that is good." Her smile was dizzy with rapture.

All followed her example, and drank it down.

"Well? What do you think?" she asked.

"It is"—James searched for the right word, the flavor still alive on his tongue—"utterly divine." Others volunteered other words: rhapsodic, ethereal, bottled light, glorious, sublime.

"What is it?" someone demanded.

Lifting the bottle, she presented the label. "It's a Château Lafite-Rothschild"—she paused, drawing out the suspense—"of the year 1878." There were gasps of astonishment all around. "When I found this, I knew we had to have it tonight. Isn't it spectacular?"

There was half a swallow left in James' glass, and he took it. But the flavor enjoyed only seconds ago was gone. It was as if the liquid in his glass had turned to ashes—flat, muddy, dank ashes. He swallowed with difficulty. "Extraordinary," he remarked. "It's gone. Vanished."

"I know." Izzy sighed in commiseration. "Wine that old

only survives a few seconds once the air touches it. But isn't it a miracle while it lasts?"

Isobel moved on to delight some more guests. The glow of that rare magic remained, however, and those who had tasted it were warmed to their very souls. James exulted in the revelry. Everyone was happy and talking, life's cares and burdens forgotten for a while. This was, he reflected, how a holiday was supposed to be celebrated but rarely was: friends and loved ones gathered around the table for a little foretaste of heaven.

A loud pop, followed by gasps of amazement, drew the attention of nearly everyone to the middle of the table where Embries was now perched on the back of his chair amidst a ring of smoke and glittering confetti. It floated down around him to the astonishment of gobsmacked children. A little further on, James saw Dougie lean over and steal a kiss from Roslyn and, still further down the line, Mr. Baxter was glowing with quiet pride as Caroline praised his good wife's culinary skill, while, across the table, Donald and the Reverend Orr were head-to-head discussing trout fishing on the Dee.

And then it was time for pudding. As soon as the men cleared away the main course plates, a cry arose demanding that the cook make her appearance with the pudding. Priddy had prepared the old Duke's favorite festive dessert of spiced figs in rum sauce and carried the first bowl in herself. This was presented to James, and seven more bowls followed. There were also five salvers of apple flan, a sumptuous rhubarb fool served up in a great silver bowl, and minted fruit salad in a crystal krater.

Dessert swiftly disappeared, the dishes were cleared—along with cases of empty bottles—and the after-dinner drinks were produced: decanters of port, sherry, and single malt, more claret, and Drambuie—along with a fresh array of crystal tumblers and goblets.

James gazed upon the celebration, feeling more and more like a monarch of old, whose hearth and hall provided shelter and sustenance, protection and pleasure for his people. *Yes,* he thought, *this is how it is supposed to be.* He looked across to Jennifer, and she glanced up just then and smiled at him, mouthing the words "I love you."

He rose to his feet at the head of the table and, with the help of Cal and several others, called the hall to silence.

"My friends," he said, "I can think of only one thing in this world which would give me greater pleasure than welcoming you here tonight, and that would be to welcome you as half of a married couple. Happily, that oversight will soon be corrected, and this time next year, when we all gather again to celebrate another New Year's Eve, I will be joined by my beautiful wife."

Turning to Jennifer, he held out his hand towards her. She rose, taking his hand, and joined him. "I am pleased and proud to announce that Jennifer Evans-Jones has accepted my proposal of marriage," he said, to a chorus of ooohs and ahhhs all around. Reaching into his pocket, he withdrew the diamond engagement ring his mother had worn and, with a kiss, he slipped it onto her finger.

She put her arms around him, kissed him rapturously, whereupon James declared, "A toast! Ladies and gentlemen, dear friends, raise your glasses to the most beautiful girl in the world—not to mention the smartest, kindest, and . . . also, the bravest . . ." This brought shouts and laughter from the guests. "My darling, Jenny!"

Everyone drank and acclaimed the couple, and suddenly the whole room was on its feet; there was a rush as the women hurried to Jenny's side to see the ring. The men congratulated James and shook his hand, and proposed more toasts to the betrothed couple.

"When's the wedding?" shouted someone.

"We haven't set a date yet," James replied, "but soon."

"Whenever you're ready," shouted the Reverend Orr, "I'll be happy to tie the knot—at half my usual fee!"

Jenny's father was next to proclaim a toast. "Ladies and gentlemen, charge your glasses!" he bellowed. There was a scurry back to the tables to refill and take up goblets and tumblers. "To our sovereign King and his future Queen—who also happen to be my own dear, wonderful daughter and future son-in-law!"

Raising his glass, Owen smiled benevolently and called, "Here's to our Royal Highness, and his lovely bride, and to wishing them both a truly splendid and joyous new year! Long may they reign!"

The hall rang with shouts of "Hear! Hear!" and "Long live James and Jenny!"

There were more toasts then. One from Embries—a rousing chant delivered in soaring Gaelic—and one from Donald, who in his best parliamentary tones raised his glass and said,

> *"Here's to the heath, the hill, and the heather,*
> *The bonnet, the plaid, the kilt, and the feather!*
> *Blythe may we a' be,*
> *Ill may we ne'er see,*
> *Here's to the King*
> *And his glad companie!"*

When everyone stopped laughing, the Reverend Orr made an ecclesiastical toast—a blessing, really—and, not to be outdone, Caroline offered one in song. Shona rose and recited the poem *"Will Ye No Tak a Wee Dram, Willy?"* which, on the last line of every stanza, requires everyone to take a drink.

She finished to uproarious applause and, as if on cue, the Deeside Drifters, the local *ceilidh* band engaged for the occasion, began to play. They struck up the *"Bowl of Punch Reel"* and instantly people were flocking to the dance floor. James crossed to Jenny and swung her out onto the floor, joining the dancers in full whirl. They danced three more reels, before bowing out to catch their breath, returning to the table for renewed congratulations by one and all.

The rest of the night passed in a giddy blur of music and motion. James danced with Jenny's cousin Roslyn, Shona, Mrs. Orr, Caroline, Isobel, and several more; and the next thing he knew he was standing with Jenny in his arms and the band was playing *"Auld Lang Syne."* The Drifters had imported a ringer for the night, a tall, slender, sandy-haired

Irishman named Brian, who played flute and pennywhistle with the wild grace of a banshee. Standing straight and tall, eyes closed, he played the old, old melody to a hall suddenly silent. The wonderful, liquid notes fell from his silver flute like snowflakes, swirling in the air and descending over the listeners like a benediction.

When he finished the hall itself seemed to hold its breath. And then someone shouted, "Happy New Year!" Jenny and James shared a New Year's kiss or three, and the dancing began again. The assembly was first-footed by none other than the Reverend and Mrs. Orr, who snuck out and very nearly didn't get let back into the castle because no one heard the bell. First-footing is the peculiarly Scottish custom whereby the first person to set foot over the threshold is welcomed as a harbinger of good luck to follow throughout the rest of the year. Accordingly, a priest bearing a blessing is especially lucky—as are blacksmiths, bakers, and, of course, brewers.

It was past three o'clock when the band finally packed it in, and close to five when the guests began departing. Not all left; sofas, chairs, and spare rooms were offered to any for whom the drive home presented a particular challenge or those who could not stand to see the festivity end. Jenny and James joined Cal and Isobel, and Gavin and Emma for a nightcap. They sat in the candlelit kitchen, clutching mugs of coffee and nibbling on leftovers. Caroline and Donald stopped by on their way to bed, and were persuaded to pull up chairs. When Embries appeared, Isobel declared she was going to make everyone her famous twice-scrambled eggs with smoked salmon.

"As this seems to be a night for announcements," Donald said, "perhaps it's a good time to let you all in on my little secret."

Grinning like a boy with a birthday prize, eyes slightly bleary from his celebrations, he leaned forward and motioned everyone closer. "I am going to save the monarchy," he announced grandly. "Two days ago I secured the necessary backing to form a new political party to be called . . ."

he paused, drawing out the suspense, "the Royal Reform Party."

He gazed brightly at the ring of faces gathered around him. "We are going to fight Waring's referendum, and we are going to win."

## ✳
# Thirty-four

$T$wo days after New Year's, James awoke to the first rumblings of the storm about to break.

"Sorry to disturb you, Your Highness," Gavin said, speaking quickly.

Awakened out of a deep sleep by a knock on the door, James had risen and shuffled to answer it without pausing to put on his robe. He stood shivering in his boxer shorts as cold air from the corridor poured through the open door.

"It's all right. What's up?" he said, glancing at the bedside clock radio. It was 6:42, and still very dark outside.

"I thought you would want to see this as soon as possible." Gavin put a folded newspaper into his hands.

Opening the paper, his eye fell upon the headline: ROYAL SCANDAL—INVESTIGATION LAUNCHED.

Drawing the paper closer in the dim light he saw the two-column story below. More curious than concerned, James sat down on the edge of the bed and snapped on the light. "Come in and close the door," he said, already skimming the article.

The *Guardian* reporters believed themselves onto a big, important story and were proceeding gingerly. Long on suggestion and short on specifics, the story insinuated that James' career in the service had been somewhat less than exemplary. Although the article did not go into specifics, the last paragraph implied that this was just the tip of a very large iceberg and that more, much more, would be forthcoming as soon as facts could be substantiated.

"Well," allowed James, "it doesn't seem too bad. My record is clean. They can look all they want—they won't find anything. Are any of the other papers involved in this mudslinging?"

"I don't know, sir, but I can find out. Shona gets quite a few delivered to her."

"Get onto it," James told him. "See what the rest of them are up to. Hurry back."

Gavin left. James put on his robe and read the article through. He was starting in on a second reading, when his bedside phone rang. It was Rhys, calling from London; he and Embries had returned to the city for a few days.

"There's a story about you in *The Daily Independent*—" Rhys began, then hesitated.

"Yes?"

"Well, it's not good, sir."

"Let's have it."

"It says that—wait, I can read it to you if you'd prefer. Let me get it here—"

"No, just hit the highlights. I'll read it myself later."

"It says that they've uncovered evidence of gross misconduct while you were in the army, and that you were brought up on charges but managed to bribe your way out of a court-martial."

"That's absurd," James told him. The idea was so ludicrous, he found it difficult to imagine anyone taking it seriously. "Not only that, it's plain impossible. Couldn't happen. You know that as well as I do, Rhys."

"There's more, sir," he said, and James caught the wary inflection in his voice.

"Go on."

"The story says witnesses have come forward who saw you do certain things in Kazakhstan—things which resulted in the charges being brought against you."

"What *things?* Do they say?"

"Not specifically, no. It does say the paper is continuing its own investigations into the affair."

"There wasn't any affair. That's *The Daily Independent,* you say—who else has got hold of this?"

"This is the only paper that comes to the house. I was just heading out to get the rest."

"Good. Call me back as soon as you've had a look. We'll do the same on this end."

James made his way downstairs and through the big house. He pottered around the kitchen by himself for a few minutes before Priddy came in and put a stop to it. In deference to his rank, however, she allowed the King to take a seat at the table while she began preparing breakfast for the household. By the time the bacon was frying, Gavin returned with Shona, her hair still wet from the shower, bearing an armload of papers. "I don't have everything," she explained, spreading them out on the table. "We can get more later."

"You do have *The Daily Independent,* I see," said James, removing one of the papers from the heap. TARNISHED WAR RECORD HAUNTS KING, read the headline. While he scanned the story, Gavin and Shona quickly sorted through the rest.

None of the other papers had anything, for which James was grateful. It occurred to him that the real story behind the story was that some enterprising con artist had discovered a way to bamboozle a load of ready cash from a couple of publishers eager for a new scandal. The fraudster was probably laughing all the way to the bank.

"Well," James said, as the three of them sat poring over the papers and sipping coffee, "it doesn't look so bad. It's all lies, of course, but at least it seems to be confined to two newspapers."

"Three," said Cal, entering the room just then. "I just read *The Scottish Herald.* Who the hell is feeding them this crap?"

Over breakfast, James, Cal, and the Rotheses—who were enjoying the last few days of their holiday at Blair Morven—discussed what to do about the story. "I don't like the smell of this," Donald declared.

Cal, angry on James' behalf, wanted to "sue the bastards' butts off."

"A robust sentiment, to be sure, Calum," Donald conceded, "but not tremendously helpful. If you like, James, I could make some calls and see what I can ferret out."

"I'd be much obliged," James told him. "Under the circumstances, you'll probably want to think twice about endorsing me."

"Not a bit of it," Donald assured him. "Tempest in a teacup. We'll weather the storm and come out stronger on the other end. You mark my words."

"I'm serious," James insisted. "You might want to wait until this blows over, at least."

"By then, I'm afraid it might be too late," Donald countered. "The referendum is less than four weeks away now. Damn the torpedoes and full speed ahead, I say."

Two nights ago, Donald had revealed his scheme to launch a new political party with the sole purpose of aiding the campaign to save the monarchy. He and James had spent many hours over the following days talking Royal Reform Party strategy, and how the organization might best use its influence and resources to help James in the run-up to the devolution referendum.

Donald excused himself to make some phone calls to his co-conspirators, and Caroline to pack for their return to London later that morning; Cal and Isobel went out for a last romantic stroll up into the hills; and James called Jenny.

She greeted him with a cheery hello, and said, "I'm up to my elbows in slurry at the moment, my love. The mixer broke down."

"I take it you haven't seen the paper this morning."

"No, why? Something slimy in the press?"

"Slimy is right. They're impugning my service record."

"That doesn't sound too serious," she suggested. "It must be some kind of mistake."

Later that night, as he waited in vain for any mention of the scandal on the broadcast news, James found himself agreeing with Jenny's assessment. The television newscasts made no mention of the story. James decided that Donald was right; it was nothing more than a tempest in a teacup. Most likely, it would all blow over by morning.

The next morning, all hell broke loose.

Almost every newspaper in the country picked up on what was now termed the King's "shameful war record." Several of the broadsheets featured the story as the day's lead item, and *The Guardian* put out a banner headline which announced SERVICE SCANDAL OF A ROYAL ROGUE. *The Sun,* as always, was much more succinct and to the point; their headline read simply KING RAT.

Below those charming words was a picture of the King himself in battle fatigues, gripping the upper arm of a dusky, young, vaguely Asiatic lovely in frilly knickers.

The photo was a fake. He'd never manhandled any civilians of any age, race, sex, or description in his life. Still, there it was in grainy poor-quality color. The camera may not lie, but photographs rarely tell the truth. And a desktop computer could make a bare-faced liar out of even the most innocent snapshot.

If the picture was bad, the accompanying story was worse. The writers, who were evidently quite accustomed to skating close to the edge, managed to insinuate an enormous amount without ever once coming right out and saying anything actionable. The story was peppered through and through with "allegedly" and "apparently" and "our intimate sources would seem to indicate." Nothing was stated in objective terms—it was all allusion, suggestion, and barbed innuendo.

The tale emerging from the welter of insinuation was that while a young, fast-rising officer assigned to the UN Peacekeeping Force in Kazakhstan, the King had become heavily involved with local gangster chieftains who paid him vast sums of money to turn a blind eye to their criminal activities—smuggling, drugs, prostitution, and so on— and that, on several occasions, Captain James Stuart had allowed these warlords to conduct paramilitary operations which resulted in the torture and execution of captured prisoners of war.

The crowning glory of this scurrilous claptrap was the

final sentence which condemned him with a question: "If His Majesty has nothing to hide, why not come clean?"

It's a simple journalistic technique, and one employed often enough in the tabloids. Never had James appreciated the devastating impact it could have on an individual. He read the damning words, and a feeling of impotent rage surged up inside that left him shaking.

Worse was to come.

Next morning's press brought a real gem: "As unanswered allegations mount, and the King continues to barricade himself behind a stone wall of silence, we may be forced to the conclusion that we have been deceived by a smooth-talking scoundrel, and that our monarch is little more than a common thug."

"Do they never get tired of slinging muck?" James growled, shaking the paper. It was early in the morning following a bad night's sleep, and he was of a sour disposition that was not improved by his survey of the day's press.

Gavin, reading from one of the dailies heaped on the table, said, "Listen to this one, sir. It says that a lengthy and thorough examination of significant documents has failed to lay the accusations to rest. They say your service record has been subsequently amended to expunge any mention of an official reprimand for what they are calling, and I quote: grievous impropriety of a criminal nature, end of quote."

"Oh, that's very clever," James grumbled. "Very shrewd. My service record is clean, so that proves someone must have tampered with it." He threw the paper down in disgust. "They must get paid by the lie."

James, restless now, and frustrated at his inability to fight back effectively, stormed up to Shona's office and had her put in a call to Embries, who was still in London. "Patience, James," he advised. "It is difficult, I know, but the truth will win out. You must believe that."

They talked for a few minutes more, and Embries assured him that he was doing everything he could to discover the source of the scurrilous stories. James hung up no better for the encouragement; the appeal to truth was all well and good, but meanwhile the accusations and allegations

mounted. The heat increased, and James simmered in a stew
of anger and exasperation. Jenny phoned regularly with of-
fers of tea and sympathy, but James insisted she was well out
of it. "You know I'd love to see you," he told her, "but if
those jackals got so much as a glimpse of you, you'd be
dragged into this quagmire with me."

"Do I care?" she replied, the defiance in her voice filling
James with pride. "If I want to see my sweetheart, I'm not
about to let a bunch of slimeball sleaze merchants stand in
the way."

"We can thank God they haven't caught wind of our engagement," James told her. "Until they do, we're going to
have to stay away from each other."

"I think it stinks," Jenny told him. "You can tell them all
I said so."

The media mob, frantic for the next new scoop, disre-
garded their previous agreement with Shona, swarming the
road, drive, and yard outside Castle Morven. The local con-
stabulary did their best to keep the journalists in check and
the merely curious moving, but there were so many it was all
they could do to maintain a clear path to let legitimate traffic through. Shona, furious at the outrageous disobedience
of her orders, flew around like a harpy in search of victims
to devour. Inundated by frenzied demands for information,
she was forced to disconnect all the phones with listed numbers in order to keep the ceaseless ringing from driving
everyone mad. Meanwhile, Cal and Mr. Baxter mounted a
ground war to keep reporters from jumping the estate walls
or sneaking down through the woods.

The photographers were growing increasingly aggressive and obnoxious. Setting stepladders against the wall,
they kept their megazoom lenses trained on the doors and
windows day and night, hollering constantly for someone
to come out and give them "five minutes, just five minutes." The mere shadow of a figure in window or doorway
was enough to trip flashguns and set motor drives
whirring.

To pass the time, the castle prisoners watched the various
news broadcasts, restlessly clicking through the channels to

catch the latest gossip—or, as one of the presenters put it: "the latest developments in this deepening crisis of confidence in our beleaguered monarchy."

"At this hour," said a reporter stationed outside in the winter darkness, "the uncrowned King sits besieged behind his high walls—high walls which cannot keep out the deepening scandal surrounding his rumor-plagued reign. Tonight fresh allegations have surfaced linking money from drug-dealing and other criminal activities to the King's Blair Morven estate.

"These new allegations bring into serious question the ability of a junior officer in the armed forces to fund a lifestyle far in excess of the salary for his rank and seniority. Further, it has been suggested that the proceeds from His Majesty's illicit dealings have, in fact, gone to finance the acquisition of Castle Morven, and subsequently played a large part in securing his kingship."

"Finance the acquisition, my butt," James grumbled. "If I had even half the money they say I've got, I'd buy my own newspaper and everybody could read about what crap merchants these hacks really are."

"Dogs running to their own vomit," said Cal. "Say the word, Jimmy, and I'll get a bunch of them in here and knock some heads together."

"Shona's working on a categorical denial," Gavin offered, trying to sound hopeful. "Don't worry, sir. We'll make them eat every column inch."

"The damage is already done," James concluded. "Even if I go on to prove every last accusation false, half the people will still believe I'm a criminal—and the other half will always wonder. Once the doubt has been created, it taints everything, *and* it lasts forever."

With each new "revelation of shocking misconduct," James' confidence drooped a little lower. Shona's, however, seemed to expand accordingly. "Some of those people out there are going to be very sorry they chose journalism for a career," she vowed darkly. "When I find out who started this libel fest, I am going to have their heads nailed to the Press Association door."

She threw her clipboard onto the untidy stack of newspapers Gavin had gathered through the day. "I've seen every story," she indicated the papers, "and I've tracked each new wrinkle as it has developed. I think I've got an idea how this is spreading." Taking up her clipboard, she handed it to the King. "I've noted a number of repetitive phrases and marked them in this column. Then, I cited individual newspapers here." She pointed to a second column.

Pulling a mobile phone from her pocket, she began punching in numbers. "I've got a call in to one of my moles. I'm going to check with him now to see what he's found out. Won't take a sec."

"I'll leave you to it."

James wandered off to the kitchen to pour a glass of wine. When he returned, Shona announced, "It's a smear job, Your Highness. Vicious and nasty as they come."

"Was there ever any doubt?"

"Sorry. I didn't mean it like that."

"Never mind. Tell me what you've found out."

"Have a look at this," she said, extending her clipboard. "Gavin's compiled a rough list, and it shows pretty much what I expected. I've put him to work tracking down the individual reporters; we'll have a list of those next."

Taking the clipboard, James saw that two phrases jumped out: "compromised command hierarchy" and "overreached UN conventions," and several others. The first had been used in no fewer than six papers, and the second in five; the others had been used in two or three each.

"Setting aside all the rest as coincidences," she said, tapping the remaining list with a short finger, "these two are proof enough."

"That the stories are made up?"

"That the stories all derived from a single source," she said, perching on the arm of the chair. "Most journalists—when they're copying someone else's feed—take care to dress it up a little. Professional pride, you know? Sometimes, though, they come across a word or turn of phrase they sort of like, right? Well, the dimmer ones can't improve on it, and the brighter ones can't resist having everyone think it's theirs. They're like magpies: they see a shiny bauble and they gotta have it."

"So this repetition means they all took their information from a single source."

"They're all singing off the same hymn sheet." She rapped the clipboard in James' hands for emphasis. "Someone supplied them with information to get the ball rolling— probably not all of them, but more than one." She paused, and James returned her notes. "My best guess is that somebody's set up a drip feed and is giving out carefully measured doses to keep everybody hooked and happy. Very crude."

"But effective, it would seem. What can we do about it?"

"I say we issue a statement and call them on it—demand to be shown the smoking gun, as it were. Challenge them to put up or shut up. If there *is* anything of substance, they have nothing to gain by keeping it from us. If they refuse to bring out the evidence, it will make them look bad. Either way, we're no worse off."

"I'll think about it," he told her.

Shona's mobile phone chirped just then. She answered it, and handed it to James. "It's Embries."

"Shona has informed me of her investigations," he said. "Added to what I have discovered, I can say that this appears to be the work of someone in, or very close to, the Waring government."

"You're sure?"

"Reasonably certain, yes. The trail, as expected, has become very muddy. There have been so many feet tramping about in this, absolute certainty is no longer possible. Rhys and I are returning to Blair Morven first thing tomorrow morning. Do nothing until I get there."

James called Jenny again later that night. They spent an hour on the phone together. He told her what Embries had said about the likelihood of the Waring government being involved in the smear campaign. "I never liked that man," Jenny replied. "I would love nothing more than to rub his face in it the way he's rubbed yours."

"I love you, too," James told her. "Embries is coming back tomorrow and we're going to figure out what to do."

They said their good-byes then, and James went to bed and rose the next morning to face yet another day of infamy in the nation's media.

# Thirty-five

The morning's crop of newspapers brought no joy. The accusation of service misconduct and subsequent cover-up was repeated in no fewer than four papers. It was cold comfort that some of the more respectable news organizations declined to run anything more than lengthy reports of the other papers' investigations.

Both *The Times* and *The Guardian,* in a rare moment of agreement, called for a full public inquiry into the King's affairs since leaving the service. *The Observer* and *Evening Standard* looked gleefully ahead to the impending referendum, and predicted a resounding victory for what they called "the spirit of new republicanism" which they insisted was sweeping through the land. The *Daily Star* offered readers a chance to win a holiday in Florida by guessing most closely the number of votes that would be cast against the King on Referendum Day.

Meanwhile, *The Sun,* anticipating a royal stonewalling, condemned the lack of communication and declared it the "silence of the damned." Carried away with their tenuous pun, they showed a computer-aided photo of James as Hannibal Lector; it looked more like a fuzzy Freddie Krueger than the King, so the insult value was minimal.

As soon as Embries and Rhys returned from London,

James called a staff meeting to decide how to respond to the continued media attacks.

"There is a psalm of King David," James began, "a king who knew a thing or two about misery." Reciting from memory, James said, " 'Be gracious to me, O God, for the enemy persecute me; my assailants harass me. All day long watchful foes torment me; countless are those who assail me. . . .' "

James leaned forward and put his hands flat on the table. "I am sick of being the media's whipping boy. I won't take it anymore."

"What do you want to do?" asked Cal quietly.

"That's what we're here to figure out," James said. He stood abruptly and began pacing behind his chair. "All I know is that I cannot and will not let it go on like this." He flipped a hand in the direction of the front lawn where the media pack was maintaining its prurient vigil. "They *allege,* they *attribute;* they speculate and implicate—they damn you to hell with insinuation. Just once I wish one of those rumormongers out there would drop the sanctimonious attitude and lay his facts on the table for the world to see."

"There are no facts," Gavin put in. "We all know there is not a single molecule of real evidence to support any of this."

"It's like a stag hunt," Cal observed. "The belling of the hounds is meant to make the stag run for cover. Once he does that, the chase is on—and it only ends one way."

Embries, slumped thoughtfully in his chair, said nothing.

"I'm not going to run. I'm going to challenge them," James replied firmly.

"We could start by giving those hyenas out there a damn good thrashing," Shona suggested. "Retaliate with a massive media blitz calling on the instigators of this hate campaign to put up or shut up—either produce the hard evidence or start making apologies pronto."

She slid a sheet of paper across the table to James. "As it happens, Gavin and I have drafted a preliminary statement. If you approve it, Your Majesty, we can get it to the BBC, independents, and satellites in time to be aired on the noon and evening news broadcasts."

James read it aloud to see how it would sound on the air. They had struck the right balance—neither too antagonistic nor overdefensive. It was a model of quiet defiance, diplomacy, and logic. Everyone agreed it was a masterpiece—except Cal, who was wearing the expression of a person who doesn't like what he smells.

"What's wrong, Cal?" asked James, laying the paper aside. "Don't you like the statement?"

"Oh, it's terrific," he said caustically. "It'll cause about as much commotion as a fart in a hurricane."

"You don't think it's tough enough?" asked Gavin. "We can give it a harder edge."

Cal shook his head. "Man, it's just words, words, and more words. We're choking on all these words. Anyway, the referendum is less than three weeks away, for crying out loud."

James stared at the statement, and thought about the presenters and reporters beavering away, hunched over keyboards in cubicles, reading copy, writing copy, filling their newspaper columns with words. Suddenly he did not want to play that game.

"Cal is right," he said, making up his mind. "We could go on trading shots with the press until hell freezes over. Meanwhile, the clock is ticking, and I *refuse* to spend what is left of my reign hiding out in this castle."

James' outburst stirred Embries from his meditations. He raised his head and gazed at James with approval. "Yes," he said, as if he had been waiting for James to arrive at this conclusion. "What else?"

"No statements, no faxes, sound bites, or phone calls," the King said. "In the Christmas interview, I said I wanted to take my message directly to the people, and that's what I'm going to do."

Shona made to object. Embries held up his hand to silence her. "Go on," he urged. "What do you see?"

"I see," said James, "getting out on the road and meeting people where they are—in schools, bus queues, and office blocks, in hospital waiting rooms, tube stations, churches, and shopping malls. I want to talk to them and let them get to know me; I want to show them the kind of person I really am—not the media-created monster they read about in the scandal sheets."

"A charm offensive," said Shona; her face crumpled in a complicated frown. "It's risky. It could easily backfire."

"I'm all for it," declared Gavin. "The King is right; we want to be seen taking positive action."

"I say we put our boy on the road and let the people decide," Cal added. "If the newspapers want to cover something, let them cover that!"

Embries added his endorsement, and Shona acquiesced, saying, "Your wish is my command, sir. Just give us a chance to draw up a list of venues and opportunities, and we'll start the ball rolling."

She and Gavin left together to begin making arrangements for James' first foray. When they had gone, Embries asked, "You were almost convinced by Shona's approach. What made you change your mind?"

"I've hidden away in my castle long enough. If I'm going to fight for the right to be King, I want a real flesh and blood confrontation. That's what I'm good at."

Embries smiled, and the tight lines around his eyes eased a little. "You sound like someone I used to know," he said.

"More coffee, Huw?" asked Donald, offering the pot.

"No, thank you, Donald—I'm floating." The leader of the Opposition glanced at his watch. "Unfortunately, we'll have to keep this brief. My driver has strict instructions to get me back to the office by two o'clock sharp. I'm chairing a meeting of the Health Services Committee."

"Well, this shouldn't take long. I just wanted to bring you up to date on some plans I've been working on for a few weeks." Taking a last sip of his coffee, he set aside the cup. The restaurant was full of businessmen, but quiet; Donald had chosen it especially. "What would you say if I told you I could make you Prime Minister?"

"I'd shout 'hallelujah!' and then ask who I have to kill," replied the burly Welshman.

As leader of the Opposition, Huw Griffith presided over a

motley assortment of splinter groups and marginal special-interest parties: old socialist Laborites; Celtic fringe nationalists; Ulsterites, who still clung to the hope that the Northern Counties could extricate themselves from the Irish Republic to re-create a new United Kingdom; radical Liberal Democrats; no-hope Greens; and the undead of the political graveyard: disenfranchised eurosceptic Conservatives.

Griffith's firm, uncompromising hand had painstakingly molded the fractious assembly into a more or less cohesive coalition. Thanks largely to his considerable skill and no-nonsense leadership, the Unified Alliance had furnished a moderately meaningful opposition to Waring's "Wall of Steel" government. Over the years, he had become extremely adept at defusing explosive situations with tact and goodwill. It was almost universally recognized among political analysts that the rotund, red-haired Welshman was responsible for single-handedly keeping all the unruly ducks in a row; if not for Huw Griffith, the Opposition would have collapsed in an unholy chaos of conflicting opinions, ideologies, and agendas.

"I am forming a new political party," Donald told him, "and I want your support."

"I'm listening," said Huw, slumping back into the deeply padded booth. Coat unbuttoned over his paunch, tie loose, he looked like a traveling salesman on the last call of a long day.

"The purpose of my new party is to promote a single-issue platform," Donald began.

"And that would be?"

"Preservation of the monarchy," Donald told him. "It's to be called the Royal Reform Party, and it's organized solely to campaign for the defeat of the referendum to abolish the monarchy."

Huw shook his shaggy head slowly from side to side. "Suicide."

"I don't think so." Donald, eager, confident, took up his coffee cup and drained it in a gulp. "I think it's high time we halted devolution before it's too late. I think you'd be surprised to find how many people agree with me."

"You're crazy, Donald. Royal Reform Party, good lord." Huw regarded his junior colleague pityingly. "The King is up to his eyeballs in sleaze. The press is crucifying him. Why do you want to go and stick your neck out like this?"

"The referendum is only about three weeks away. It must be stopped. It's as simple as that. Moreover, I think you'll find a groundswell of public opinion that this is a referendum too far. I'll be the first to admit we've had some lousy monarchs, but with this new King, I believe we've got a new chance, and I think it would be unconscionable to proceed."

Huw, a battle-hardened veteran of parliamentary politics, looked at his watch. "So, you've got the hots for this new King. To tell you the truth, I rather like him myself. But if it comes down to him or me, it's no contest. King or no King, I will not put the party through another election defeat. Waring is weak, and his support is failing. A few more months and we should have the clout we need to bring his government down."

"You disappoint me, Huw."

"Sorry, but that's the way it is. A new party is not in the cards right now. Take my advice, and just forget it. Forget all about it."

When Donald did not respond, the Opposition leader leaned forward earnestly. "Listen to me, Donald, I'm serious. Waring is on the ropes. It's taken years, but we've finally got him right where we want him. The British Republic Party has all but lost its majority. Next election is ours. And if you think I will stand idly by and watch you or anyone else ruin our chances, think again, my friend."

Realizing he had been ranting, he lowered his voice, and added, "Now, I am sorry to be so blunt, but . . . Donald, we're *this* close to victory. As of this week, Waring's majority is down to four seats—*four,* for crying out loud!"

"I heard about Alfred Norris' heart attack," said Donald. "Who is the other?"

"Belknap," announced Griffith. "The old pinch fist has been called before the audit committee over an offshore tax shelter scheme. Waring is pressuring him to take the heat, but my moles tell me he will happily trade resignation for prosecution. Moreover, we can get his name on the dotted line before the end of business tomorrow."

"Then that makes it even easier," began Donald.

"Not if you go through with this party of yours it bloody well doesn't," Griffith told him flatly. "You'll split the Opposition, effectively *increasing* Waring's majority at the very moment when he's most vulnerable. Does that make sense?"

"I had hoped you would see the possibilities," Donald said. He signaled the headwaiter, who approached with a small wooden box. Opening the box, he offered it to Huw. "Cigar?" asked Donald. "Direct from Havana by way of Jermyn Street."

"Thanks." Huw accepted the cigar, drew it along his upper lip as he inhaled deeply, then twirled the end in his mouth. Donald selected a cigar for himself; the headwaiter offered a small guillotine to chop the end off each cigar, and placed matches and a crystal ashtray between them on the table before retiring.

"So tell me. Why should we all line up and sing 'God Save the King' for you?" Huw asked, taking a long puff on his cigar.

This was the moment Donald had been waiting for. He felt his heartbeat quicken and his blood begin to race. "Because," he said slowly, "in return for supporting my new party, I will deliver two of Waring's seats to the Opposition."

"Two seats?" The Welshman's unruly eyebrows shot up. "Donald, my haggis-hurling friend, why didn't you say so in the first place?"

"Take away two from Waring's column, add two to your side of the ledger, and what have you got?"

"Given Norris' demise, and Belknap's disgrace—a stand-off."

"We have a name for that in Whitehall, I believe," suggested Donald lightly.

The light came on in Huw Griffith's eyes. It was the rosy dawn of his day of deliverance. "Hung Parliament." He said the words as if whispering a magic formula.

"Simple mathematics," Donald confirmed, tapping ash

from his cigar. "The vote is deadlocked. As leader of the Opposition, you could instantly call for a confidence vote. With two new seats at your command, you could win that vote. Then it would be up to the King to dissolve Parliament and order a general election."

Huw blinked at the beauty of it.

"Hey, presto! The 'Wall of Steel' collapses," Donald concluded triumphantly, "a grateful population weeps, and you are swept into power on a tidal wave of change."

Griffith sat for a moment regarding Donald with cautious anticipation. "You could get the King to go along with this? It would mean compromising his constitutional impartiality."

"The King would certainly see the wisdom of replacing a government which has outlived its usefulness," Donald replied. "I could get him to do it, but if the Act of Dissolution goes through, it will be 'Good-bye, King,' and 'Hello, President,' forever."

"Ah," said Huw, "so that's what it's going to cost. Saving the monarchy."

"Obviously, he can't dissolve Parliament if he's no longer King," replied Donald simply. "We save the monarchy, and all the rest follows."

"There is another way," suggested Huw, blowing smoke into the air. "Don't wait for the referendum."

"Go for a hung Parliament now, you mean?"

"As soon as possible. Parliament reconvenes in two days. We do it then."

Donald smoked thoughtfully. He had not anticipated this wrinkle.

"Listen, Donald," Huw said earnestly, "your plan is sound as far as it goes. But we could campaign like blue devils and still see the referendum succeed by a country mile. On the other hand, we'd stand a far greater chance of defeating the vote if Waring and his henchmen were not around to sabotage our efforts at every turn. You said it yourself: we have to act while there still *is* a king. We do it now."

"I don't know, Huw. . . ."

"Very well," said the Opposition leader, leaning over the

table, "off the record, just between you and me, what's it going to take to get you to see things my way? Higher profile in the new Government? You want a seat on the front bench? You got it."

"I think," Donald replied slowly, "you may have misunderstood my intentions. I'm not seeking any personal advancement out of this. I want to see the Waring government assigned to purgatory as much as anyone, but not at the cost of the monarchy. I want the referendum to fail and the Act of Dissolution to disappear."

A man in a dark suit entered the restaurant and was met by the headwaiter, who came to the table. "Sorry to disturb you, gentlemen," he said. "Mr. Griffith's driver is here to collect him."

"Thank you, Raymond," replied Huw. "Would you mind telling him to wait? Won't be a moment." When he had gone, he turned to Donald and asked, "Well? What do you say?"

Donald hesitated. It was not all he wanted, but it was close. And time was running out. "All right," he agreed. "You have a deal."

The Welshman made no move to get up. "Good. There is a bill coming up for vote on the Wednesday following the holiday recess—it's the Motorway Compliance legislation."

"Changing all the highway numbers to conform to the European system."

"That's the one." Huw was already racing down the road towards the Holy Grail he saw shining in the distance. "Here's how it will work: I'll have the Chief Whip issue a three-line whip for that vote, and I'll instruct the membership to vote no. Tell your defectors to be ready to jump ship. Once they're safely aboard, I'll welcome them with open arms."

"You're certain you can deliver a coalition-wide 'no' vote?" asked Donald.

"Don't you worry about that. I'll break heads if I have to."

Huw Griffith smiled expansively, leaned back, and stretched his arms across the back of the chair. "If you help us oust Waring, I will personally see to it that you get all the help you need to defeat the referendum." Huw slid his bulk along the leather bench and stood up beside the table. He stuck out his broad hand. "Well, how about it? Have we got a deal?"

"We do, Mr. Griffith," replied Donald, rising to clasp the offered hand. "Indeed, we do."

They shook hands, and Donald walked his guest to the foyer where the driver was waiting. Griffith sent the chauffeur on ahead, saying, "I'm right behind you, Archie."

"Very good, sir," replied the driver.

Stepping to the door, Huw said to Donald, "Just between you and me, Donald, I'm not convinced the monarchy is worth saving. But I can live with this James Stuart character as King of Britain a hell of a lot better than I can with Thomas Waring as the first president of the British Republic."

"It doesn't bear thinking about," observed Donald.

"I've given you my word. You deliver those two seats, and I'll put the party to work on the defeat of the last referendum. But it's got to be one step at a time. We can't let Waring get wind of any of this."

"I understand," Donald assured him, catching the undercurrent of the Opposition leader's concern. "I won't announce the new party until after the vote."

Griffith stepped out onto the pavement. "Thanks for a most interesting lunch, Donald."

"I'll walk you to your car."

"No offense, but I think it's best if we are not seen together until after Wednesday's vote. We'll have a drink together afterward to celebrate our victory."

"I'd like nothing better."

Donald stood in the doorway until the car was out of sight. Then, stepping back inside, he dashed to the nearest phone to call James with the good news.

## ✳

# Thirty-six

Rising early, Donald arrayed himself for battle, donning his best kilt—the Dress McKenzie—short black jacket with silver buttons, white ruffed shirt, sporran, heavy wool socks, and high-laced dress shoes. He looked every inch a Scottish baron on his wedding day. In fact, he had worn the same outfit on that occasion, too. A kiss from Caroline, and he was off in a cab to the Palace of Westminster, where by carefully contrived means he sent his co-conspirators their final instructions.

This occupied him through the lunch hour; he had sandwiches sent in, purposely keeping out of sight until Parliament was convened at half past two. Not wishing to appear too eager, he lounged for another hour, waiting for the first items of business to be concluded: the Speaker's announcement of Alfred Norris' death and the motion for a writ for a by-election to replace him. Next, there were three private bills to be read, and then departmental questions would be considered, by which time it was approaching four o'clock, and Donald, unable to wait any longer, decided to join the proceedings.

He walked down the long corridor and entered the chamber, bowing to the Speaker's chair before taking his customary seat three up and on the aisle behind the leader of the

Opposition. He settled back against the green leather bench, took a calming breath, and tried not to think—for the ten thousandth time—that today was D day, the day they ripped a hole in the famed Waring Wall of Steel.

While a Treasury minister answered technical questions about apparent funding anomalies discovered in a recent departmental audit, Donald occupied himself with a quick survey of the benches. As expected, it was too early to tell much one way or the other; neither side of the House was anywhere near full capacity. Judging from all the vacant places and the nearly empty galleries, the Government side was at about a third of its strength, while the Opposition was only showing about a fourth.

Well, he told himself, it is early yet; there is still plenty of time to get the troops into position. Turning his attention to his order paper, he saw that the Highway Compliance Bill was last on the agenda. Two other items stood ahead of it. The next hour was taken up with matters of constituency concern, and a few more members drifted into the chamber in preparation for the day's main business.

When the Defense Secretary, an austere and normally very quiet member of Waring's cabinet, rose to make a ministerial announcement regarding the Government orders for two new submarines, Donald began to suspect that his bombshell had been discovered. His suspicions deepened when the lengthy ministerial announcement was followed by two more time-wasting statements—one from the Environment Secretary putting forth the Government's intention to request funding for a feasibility study of commercial sale of Northern Isles wind-generated power, and the other from the Education Secretary, who issued a statement on the revision of Government policy regarding harmonization of A-level testing of modular subjects.

Donald could not understand what Waring expected to gain by employing such lame tactics. Did he actually hope to delay the bill coming to the floor? Waring would know better; the Opposition would simply call the question and demand the vote. Then, as Donald looked around the chamber, trying to catch a glimpse of his co-conspirators on the

Government back benches, the explanation occurred to him: the delay was not to avoid the vote but to discover the traitors within their ranks.

Somewhere in the bowels of Whitehall, he thought, the Government Whip's office must be knee-deep in blood. Donald had only been called to the Opposition Whip's office once, and that was for a more or less friendly chat regarding a personal matter. Even so, he left the interview a firm believer in the power of the Chief Whip and his own utter insignificance in The Grand Scheme of Things. He had heard of grown men weeping and offering up firstborn offspring to appease an irritated Whip. In the parliamentary firmament, the Whips were archangels charged with divine retribution, and their ability to extract obedience was nothing short of miraculous.

As Donald sat contemplating the horror facing his co-conspirators, a sick dread crept over him. What if his revolt had been discovered and his secretly royalist friends caught?

There had been no way to disguise the three-line whip. For a politician of Waring's acumen and experience, it wouldn't have taken the usual spies or moles to tell him a major confrontation loomed. When a simple straightforward, noncontroversial bill enjoying full cross-party support was suddenly subjected to a three-line whip—a signal requiring every voting member *without exception* to attend and toe the party line—alarm bells would have run at Number Ten. Accordingly, Waring had issued his own three-line whip to counter the Opposition, and prepared for a showdown.

It was Donald's dearest hope, however, that in the hours between learning of the Opposition's maneuver and the convening of Parliament, Waring had not been able to ferret out the traitors and turn them once more to the Dark Side.

More MPs arrived in the chamber and took their places; the galleries began to fill up with journalists and friends of Parliament. Now Waring's cabinet was assembled in force on the front bench across the House divide. Grim-faced, haggard, sweating in their expensive suits, they had the look of men who had been stoking coal-fired furnaces with shovels two sizes too small. The image gave Donald a fleeting comfort. *Get used to it, lads,* he thought, *this is just the beginning.*

By six o'clock, the chamber and galleries were at standing-room-only capacity, with members and essential officials still crowding in. The press pack, scenting blood on the wind, had assembled in full force; if history was going to be made, no one wanted to miss a moment. Donald looked in vain for his co-conspirators, but could not locate them in the throng.

At twenty past six, Prime Minister Waring entered with his three closest advisors. He moved with confidence to his place on the front bench and, after a brief exchange of words with those around him, sat down. Of all the Government MPs, only Waring himself seemed anything other than miserable; he looked edgy, angry, itching for a fight.

At Waring's appearance, the Government launched its first attempt to keep the Highway Bill from coming to the floor. The Home Secretary led the first attack. "Mr. Speaker," said Patricia Shah, "it has come to this government's attention that a recent cold snap in the northern counties has left a considerable number of elderly and homebound citizens without adequate heating. It is this government's duty to put forward emergency legislation to provide for an increase in home energy allowances available to old age pensioners and those on disability benefit. Therefore, Mr. Speaker, I do move to suspend the business before the House in order that we might put this time-sensitive legislation through while it is still possible to do some good."

The opening volley was particularly well aimed, thought Donald. They had attacked a place where the Opposition was traditionally weak—their advocacy of the poor and infirm. In effect, they were attempting to bribe the weaker Opposition members with valuable constituency propaganda. *Give us the Highway Bill,* they were saying, *and we'll let you have some votes for your marginal seats.*

Waring knew full well there would be those in Huw Griffith's camp who would find resisting such temptation very difficult indeed.

It was Huw Griffith himself who picked up the gauntlet. "Mr. Speaker," he bellowed, taking his place at the dispatch-box, "while we grant that an increase in home energy allowance is desperately needed, we cannot agree that this motion is of sufficient urgency to suspend the day's business. If it had been so, we believe this government would certainly have introduced it properly under standing order number twenty. However much we would like to accommodate the Government on this point, I beg the Speaker to disallow the motion and proceed with the business before the House."

Speaker of the House Olmstead Carpenter agreed with the Opposition that the application for an emergency debate should have been made prior to commencement of the day's business, and suggested that introduction of the proposed legislation at this point amounted to an unnecessary delay.

The Government took the denial of its motion without grumbling, but swiftly made two more motions to set aside the day's business. The clock ticked slowly on, and the great shambling Welshman stood to his work; with patience and skill, Huw Griffith doggedly met each stratagem with cogent and plausible arguments. Although it took the better part of another hour, by seven-thirty he had cleared the way, and the House moved on to the first agenda item.

By prior arrangement with Opposition backbenchers, legislation was allowed to proceed unopposed, which brought the Highway Bill to the floor at last. The Government, desperate now, objected on the grounds that, owing to the lateness of the hour, the bill would not get its full share of final debate.

"Mr. Speaker!" shouted Charles Graham, leader of the New Conservative Party and Huw Griffith's loyal shill. "As this legislation has already received two complete readings, I suggest the Government's motion amounts to an egregious waste of time and taxpayers' hard-earned money. I must therefore object, in the most strenuous terms, to any further delay in bringing this important and necessary bill to a vote."

The Opposition benches erupted with "Hear! Hear!" and, "Bring the bill!"

When relative order had been restored, the Speaker of the House ruled that there was no compelling reason not to proceed with the vote. "The Government will bring the bill," he commanded sternly.

Prime Minister Waring, icily calm on the front bench, nodded slowly, and the Transport Secretary, Michael Gowring, took his place at the dispatch-box. "Mr. Speaker," he said without enthusiasm, "I move that the bill before us be now read for the third time."

He then proceeded to read out the bill in all its tongue-tied legalese, and closed with the standard recommendation that the bill should be passed as read, whereupon the question was opened for the third and final debate. As expected, there was no real debate at all. While no one liked it very much, the renumbering of British motorways to conform to the European highway numbering system was a foregone conclusion; it had to happen if Britain expected any future EU money for roads.

When no members stood to speak, Charles Graham rose and said, "Mr. Speaker, I move that the question be now put."

Division bells were run throughout Westminster, and in all Commons rooms. There followed eight interminable minutes during which those already in the chamber shifted restlessly in their seats while the few stragglers were rounded up and herded in. When the Speaker called the question, instructing the members to vote aye or no, each MP reached for the pager-sized keypad on the bench before him and, after entering their personal ID number, pushed one of two buttons: green for yes, and red for no.

Donald, almost faint with anticipation, tried to read the expression on the face of the Clerk of the Chamber as the latter watched the electronic counter installed in his podium; but the man gave nothing away. Olmstead Carpenter called for the votes to be submitted, then asked for the result.

The Clerk turned to the Speaker's chair, and declaimed in a loud voice, "Mr. Speaker, the vote has been cast and tallied. The result is as follows: for the ayes, three hundred and forty-five. For the noes, three hundred and forty-five."

A moment of complete silence followed the announcement, and then the chamber erupted in roars of triumph and groans of defeat, over which the Speaker pounded his gavel, shouting, "Order! Order! Order, ladies and gentlemen, please! Order!"

When some semblance of decorum had been restored, Carpenter, in his stentorian voice, repeated the numbers, and added, "It would appear, Honorable Members, that the chair must cast the deciding vote." He paused, considering, perhaps, the effect of his next words. "The Chair elects to maintain the *status quo* by registering a 'no' vote. The bill is hereby defeated by the margin of three hundred and forty-six to three hundred and forty-five."

Pandemonium instantly returned, and the Speaker's efforts to restore order went unheeded.

"Yes!" Donald sank back into his chair. It was official: the Wall of Steel had been breached.

Across the divide, Waring and his cabinet sat immobile with shock. Not so Huw Griffith, who was on his feet instantly, waving his order paper and shouting above the joyful clamor of his colleagues to be recognized.

The Speaker finally succeeded in calling the chamber to order and granted the Honorable Member's request to speak. "In light of the vote just taken, Mr. Speaker," Griffith said, "it would seem that the Government in power has lost the ability to put through its legislation. Therefore, as leader of the Opposition, I beg to move that this House has no confidence in His Majesty's Government."

The chamber roared, each side shrieking its position so thunderously that it took the Speaker a full five minutes to quiet the noise sufficiently to recognize the leader of the Opposition's motion.

Waring was on his feet before the Speaker finished. He launched into an impassioned speech which amounted to a plea for party unity—laced with subtle threats for those who failed to fall in behind their elected leader. Then, unexpectedly, he sat down, yielding the floor to his enemies.

Perhaps it was a show of confidence; then again, perhaps, fearing full-scale revolt, he chose to forestall debate before the waverers and floaters had a chance to think things through and turn a simple defection into a rout.

Once more there arose a mighty din, and when at last the clamor subsided, Speaker Carpenter said, "It would seem the Honorable Member's motion has been debated with admirable brevity. Unless the Opposition have a further point to make, I will entertain a call to put the question."

"Mr. Speaker," said Charles Graham, rising to play his part, "I move that the question be now put."

Again, the commotion was so loud that the Speaker, despairing of restoring order, instead ordered the Clerk to sound the division bell. Eight more minutes elapsed before the vote; but this time the atmosphere was raucous with jibes and challenges across the divide. And then the moment of truth: codes were dutifully entered, and votes electronically cast.

It was all Donald could do to force himself to sit still and listen to the Clerk's tally. Even so, what with the turmoil all around, and the loud thumping of his own heart, it was several seconds before the Clerk's announcement made sense.

". . . three hundred and forty-five . . . and for the noes, three hundred and forty-two. Honorable Members of the House, the ayes have carried the motion."

At first Donald did not believe he had heard correctly. The tally didn't add up—fewer members had voted this time than last time. But, as the Speaker repeated the tally, Donald realized what had happened: three Government MPs—three of Waring's floaters—had abstained. The no-confidence motion had passed.

Donald gazed around him as the Opposition benches erupted in ecstatic jubilation. MPs threw their order papers in the air and cheered, dancing and hugging and kissing one another. Meanwhile, Waring and his cabinet slumped on the front bench like train-wreck casualties, staring in numb disbelief at their jubilant counterparts on the other side of the chamber.

In time, the rejoicing quieted sufficiently for the Speaker

to be heard. "The Chair has duly noted the motion's passage," Olmstead Carpenter said, sounding like the voice of God, "and on the evidence of the vote it would seem that His Majesty's Government is no longer in a position to conduct the ordinary business of this House. Therefore, I request and do hereby declare this Parliament to be suspended until such time as it shall be reconvened by His Majesty the King."

Rising from his great, thronelike chair, he said, "This House is adjourned." With that, he stepped down from his chair and left the chamber.

Donald breathed a silent prayer of thanks, then rose and walked down the steps to congratulate Huw Griffith on their joint victory. "It was your call, Donald," Huw said, clapping him soundly on the back. "Well done. Are you still going to announce your new party tonight?"

"As soon as possible," he said, elation beginning to swell inside him. "Care to come along?"

"No, you earned your moment in the limelight," Huw replied, his red face radiant with joy. "Take your bow, Donald; you deserve it. Join us for a drink in the Commons bar afterward. We have a general election to discuss."

The Opposition leader was pulled away just then, and Donald went in search of his co-conspirators to welcome them into his new party and, more important, reassure them. It was no mean feat to help bring down a sitting government, and he suspected they might be feeling fretful and forlorn.

He located the two ex-Government MPs, and moved them smoothly and swiftly out of the chamber and into the corridor, away from potentially hostile colleagues. He thanked his co-conspirators for their support and expressed his admiration for their courage, saying that he hoped the thought of a glorious future with the new party would take some of the sting out of the flogging they were sure to receive from their former party bosses. "You've done the right thing," he told them. "I'm going to announce the Royal Reform Party now. Come along, and stand with me."

While His Majesty's loyal Opposition decamped to the House of Commons lounge for celebratory drinks, Donald steered the first members of his new party through the crush of well-wishers, and hurried down the long corridor towards the Commons entrance. Pausing briefly before opening the door, he said, "Ready? Here we go!"

Emerging from the building, the three of them were instantly mobbed by the waiting reporters—Donald's first spontaneous press conference in all his years of government work. "Lord Rothes! A statement, Lord Rothes!" they called, showing a marked respect heretofore absent in his dealings with the media. And then someone from the rear of the pack shouted, "Donald, where's yer troosers?" and he knew he had finally arrived.

"If you don't mind," he said, speaking into the glare of television lights, "I have a prepared announcement I would like to read, and then I'll take questions."

Withdrawing the paper from his jacket pocket, he unfolded it and began to read. " 'It gives me great pleasure to stand before you today and proclaim the formation of a new political party, the Royal Reform Party. I would sincerely like to extend membership to any who wish to help preserve the inestimable benefits of the constitutional monarchy for ourselves, for our children, and for posterity.' "

There came a flutter of questions at this declaration. Ignoring the commotion, Donald continued, " 'Towards that end, as leader of the Royal Reform Party, I hereby declare our principal aim and political ambition shall be the defeat of the referendum for the Act of Dissolution of the Monarchy. That campaign begins here and now, and I cordially invite any like-minded individuals to join us in the struggle.' " He looked up from his paper. "My colleagues and I thank you for your kind attention."

The closest journalist thrust a microphone into his face and said, "Rumor has it that you and Huw Griffith orchestrated the collapse of the Waring government—would you care to comment?"

Before Donald could answer, someone else called out, "The King's a rat!"

There were raucous shouts of "Down with the King!" and "Stop the rat!"

A reporter in the front row shoved forward. "In light of recent revelations," he said, "it would seem the monarchy is finished."

"Don't believe everything you read in the papers," Donald remarked.

"Seriously," insisted the reporter, "why beat a dead horse?"

Donald, half-blinded by the TV lights and camera flashes, hesitated, choosing his words carefully. During the ensuing pause, a third reporter called out, "Did the King put you up to this? How much did he pay you?"

The question sparked an instant reaction inside him. He leaned forward into the banked microphones and replied, "You know, you've just reminded me that when I began my political career in the House of Lords, I wore my title proudly. Yet, when that lofty—and, to be honest, outmoded—institution was dismantled to make way for the coming devolution, I could not have cared less, because, like a lot of people in this country, I had long since lost any sense of honor or respect I might have had in my title.

"After all, what is nobility worth when it is debased daily in the eyes of the watching world by a randy old profligate who cannot bring himself to reside in the land that gave him birth, to live among the people who nurtured and sustained him in his youth, and furnished him with his position, wealth, and purpose in life? What is nobility, then, when it becomes a byword for indulgence and excess, a laughing-stock for the professional comedians of the world, and an embarrassment to those who still possess a sense of moral indignation?

"Like many of my countrymen, I felt that the crown of Britain had become both source and symbol of all that is sordid, shabby, and salacious. In consequence, I held my own title lightly; I considered it a thing to be despised and, when the third referendum dissolved the House of Lords, I welcomed it. Instead of railing against the injustice of a short-sighted, unthinking government—as did many of my ermine-wearing colleagues—I went on the campaign trail and got myself elected to Parliament where I thought I might do some good.

"Now, you might well ask me why I started a political party with the sole purpose of restoring and preserving the monarchy. Why try to revive that dead horse? I'll tell you this: I did it because our nation desperately needs a champion to rescue it from the creeping pessimism and distrust of our age. Our country, our world, needs the inspiration of true nobility, the example of a sovereign king who can redeem our highest hopes and aspirations.

"Why did I do it, you ask? I did it *not* because I desire the reclamation of a shallow, self-interested monarchy, but because I crave the restoration of our better selves."

Donald finished in silence. The reporters had caught the edgy enthusiasm of his tone, and were much affected by it in spite of themselves. He had not intended to say all that, yet when pressed to respond, a lifetime of yearning had boiled up and overflowed.

The moment passed, and the press pack recovered its voice. They began clamoring and shouting more questions, but Donald merely replied, "I have nothing more to say right now. Thank you very much for listening." Turning to the members with him, he said, "I'll turn you over to my colleagues now. Perhaps you have some questions for them."

With that, he pushed on into the crowd, which gave way grudgingly to let him by. They continued flinging questions at him as he passed, and no doubt would have pursued him from the parking lot if they had not been distracted by the appearance of Huw Griffith and Charles Graham, who emerged from the House of Commons just then. The mob abruptly abandoned Donald, and raced to gather sound bites from the major players in the day's monumental drama.

Donald found himself quickly alone, and hurried towards the Commons taxi rank, hailing a cab as he went. The day's result had exceeded his wildest imaginings, and he was anxious to share his moment of triumph with Caroline. Also, he had promised to call James and Embries with a full report as soon as practically possible.

As the black cab drew up, he opened the rear door, bending forward to tell the driver his destination through the half-open window. As he did so, a young woman appeared and quickly slipped into the cab through the open door.

"Excuse me, miss," he said, "this cab is taken. I'm sure there will be another along shortly."

"I heard what you said just now," answered the young woman, "and I want to talk to you about it." She slid further into the cab, and patted the seat beside her. "Come on, don't be afraid. I won't bite."

"It's not that," Donald protested. "Look, it's been rather an eventful day, and I'm exhausted. I'd really just like to get home, if you don't mind."

"I don't mind in the least. We can talk on the way." She opened the bag at her side, and withdrew a microphone which was attached to a tape recorder inside. "Please? It would make my editor a very happy man, and I would be forever in your debt."

"I've said all I intend to say at the moment," Donald informed her.

The taxi behind them, having picked up a fare, gave a sharp blast on the horn to move them along. "What's it going to be, mate?" called the driver, losing patience. "Going, or staying—make up your mind."

"No detours—I only want as much as you can tell me on the shortest route to your place," the reporter promised cheerfully. "Please?"

"Oh, all right. Just this once." Donald put his foot into the cab, then hesitated. "Let me see some identification first," he said to the woman. "Simple precaution. I hope you don't mind."

"Not at all. One cannot be too careful these days." She put down the microphone and rummaged in the black bag. "Here it is," she said, withdrawing a plastic-laminated ID card.

Satisfied, Donald handed the card back and climbed into the cab. "Is this a common method of securing your interviews," he asked, as the taxi pulled away, "kidnapping your subjects, Miss Morgan?"

She put back her head and laughed, her voice rich and throaty and seductive. "Not at all," she replied. "I take whatever opportunity presents itself. I work purely by instinct, and my instincts tell me that you are a very complicated man, Lord Rothes."

"You must be careful," he warned lightly. "Flattery can be construed in some political circles as a bribe."

"I'm merely stating a fact." She smiled warmly, sliding a long silver pen from her bag. "My sources tell me you're one of the chief architects of the royalist revival—"

"Hoped-for revival," corrected Donald.

"Quite." She withdrew the cap from the pen. "I thought we might talk about the resurgence of the royalist sentiment."

"Very well, Miss Morgan," said Donald, easing back in his seat, "for the next ten minutes, you have my undivided attention. How can I help with your story?"

## ❋

# Thirty-seven

The body of Donald Rothes was found floating in the waters of St. Katharine's Dock at half past eleven on the night of his great parliamentary triumph. He was discovered by a young couple who, emerging from the Dickens Inn on that particularly crisp, clear January night, had paused on a wooden footbridge to look at the lights of Tower Bridge reflected in the water.

They noticed something bumping against the hull of one of the sailboats and, growing curious, walked around the dock for a closer look which confirmed their worst suspicions: the object was a person lying facedown in the water. At first they thought it was a woman, but when the police arrived and fished the body out of the water, they discovered the body was that of a man dressed in a kilt.

At Blair Morven, James and Jenny had been watching TV in James' room, flicking through the channels to catch the latest word on Donald's triumph. The collapse of the Waring government knocked every other story off the schedule; most channels were running in-depth coverage of the extraordinary events of the day. BBC Two had abandoned its regular programming to bring in-depth reporting on what they were calling the "Waring revolt." The regular ten o-clock broadcast had been extended into the night with continual replays of the crisis in Parliament, interviews with MPs, and endless speculation by political pundits of various stripes.

James had been following the unfolding drama from the moment coverage of the parliamentary session began. By six o'clock, the British networks were on the air and giving the play-by-play of the vote. Jenny had braved the entrenched journalists outside the castle to join the King and, together with the entire staff of Blair Morven, gathered in the library before the big-screen TV, they watched the collapse of the Waring government live and in color. They popped a cork in Donald's honor when he announced the formation of his new political party outside the House of Commons.

Later, they had supper in James' apartment and settled back to enjoy an evening's televised news. Both agreed that Donald had acquitted himself well, and his announcement speech struck just the right note. Several broadcasts featured Donald prominently in their coverage of the day's developments. ITV devoted a ten-minute segment to reporting on the new party, and Donald's speech was replayed in its entirety.

Still exhausted from the day's heady events—and slightly buzzed from the champagne—the royal couple found it somewhat difficult to come down from the high. Jenny, remote control in hand, was sitting cross-legged on the edge of the bed, restlessly channel hopping in order not to miss anything.

"He just might pull it off," Jenny was saying as the phone rang.

James answered, thinking it must be the man himself wanting to share the golden moment. He had been expecting a call all evening, and reached for the phone with congratulations on his lips. A woman's voice came on the line, speaking so quickly he could not make out what she was saying.

"Caroline? Is that you?" he said.

At these words, Jenny turned to look at him and saw James' expression change instantly to concern. "What's wrong?" asked Jenny.

"Yes, by all means, Caroline. I'll tell him."

He hung up. "Donald's missing. She hasn't seen him since he left for the House of Commons, and he hasn't called or anything."

A few moments later, Embries was on the phone trying to calm an increasingly distraught Caroline. "Call the police," he instructed. "No, do it now. Ask for Chief Inspector Kirkland. Then call me back as soon as you've spoken to him." He paused. "That's right. We're on our way."

They received word of Donald's death a little after midnight, and were in the air within minutes of the dreadful news: James, Embries, and Rhys. Calum was left to coordinate security at Blair Morven, which had suddenly taken a much higher priority.

The Tempest landed at Ealing's small airfield, and they sped by taxi straight to Kenzie House through nearly deserted London streets. They arrived to find the entire street blocked by police cars, television vans with satellite equipment, a few dozen photographers, a score of journalists, and several neighbors wearing coats over bathrobes who obviously could not sleep for all the commotion.

Stepping from the cab, they moved quickly to the house, pushing through the crush of cameramen and reporters shouting questions: "Is it true Lord Rothes is dead?" they cried. "Was it suicide or an accident?"

Rhys shoved his way to the door, where they were immediately ushered into the house by a police constable, who closed the door quickly behind them, saying, "You are expected, Your Highness."

The foyer was full of people, mostly policemen and detectives, but several of Donald and Caroline's friends and neighbors as well. Caroline and Isobel were in the sitting room, shoulder to shoulder in front of the fireplace in which a blaze was roaring. As James and Embries entered the room, they turned and the look on the women's faces made the skin on the back of James' neck tingle; his shoulders felt as if an electric current were passing through his body.

Time seemed to recoil as he stepped through the doorway. The darkened, firelit room took on a dreamlike quality. The quivering firelight illuminated a glowing rectangle on the figured carpet where Caroline and Isobel stood. The light shimmered, surrounding the women in a radiant halo as they wept. At the sight, the *fiosachd* awakened and James heard, as if from far away, the wind sighing over a distant battlefield.

Into his mind came the image of a darkened, moonlit plain, strewn with the huddled shapes of fallen warriors. There were figures walking among the dead, stoop-shouldered, bent low to peer into the faces of the corpses—women searching for their men. On the wind he could hear the broken sobs of those whose search had ended in cruel discovery. Here and there, the moonlight picked out a shield boss, or spear tip, and glinted with a melancholy gleam.

The sitting room dissolved around him: James was there on that windswept plain once more. The tang of smoke filled his nostrils, and he turned to see a fire on the riverbank a short distance away. The wounded had gathered there to warm themselves and have their injuries cleaned and bound.

As he stood looking on, a great grief descended over him—sadness heavy, cold, and unyielding as a cloak of iron. He could not stand. He sank to his knees and fell forward onto his hands, as a cry of sorrow, quick and sharp, tore from his throat. In this torment, he cried once and again; releasing the third cry, he heard someone call his name.

"Arthur!"

The call startled him, stifling his cry.

"Arise, Arthur. Take up your sword and stand."

Raising his head, he looked up to see a tall, upright man approaching. His cloak was dark, trimmed with wolf skin. His eyes were stern, and glimmered in the moonlight like pale gold. He came to stand before him, and Arthur looked up into the face of his Wise Counselor.

"I grieve, Myrddin," he told him. "When will I mourn my Cymbrogi, if not now?"

"You are the Pendragon," Myrddin replied sternly. "While others mourn you must prepare for the battle to come. The enemy will not be stopped by your heartfelt tears of sorrow, but by the sharp blade in your strong hand."

Stretching out his hands, he spoke a word in the old Dark

Tongue, and the King felt strength returning. Seeping up out of the ground and into his bones it came, driving out the dull, clinging weight of grief that hung upon him. The black mist of sorrow lifted; he could see clearly once more. Gathering the raveled threads of his courage, he reached for the sword lying beside him on the ground. Arthur pushed himself up, and stood.

Myrddin placed one hand on the King's shoulder and raised his staff over his head. "Though grief be your constant companion, Arthur, it is not for you to mourn. You are the strength of your people; you are the mighty tower of their hope and the fortress of their trust. Therefore, harden your heart, seal up your tears, and set your face to the morning."

He pointed across the plain with his staff. The Pendragon looked and saw the pearly pink blush of sunrise tinting the eastern sky.

"Come away, Arthur," said his Wise Counselor. "It is the living who have need of you now, not the dead."

He turned and moved away towards the campfire and the wounded gathered there. The King followed, feeling the solid strength of the earth beneath his feet. He heard the sound of a monk's bell, and the plain faded, becoming the sitting room once more.

James went to Caroline and Isobel, and gathered them in his strong arms. "I'm so sorry," he said, his voice cracking with emotion. "I'm so very sorry."

Caroline nodded, and pulled away, wiping her eyes with a damp handkerchief. She straightened to her full height and, drawing her arm around Isobel, said, "He didn't commit suicide. That's preposterous. And he didn't get drunk and fall into the water. That Inspector Kirkland implied as much—as if Donald were a lager lout with nothing on his mind but . . ."

Embries, silent and dark beside James, spoke up then. "There will be an autopsy. The truth will be established. Take no heed of the fools who gather outside your door. Be strong."

Caroline nodded again, and Isobel began to weep softly.

"Be strong," Embries urged, placing a hand on Isobel's

shoulder. "The enemy is near. The battle is soon joined." Turning, he walked swiftly to the door.

James kissed Caroline on the cheek, then Isobel, and hurried from the room. He caught up with Embries as he opened the door of the black Jaguar parked in the private driveway behind the house. "You know what happened to Donald," he said. "He was killed, wasn't he? I'm going with you."

Embries gave his head a slight shake. "This is my fight. I will go alone."

"You'll need me with you," James insisted. He started to move around the side of the car.

Embries grabbed him by the arm, and held him. "This fight is mine!" he growled angrily. "You have more important things to do right now."

"What is more important than finding out what happened to Donald?"

"Dissolving Parliament," Embries answered. "Schedule your meeting with the Prime Minister for around three. Rhys should have no difficulty looking after you."

James resisted. "But I want to do something. I want to help."

"Then pray!" he snapped. "And do as I say."

Embries softened somewhat and placed a hand on his shoulder. Looking into James' eyes, he said, "You are the King, the life of your people. It is not for you to mourn."

At his words the ancient vision flickered, and James glimpsed again that moonlit battlefield. The air was heavy with smoke and the stink of blood. All around him men were moaning softly, but his Wise Counselor was right: there was work to be done. Hardening his heart to the grief he felt for his fallen Cymbrogi, James returned to the house, and to his duty as King.

✳

# Thirty-eight

The drive from London took longer than Embries anticipated, but he did not hurry. There was plenty of time before
dark to do all that was required. Upon approaching the town,
he turned off the busy highway and proceeded along the sin-
gle-track farm roads. He much preferred the old, low, winding lanes when traveling in this part of Britain. Some of
those deep hollow ways dated from Neolithic times, and he
felt the immense age of the place seep into him whenever he
used them.

He stopped a little way off from the hill itself, retrieved
his staff and rucksack from the boot, locked the car, and
continued the rest of the way on foot. The sky was dark and
brooding, overcast with a single mass of formless cloud the
color of ancient pewter. The wind out of the northwest had
a damp, icy scent—rain at least, perhaps sleet in the offing.
The sound of the crows gathering in winter-bare trees
across the empty fields filled him with a strange melancholy—a lonely nostalgia for all the times he had come to
this place.

And then he saw it—rising suddenly before him, green
and looming against the blank sky—the Tor, with its solitary
tower, like an omphalos pole marking the center point
around which the entire world revolved. The sight always

371

made his breath catch—not because it was so arresting in itself but for how he remembered it to have been long ago. Perhaps for this reason he always felt more at home here than anywhere else in all Britain.

Glastonbury Tor . . . Ynys Witrin, the Glass Isle of old . . . the curious conical hump of earth and stone had worn various names throughout the ages. Some even called it Avalon. Embries knew it first as Ynys Avallach, and that is the name he still preferred.

He let himself through a rusty iron gate, and walked across the field below the Tor. Once the field would have been under water; if not for the extensive range of drainage ditches, the Tor would still be surrounded on three sides by lake water even now. Looking across the field to the low hill sheltering behind the Tor, he marked the place where the shrine had been and, near it, the first abbey. Those ruins were long gone; constructed of timber, wicker, and mud, there was little more than a bump on the hillside where they had been.

Reaching the end of the field beneath the Tor, Embries climbed the stile and walked along the road until he came to a tiny, quick-running stream. There, he stopped and took off his shoes and socks; stepping into the icy water, he waded into the middle of the stream, feeling with his feet and toes in the soft mud of the streambed for the stones he knew were there. Whenever he found a suitable stone, he retrieved it, rinsed it, and put the smooth, egg-shaped rock into a net bag he had taken from the rucksack on his back. By the time he had collected enough, the dim, misty daylight was beginning to fade.

Returning quickly the way he had come, he climbed from the stream, put on his shoes and socks once more, and hurried on to the Tor. He pushed through the lopsided metal gate the National Trust had put up generations ago, and entered the sacred precinct of the hill. Squatting on his haunches, he waited, watching the road and listening to the mournful moan of the wind as it flowed over and around the smooth grassy heights above. When he was certain he would not be interrupted, he took up his staff and began the first circuit of the Tor, walking quickly in a sunwise circle around the base of the great mound.

The completion of his first round told him there was no one either on or near the Tor—the place had become such a magnet for New Age hippies, neo-druid wannabes, crypto-feminist Earth Mother goddess worshippers, magic mush-room devotees, and latter-day pagan revivalists, he was never sure he wouldn't encounter someone coming or going on the hillside. The presence of these airy-fairy dabblers was more than irksome to him; it was potentially dangerous—not to himself but to the cheerful ignoramuses who might stumble into far more than they bargained for.

The second circuit confirmed the fact that he had the place to himself. The third circuit was accompanied by a chant of isolation, and upon its completion, he relaxed. He would not be disturbed or interrupted now.

Opening his backpack, he carefully withdrew three bun-dles. The first was a voluminous, long-sleeved blue tunic, seamless, woven of hand-twisted linen, which, once he'd drawn it over his head, reached from his chin to his ankles. The tunic was gathered in by a wide cloth belt—also blue, also woven of hand-twisted linen—which he passed three times around his waist before tying.

The second bundle was a cloak—so old and ragged that it hung about his shoulders in straggling, featherlike tatters that rustled and fluttered as he walked. Lifting it onto his shoulders, he fastened it at the neck with a silver brooch and pin. And then, taking up the oaken staff, he tucked the third bundle under his belt and started towards the Tor, leaving the rucksack behind but taking up the bag of stones he had col-lected.

A path leads up the side of the Tor, with improvised steps cut in the turf, for those visitors who care only to bolt to the top for the view. But there is another, far older pathway, the remnants of which form a series of deep, sinuous ridges around the flanks of the hill. This can be trod by anyone who wishes to take a more leisurely climb, but it is effective only to those of the Learned Brotherhood who know the proper chants and invocations to make along the way.

For the old path is in reality a maze—a means of concentrating both the mind and spirit to the task at hand. Through seven circuits the Seeker, or Initiate, winds his slow way around the hill, moving in a sunwise direction, only to double back the opposite way on the next circuit. At various places the Initiate pauses to make ablution, propitiation, or invocation as necessary, depending on the nature of his particular quest.

Embries moved to the foot of the Tor and, taking his staff in both hands, raised it before him. "Great Light!" he called. "Creator of all that is moving and at rest, hear me now! The path grows dark before me. Illumine my steps with the light of your presence, and guide me in the way of truth."

So saying, he put his foot upon the path and began walking with slow, deliberate steps along the deep-grooved ridge. At the end of each circuit of the maze, he stopped and offered up a rune of protection: "Michael Valiant, Protector and Defender of souls, draw near me this night, and shelter me beneath your strong shield. Put your fiery sword between me and all who wish me evil; guard me with a mighty protection."

A murky, howling darkness swarmed out of the wintry sky, swiftly descending over the Tor. The wind hissed through the long grass, spitting tiny ice pellets over him. Hardening himself to the gale, he moved on, repeating the old, old pattern of the eternal dance traced out on the rising slopes of the Tor.

He finished the climb in complete darkness, and came to stand inside the tower to escape the buffeting of the wind. St. Michael's Tower, as it was known to the locals, was the sturdy remnant of a medieval church which had once occupied the auspicious site. The square stone room was empty, and open at either end, but allowed some small protection from the elements. What is more, among the dank odors of damp earth and decaying stone, the odor of stale smoke still clung to the walls. He could smell dog's urine, too, and knew that someone—tramp or traveler—had recently spent the night atop the Tor and lit a fire to keep warm.

Stepping into the center of the tower, he bent down and put his hand to the floor. After a moment's search, he found what he was looking for: a small heap of soggy ashes from the twig fire the tramp had made. He rose and, stretching his staff over the damp heap, began speaking in a low voice. As the words of the Dark Tongue echoed in the hollow chamber, the ash heap began to warm. Raising his voice, he repeated the charm, and embers awakened and began to wink and glow like the eyes of nocturnal animals.

Moving the staff slowly over the ashes, his voice ringing in the chamber, he saw the first slender blooms of flame appear—one, then another, and more. Pale and weak, they fluttered to life, gathered strength, and finally burned with a firm and steady light. In a few moments, the fire was reconstituted from the ashes it had formed. Lowering his staff, Embries squatted down to warm himself.

He sat a long while, listening to the snap of the flames and the vacant shriek of the wind as it restlessly circled the tower. He thought about the ordeal before him, rehearsing each movement in his mind. When at last he judged it was time to begin, he rose and went outside, taking the stones with him.

Pacing off thirty steps from the tower's entrance, he dropped the net bag and, holding the staff in both hands, drove it down into the soft earth of the hilltop. He retrieved the bag of stones and paced off three more steps from the standing staff, laying the first stone where he stopped. Raising his right hand over his head, he spoke a rune of protection: "As I place this stone, I am placing myself, body and soul, beneath your protection, O Lord of Hosts."

Retracing his steps, he walked three paces from the staff and placed another stone directly opposite the first, repeated the rune, and returned to the staff. In this way, he quartered the circle, placing a stone at each point of the compass; when that was finished, he proceeded to quarter the quarter. After establishing the eighth stone, he repeated the rune twice. Then, taking up the bag, he moved around the circle laying a stone between each one already placed until the bag was empty.

Satisfied with the circle he had created, he returned to the
center and, taking hold of the staff, he looked to the storm-
wracked sky and called aloud:

> *"High King of Heaven! My shield, my defender,*
> *be the strong tower of my strength*
> *This night, this hour, and always.*

> *"Be Thou the cloak of Colmcille over me,*
> *Be Thou the cloak of Michael militant about me,*
> *Be Thou the cloak of Christ, Best Beloved,*
> *safeguarding me.*

> *"High King of Heaven! Great of Might,*
> *hide me in the hollow of your Swift Sure Hand,*
> *in the hour of my torment and travail.*

> *"An isle art thou in the sea,*
> *A hill art thou on the plain,*
> *A well art thou in the wilderness,*
> *A tower art thou in the camp of the enemy.*

> *"High King of Heaven! Brother of the Helpless,*
> *be near me, uphold me,*
> *place your angel host around me,*
> *encircle me with Heaven's bright war band:*
> *this night, this hour, always and forever.*

> *"As thou wast before*
> *At my soul's shaping,*
> *Be thou too*
> *at my journey's close. Amen!"*

Lowering his hand, he turned his face to the wind, gathered his cloak around him, and sat down with his back to the
standing staff. Eyes closed, he sat motionless, slowing his
breath, calming the inner turmoil of his heart, clearing his
mind of every thought save one.

He repeated the thought over and over until he could feel

the rhythmic pulse of power begin to ebb and flow within him. He gathered the power to him, holding it, until he could not contain it any longer. Then, placing the full force of his volition behind this single concentrated thought, he put forth his hand as if flinging a bird into the teeth of the storm.

In the same instant, he released the thought: *Come, Morgian, I summon thee!*

The gale howled, scouring the bare hilltop, but he pulled his cloak more tightly around him and hunkered down to wait for an answer. Far above the all-obscuring cloud, the cold stars wheeled through their ceaseless courses, revolving slowly around Heaven's Nail, which itself was pierced by Embries' staff.

She gave no warning of her arrival.

Embries sensed a subtle quickening in the storm-wrent air, and opened his eyes to see her walking towards him: a young woman, wrapped head to foot in a heavy black coat so that only her face and one pale hand showed where she clutched the coat at her throat.

His heart froze as he beheld her. His hands grew numb and his spirit shrank back in dread and revulsion.

She smiled when she saw him, her smile as mocking as her glance. Although her appearance had altered since he'd last seen her—her hair was red now, her youthful face more round, her features more generous—she was as beautiful as ever.

He climbed quickly to his feet and put up his hand to halt her. "Stop there," he said. "Come no further."

Glancing at the circle of stones, she halted. "A *chaim*— why, I haven't seen one of those for *ages*. How quaint." She laughed, her voice sultry and low. "But then, you always were something of a romantic old fossil."

"This is not about me, Morgian—or should I say, Moira?"

She laughed again, and the darkness seemed to contract around her. "Oh, well done, Merlin. It took you long enough," she said brightly. "Don't tell me you are afraid of me, dear heart."

"No," Embries said softly. "I do not fear you."

"Maybe you should," she replied. Embries marveled; she had lost none of her arrogance . . . and none of her venom. She turned and began walking around the stone circle. "You know, I've been to Llyonesse. I couldn't wait. I wanted to see it before it was crawling with tourists."

"There's nothing there for you anymore," Embries told her, trembling inwardly.

"Are you certain?" she said, arching an eyebrow provocatively. "I wouldn't stake my life on it if I were you, Merlin. You're bound to be disappointed. But then, you always were something of a loser, weren't you? Perhaps that's why I find you so irresistible."

"It won't be like last time," he warned.

"Oh, don't be tedious, Merlin. I can't stand it—I really can't." She stopped walking and turned to face him. "Look at you, hiding like a hermit inside your pitiful stone circle. You poor, deluded little man. Do you think I have not anticipated this moment?"

"Listen to me, Moira," Embries said, "I will only say this once: the killing will stop. It is me you want. Leave the others alone."

"Is it getting to you, pet?" Her voice took on a steely edge. "Oh, dear, oh, dear"—she clucked her tongue in mock sympathy—"and here I was just getting started! You haven't seen anything yet."

"Take me, kill me—if you can. But leave the others alone."

"My, how you do flatter yourself," she replied. "Do you really think your pathetic life means anything to me? Your delusions will be the end of you, I really do believe. Anyway, I could have had you a thousand times, dear heart, but the truth is, your insignificant existence does not interest me in the least."

She began walking again around the *chaim*. "I have other plans for you, Merlin, dear heart. I want you to live long and watch the destruction of all your fondest hopes. And then, one by one, I will destroy your happy little band of dreamers."

"No. It is finished." Raising his right hand, palm outward,

Embries declared, "In the name of Christ, I do bind you, Moira."

"Stop it!" she screamed, losing her temper. "How little you know me if you think *that* tired old singsong will restrain me."

"In the name of Christ, Lord of this world and the next, I do bind you."

"Bloody idiot!" she sneered, her voice savage and raw. There was a movement around her like a rush of unseen wings. The darkness seemed to shudder and writhe, tightening around her. "You cannot stop me. No one can."

All at once, her demeanor changed. As if remembering herself, she said, "Put aside your childish tricks, and I will give you one last chance. Join me, Merlin. We could rule together, you and I. We could restore Llyonesse. The Lia Fail is still there—I know it is. We can find it, and the world would be ours for the taking. Come, cousin, what do you say?"

She extended her hand, and her coat fell open, exposing an exquisite white flank and rose-tipped breast. "Why go on denying what you've always wanted? Come to me, Merlin. Take me. Love me." She held out her arms and beckoned him to step outside the protecting circle of the *chaim*. "Worship me."

Poor, demented Morgian, he could almost pity her, forever relying on the same crude tricks. Unmoved, Embries doggedly repeated, "In the name of Christ Jesus, King of Heaven and Earth, I do bind you and compel you to desist."

Moira turned her hands, thrusting them out in front of her as if to ward off blows. Embries noticed that a crude eye had been carved in the flesh of each palm. Raising her arms, she crossed her hands over her head, and began spitting words at him. *"Exis velat morda! Exis velat morda!"*

The wind shrieked, swirling down from the black sky as from the pit. Hair streaming out from her head like living snakes, her eyes wide and bulging with loathing and disgust, she screamed her incantation at him, loosing the power of her fury. *"Exis velat morda! Gorim exat morda!"*

The raw force of her malice hit him like a gale gusting hot from some godless desert waste, arid and empty, withering the very flesh on the bones. He staggered back a pace, and felt his staff at his back. Closing his eyes, he turned his face away and put out a hand, took hold of the stout oak and gripped it hard. Here in Britain's sacred center, the center of the world, he would not be moved. Holding tight to the oaken staff, he faced the corrosive blast of Moira's hatred. "In the name of Christ Triumphant," he cried—the wind seized his words and hurled them back in his face—"I do bind you and compel you to desist!"

Moira screamed. Whether in frustration, rage, or pain, Embries could not tell. But it was the sound of a wounded animal that knows it must either fight to the death or flee.

Inside the tower, the fire guttered and went out. The feeble light vanished, overwhelmed by the darkness. Embries drew a breath and braced himself for the final onslaught.

"High King of Heaven! Great of Might," he cried, "hide me in the hollow of your Swift Sure Hand. In the hour of my torment and travail, defend me and preserve me!"

The gale howled like an enraged beast, lashing at the exposed flesh of his face and hands. He heard Moira scream, agonized and furious. The earth and sky seemed to change places and the Tor to spin on its axis. Still, he clung to the staff in the center of the sacred circle.

It took a moment for him to realize that the sound he heard was not Moira's demented scream but the wind's cold wail as it tore itself on St. Michael's unyielding tower battlements.

Although the wind continued to assault him, he knew Moira was gone. Still, he waited, gazing into the storm-black night and listening for any sound that might betray his enemy's presence. He heard nothing, save the empty, aching whine of the wind, and that was rapidly dwindling away.

Myrddin sat for a long time, pondering what had taken place. The enemy had been delivered into his hand. In revealing herself, she had revealed her true strength. Unable to resist his summons, she had tried to use it to her advantage. She had directed the full force of her dire power at him; he had faced it and survived. She was deadly dangerous, but far from invincible.

Towards dawn the gale, having exhausted itself, died away. The clouds thinned and then parted, allowing a thin, watery moonlight to illumine the hilltop; only then did he dare to move from the protection of the *chaim*.

*Great Light,* he thought, *all praise to your glorious name! The power of your presence is sufficient to the day. Remember mercy, Lord, and do not hold your servant's frailty against him. Rather, give me strength to face the trials ahead. So be it!*

Stepping to the perimeter, he bent to the first stone and removed it, breathing a prayer of thanksgiving as he lifted it from its place in the ring:

> *"In praise of the Gifting Giver,*
> *In praise of the Shielding Son,*
> *In praise of the Quickening Spirit,*
>    *I am plucking up this stone of mercy,*
>    *the needful rock of thy salvation."*

He did this for the other stones, too, each in turn until he had collected them all and replaced them in his nylon bag. Taking up his staff, he returned to the tower to scatter the embers he had awakened. He walked to the edge of the Tor and looked out over the still-dark hills. Overhead, stars glimmered dully in patches between the slowly dispersing clouds; away to the east, night was easing its grip on the land. He could make out the undulating landscape beneath the blue-gray sky.

Lifting his staff, he blessed the coming light. Then, gathering his cloak around him, Embries started down the hill. If he hurried he could be back in London before the city began to stir.

## ✳

# Thirty-nine

He tossed back the contents of the crystal glass, and quickly poured himself another—pouring rather more than he'd planned, but what the hell? It wasn't as if he had a country to run anymore. The way things were going, he'd be lucky to hold on to his own parliamentary seat. He took a long pull on his drink and shoved the half-empty bottle aside; he walked the few paces to his chair and collapsed.

The visit from the King informing him that his government had failed was far and away the worst moment of his entire political career—a distinction previously held by the night he'd come third in a midterm by-election to a Socialist and a neo-Nazi. He'd been a young idealist then, and losing was part of the learning curve; it went with the job. Now, however, that humiliation was dwarfed by the great hulking failure of his inability to prevent desertion in the ranks the previous evening.

Shit, what a lousy day.

It had begun badly—actually, it had not properly begun at all. After an all-night disaster analysis and damage-control meeting involving the full cabinet and a host of advisors, he had emerged to receive the news of Donald Rothes' death.

"Sorry, PM," said his private secretary, darting up as Waring stepped into the lift; he needed a shower and a change of clothes. "We've had a call from Scotland Yard. I didn't want to disturb you while you were—"

"Just tell me, for Chrissakes, Leonard. What'd they want?"

"Apparently, Donald Rothes' body has been found floating in the—"

"Oh, bloody hell." His stomach knotted into a hard lump.

"Would you like to speak to—"

"Get Martin to knock out a statement right away. Say we've just received word, and we are shocked and dismayed by this tragic and senseless . . . and so on. Tell him to be sure to say I will instruct the Home Office to make this a high-priority investigation. Got that?"

As DeVries performed an about-face and headed away, Waring called after him. "How did it happen?"

"They're not saying at the moment. I can put a call in if you want to speak to someone about it."

"Later. Just get that statement out as soon as possible. I want it broadcast concurrently with news of Rothes' demise."

He went up to his rooms, took a quick hot shower, changed his clothes, and prepared for a long, hard day of media manipulation. As if losing his majority to that scumbag lord's one-horse party wasn't bad enough, he would now have to spend valuable airtime telling everyone how shocked and sorry he was that his dear Opposition colleague had gone and got himself killed. Served him right, the meddling, toffee-nosed git.

After a snatched breakfast of coffee and more coffee, he had summoned his constituency committee to an election-strategy planning session. He told them he wanted to hit the ground running as soon as the formalities were over. If he could steal a march on the Opposition—hell, *he* was the Opposition now!—catch them basking in the glow of their victory, he just possibly might gain back some of the ground they'd stolen. In the next week, he wanted to transform his office into a lean, mean electioneering machine. He wanted that fat bastard Griffith to smell the smoke and feel the heat.

In his heart, he knew that the sooner he could devote his

full attention to the campaign, the better he'd feel about the situation. Until then, there was just the little matter of receiving the official announcement from the King. When the call came at two o'clock, he accepted his fate with the fatalistic fortitude of a Stoic.

At two minutes to three, Waring stood in the vestibule and watched the King's arrival on closed-circuit television. He saw the plum-colored Range Rover as it was waved through the crush of reporters and cameramen outside the high iron gates to Number Ten, he saw it pause at the blue security kiosk to be identified—and to allow the camera crews to get some good footage of the King's arrival—before proceeding up the street and pausing again to wait for the antiterrorist barrier to be lowered.

Two junior aides were waiting for the King on the steps, along with the Downing Street head of security, who doubled as doorman, and opened the rear door of the vehicle. The day had deteriorated somewhat, and a dreary drizzle was leaking out of the low, dull clouds. One of Waring's aides held an umbrella over the King, and he was conducted straightaway into Number Ten.

Waring turned from the TV screen, closed the door, and took his place beside his Deputy Prime Minister and private secretary. He stood with his hands clasped behind him, staring balefully from under his brows.

"Good afternoon, Prime Minister," the King said, and a wave of revulsion licked up around Waring's thighs and belly.

"Come to gloat, Your Royal Highness?" he replied, his voice thick with sarcasm. Deputy PM Angela Telford-Sykes looked abashed, but said nothing. "Get it over with."

Give him credit, the King did not rile easily. Waring could even envy the young man's calm dispassion. He stood looking crisp and cool, and very much in control of himself and the situation. Waring hated him all the more.

"In accordance with established precedent," James said, "it is my right and duty to inform you that, owing to the failure of your government to maintain a voting majority, as Sovereign King of Britain, I am exercising the royal prerogative to dissolve the current Parliament."

Although Waring knew the blow was coming, it still knocked the wind out of him. His face, already gray, grew ashen. "Go on then," he muttered.

"As of this moment, Prime Minister Waring," the King continued, "your government is no longer in power. In the fervent hope that a new government can be speedily formed, I instruct you, and will so instruct the leadership of the Opposition parties, to prepare for a general election to be held in six weeks' time."

Waring glared at the young man before him. An old boxer with his back to the wall, he went down swinging. "This won't change anything," he said thickly. "You won't stop the referendum—it's going ahead as planned."

"I don't want to stop the referendum," the monarch replied. "Two weeks from now, I may not be King. That is for God and the country to decide. But I can tell you, Mr. Waring, that as of this moment you are no longer Prime Minister."

Waring gave his chin a sharp downward thrust. "Was there anything else, Your Majesty?" He spoke the title like a curse.

"I have nothing more. Good day to you," the King said; he nodded in the deputy PM's direction and turned to the door. The security officer snapped to and saw him out, holding the umbrella while the police constable on permanent duty outside Downing Street opened the rear door of the car.

But instead of climbing into the vehicle, the King walked to the front gate to deliver a short announcement to the press. He said, "A few minutes ago, I officially dissolved Parliament. I have informed Mr. Waring of his government's failure and have accordingly called for a general election to be held in six weeks." He paused, as the camera flash lit up the dreary day. "This matter is concluded. I have nothing further to add."

As he turned to make his way back to the Range Rover, a journalist called out, "What are you going to do now?"

The King half turned and called over his shoulder, "Why don't you come to Hyde Park Corner tomorrow and find out?"

Waring watched the impromptu press conference on the closed-circuit television. Although the announcement of his government's failure made him writhe with resentment, anything was better than standing another second beneath the insufferably superior, condescending gaze of the monarch.

Dismissing his deputy and aides, Waring had then gone directly into yet another meeting—with the Chief Whip and party chairman this time—to begin drawing up a preliminary election platform. It was after seven o'clock when that meeting broke up; and he allowed the Chief Whip, Nigel Sforza, and Albert Townsend, a party mogul, to talk him into dinner at the British Republic Party's private bolthole, the Balthazar Club. Once there, they were joined by three junior members of the Chief Whip's staff and Albert's trophy wife, Francine.

Over steak and *pommes frites* they had made a valiant attempt at drowning their sorrows in Balthazar's commendable claret. The effort fell short, however, and Waring was deposited back at Number Ten feeling only marginally better. Nigel had offered to keep him company; but the PM refused, saying he wanted nothing more than to go to sleep and let this wretched day end.

That had been over two hours ago, and he was still awake and wallowing in his misery. He had tried to watch the evening's news programs, which had been taped for him— but the continued dissection of his government's failure and the dissolution of Parliament made him angry, so he gave it up. He decided to take a hot bath and try to go to bed.

He had unbuckled his belt when he heard the door close in the room he'd just left. Thinking it must be the night duty officer, he turned from the closet to see a woman appear in the bedroom doorway.

"Moira," he said without enthusiasm, "don't you ever knock?"

"I thought I'd surprise you, darling."

"How'd you get in here? Who let you in?"

"The door was open, so I just came on up. Aren't you glad to see me?"

"I mean," Waring said with exaggerated patience, "who saw you? Who'd you talk to?"

"Oh dear, we *are* anxious, aren't we? Relax, my sweet, I was *très discret*."

"Forgive me if I don't ask you to stay," Waring said bluntly. "I've been rather busier than I hoped to be the last two days. I'm beat."

"Darling," Moira said, purring, "I couldn't stand the thought of you sitting up here alone feeling sorry for yourself. I came to cheer you up."

Waring eyed her with guarded approval. She was wearing his favorite outfit: the red satin jacket with shimmering see-through blouse beneath and the short red skirt that showed off her long legs to devastating effect. Still, he was dead tired and disinclined to entertain her tonight; he was also miffed that she had taken so long to come around. He had called her weeks ago. Why did she have to show up tonight, of all nights?

"I'm sorry, Moira," he said, softening a little; he didn't really want to start a fight with her. "You've caught me at a bad time. I was just getting ready for bed."

She moved into the room and stood seductively before him. "Great minds think alike, I hear." She put her hands on his chest and brought her face close to his. Her perfume was subtle but intoxicating. "I've learned a new trick, darling."

"Sorry, not tonight." He removed her hands.

"You're angry," she said, pursing her lips in a pretty pout. "Is it because Moira kept you waiting?"

He stared at her, refusing to rise to the taunt. Gorgeous as ever—so cool and elegant, so clever. Once he had contemplated marrying her; she would have given his presidential image a shot in the arm. Now, however, he was glad he had resisted that particular temptation; she was too demanding, too unpredictable, too impulsive. He didn't need any more loose cannons on the deck of his storm-tossed political ship.

"Thomas, darling, did you think I was a pet? That all you had to do was whistle and I'd come running?"

"I honestly don't know what I was thinking," replied Waring testily. "Right now, I could wish I'd never laid eyes on you."

"That's not what you used to say," she replied sulkily. "In

fact, it was always: 'You're fantastic, Moira. You're a beauty, a goddess. I have to see you, Moira. Come rescue me.'" She laughed, her smile beguiling.

"Well, it might have been useful if you'd have come sooner. As it is, we have very little to discuss." Waring could feel himself growing peevish and defensive. He didn't want to argue with her; all he wanted was for her to leave him in peace. "You may have noticed Parliament's been dissolved and I've got a general election to fight."

"And you'll win, too, darling. I predict the largest majority of your career."

"I'm glad you think so. No one else rates my chances so high just now."

"Public opinion can change in an instant," she said with a snap of her long fingers. "Why, I shouldn't be at all surprised if tomorrow's bravado proves to be the worst mistake of the King's short career."

Cold dread spread through Waring's stomach. "What have you done?"

She smiled wickedly. "You never wanted to know before."

"Before? What are you talking about, Moira? There was never any 'before.' I never asked you to do anything for me."

"You didn't have to ask, darling." She moved across to the bed, sat down, and leaned back provocatively. "It was understood. I told you I would help any way I could."

"Teddy blew his brains out. It was suicide. There was no one with him."

"Believe what you will," Moira replied. "But do you really think a bumbling ne'er-do-well like Teddy could have managed that on his own?"

Waring stared at her. "I didn't hear that."

"Did you not, my darling?" she asked, affecting a thick Portuguese accent. "It's a little late in the day to become squeamish, don't you think?"

Waring felt his flesh crawl. "My God, Moira, if there is ever so much as the slightest whisper of a doubt that Teddy's death was anything but a simple suicide—"

"Now, Thomas," she chided prettily, "you worry too much."

"Maybe you should worry a little more," he told her. "This is not a game. I can't be remotely implicated in that man's death."

"Afraid of a little blood, my pet?" She laughed, letting her head fall back, exposing her long, lovely throat.

Her casual wantonness astonished and frightened him. She had as much as admitted causing Teddy's death—what else was she capable of? Had she killed Donald, too? No, it was too absurd.

"Anyway," she was saying, "after tomorrow your worries are over. No one will have any use for that tin-pot King and his pissant advisor."

"What happens tomorrow?" demanded Waring. "What have you done, Moira?"

She sat up straight. "Oh, look at you." She laughed, teasing. "Suddenly interested in your Moira again."

He stepped towards her. "I'm not in the mood, Moira. What have you done?"

"Are you *sure* you want to know?" She smirked. "A second ago you weren't so keen."

"I mean it. Either tell me or get the hell out."

"You're no fun," she complained sulkily, winding a lock of her auburn hair around her finger.

"Tell me, goddammit!"

"Live by the press, die by the press—isn't that what they say?" She laughed again, and lay back on the bed, letting her short red skirt ride up her shapely thighs.

"The press—" He stared at her dumbly. "You know about that?"

"Of course. What did you think?" She gazed up at him playfully. "But don't worry, your secret is safe with me. I won't tell a living soul." Her slight emphasis on the word "living" made his scalp tingle.

"Well, if you're not going to take me to bed," she said, sitting up again, "at least you could get me a drink."

"Look, maybe we should just break this off. It's late, and I'm tired, and for the next six weeks I'm going to be up to my neck in an election campaign. We wouldn't be able to spend any time together. Maybe we should just call it quits."

"Just like that," she said, watching him begin to pace back and forth in front of the bed.

"A clean break. That would be best."

"Oh, no you don't, my sweet," she said, rising onto her knees. She knelt on the bed, staring at him. "We're in this together. *You* were the one who called *me,* remember?" Her voice had grown as brittle as glass. "You can't get me to do all your dirty work and then toss me aside when you feel like it."

"I'm not tossing you aside. I just don't think it's working out, that's all. It's time to go our separate ways."

"You worm!" she shouted, suddenly furious. "I am not one of your whores. We made a bargain, my sweet. We are partners. You need me far more than I need you. Don't ever forget that."

The force of her anger halted Waring mid-step. He glanced at her and saw how the rage twisted her face into a rigid mask of hate. The expression passed at once, and her mood altered. "You're worried about the election, Thomas," she said softly, suddenly reassuring. "You're under a lot of strain. I understand."

"I'm worried about the election—simple as that, is it?" He shook his head slowly. "You don't have a clue. The election isn't half of my problems. That idiot Rothes started a brand-new royalist party and then went and got himself killed. Ordinarily, I wouldn't mind so much; unfortunately, he will now be seen as a martyr to the cause, and that can only increase public sympathy for the bloody fool and his bastard King."

"If you ask me, Rothes got precisely what he deserved," Moira replied. "Consider it a warning to anyone tempted to interfere in affairs that do not concern them."

Waring felt himself growing cold, as if the temperature in the room had suddenly plummeted. What *did* she know about Donald Rothes' murder? He thrust the question firmly aside; after all, if she was even half as deeply involved as he suspected, did he really want to know the details?

"Relax, Mr. President," she cooed. Sliding off the bed, she came to stand before him again, gathering him into her forceful embrace, pressing herself against him. He felt the heat of her body stirring him. He wanted her, and was too tired to fight it anymore. "You don't have a worry in the world. Trust me, darling. Trust your Moira."

# Part V

# ✳
# Forty

"I appreciate your coming along," said James as the black Jaguar inched through nearly gridlocked traffic. "But you didn't have to—especially if you're not feeling up to it."

"True," agreed Cal. "We could have handled it ourselves."

Embries, brooding and silent since his early-morning return from Glastonbury, sat like the shadow of death in the front seat. At James' suggestion, he half turned to look at those behind. "From now on, we underestimate the enemy at our peril."

"What enemy?" asked Cal. "Man, what did you do last night?"

Embries turned his face towards the front window without answering.

"It's to do with Donald's accident, isn't it?" suggested Jenny. Following Donald's death, she and Cal had flown down to London to help lend whatever aid and comfort they could.

"It was no accident," muttered Embries; he kept his gaze fixed on the slowly moving traffic outside the window. "That, at least, is beyond doubt."

"Then it was murder—is that what you're saying?" When no more was forthcoming, James said, "Look, if you're not going to tell us anything—"

"There are forces arrayed against us," Embries said sharply, "powers, principalities, rulers of this dark world, which would see the sovereignty of Britain destroyed forever." He turned in his seat, agitated and upset. "Last night I tried to bind the chief exponent of power. . . ." He paused, his expression turning desolate once more. "God alone knows whether I succeeded."

"This is a person we're talking about, right?" said Cal. "Not a ghost or banshee or anything?"

"You scoff because you do not know," Embries grumbled. "You haven't the slightest idea what you're talking about."

"So tell me," said Cal stubbornly. "I want to know."

Embries stared out the window, shaking his head slowly. "Like me, she is a relic of a forgotten time," he muttered at last.

Before anything else could be said, Rhys announced, "We're almost there, sir. And it looks like it's going to be a scrum."

"Maybe this wasn't such a brilliant idea after all," said James, looking at the swarming mass of people awaiting his arrival.

"You'll be wonderful," Jenny assured him. "After today, the whole world will know what kind of man you are."

"Pray that is so," murmured Embries darkly.

Thus, the typical Saturday-morning turnout for the nation's traditional observance of democracy in action—also known as Speaker's Corner, where mostly harmless eccentrics unburdened themselves to a chorus of robust heckling—had ballooned from the normal few dozen diehards to several thousand. From the look of it, the King would have a sizable audience for the launch of his charm offensive.

The closer they got to Hyde Park, the greater seemed to be the crowd converging on Marble Arch. *Why not?* wondered James. It was a brilliant winter day: mild and sunny, and with a strong whiff of royal disgrace in the air. People by the hundreds were streaming towards the site. Come what may, he'd have a full house to witness his performance. At least, he concluded gloomily, the masses might be entertained by the sight of their King ahoist on his own petard.

The Jaguar crept to a halt before a police cordon, and Rhys leaped out to open the King's door. "Nothing ventured, nothing gained," said James, taking a deep breath. "Here goes." Jenny gave him a kiss for good luck, and he stepped from the car to face a sharply ambivalent public.

The Metropolitan Police, anticipating a larger-than-usual turnout, had set up barriers along the pavement; and, although James could see a few dark-blue uniforms scattered in among the crowd, the police presence was minimal and seemed to be concentrating mostly on keeping traffic moving. Several TV crews and a host of journalists and photographers were ready and waiting at the end of a small walkway formed by two double-length sections of barriers. James was quickly met by two bobbies, who greeted him and conducted him to the official Speaker's Corner soapbox, a sturdy wooden red-painted box about a meter square.

At James' appearance, people began to clap and shout. Many people lining the police cordon had brought signs and placards; a quick visual tally revealed roughly as many for the monarchy as against. James was heartened to see that the Save Our Monarchy activists—presumably, the ones who had decided a scandal-ridden house of Moray was better than no house at all—had turned out in force. Although, amid the applause there were shouts of "Down with the King" as well.

Here and there, clusters of balloons swayed in colorful profusion above the heads of the crowd, and James could smell roasting chestnuts on the air. Whatever else happened, a few enterprising souls would make a bob or two out of the event.

Escorted by two police officers, walking in slow procession through the tightly packed, gawking throng, James felt like a condemned man being led to the gallows. The feeling increased as he reached the soapbox to a crescendo of catcalls. The hostility and anger on their faces as they ranted and screamed seemed to James all out of proportion to any actual crime he might have committed. It was more on the order of the sort of outrage usually reserved for child molesters or dangerous perverts. Looking at all those hate-

twisted faces, he could only conclude that there was something else at work in people's hearts and minds—something
far deeper and much more significant than anything he
might have done. Who, after all, gets so worked up over
events that may or may not have happened years ago to people no one ever knew or saw or cared about in the first place?

The police had established a clear zone extending in an
arc from the foot of the soapbox to a barricade line ten meters away. Pressed up against the barriers were television
cameramen and other media types; he could see no sign of
Jenny, Cal, or any of the others.

James mounted the small wooden platform and looked
out across that narrow divide, and saw the people gazing
back at him, their faces pinched with sharp expectation. So
like children, he thought, angry and frustrated because they
wanted something but did not know what it was or how to
ask for it. This nameless yearning had soured inside them
and made them bitter.

"You will have heard it said," he began, speaking with
slow and deliberate emphasis so his words would not be lost
or misunderstood, "that I dishonored myself and my country
while serving as an officer in the army."

He paused, to allow this to sink in. Someone in the crowd
yelled, "Abdicate!"

"You will have heard it said," James continued, unperturbed, "that I participated in criminal and immoral activities, and enriched myself with the proceeds. You will have
heard these and other allegations about me, my friends—"

The heckler shouted, "We're no friends of yours! Bastard!"

"These accusations are lies," James declared sternly, then
repeated it for emphasis. This assertion was met with a fidgety silence, which he took as a good sign, so he continued,
saying, "I come before you this morning to put an end to
these rumors and to stop the lies. More important, I come
before you this morning to tell you something of the vision
I have for Britain."

"Who cares?" shouted another heckler.

"I'll tell you who cares," replied James evenly. "Every sin-

gle person here today cares; you wouldn't be here otherwise.
You care, or you wouldn't have bothered to come down here
to make your feelings known. Every single person here today
cares very deeply; I know because I, too, care very deeply
about this country of ours and what is happening to it."

Out of the corner of his eye, James saw Cal and Jenny
slide into the front row behind a nearby barrier. Cal gave
him a thumbs-up sign, and Jenny gave him a wink.

"Most of you believe that the monarchy is dead and ought
to be buried, that it's an institution well past its sell-by date,
that it is nothing more than a holdover from a once-grand
past which has long outlived its usefulness. But I'm here to
tell you that you're wrong.

"This nation needs the monarchy—perhaps now more
than ever before," James declared.

"We don't need *you!*" someone shouted.

"My friend," said James, "I am precisely the one you
need. You need me because I am all that stands between us
and a system of government which will effectively obliter-
ate the last vestiges of British sovereignty. Once the monarchy is gone, there will be nothing to prevent the proliferation
of parliamentary power—or its escalating abuse."

The words were still on his lips when James felt a sudden
twinge between his shoulder blades—a piercing ache so
sharp he thought he'd been stabbed. Never had the *fiosachd*
come upon him with such force.

The flesh on the back of his neck writhed. He turned
quickly and scanned the crowd. He saw a woman with striking red hair pushing through the crush of people. He had but
a fleeting glimpse of her face as, in the heightened awareness of the *fiosachd*, darkness descended like a cloud, and he
was overwhelmed by a feeling of fearful oppression. Into his
mind flashed the image of blood pooling in the street, and he
heard as in a dream the droning whine of sirens and the
screams of the people as they fled.

He looked out on the unsuspecting crowd and felt a crush-
ing weight settle upon his chest. Death was here.

"Ah, well," James concluded lamely, "I guess that's all I
have to say right now."

Stepping quickly down from the speaker's box, he crossed to where Cal and Jenny were standing. She saw the set of his jaw and asked, "What's wrong, Why did you stop?"

"Where's Rhys?"

"He's waiting with the car," replied Cal. "Why?"

"There's trouble."

"What do you want me to do?"

"Get Rhys on the mobile. Tell him to get over here fast. Then follow me."

"What about Jenny?"

"Don't worry about me," Jenny told him. "I can take care of myself."

"Just get hold of Rhys," said James, "and then follow me!"

Even as he spoke, James became aware of a movement in the crowd—like a ripple in a stream as water flows around an obstacle. He caught a glimpse of black leather and the cold metallic glint of chain and, emerging from the close-gathered throng, a man dressed in black tee shirt and jeans, his feet laced into heavy steel-toed bovver boots. His head was shaved completely, and he had a black tattoo of a dagger on the side of his neck. A painted red swastika glistened on his forehead like a wound.

More thugs pressed in behind the first; each with a length of pipe or a section of chain. Their shaved heads and tattooed faces gave them the look of barbarians of another age.

Embries, ever alert to the transient moods of every situation, appeared and stepped quickly to James' side. "You've seen something."

"Skinheads—they've come to disrupt things," James replied. "Get the police over here *now*." James turned and made to step back onto the box when a brick smashed on the pavement at his feet.

Another brick struck the side of the soapbox. This one was accompanied by a shout: "Death to the King!"

The crowd gave a shudder and edged back in alarm.

The first of the gang had almost reached the barrier. People were shoving back, trying to get out of the way. Moving towards the commotion, James saw three skinheads climb over the barricade and step into the cleared zone. The two nearest police constables were running to stop them. As the bobbies approached, the three intruders suddenly squatted down; two more rose from the crowd behind them and let fly with bricks. One missile caught the foremost policeman full in the face; his legs buckled and he toppled backward onto the pavement. His partner was struck in the chest and went down; he lay writhing and clutching his heart. Instantly, the nearest thug was on the wounded officer, kicking him and beating him with a length of lead pipe.

"You're mine, friend," James growled and started for the fray.

"James, wait!" Jenny shouted as the King darted to the injured man's defense.

# ❊

# Forty-one

James reached the injured policeman just as his attacker landed an expert kick in the officer's stomach. When the thug drew back his boot to launch a kick at the bobbie's unprotected throat, James seized the skinhead's ankle from behind and yanked it hard up towards the small of his back, throwing him forward. His face struck the pavement; and he came up gasping and spluttering like a crimson geyser, blood spurting from his nose and mouth. James applied a firm tap to the base of his skull, and he subsided with a groan.

The two remaining skinheads saw their chance and advanced. The first lunged clumsily, swinging at James' head with a length of pipe. James easily sidestepped the blow, took hold of the thug's arm as it swung past, and gave it a sharp downward yank. The thug sprawled forward onto his hands and knees, and the pipe went spinning out of his grasp.

Before James could remove him from the fight, however, the second was joined by another. James did not wait for them to make the first move but met them on the run, taking the nearest head-on. The skinhead had a meter of rusty chain in one hand and a lead pipe in the other, so James aimed a swift kick at his kneecap. The ruffian shrieked in pain and dropped the pipe to grab his leg. His descending chin met James' knee on the ascent, and the attacker's mouth snapped shut with a teeth-shattering clack.

The bruiser's companion gave a shout and loosed a wild roundhouse with his chain—which James easily ducked, coming up with a fist under the hood's ribcage, driving the air from his lungs. He gasped for breath, and James seized his throat, closing off his windpipe. The skinhead's eyes bugged out and his mouth gaped open for breath, but James held him just a little longer and then shoved him into the path of two more skinheads, who had darted into the walkway behind him. One tripped over his gasping partner, forcing the other to dodge awkwardly.

James went for the awkward dodger first, stiff-arming him in the chest as he tried to charge. Already off balance, his feet flew out from under him and he smacked the street with his backside. James heard a crunch that might have been his spine giving way, and the bully fainted.

James stepped back, looking for the police and wondering why they were so slow in responding to the situation. He was starting back towards the injured constables when someone shouted, "Behind you!"

He pivoted, jerking his head from the path of a downward arcing section of pipe, taking the blow on his shoulder. The pain brought tears to his eyes, and he fell onto his side and tried to roll away. The skinhead gave a wild shriek of triumph and leaped forward. James saw the pipe swing up into the air, and threw his arms over his head to protect his skull.

As the pipe started down, however, a strange thing happened. The troublemaker's arm seemed to fold inward upon itself—as if he had suddenly developed a second elbow in the middle of his forearm. The lead pipe spun with a dull clank to the ground as the bully grabbed his broken arm, his face alive with wonder. There came a meaty thwack, and the skinhead's eyes bulged with pain; he fell, clutching his shin, a curse between his teeth.

James lowered his hands and saw Jenny with her fist clenched tight around a section of pipe. She stood over the thug, breathing hard, silently daring him to get up. Cal scrambled up behind her and stooped down to help James to his feet. "Man, can we no' take you anywhere?" he said.

"Where is the riot squad when you need them?" asked James, rubbing his throbbing shoulder.

The skinheads who had come through the barricade were hugging the pavement. "That looks like the lot," Jenny observed with relief.

"Maybe we should get you two to the car," said Cal.

"Let's see to these injured officers first," James replied, turning to the bobbies on the ground. The first was still out cold; the second had stopped writhing, but his face was ashen, and he was having difficulty breathing. "Rest easy," James told him, kneeling down beside him. "We'll get some help over here right away."

From somewhere beyond the barricade, there came a shout to clear the way. "Over here!" shouted Cal, waving his arms. "Get an ambulance!"

Policemen were trying to clear a path. The crowd, like an ocean wave, had recoiled upon itself during the attack; now it was surging again and flowing confusedly around the scene of the fight. From the speaker's box, Embries called on everyone to remain calm. There had been an incident, he said, but it was over now. Everything would soon be back to normal if everyone would just remain calm and allow the police to do their jobs.

And then James heard sobbing: desperate, uncontrollable. Instinctively, he moved towards the sound. Jenny started after him. "Stay with Cal," he told her.

"No way," Jenny said, laying her hand gently on his injured shoulder.

As she spoke, an image flashed into James' mind: a dark-haired young woman dressed in gleaming mail, a small round shield at her breast and a slender spear in her hand. There was sweat on her brow and grime on her cheek as she regarded him with amused admiration.

"Suit yourself," James relented. "Follow me."

They waded into the crowd together. A number of people had been knocked down when those in the front had tried to retreat. Many of them were still on the ground, dazed and frightened as the onlookers streamed around them. There was a young woman on her knees beside a mangled baby stroller. She was bleeding from a cut on her cheek, and her chin was bruised.

As James reached the young woman, he saw Rhys' head and shoulders struggling through the mass of people. "Rhys! This way!" James shouted. Kneeling beside her, he said, "Can you stand? Here, let's get you on your feet."

Rhys was beside them a second later, and together they lifted the woman to her feet. "That's better," Jenny soothed, trying to comfort her. "Are you hurt?"

The woman stared at them with terrified eyes. Clutching at Jenny's sleeve, she wailed, "My baby! I can't find my baby!"

"We'll find your child," James said. "What's the name?"

"Hannah." The woman sobbed, trying to get control of herself. "She's only three. She's wearing a red jacket. Please—"

James stood and made a quick survey of the area, but could see no toddler. There were so many people milling about that it was difficult to see. "We'll circle the area," he told Rhys. "You go left, and I'll go right."

"She has a yellow woolly hat," called the mother as they started away.

The search was made more difficult because many people, recognizing James, stopped in his path and wanted to shake hands or accost him. "We're looking for a lost child," he told them, when they tried to greet him. "Please help us find her."

By the time they completed the first circuit, he had recruited six or so other searchers, but had not found the little girl.

"Go around again," James told Rhys. "Make the circle wider this time."

"Your Majesty!" called a fresh-faced police constable as he jogged towards the King. "We can take it from here. Allow us to escort you to safety, sir."

"I'll go when the little girl is safe," James replied. "Help us search."

Within moments, the area was ringing with shouts of "Hannah! Where are you, Hannah?"

Halfway around the second pass, James met Cal, and quickly explained who they were looking for. "Tricky, these little'uns—they can get around faster than you'd think."

"Well, find her then—if you know so much," James snapped, casting a quick look back at the mother leaning in distressed immobility against Jenny. Cal squatted down and gazed around at roughly the eye level of a three-year-old toddler. "There!" he said. "That's where I would go if I was a bairn on the loose."

James looked where he was pointing and saw a cluster of helium balloons fifteen or twenty meters away. The vendor had probably abandoned them in the stampede and, tethered by their strings to a weight, they were bumping along the street. Cal and James started for the place together, side-stepping the glad-handers and reporters; they had covered half the distance when James caught a glimpse of a small red figure a few yards ahead. "There she is!"

"Got her," said Cal.

Suddenly, the crowd was streaming around them, and James saw why: five more skinheads had appeared on the scene; dressed in black jeans and leather jackets, the two leading the group had dogs on the end of heavy chains. The rest carried cricket bats and sections of pipe.

James took one look at the dogs and their vile, flat, brown, beady-eyed heads, thick necks, bow legs, and bulging haunches, and his stomach tightened with disgust. "God help us," he muttered. "They've got pit bulls."

"Cursed beasts," spat Cal. "Damn them all."

The horrified crowd scattered in every direction. People fled to either side, screaming, shouting, desperate to get out of the way of the advancing skinheads and their snarling dogs.

Suddenly, as if it had been carefully choreographed and scripted, it was Cal and James on one side of a small clearing, and the hoodlums with their pit bulls on the other—and Hannah between them. Even before the thugs' hands moved to the collars of their dogs, James knew what was going to happen. The horrified crowd moaned as little Hannah caught sight of the dogs and headed straight for them.

The pit bulls saw the toddler, too, and the instant they were loosed, went for her. James put his head down and ran for all he was worth; Cal loosed a whoop to distract the dogs, and raced after him.

The pit bulls charged ahead like low-flying cannonballs. Hannah, oblivious of the danger, reached out her tiny hands and stumbled forward on unsteady legs as the dogs sped nearer.

The first dog loosed a vicious, slavering growl and dove headlong for the infant. James saw the jaws open . . . the glimmer of white teeth slashing through the air. . . .

At full stretch he lunged, snagging the hem of the child's red coat. His fingers caught the soft cloth, and he jerked the infant up off the street as the dog's teeth snagged her sleeve. The animal's head came up as James lifted the little girl, so he kicked out at the repugnant creature's throat and managed to get it to release its hold. The dog fell back with shreds of red cloth hanging from its mouth.

The child, terrified now, wailed.

"Catch!" James shouted, lofting the toddler laterally to Cal. She sailed a short distance in the air before falling safely into Cal's hands. Wrapping Hannah in his arms, he spun on his heel and shot away.

There came a strangled snarl, and James felt a pain in his leg. The pit bull, denied its prize, had attacked him instead. Missing his groin, it had fastened its teeth in his upper thigh. Lacing his fingers together, he brought both hands down hard on the back of its thick neck at the base of its odious skull. The dog yelped and fell onto its side.

James had no time to finish it off, for the second dog was on him in the same moment. This one made a leap and caught him just above the wrist, almost yanking him off his feet. He felt the teeth penetrate the cloth of his suit coat and sink into his flesh.

The pain was fierce, the grip of the animal's jaws tremendous. Pulling up with all his strength, James lifted the dog's forelegs off the ground. At the same time, he withdrew his free arm from the sleeve of his jacket, jerking the coat over his shoulder and down his arm, covering the dog's head.

Unable to see, the creature loosened its hold for an instant. James pulled his arm free. Shaking furiously, the pit bull tried to shed the coat. James seized the struggling beast and drop-kicked it across the clearing, only to realize he now had five more skinheads to deal with.

They rushed him all at once. James succeeded in dodging one and eluding another, but a third launched himself with a feetfirst football tackle, sweeping James' feet out from under him. He hit the street, landing heavily on his hip. There was a flash of silver in the air, and James twisted away as a chain struck the pavement, dashing sparks before his eyes.

As the hooligan raised it to swing again, James reached out and grabbed the end of the chain. The thug reared back, trying to jerk it from James' hand, but James held on. The skinhead pulled harder . . . and James let go. The ruffian reeled away, and the King rolled to his feet as the fourth skinhead took a swing at his head with a cricket bat.

Seizing the thug's arm, James pulled him forward, planting his knee in his groin. His face turned blue, and he sank to his knees. James had a glimpse of him vomiting in the street before the fifth attacker was on him.

James turned to meet him, and caught the glint of metal in his hand as he dived. Throwing himself to the side, James heard, rather than felt, the ripping of shirt fabric as a knife carved a gash along his ribs. James hit the pavement beside the retching skinhead and snatched up the cricket bat he had dropped.

Twisting on his knees, he swung the bat around his head, driving the knife-wielding thug back. The skinhead dived at him again. James parried his thrust with the side of the bat, then gave him a solid thwack on the leg with the follow-through stroke. The thug gave out a yelp and a curse, shoving the knife at James' face. Knocking the knife hand away, James drove the bat end-first into his attacker's solar plexus. Once, and again. The killer went down gasping for breath.

James struggled to his feet as Cal appeared with half a

dozen policemen, who commenced sorting out the attackers. The two toughs James had eluded decided to leg it while they had a chance, and several officers raced in pursuit.

"Where were you?" James gasped, as Cal skidded to a halt beside him.

"Baby-sitting," he replied, wiping sweat from his face. Glancing at the squirming pit bull with its head stuck in the sleeve of James' suit coat, Cal said, "It looks like your furry friend still wants to play."

Just then the dog managed to shake off its restraint; growling and snarling, the creature dashed stiff-legged to the attack. Taking the cricket bat from James' hand, Cal cocked the bat. "Get behind me," he instructed.

The dog leapt, jaws snapping, and Cal smashed the venerable willow into the side of the animal's head with a near-perfect double-handed swing. The creature's hind legs kept churning, but its front legs folded under it like the broken landing gear of an ugly brown airplane. The beast drove forward, its snout dragging on the street. Cal swung again, and the thing rolled onto its back with a groaning whimper.

Another contingent of uniformed policemen came running to surround the King. "We'll take over here, Your Majesty," the sergeant said, eyeing the cricket bat dubiously.

"Welcome to the party," James said. "We were beginning to think you'd mislaid your invitations."

The policeman stiffened. "Dreadfully sorry, sir. The crowds have impeded our efficiency to an unacceptable extent. My apologies, Your Majesty. I can assure you it won't happen again."

"Impede yourself," sniffed Cal. Taking James by the arm, he began leading him away. "Come on, Jimmy, let's get you fixed up."

Cal and two constables led the King back through the gathering crowd. By this time, police cars were arriving in swarms, sirens wailing, and the first of several ambulances was making its way up the pavement towards the arch. People were milling aimlessly about, some looking distinctly shell-shocked; police were trying to impose an orderly evacuation of the area, and were being largely ignored.

They reached the place where Cal had left little Hannah with her mother and Jenny. The child still had tears on her chubby cheeks, but she had stopped crying, and was fascinated by Jenny's long black hair. She had a handful of it and was separating it out by strands. "You saved my Hannah's life," the mother gushed. She drew herself up and kissed James on the cheek. "Thank you, Your Highness. Thank you so much."

"I'm glad she's safe," James replied as a television crew shoved towards them.

"Your Majesty! Excuse me!" the reporter cried. "Excuse me! Could we have a statement, please?"

"Sorry," James said. "No statements." The police, anxious to get the King out of harm's way, started moving him along.

James reached out to Jenny and, as he made to put his arm around her shoulders, the movement caused a sudden cascade of pain down his side. He put his hand to his ribs and discovered the side of his shirt was soaked with blood. "James!" gasped Jenny, taking hold of his arm. "You're injured."

"Get the camera on that!" shouted the reporter. "The King is wounded. Hey, wait a tic. We just want—"

James turned away, and the reporter shoved a microphone into the mother's face instead. Cal stepped beside him and Jenny slipped her arm around his waist, and the police conducted them quickly to the nearest ambulance. Cal hailed the attendants as they stepped up to the open doors of the vehicle, and two veteran paramedics snapped to attention.

The sight of the King receiving medical attention for wounds received in a street fight proved too much to resist; cameramen flocked to the ambulance like gulls to a trawler. They started pushing and shouting questions over the top of one another.

Embries, stepping quickly to the rear of the ambulance, joined Jenny and Cal. He saw the crease in James' side, and said, "We're taking you to the hospital."

"Not until I finish my speech," James told him, stepping up into the ambulance. "You wouldn't want me to disappoint all my fans, would you?"

"Go on then," said Embries. "Get yourself bandaged up, and I'll have Rhys see to the car. We're off to casualty as soon as you're finished."

A reporter plowed forward, holding out a microphone. "A statement, Your Highness!" he shouted, as the police muscled him back. "Give us a statement!"

This started a scuffle among the cameramen jockeying for position. Instead of calming down, the atmosphere was, if anything, growing more chaotic as onlookers pressed in to see what was happening. As James was out of reach inside the van, the cameras went for Cal and Jenny. Some of the photographers were calling for her to give them a smile; others were shouting questions. "Are you the King's girlfriend? Were you afraid for your life? What was going through your mind when you saw the King struck down? Did you think he would be killed?"

"Cal," said Embries, "let's get these doors closed and give them some privacy." He helped Jenny into the ambulance as the medic lifted James' shirt and began cleansing the knife wound.

Cal closed the ambulance doors, and stood guard outside while the medics bandaged James. They cleaned the stab wound and attached butterfly tapes to hold the cut closed, then wrapped gauze around his middle. They treated the bites on his thigh and wrist, cleansing them and applying disinfectant, gave him a tetanus jab and extracted a promise to see a doctor right away.

James thanked them and rapped on the door for Cal to let him out. Under a hastily arranged police escort—fifteen officers with riot shields and truncheons at the ready—they returned to the speaker's platform where they were met by the officer in charge of the police detail for the event. "With all respect, Your Majesty, I do think it would be best for all concerned if you would desist from speaking," he said. "It would allow us to move everyone along, sir."

"You are right to be concerned, Sergeant," James replied. "But the disturbance was meant to silence me. If I don't finish what I started, the skinheads and those who undoubtedly hired them will have won. We can't allow that to happen at Speaker's Corner, can we?"

The police officer frowned, clearly unhappy with this line of reasoning. The breakdown of security and crowd control had shaken his confidence in their ability to maintain order. "We cannot take the respon—" he began.

"The King is right," said Jenny quickly. "If they win this one, you will have let a bunch of thugs dictate terms. No one wants to see that happen."

The officer relented. "I suppose not, miss." To his constables, he said, "Right, boys and girls, you heard the King. Let's see it doesn't get out of hand this time, shall we?"

James mounted the soapbox once again. There was a smattering of applause, and he began to speak about what had just taken place.

"My friends," he began simply, "there are forces in the world which do not love goodness, do not love compassion. There are forces of darkness, which do not love charity, or mercy, or justice, and which will not rest until these virtues are extinguished by all-encompassing night. Whenever any good or worthy thing is contemplated, the agents of evil seek first to destroy it; failing that, they seek the destruction of any who champion virtue and right. We saw that here today.

"But I tell you that as long as I am King, those whose minds are bent on hate and destruction have a foe who will not retreat. In the King of Britain, the agents of evil have roused an adversary who will take the battle to the grave. I will not be bowed. I will not give in. I will not surrender to the forces of night."

He finished by saying that in the final days before the referendum he would be taking his vision of Britain directly to the nation. He asked those listening to think about what he had said, and if they found themselves agreeing, then he asked for their support. "Britain was exalted once, and it can be again," he said. "Join me in the fight. Together, we can make Britain the place it was always meant to be. We can make the dream of Avalon into reality."

※

# Forty-two

That night Prime Minister Waring, along with several million other viewers, sat transfixed before the Six O'Clock Report and watched the gallant young King snatch a toddling child from the jaws of ravening attack dogs, and then take on not only savage pit bulls but a gang of rabid neo-Nazi hoodlums as well.

Had the attack been painstakingly planned and rehearsed, it could not have been better stage-managed. The scandal had made the monarch the center of attention; the impromptu Speaker's Corner appearance had guaranteed sufficient media involvement; the attack, so sudden and brutal and wanton, had made him an instant hero.

The trouble, from Waring's point of view, was that it hadn't been an act. The pipes and chains were real, the dogs frighteningly real, and so was the courage that had faced them down. In media terms, it was an unassailable demonstration of the King's personal integrity, an unanswerable argument for his character.

Next day, the nation's Sunday newspapers displayed magnificent full-color photos of the valiant King cradling young Hannah in his arms, heedless of the leaping pit bull. Nearly every front page of every newspaper in the land extolled the King in banner headlines. Several seasoned paparazzi cap-

tured the precise moment the airborne toddler fell into the
safety of Cal's arms, thereby making Calum McKay a sec-
ondary hero in the drama.

*The Sun,* heretofore the monarch's biggest detractor, ran a
seven-page photo supplement on the attack—which they
called a "mob riot"—complete with diagrams and a minute-
by-minute timeline. Two pages were devoted to the role
played by the King's mysterious fiancée; the main photo
showed Jennifer comforting a frightened Hannah, their faces
nose to nose, tears still glistening on the child's round face,
her tiny hand tangled in Jenny's long black hair. An intensely intimate moment, that single picture did more to en-
dear the heretofore unknown woman to the nation than any
number of silky soft-focus glamour portraits so adored by
previous royals.

Not to be outdone, the *Observer* proclaimed ARTHUR
LIVES! The headline was run above a photo of the unarmed
King in hand-to-hand combat with a gang of marauding,
chain-swinging, pipe-wielding skinheads. The reporter, also
an eyewitness, fell all over himself praising the King, and
declared with solemn sincerity, "In our brave new King,
Britain's ancient code of chivalry is revived." He ended the
piece proclaiming, "The spirit of Arthur lives again!"

Clips of the attack were run and rerun on news programs
for the next few days. Waring couldn't turn on the television
without seeing yet another replay of some aspect of the
Hyde Park incident. Every man, woman, child, and tourist
within a mile of the place must have had their video cameras
grinding away, because there seemed to be no end of fuzzy,
poorly lit, herky-jerky footage of Good King James beating
the living snot out of the bad guys for the glory of Great
Britain. Eyewitness interviews seemed to have included half
the population of greater metropolitan London, and the other
half was phoning up radio talk shows to discuss it in depth.

If that weren't bad enough, the King proceeded to take his
absurd naïve primitivistic message on the road. On Monday
morning, he joined the London commuters on train platforms to chat with them and receive their promises of support; Monday afternoon saw him in the City, speaking to

businessmen and -women lunching in pubs, cafés, and the restaurant haunts of executive high flyers; by Monday evening he was working the poorer housing estates of Tower Hamlets and the East End.

On Tuesday the King turned up in Birmingham and was featured live on the morning breakfast shows as he talked to Asian market-stall merchants, shopkeepers, and cabdrivers. By Tuesday afternoon he was on the move again, this time to Manchester, where he visited two hospitals, three schools, and the UMIST campus. Tuesday night found him in Liverpool, doing the clubs and taking in the street scene, talking to young people, winos, and police on the beat.

Meanwhile, the King's unofficial entourage of press and paparazzi scrambled frantically to keep up with him, faithfully reporting his every move—a process made more challenging by the fact that he refused to announce his next destination. This engendered intense speculation among professional pundits, and became a fascinating game for viewers and listeners at home as everyone tried to guess where the King would pop up next and what he would say.

Wednesday dawned, and an intensely curious nation awoke to learn where the King had surfaced again; his destination this time was Newcastle, where he was videotaped addressing a special meeting of the long-haul truckers' union. People all over England, Wales, and Scotland went to work with the King's stirring words of challenge and hope ringing in their ears. Lunchtime found him in Gateshead at a shopping mall, visiting merchants and customers, and posing for pictures with shop assistants and food court diners. Then it was on to Middlesbrough for tea and sandwiches at a retirement home and an early supper backstage with the cast and chorus of the English National Opera touring company in Durham. He ended his hectic day in Glasgow at a night shelter for the homeless, where he spoke at length on his vision for a Britain where all such shelters would close, not for lack of funding, but for lack of need.

Waring watched all this with a dull, burning hatred that mounted almost hour by hour, as the relentless, tireless press reported the King's every move throughout the day. He watched as slowly, gradually, the charismatic new monarch began to turn public opinion. He watched as the King's popularity waxed, and his own waned in almost direct proportion. The ex-Prime Minister watched with the growing desperation of a man who feels the deck tilting dangerously beneath him and knows there is nothing he can do to bring the ship around.

On Thursday, the King returned to London for the funeral of his friend and supporter, Donald Rothes, and Waring breathed a sigh of relief. At least, attending the funeral would slow the media juggernaut somewhat, and for once the blasted King would not be the center of attention. As a parliamentary colleague of the former MP, Waring would also attend the service. In light of the opportunity provided, he intended to make the most of the situation; he had his press secretary prepare a speech ripe with juicy sound bites guaranteed to tempt the media back into his camp. Given only the slightest chance, he would be well on his way to restoring the shambles of his collapsed government.

Donald Rothes' funeral service was held in St. Margaret's—the gray stone church that huddles in the shadow of mighty Westminster Abbey. As a sitting Member of Parliament, he was accorded as much pomp and ceremony as precedent allowed. All of his Commons colleagues attended. The former Prime Minister and his cabinet cronies, and Huw Griffith and the rest of the Opposition party leaders were given choice seats in the choir; the rest of the backbenchers and junior members filled in behind according to their own peculiar pecking order—much as they did in the chamber. Add to this number several score friends and numerous relations, and the church was quickly crammed to standing-room-only capacity. The media newshounds, who were not allowed inside the church, joined the throng crowding the entrance and square, impeding the flow of traffic through and around the abbey precinct.

Caroline and Isobel, grim and dour in their black mourning hats and veils, sat on the front row of chairs lined up on either side of the coffin. With them were some of the

Rotheses' close friends and relations—his younger brother, Alexander, and a few of Donald's business associates and neighbors. Jennifer and Calum sat four rows behind the family and friends; Embries, Rhys, and Gavin stood at the wall behind the mourners. As a speaker, James sat on the dais beside the Archbishop of Canterbury, who had volunteered to deliver a sermon. At Caroline's request, James had prepared a simple eulogy, and the vicar of Donald's local parish had been asked to lead the service itself.

It was a morning service, following which the casket would make its way up to the family estate at Glenrothes in Scotland, where Donald would be buried in the family plot. The day was suitably subdued, the sky crowded with heavy low clouds allowing only rare bursts of sunlight. Outside the church, the funeral cortège of black limousines sat waiting to begin the long trip north.

From where James sat, he could observe those in the front rows quite easily. He noticed that although most of the congregation appeared dutifully solemn and pious, Waring looked distinctly haggard and ill at ease. Was it, James wondered, anything to do with the fact that two of the nation's most highly respected newspapers had come out in support of the Royal Reform Party on the day of Donald's funeral?

The service started promptly at ten. The hymn "Amazing Grace" was played, and the Reverend Samways led an invocational prayer. The congregation sang "We Rest On Thee," which was followed by a passage from St. Paul's Epistle to the Romans; there was a short liturgical reading, after which Samways introduced the King. James stepped to the pulpit and read a few verses from the Book of Revelations about the final judgment every human being must one day endure. He then delivered the eulogy—which he hoped was as much a celebration of a fine man's life as it was a lament for his needless, wasteful death.

He sat down to respectful silence, wishing he might have done more. This feeling was short-lived, however, because the Archbishop spoke next. A man of imposing stature and a full head of snow-white hair which billowed in waves over his high-domed skull, Archbishop Peter Rippon looked out upon the world through disconcertingly direct blue eyes. In manner and appearance, he reminded James of one of those energetic oldsters who take up bungee jumping or join the Polar Bears; he looked as if he might suddenly sell up, buy a caravan, and head for the cheap casinos of Costa Brava.

Rippon began in the time-honored, if slightly stuffy, way of Anglican clergymen, but quickly departed from the stylized form. "Observe the oak coffin before you," he said. "Soon it will be removed from this place and laid to rest, and we will all go back to our daily chores and occupations. Life goes on, we'll say; and it's true. But for now, for this one brief moment, while the coffin stands before us, I would have you feel with me the heartrending tragedy of a life cut down in its prime."

The Archbishop went on to say how deeply he had been affected by news of Donald's death following, as it did, the announcement of his new Royal Reform Party. He then brought the congregation bolt upright with the declaration: "As a lifelong royalist, I have no doubt whatsoever that Lord Rothes' murder was a direct result of his desire to save the monarchy."

This bald statement sent ripples of chagrin through the largely government-comprised congregation. Many of the Archbishop's listeners—not least Waring and his cohorts, who had not anticipated being accused of complicity in their former colleague's murder—blinked in astonishment at this unexpected revelation.

"Now that I have your complete attention, perhaps you will allow me to explain," the Archbishop continued. "Where the blame for our brother's death will ultimately come to rest, God alone knows. Nevertheless, the *reason* for his death is no mystery at all. I put it to you that our dear brother was killed because he dared take his stand on the side of the angels. He was murdered because he defied the corporate wickedness of the current political system."

The congregation squirmed.

"I see that some of you are upset by my blunt speaking. Good!" Archbishop Rippon declared, leaning out from the pulpit. "Good for you. We *should* be disturbed in the face of such pernicious evil. All the same, it should come as no surprise to anyone here that we live in an exceedingly evil age. My friends, I remind you that our fight is not against flesh and blood but against the principalities, against the cosmic powers, against the rulers and potentates of this present dark age, against the supernatural forces of wickedness in high places.

"I dare say some of you will think I am overstating the case; you will think I am assigning cosmic causes to simple worldly problems. 'Now wait a minute, padre,' I hear you say. 'Accidents happen. It's just the way of the world.'

"Let me tell you something, ladies and gentlemen: the way of the world *is* evil. It does not become any less evil because we disguise it with harmless-sounding phrases like 'status quo' or 'business as usual'—it merely makes the evil more palatable to us. Therefore, I'll say it again: Donald Rothes died because he dared speak out against the way of the world. His voice was silenced by the very evil he sought to uproot."

He gazed out upon the captive audience with steadfast defiance, all but challenging anyone to disagree.

"Does this assertion seem overwrought to you? Is it too presumptuous, perhaps, too melodramatic? Well, maybe it is," he allowed, drawing the doubters in. "Then again, maybe it is we ourselves who have become so jaded, so worldly-wise, so knowing, that the merest mention of righteousness, goodness, and truth—or their counterparts evil, wickedness, and sin—makes us writhe uncomfortably in our seats. But tell me now, what do you call it when good, well-meaning men are silenced for daring to challenge the status quo?"

He let the question hang in the air.

James looked at Waring, who merely stared ahead, legs crossed, hands folded on his lap, his features drawn but impassive. A case-hardened political trench fighter, he was giving nothing away.

"Now then," the Archbishop continued, "some of the more sensitive among you will no doubt be thinking: 'Such a waste. He died in vain.' But you're wrong.

"You see, I believe that no man dies in vain who has staked his life on a godly principle. Some of you may choose not to believe that. Others might be skeptical of such an assertion; you will be asking yourselves, 'On which godly principle did Donald Rothes stake his life?'

"I'll tell you: Donald Rothes recognized that earthly sovereignty is a provision of the divine order, an important part of God's plan for the good governance of his people. More specifically, he saw a sacred institution under attack and tried to defend it. He saw the monarchy of this nation—much abused, forsaken, defiled, and debased, to be sure—besieged by the enemy, and he dared to believe the monarchy could be redeemed." Extending his hand towards the flower-covered casket, the Archbishop said, "Donald Rothes believed in the monarchy as a sacred institution, ordained by God; he saw it in deepest trouble, and sought to defend it. For that he was killed, and his body lies before you in that coffin."

The congregation was growing restive under the Archbishop's unrelenting barrage. They had come to hear a few platitudes in praise of their fallen comrade, not to be lectured by a cleric with an axe to grind. Rippon, not to be deflected, steamed on.

"Sacred institutions, divine order—what old-fashioned notions, completely irrelevant to the modern world of e-mail on the Internet, Martian probes, and genetic engineering. That's what most people think. And, if you're anything like the ninety-three percent of the population that owns a television set, subscribes to a newspaper, and listens to at least one hour of radio per week, then that's what you think, too.

"If so, you only have to ask yourself: Does love go out of fashion? Do kindness and compassion and simple virtue wax and wane with the transitory trends of fashionable society? Is the longing for something good and decent and trustworthy in life merely a mirage, a delusion, a pacifying illusion in the service of 'business as usual'?"

Archbishop Rippon let his gaze sweep across the assembly; he let them feel the weight of the questions.

"If the things we value are not ephemeral—if we recognize that there *are* some eternal truths, some everlasting principles at work in our broken world, then we must refuse to give in to the status quo, to surrender to the way of the world. My friends, we must refuse to allow our voices to be silenced when we stand up for goodness and righteousness. We must demand that godliness gets an equal share in the day-to-day commerce of our lives. We must refuse to cast aside the very principles which have become the foundational truths of our great nation, which so many of our best citizens have given their lives to defend."

With that, the Archbishop took his seat. He glanced at James and favored him with a knowing look, as if to say *Let them chew on that awhile*.

The Reverend Samways closed the service with a prayer, and the congregation sang a final hymn; then the pallbearers came forward and removed the coffin, carrying it slowly back up the aisle.

Following the service, the casket was taken by cortège to Stansted Airport where it was transferred to a plane and flown to a private airfield in Fife. There, three black limousines and a hearse would be waiting to collect the casket and mourners, and the funeral party would be conveyed to the ancient family home, Balbirnie, a turreted sixteenth-century mansion in the Scottish baronial style. In the churchyard on the estate a few miles north of Glenrothes, Donald, sixteenth Earl of Rothes, would be laid to rest.

For James, however, the funeral was but a momentary lull in his relentless mission to save the monarchy. He and the royal entourage watched the limousines out of sight, and then prepared to drive to Cardiff where he would address a conclave of Welsh National Party leaders and rank-and-file faithful who had offered to work their small but influential patch on his behalf.

As he was about to climb into the black Jaguar, he heard himself hailed from the church entrance, and turned to see the Archbishop signaling to him. Amid the shouts of reporters, the King stepped quickly back into the vestibule for a word with the churchman.

"Thank you for the good word, Your Grace," James said. "It was certainly very kind."

"Not at all," the Archbishop replied quickly. "What I said today was the simple truth, and I meant every word of it. You see, over the years I have become a very good judge of character. I have been watching you very closely in the last few days, and I don't mind telling you, I like what I see. I like it very much. So much, in fact, that it makes me a little afraid."

He frowned thoughtfully. "If you can spare a minute, I'd like to talk to you. Please? It'll only take a minute or two, and then you can be on your way."

"Of course," replied James, "it would be a pleasure." He signaled to Rhys, who was waiting at the church door, and then joined the Archbishop; the two men moved a little further into the church, away from the cameras and microphones of the waiting journalists.

"You know," said the Archbishop after a moment, "people assume a churchman's life is dull as dishwater, that we glide blissfully from one placid appointment to the next with nothing more exciting than the occasional homily to liven our luxuriously empty days."

"What?" James asked in feigned surprise. "You mean it's not like that?"

"Not by a long shot," Rippon declared with a flat chop of his hand. "I'm here to tell you it's a snake pit—worse than that even. Most reptiles only strike in self-defense, but our variety bite for the sheer joy of inflicting pain. And the parishioners are almost as bad." He paused, shaking his head, then said, "I love it. God knows I do."

"You surprise me, Archbishop," replied James, warming to the man by the moment.

"The much-trumpeted cut and thrust of party politics is mere child's play compared to Church House administration. Believe me, most senior career politicians wouldn't last a general synod." He smiled with sudden animation. "It's war, but without the blood and bombs. When I was a lad in Berkshire, I used to dream of one day commanding a fighting ship on the high seas. God certainly has a wicked sense of humor, because my ambition has been fulfilled in spades. The only difference between an archbishop and an admiral is that an admiral in the Royal Navy doesn't have to engage in daily hand-to-hand combat with his own shipmates."

James laughed at the thought of bishops tussling in their cassocks.

"I would have been wasted in the navy," Archbishop Rippon continued. "Too docile, too pedestrian. Give me a laity missions conference any day."

"The Admiralty's loss is definitely the Church's gain, I'd say," James observed sincerely.

They arrived at the end of the aisle. The churchman stopped and turned to James, serious once more. "I said I was afraid just now," he confided. "You see, Your Majesty, disappointment is something I've never taken very well."

"You're afraid of being disappointed by me, is that it?"

"Let us say I am afraid of hoping too much." Addressing James squarely, he came at last to the heart of his concern. "It comes down to this: are you the man you say you are?"

"Contrary to what many seem to think," James replied, "I did not ask to be King of Britain; it was not something I chased or coveted for myself. But it is something I believe in; and the more I see the need in this country, the more deeply I am convinced of the urgent, aching necessity for someone who stands above and beyond the continual, corrosive powermongering and compromising that is modern government." He smiled. "Archbishop Rippon, I am that man."

The Archbishop's grin was wide and genuine. His clear blue eyes grew moist with emotion. "You'll have to excuse me," he said, dragging a handkerchief from his pocket. "It seems I grew up with the now-unfashionable notion that Britain was great because it was a nation that believed deeply in the sacred and reverenced the divine. That our little island held a special place in God's heart because Britain held fast to the twin pillars of nationhood—the church and the monarchy—when the spiritual storms of the Renaissance and the Enlightenment raged through Europe and blew the rest away. To this day, I believe Britain endured and survived with our culture and heritage intact because our ancestors refused to sacrifice sovereignty to the gods of humanism and materialism.

"But now," the Archbishop continued, stuffing the handkerchief back into his pocket, "now the enemy seeks not just to replace the faith of the nation with a different faith, or many faiths, but to destroy faith completely. To accomplish this, the enemy attacks both the monarchy and the Church, ruthlessly, relentlessly, dismantling them piece by piece."

Turning to James, he put out his hand in a gesture of appeal. "Alone, we're finished, you and I. Together, we have a chance. What do you say, Your Majesty?" He smiled mischievously. "We may not win the battle, but we can sure give the devil a hell of a fight."

"Archbishop Rippon," James replied, "I've never dodged a fight in my life. You can count on me."

Peter Rippon reached out and took the King's hand in his own. "God bless you, Your Majesty. I will pray for you."

"Thank you, Archbishop. I can use all the help I can get."

"What is more," added Rippon, "I will put feet to my prayers and do what I can to mobilize the Church in support of the monarchy. It may be that, come referendum day, we will have our own small part to play."

"I would very much appreciate it," James told him.

Then, taking hold of the cross which hung on the chain around his neck, the Archbishop raised it before the King, and said, "May the God who has called you bless you richly and prosper you in all things. And may He grant you the gifts of grace and wisdom to perform aright the duties which belong to the grave and sacred trust you have undertaken. And may the Lord of Peace, who raised our Lord Jesus from the dead so that we might know salvation, give you vision, courage, love, and strength to do His will. And may the blessing of the Almighty Creator be upon you and remain with you always. Amen."

"Amen," echoed James, his head bowed to receive the blessing. He thanked Rippon and, after promising to keep in touch regardless of the referendum's outcome, rejoined Rhys at the door. Then, braving the crush of reporters, he dived into the back of the black Jaguar and drove on to Cardiff.

## Forty-three

The next six days passed for James and his entourage in a dizzying swirl of meetings, addresses, assemblies, convocations, confrontations, and gatherings both formal and informal. In the end, there wasn't a county from Land's End to John o' Groats that had not been invaded by the King and his rolling media circus. When, on the day before the referendum, he finally turned and headed north once more it was with the knowledge that he had done all that was humanly possible to get his message heard by the nation's voters. By dint of tireless barnstorming, he had made direct contact with more of the country's population than had the last five British monarchs combined, and his winsome personality had been displayed to stunning effect.

Whether the effort had been enough to sway the undecided masses was anyone's guess. Most of the reputable polls maintained that it was too close to call. Shona and Gavin's unofficial reading indicated more or less the same thing. James had given it his very best, and now it was up to the people to decide.

He arrived in Braemar just before noon, and went directly to Blair Morven, where Jenny was waiting. Shona and Gavin, who had joined the King in London the week before, fended off the reporters, while James went in for a well-deserved rest. He and Jenny settled down to the first peaceful, uninterrupted lunch the King had enjoyed since his campaign blitz began. In almost two weeks he had not taken a bite or had a drink in private, and the thought of a quiet meal with his beloved had become an obsession.

The moment he closed the door and Jenny came into his arms to welcome him home, however, all thoughts of food and drink evaporated in the heat of her passionate embrace. Instead, James found himself whispering, "Let's get married."

"Of course, my love. Set a date, and I'll meet you at the church." She kissed him. "Anytime."

"How about right now?"

"Now?" She laughed. "Now you want to make an honest woman of me?"

"I mean it," he insisted. "Right now. Today. This minute."

"James," she said, pushing back as his arms drew her tight, "we can't possibly. It would take a month to plan at least, and then there's—"

"We don't have to plan a thing. We could run away. We could elope."

"We can't run away. You're the King of Britain."

"I am now, but by this time tomorrow, who knows? Jenny"—he took her hands in his—"look at me. Tomorrow is the referendum, and I have no idea how the vote will go. But whether I am King or not the day after tomorrow, I know I want to wake up next to you." He kissed her and rested his forehead against hers. "Marry me. Now. Tonight."

She stared at him, slowly shaking her head from side to side. "I don't know whether to laugh or cry. But you— you're serious about this."

"I can't do it anymore without you, Jen. I need you beside me."

She swallowed. "You could give a girl a little notice."

"Does that mean yes?"

She nodded.

James gathered her in his arms and kissed her. "We'll ring up Reverend Orr, and get him to come over and perform the ceremony right here. It won't be the first wedding to take place in the castle. We can have—"

"Hold it right there, boyo," Jenny said bluntly. "I'm having a proper church wedding and honeymoon, or nothing doing." Taking him by the hand, she led him to the table and sat him down. "Have a sandwich and collect yourself. I've got a wedding to plan."

She swept from the room and, as James took a bite of his ham sandwich, he heard her in the corridor beyond, calling for Shona to get her mother on the phone.

Strings were pulled, mountains moved, and favors called in—Archbishop Rippon cheerfully granted a Special License for the wedding, and the Banchory florist contributed her entire stock of cut flowers—and by six o'clock that evening, everything was ready. Despite the fiendishly short notice, there was standing room only in the church. The Glen Dee grapevine had performed its usual service—every seat in every pew was full, and the back of the church packed with friends, relations, and well-wishers. The sanctuary was lit entirely by candles, which imparted a cozy glow and also served to hide the lack of decoration; nevertheless, James thought the little church had rarely looked lovelier. Reverend Orr was in fine fettle as he began the service.

Taking his place at the front of the church, James, splendid in his dress kilt—complete with a genuine badger-skin sporran, and his father's dagger tucked into the top of one tall sock for good luck—waited nervously through the organ prelude. And then, there she was, standing in the center of the aisle, his bride, looking radiant and lovely in the candlelight. Two of her workers from the pottery joined her as bridesmaids and, at their appearance, the "Wedding March" commenced.

James gazed with pleasure at Jenny's lovely face, so calm and composed, feminine and beautiful, her blue eyes shining with love and delight as she walked down the aisle. She paused to allow her father to step beside her and take her arm. Instantly, James was put in mind of his parents, and how much his mother would have loved to have seen Jennifer come down the aisle, gorgeous in her snow-white froth of lace and satin. He had no idea how or where she had found the dress, but he knew his father would have been proud to have welcomed such a beautiful daughter-in-law into the family. He thought about his and Jenny's future together, and wondered what kind of future it would be.

He became so engrossed in his thoughts that the next thing James knew, Reverend Orr was leading them in their vows. He heard himself saying "I do," and the preacher asking for the ring; he fumbled in his jacket pocket before Calum, his best man, placed it squarely in his hand. Next came the stirring pronouncement of "man and wife" and a thundering swell of organ music. The happy couple kissed, and the congregation erupted in wild applause. Most of Braemar, James realized, had probably been anticipating this particular wedding for years, and the long-suffering townsfolk were relieved to see it accomplished at last.

Embries and Gavin, working with Agnes and Owen, had laid on a slap-up reception at the Invercauld Arms Hotel just around the corner from the church. The ballroom was festooned with appropriate splendor, and the meal a genuine highland feast. There was music and dancing—Douglas, swiftly pressed into duty, had arranged for the Deeside Drifters to play—and champagne, silly speeches, and round after round of wedding toasts to the new couple.

Most of the town was there, which made it good fun. After so many days on the road, James relished the easy conviviality of the reception, and almost felt it a shame when at last the time came for the newlywed couple to leave. But leave they did, or else they would have had no honeymoon at all.

With Cal and Douglas' help, they enacted a simple ruse to draw the ever-present paparazzi away. Dougie and some of the band members had decorated Embries' Jaguar—filling it with balloons and tying crepe streamers to the rear bumper and door handles. At the prearranged signal, the car pulled up to the hotel entrance. There was a sudden flourish at the door, as people rushed out throwing confetti and shouting as the black car sped away; the newshounds gave chase, and in the confusion, no one noticed the battered blue Land Rover quietly leaving from the back of the hotel.

The couple drove out onto the Pitlochry road and headed for the Spittal of Glenshee, where Cal had booked them the bridal suite at Dalmunzie House. The night was cold and clear, with only a few broken clouds passing over the bright starfield. Once away from the town, the snow-covered tops of the hills glowed ghostly white in the dark. The road was deserted and fairly dry, with only a few patches of rough ice along the shoulders and center line.

They came into Glen Clunie and started up the long rise towards the Cairnwell Ski Center. They could see the glittering lights of the ski lodge at the top of the hill, and Jenny said she thought it looked like the night skiing crowd was having a bash. Yet, when they reached the ski center, the parking lot was virtually empty; the restaurant was dark, and the only interior light they saw came from the pub.

"The chairlifts must be out of commission," remarked James as they drove past. "That's a tough break. The snow looks perfect."

They crested the hill and started the steep descent into Glen Beag. The patchy clouds had parted enough to let a bright crescent moon spread a pale sheen of silver on the ice and snow. The road narrowed as it coursed down the shoulder of the mountain, bounded by a steep rock bank to the right, and an abruptly angled drop into total darkness to the left. A low ridge of dirty snow left by the plow marked the edge of the highway.

Approaching the treacherous switchback turn of the Devil's Elbow, the skin on the back of James' neck began to twitch. An instant later, Jenny cried, "James! Look! There's someone down there."

James was already slowing the Land Rover as, just beyond the beam of the headlights, he glimpsed movement at the side of the road: a figure was toiling up the steep slope.

He slammed on the brakes and pulled over sharply as a woman staggered onto the highway. Dressed in a long, dark coat, she hastened towards them, hands outstretched, her face white in the headlights, half running, half limping; her mouth was open, and she was calling to them.

James threw open the door and started towards her, with Jenny a step behind.

"Help me!" wailed the woman hysterically. "My boyfriend! My boyfriend's down there. Help me! He's hurt! Please!"

"What's happened?" asked James, running to meet her.

"He's dying!" the young woman shrieked. She was bleeding from a split lip and from a small cut above her eye. "You've got to help me save him."

"We'll help you," said Jenny, trying to calm her. "Tell us what's happened."

Stepping quickly to the side of the road, James looked over the edge into the ravine below. There was a car near the bottom of the deep gorge; the lights were still on, bathing a narrow slice of the rocky hillside and the black, ice-bordered stream in pale yellow light.

"She's gone off the road," said James. "Take her to the ski lodge and call an ambulance."

"No!" said the woman, clutching wildly at James. "There's no time. I have to save my boyfriend! Both of you—this way! Hurry!" She turned and fled back down the slope.

Jenny made to follow, but James held her back. "I'll go down. You go to the lodge and call for help."

"I've got my mobile in my purse," said Jenny, already darting away.

"There are flares in the box under the rear seat," he called after her, then turned and started down into the ravine after the woman.

The snow was not deep and served merely to disguise the rocks as James stumbled and slid down the sharp, boulder-strewn slope. It was darker in the shadow of the hillside, and James could barely make out the woman as she flitted down the slope ahead of him, heedless of the ice-slick rocks. "She'll break her neck," he murmured, and called for her to take it easy.

As far as he could tell, the car had come off the highway at the turn and plowed straight down the incline. From what he could see in the darkness, the vehicle was on its side at the base of a huge boulder that was perched above the stream a short distance below.

Sliding and sprawling, his dress shoes slipping with every skidding step, James plunged down the sheer slope of the ravine, bashing knees and hands against the half-covered stones. His short jacket split at the seams, and his kilt flew around his legs as he stumbled on. The young woman, with an agility born of desperation, fairly flew over the craggy terrain, reaching the car well ahead of him.

"Hurry!" she screamed, floundering, falling, picking herself up and dashing on.

James, the *fiosachd* tingling and squirming, followed, trying to discern the nature of the warning he was receiving. And then, as he drew near the car, he smelled it: gasoline.

The car's petrol tank had ruptured, spilling fuel down the hillside. One spark and the car would explode, taking everyone with it.

"Wait!" he shouted. "Stop right where you are!"

Heedless of the danger, the young woman ran on, disappearing around the side of the overturned car. James caught up with her a few seconds later as, standing on a nearby rock, she tried to pry open the caved-in rear door with her fingers.

The stink of petrol fumes was almost overwhelming. No sound came from inside the car.

"Calm down, now," James said softly. He came to where she was standing and took her arm. "You'd better let me do that."

He helped her down from her slippery perch, and moved her aside, saying, "The petrol tank is leaking. We've got to be very careful, or we're in for a nasty surprise." He held her hands, speaking slowly and earnestly. "Now, you just stand here, and let me have a look inside. All right?"

He made to step away, but she clutched at him, holding him back. "Don't leave me!"

"I'm not going to leave you," James assured her, gently

removing her hands. "I'm just going over here and see if I can get your boyfriend out of the car. All right? Now you stay right here."

He turned and hurried back to the wreck. The car seemed to be wedged in tightly between two big boulders. He could hear the tick of hot metal and the liquid drip of petrol splashing onto the rocks somewhere at the rear of the vehicle. He tried the door handle, but either the door was locked or the frame was so badly damaged the door was jammed shut.

Raising his foot, he found a toehold on the undercarriage and pulled himself up onto the side of the car. Lying on his stomach, he peered in through the shattered window but saw no one in the front seat. As he squirmed to look in the rear side window, he heard a distinctly familiar metallic click which caused the flesh at the nape of his neck to tingle anew.

Lowering himself off the vehicle, he turned to see the young woman now in absolute control of herself. Dry-eyed, calm, she regarded him with a slight, knowing smile. Her hands were doubled beneath her breasts, and as he turned he saw the moonlight glint on the black metal barrel of a handgun.

*Fool!* he thought, inwardly kicking himself. The danger posed by the wrecked car had masked any other threat; the *fiosachd* had tried to warn him, but he'd failed to look any further.

"That's right," the woman said. "Stand easy."

"You're very good," James told her. "You had me convinced."

"It's a gift," she replied blithely.

"So what happens now? Robbery? Maybe I should have told you, I don't have any money."

The young woman's lips framed a generous smile, but her eyes remained mirthless and hard. "I know—royalty never carries cash," she replied. "It's not your money that I want, Your Highness."

"What then?"

"I want what anyone wants, really. A little recognition,

appreciation, understanding. Is that too much to ask?" She moved a step closer. He caught the glint of auburn hair and saw her face in the half-reflected glow of the headlights and knew he had seen her before—at Hyde Park? Had she been in the crowd that day?

"Call your pretty wife down here. We don't want her to miss all the fun on her wedding day."

"No," James said firmly. "You might as well shoot me now and get it over with. I won't do it."

"Shoot you?" The red-haired young woman moved a half step to the side. "You've been watching too much cheap television. I have no intention of shooting anyone."

"You're the one who killed Donald Rothes," James said. "You killed Collins, too."

Her smile widened and she stepped nearer; the wild gleam in her eyes sent a quiver rippling along James' ribs. "Did you work that out all by yourself?" she said. "Or did Merlin help you?"

"Who are you?" asked James, a sick feeling spreading through his gut.

"Most people call me Moira," she replied casually. "But you and I both know how misleading names can be."

"Is that supposed to mean something to me?" he asked.

"You can do better than that, surely," Moira replied. "Do you mean to say that after all these years you don't remember me?"

"Should I?"

"Don't be tetchy, dear heart," she said. "You'll spoil my good opinion of you."

"Who are you?" he asked again.

Just then there came a call from the roadside high above. "James . . . can you hear me?"

"Tell her to come down," the woman instructed. "Tell her you need her to help you right away. Just get her down here."

James half turned and put a hand to his mouth. "Stay up there, Jenny!" he shouted. "There's petrol spilled all over. Don't come down here!"

The butt of the gun caught him a glancing blow on the side of the head, which knocked him to his knees. "You stupid—" she shrieked, her voice echoing like a shot across the glen. She regained possession of herself instantly. "Oh dear, oh dear," she tutted regretfully. "Now you've made it that much harder on yourself—and on your dutiful little wife. I was going to let you buy her life with yours, but now she'll just have to take her chances."

"If that's meant to frighten me, save your breath," James said. "Jenny's a big girl. She can take care of herself."

"And they say chivalry is dead." Moira shifted the gun to her left hand. "But, then, you never were much of a romantic—were you, Arthur?"

The sound of the name made the small hairs prick up on his scalp. Into his mind flashed the image of a woman dressed all in black standing on a deserted sea strand, the waves tumbling the pebbles along the shingle. The day was clear, the sky high and bright and windswept, and the woman with the golden hair was pleading for her life.

The wind was blowing her long hair across her face as she spoke, wildly, violently, spitting hate-filled lies at her accusers. Cal was there—and yet it was not Cal, but Cai—and Gavin, and Jenny, and several others, who also were and were *not* the people James knew. They had gathered to hold the woman to judgment for her crimes. A name came to him. "Morgian," he whispered aloud.

"Yes," she replied with evident pleasure. "Like you, I'm back. Did your precious Merlin never tell you?" The answer to her question appeared on his face. "No? Oh, what a shame. Not that it would have helped you very much."

The wind gusted, swirling through the glen, and James imagined he heard the rustling sound of wings as carrion birds gathered. Wrapping his arms around his chest, he hugged himself for warmth. "Look, Morgian . . . Moira—or whoever you are—whatever it is you're going to do, I wish you'd hurry up. It's cold out here. I'm freezing."

From the highway came another call. "James? Are you all right down there?"

"Stay where you are, Jenny!" he called back. "It's under control."

"Help is on the way," Jenny shouted down to him. Her

voice sounded as if it were falling from the top of a mountain. "I called Rhys—they'll be here any minute."

"You heard her," James said. "They'll be here any minute."

As he spoke there came the thrumming rumble of a helicopter engine in the distance. "Make that half a minute," he amended. "In which time this glen is going to be a very busy place."

"A few more seconds is all I need," Moira replied sweetly. She slipped a gloved hand into her pocket and drew out a single cigarette. Placing it between her lips, she took a plastic cigarette lighter from the same pocket.

"Don't—!" James began.

"Worried now, are we?" She flicked the wheel on the lighter, and it sparked to life. The small blue flame guttered in the fitful wind, then took hold. She lit the cigarette, took a deep drag, and exhaled the smoke out through her mouth.

"Farewell, Arthur," she said, blowing the tip of the cigarette to red brilliance. "I don't expect we will meet again—in this lifetime, anyway." With a practiced flick of her fingers, she sent the cigarette flying.

James watched the glowing tip of the cigarette as it spun through the air towards the back of the car, but the fumes, dispersed by the erratic wind, failed to ignite. The cigarette fell to the snow where it merely sizzled and went out in a wisp of white smoke.

"Well," said James, climbing quickly to his feet, "I guess things aren't working out the way you'd planned, are they?"

"We can't have everything," Moira replied, her face glacial, her eyes livid with hate. She raised the gun, aimed at James' chest, and pulled the trigger.

✳

# Forty-four

James threw himself forward as the gun fired, the percussive crack loud in the rocky glen. He felt a hard jolt hit his shoulder as he fell, and he was already rolling to his feet as Moira fired again. The second bullet tore through the fabric of his kilt, carving a gash in his hip. He heard the slug smack into the undercarriage of the car with a strangely wooden whack as he dived.

The momentum of his scrambling leap carried him into her; he hit Moira square in the ribs with his shoulder and they both went down. James landed heavily on top of her, and she rolled from side to side, trying to shake him off, while sideswiping his head with the gun barrel. She managed to land one solid blow above his left ear, but James took the blow and grabbed her wrist, forcing her arm over her head. She raked at his eyes with her free hand, and James grabbed that, too, and hung on.

They struggled for a moment, and James became aware of someone shouting from the road high above. It was Jenny, alarmed by the shots. She was calling for him. "Stay there!" he cried.

In the distance, he could hear the thrum of the helicopter, and knew that if he looked back along the glen towards Braemar he might see it now. "It's over, Moira," he said.

"You might as well give up and save yourself an injury. I'm not letting go of you."

"Fool!" She spat at him. He felt the heat of her hatred lick him like a flame.

"Give it up. Rhys will be here any second," he said, and felt her go limp beneath him—as if she had suddenly abandoned all strength. She closed her eyes and stopped breathing.

He looked at her face in the headlights' glare; she seemed to have lost consciousness. "Moira!" he said sharply, not daring to release his hold just yet. "I don't know what you think you're—"

All at once her body went rigid. Her eyes flew open. *"Exis velat morda!"* she screamed. *"Gorim exat fortis!"*

At the last word, James was blown bodily away and hurled onto his back a few yards distant. He landed hard against the rock upon which the overturned car rested. By the time he scrambled to his knees, Moira was already on her feet, and the gun was trained on him once more.

In the ravine behind them, the searchlight of the helicopter scoured the slope; the boom of the engine filled the glen with the sound of a great rushing cataract.

"I guess this is good-bye," Moira said, her lips curling back over her teeth as she extended her arm and squeezed the trigger.

James' fingers closed on the dagger in his sock. The *sgian dubh* was in the air before Moira knew he'd thrown it. The blade struck her above the right breast just as she fired the gun. The shot went wide, striking the back of the overturned car.

In the same instant, James felt rather than heard a whiffling rush—as if a missile were streaking toward him. There was a sudden shudder as the air convulsed, and he felt the heatflash bloom across his back.

Moira's astonished face was illumined in the dirty yellow flare of the gasoline explosion. The blast threw him onto his face and filled his lungs with searing fumes.

When James came to, he was lying beside the freezing stream twenty meters from the burning car. His clothes were smoldering, and his bare legs were singed. His mouth tasted of petrol and smoke, and the cold air stung his lungs. He coughed and spat, each breath an agony in his throat—as if the inside of his windpipe were being flayed with knives.

He was aware of a small buzzing sound in his ears and he felt something snatching at him. He thought of crows picking his flesh—carrion birds stripping meat from corpses on the battlefield. He turned his head and lifted an arm to shoo the birds away. His sword—he must have dropped his sword—he had to find it before the Saecsens returned.

Pushing himself up on his hands, he looked across the black-watered burn. Behind him the fire still raged; he could feel the heat, and the dancing flames made his shadow quiver on the snow and rocks. He made to stand, but his legs would not obey. He was bleeding from a wound in his shoulder, but he could not remember being speared.

It had been an ambush. Cerdic and Hengist had been waiting in the glen, and he had ridden in unaware. He could remember nothing of the battle itself, and wondered what had become of the Dragon Flight. His warriors would never have left him for dead. He glanced around in the darkness, but the only sign of the fight was a single set of footprints in the snow—leading down the rocky bank to disappear in the black water of the swift-flowing Clunie stream.

*Bedwyr! Where are you? Cai!*

Perhaps they had pursued the enemy or maybe they had gone for help. Where was Myrddin? Where were Rhys and Gwalchavad?

No . . . not Cerdic . . . not Hengist or Horsa. This time it was dread Morgian, Queen of Air and Darkness. He gazed around the circle of firelight, but could see no sign of her; nor could he feel her stifling presence. She was gone.

Dragging his legs under him, he raised himself into a sitting position. Taking up handfuls of snow, he rubbed his raw legs. The cold felt good on his blistered skin. The buzzing sound had not abated; the only sound to break the unnatural silence, it seemed to be coming from somewhere high on the ridge above. He turned his head towards the noise and saw a bright light—like a dazzling star—hanging just over the ridge top. In this strange, intense starlight, he saw a figure moving down the sheer, rock-covered slope of the ravine. Someone was hurrying to his aid.

He looked down at himself. He was covered with filth and his clothes were rags. There was nothing he could do about that, but it was not meet that anyone should find him wallowing in the mire like a common swineherd. He was the High King of Britain. He would stand.

It took all his strength and determination, but he forced his unfeeling legs to his will, and climbed somehow onto his feet beside the rushing burn. He heard someone shouting; the sound was all but swallowed in the silent roar that filled his head. He looked up and saw a woman running over the slippery, uneven ground. Relief and apprehension mingled in her expression, and there were tears in her eyes.

As she came into the light, he saw the long dark hair and, although her clothes were strange, he recognized his beloved, and his heart stirred. He squared his shoulders and sought to reassure her with a smile. "It is well," he said, his voice sounding hopelessly small and distant inside his head. "I am alive."

She came into his arms in a rush, and he allowed his bruised body to be gathered into her embrace. "I knew someone would find me," he whispered, the air rasping harshly in his throat. "I did not know it would be you, my Queen." He put his face against her hair. "Ahh, Gwenhwyvar . . ." He sighed, feeling the immense weight of fatigue descending on him. "We have been apart far too long. I want to go home."

James spent what little was left of his wedding night in the emergency room of the Pitlochry Infirmary. Embries had wanted him to be taken to the hospital in Aberdeen, but neither James nor Jenny would hear of it. "If we go there," Jenny said, "there will be no way to keep it out of the news. This way, we have a chance."

"Keeping it out of the news is the least of our concerns at the moment," Embries said sharply.

"He wants it this way," Jenny insisted. "Look, just find

that woman—she's got to be down there somewhere. Find her and get her out."

"We will find her," Embries replied. "Cal and I will see to police matters here, and follow along as soon as we can." He gave Jenny's hand a squeeze. "Go with God."

She climbed into the back of the Tempest and settled in beside James, who was wrapped in a silver-foil survival blanket. At her instruction, the engine spun to life; Rhys adjusted the angle of the blades, and they lifted off a few seconds later.

The helicopter had arrived at Devil's Elbow moments after the explosion. Rhys landed on the edge of the highway and trained the spotlight down the slope of the ravine. Jennifer was already halfway down to the burning wreck by the time he and Embries started down. The ambulance Jenny had called arrived two minutes later with Cal right behind.

The paramedics had quickly stabilized the King and, strapped to a rescue board, they had hauled him out of the ravine and secured him in the back of the helicopter for the short ride to Pitlochry. A police car dispatched from Braemar rolled up as the helicopter disappeared into the night. Embries dealt with them quickly and efficiently; he gave them Jenny's description of the woman she and James had been trying to help, and directed them to comb the area for her body. He then joined Cal for the anxious ride to the infirmary.

"A hell of a way to celebrate your wedding night," Cal observed, nosing the car around the turn and heading down toward the Spittal of Glenshee.

"Better a hospital than a morgue," Embries remarked.

"Oh, aye," Cal agreed. "What on earth happened down there? I couldn't make head nor tail of it. Strange women, and cars off the road, and who knows what all. Jenny was pretty rattled."

"The relevant facts have yet to be established." Embries turned to regard his traveling companion. "But we might as well start with you."

"Me?" Cal glanced sideways at his passenger. "Man, I know less than you do about this."

"Indeed. Is that so?" inquired Embries pointedly. "Then I suppose it's no use asking *you* who arranged for the King to sneak off unattended?"

"Well, that—" Cal blustered. "It was his wedding night. Even the King is entitled to a little privacy on his honeymoon. I couldn't very well allow the newlyweds to be hounded by a pack of wild paparazzi, could I?"

"It was a foolhardy risk."

"Come on," pleaded Cal. "It's his honeymoon. Anyway, James knows his way around. They were only heading down the road a wee way. It wasn't like they were going off to war, or anything."

"That," Embries snapped, "is where you are naïve—and wrong!"

Cal turned his head and looked at Embries, his face hard in the dim light of the dashboard. "Just what *do* you think happened down there?"

Embries was silent for a moment before answering. "I think," he said at last, "the only person who knows for certain what happened is James. We will have to wait until he feels like talking to ask him."

It was several hours before they were finally able to see James. He was sitting up in bed, but his eyes were closed and he seemed to be asleep. His left shoulder was heavily bandaged, and one side of his head and neck glistened with ointment for his burns.

Jenny was in a chair beside him holding his hand, and in a much more tranquil frame of mind. She smiled as they came into the room. "He's going to be all right," she told them. "One bullet passed through his shoulder below the clavicle—muscle damage, but it missed the bone and major vessels—and the other one just grazed his hip. The struggle opened up his knife wound, though, and that's not so good." She turned to look at her husband, rubbing his hand. "All in all, he's very lucky."

James opened his eyes. "Can you get me out of here?" he asked, the words slightly mushy in his mouth. "All things considered, I'd really rather be at Blair Morven."

"Sorry, no can do," Cal replied. "The doctors want to keep

you around awhile. They say you're not out of the woods yet and, unless you start showing some improvement, they may send you to Aberdeen."

"Some honeymoon," James said. Raising Jenny's hand, he brushed her fingers with his lips. "Sorry."

"This isn't the honeymoon," she replied. "We're still on the way *to* the honeymoon." She squeezed his hand. "We'll get there yet."

"What time is it?" asked James, sinking back against the pillows.

Cal glanced at his watch. "Twelve minutes after one. Look at that—the polls open in just five hours."

"Don't forget to vote, Cal," James said. His voice cracked with fatigue. "I'm counting on you."

## ✳
## Forty-five

Jonathan Trent gazed with ardent solemnity into the camera and began his broadcast with these words: "Tonight, a major political battle rages for the heart and soul of a nation. Tonight, the future and fate of Great Britain's monarchy hangs in the balance."

He paused, tapped his sheaf of papers expertly on the desk, and continued. "Good evening, ladies and gentlemen. All day long, Britain's voters have been deciding the fate of the monarchy. With a little under two hours until polls close around the country, we can tell you that voting has been exceeding all expectations, with many polling places registering record highs in voter turnout." Turning to the monitor built into the desk beside him, he said, "To bring you more on this story, we go now to Kevin Clark in Glasgow. Tell us, Kevin, how is the turnout in your area?"

The picture switched to young Kevin Clark standing before what appeared to be a school building in a district that had seen better days. Light drizzle beaded up on his raincoat. "Yes, Jonathan," replied Kevin enthusiastically, "well, what can I say? Voter turnout here—in this large residential district, dominated by the Kirkallan Council Estate—has already reached an unprecedented seventy-three percent of registered voters, and there are still queues of people wait-

ing patiently in the rain. Officials are forecasting a final figure in the seventy-eight to eighty percent range—and this
for a precinct not known for its, shall we say, democratic enthusiasm. In fact, polls may close before everyone has had a
chance to cast his ballot—a development which has caught
the election commissioners on the hop. Rumor has it that
there is a time extension in the works; we should have a decision on that shortly."

"Remarkable, Kevin," observed Jonathan, beaming with
obvious delight.

"Other precincts have been likewise affected by heavy
voter turnout," Kevin Clark said. "I'm told that this same
pattern is being repeated all over Scotland generally." He
smiled and nodded. "Back to you, Jonathan."

"Thank you, Kevin," replied Trent affably. "Continuing
this report, we go now to Deirdre Mulhaney in Birmingham."

The screen switched to a dark-haired young woman in a
green coat standing inside a civic hall. Behind her were
ranks of yellow canvas polling booths, before which election
officials with stacks of registration printouts were seated at
folding tables; long lines of voters picked up their ballots
and shuffled from table to booth.

"Records are tumbling tonight," Deirdre intoned
solemnly. "Election officials in this mainly working-class
suburb expected a high turnout, but today's voting has exceeded all expectations. The old record—an astonishing
seventy percent of registered voters—achieved in the defeat
of the European common currency referendum—fell early
this afternoon, and it looks like this tight-knit working community might just carry away top honors again."

"Incredible, Deirdre." Trent shook his head in studied disbelief. "To what are they attributing this extraordinary showing?"

"Most people I've talked to say they feel this is an important decision in our country's history, and they wish to make
their opinion known. I'm certain that is the case, but there is
another, rather intriguing, possibility. Early this afternoon,
we began hearing reports about the involvement of the

Church. I've been checking this out, and the rumor does indeed seem to be true. In fact, a fairly high proportion of the voters I've spoken to indicate that their local parish church has organized transportation for their members."

"Yes, Deirdre," agreed Jonathan. "We have been getting similar reports from other regions of the country. In general, it would seem that a great many of the nation's churches—from the Church of England, to Roman Catholic, Methodist, Baptist, and also Jewish congregations—have organized transportation for their members. Many mosques have added their weight to the 'vote no' campaign as well."

"That's right, Jonathan," replied the reporter. "The entire referendum might very well swing on the influence of the grassroots religious community of Britain—which appears to be a much-underestimated power in this country. I very much doubt whether the political pundits and spin doctors reckoned what might be termed the 'spiritual quotient' into their calculations—but it is beginning to look as if they should have." She smiled, signaling the end of her report.

"Thank you, Deirdre," said Trent. "We'll be coming back to you as soon as polls close for an early exit-poll survey."

"We'll be ready and waiting, Jonathan."

Trent swiveled back to look at the main camera. "We will of course be bringing you full coverage of today's historic voting on the fifth and final referendum which will decide the future of the monarchy of Britain. We invite you to tune in at nine o'clock for our extended broadcast, 'The Monarchy: A Nation Decides.' "

Taking the top sheet of paper, Trent turned it over and placed it facedown on his desk. "In other news tonight, scientists report yet another minor earthquake off the Cornish coast in the area which has been dubbed 'Avalon' by the popular press.

"Although the tremor—the fifth in almost as many days—measured only two point three on the Richter scale, it produced the extremely rare effect of reversing the flow of many of the southern region's rivers and streams. Normal flow was reversed in tidal basins from the Severn estuary in the west to the Thames in the east. Geologists and oceanographers, many of whom have been studying the region in extensive detail over the last few months, are warning that these minishocks may be a prelude to a major seismic event."

Gazing into his desk monitor, he said, "We have this report from Ronald Metcalf, filmed earlier today aboard the research vessel *Polperro* in the Celtic Sea."

The picture changed to a gray expanse of water beneath a colorless sky, and a scattering of low rocks around a larger island which was itself a barren rock in the middle of the sea.

"For the crew of the *Polperro*," Metcalf began, "it is business as usual: measuring the effects of the phenomenal forces which are involved in creating nothing less than a new landmass off the southern coast of Britain. Before setting off, I talked to the project coordinator, Dr. Christine Fuller, Director of . . ."

Prime Minister Thomas Waring aimed the remote control, and the television set flicked off. He could not care less about any new landmasses; it was landslides he was worried about. If the referendum was defeated, it would effectively end his political career. Delivering an election victory for the British Republic Party after a setback like that would be tantamount to raising the *Titanic*.

Who would have imagined the Church to wield such influence? Could it be true? Waring passed a hand over his tired eyes. The Church—he had never even remotely imagined it might be a factor one way or the other. And now it was too late.

The phone balanced on the arm of his chair rang; he punched a button on the console. "Waring."

"We've got some new indicators, PM." It was Dennis Arnold again. He had been calling periodically through the day with reports from his various sources. When Waring failed to respond, Arnold said, "You wanted me to call as soon as I received the latest projections."

"Of course," Waring replied softly. "What have you got?"

"Good news," Arnold said. "We've picked up a point and a half, maybe even two."

"Terrific," Waring muttered.

"Two points," repeated Arnold. "We can still pull this off."

"I don't call two points a vast improvement, Dennis. We went into this referendum with better than ninety-percent support from an estimated thirty percent of registered voters. We're struggling to hold on to a two-point lead with every bleeding housefrau and pensioner in the country standing in the rain waiting to vote—and you think that's good news. I'll tell you what I think: I think it's a flaming bloody disaster."

"So it's close. What the hell? The trend is running in our favor," Arnold argued, "and there's still two hours to go before—"

Waring replaced the phone. He didn't want to debate the issue. The unarguable bottom line was that in less than two weeks the anti-monarchy camp had lost 40 percentage points. In his book, that was a catastrophe—and all the spin doctoring in the country would not convince him otherwise. For the past 48 hours the pollsters had been trying to pinpoint when it was that the mood of the people had changed.

Waring did not need any opinion surveys to tell him when the slide set in. He *knew* the exact moment—hell, the precise nanosecond—that public opinion had begun to shift and his dreams began to crumble: when the young monarch climbed back onto his soapbox and stood, bloody but unbowed, before the shocked Hyde Park crowd and told them that Avalon was waiting in the wings.

Confronted with such a fresh and indisputable example of his personal courage and integrity, the hardheaded media muckrakers had crumbled into a limp, groveling heap. Even the harshest critics of the new-style monarchy had embarked on a sycophantic frenzy of royalist propaganda. Where, two weeks ago, the success of the final referendum had been a foregone conclusion, the King's spectacular barnstorming performance had turned the tide of public opinion in mid-flow even as his heroism had revived the moribund monarchy. Quite simply, people had never seen anything like it from a royal and were astonished and elated. Who could blame them? Waring had never seen anything like it, either.

A body couldn't move three paces in the capital without bumping into another fresh convert to what the media were calling "the rejuvenated monarchy." Like all new believers, they carried the gospel with unflagging zeal. London cabbies had traded the usual weather banter for, "How about our King, then?" Suddenly every commuter on the Underground was an expert on constitutional monarchy. Even the Leicester Square winos took a newfound personal pride in defending the King's character to all comers. "You can say what you like 'bout the rest, mate. But don't go takin' the piss outta our Jimmy."

There were usually only two things a politician could do when confronted with such an enormous inundation of goodwill: stand aside or be swept away. So Waring stood aside and watched as public sentiment underwent a dramatic sea change and his once-invincible lead in the opinion polls dwindled away point by precious point. Any attempt to counter the tideflow would have been like trying to divert an avalanche with a paper fan.

The phone rang again, but Waring switched off the ringer. He got up from his chair, went into his bedroom, and stretched out on the bed. He closed his eyes and tried to sleep. After twenty futile minutes, he abandoned the attempt, and decided to go down to the kitchen and arrange supper instead. He was supposed to dine with Nigel, Dennis, and Martin tonight. They had planned an all-night referendum vigil, but any interest he might have had in such an event had withered and died days ago. An evening of forced bonhomie seemed dire beyond endurance. He decided to have one of the aides downstairs call around and cancel it.

He walked to the lift and was about to step into it when the buzzer sounded at the apartment door. He answered it without enthusiasm.

"Sorry, I'm early, PM," said Nigel Sforza, stepping into the room with a plastic carrier bag in his hand. "I tried to call a little while ago, but your phone is switched off apparently, so I just came on ahead." Hoisting the bag, he said, "I brought beer. I hope that's all right. Here." He handed two tall cans to the Prime Minister. "Martin should be along shortly. I'll just pop the rest of these in the fridge till he gets here."

Sforza proceeded to the small kitchen in the rear of the apartment. Waring watched him for a moment. "Sure, come on in, Nigel. Make yourself at home."

"Anything wrong?" came the voice from the other room.

Idiots and imbeciles, thought Waring hopelessly; they were all idiots and imbeciles, boobs and bozos. "Not a care in the world," he replied, and added under his breath, "not after tonight, anyway."

"What about having Chef send up some of those buffalo wings, or whatever they're called?"

"Anything to make you happy, Nigel."

Dennis Arnold and Martin Hutchens showed up around seven-thirty. By nine o'clock they had drunk all the beer Sforza brought and sent down to the kitchen for more. They had eaten two dozen hot and spicy chicken wings, a large pizza, and huge plates of the chef's special Caesar salad, and were well-fortified to begin the night's vigil.

They decided the BBC had the best coverage, and switched on the set in time to hear Jonathan Trent say, "Voting records were shattered today in what surely must have been the largest turnout in the nation's history. Early indications from exit-poll surveys point to a referendum victory by the narrowest of margins."

Trent, sober before a subdued purple backdrop with the words "Royal Referendum" and the logo of a crown above a question mark, turned to his left and said, "With me in the studio is Peter Bancroft, our veteran exit-poll analyst, to explain the state of play. Peter—"

The picture switched to a middle-aged man with hair like an Albert Einstein fright wig. He was whizzing around before a large screen on which two computer-generated columns—one purple, one blue—of roughly equal height were superimposed.

"Thank you, Jonathan," said the resident expert. "As we can see from this graphic, the evening begins with both sides at extremely level pegging. The blue, which represents the 'yes' vote to abolish the monarchy, and the purple, which represents the 'no' vote, are within half a percentage point of each other—the advantage at this early hour going to the 'yeses.' However," he quickly pointed out, gesturing with blithe incoherence, "we should remember that when a plus or minus accuracy rating of three percent is factored into the equation, that slight advantage disappears, and we can see that this referendum could go either way."

"Christ," groaned Waring, sinking further into his seat.

"He's blowing hot air," Arnold declared. "Our own surveys show a solid eight-percent advantage."

Waring turned his face to regard the Special Committee Chairman skeptically. "You told me two percent a little while ago."

"I said it was a *trend,* remember? You're just going to have to cheer up, my friend," Arnold chided jovially. "We're going to win this referendum whether you like it or not."

The next hour improved the picture considerably. As the voting precincts began reporting their tallies, the blue areas on Peter Bancroft's computer-generated map of Britain began to spread. By eleven o'clock it looked as if the greater London region would remain true blue with Kent the only holdout in the southeast.

Waring's hopes began to revive. If they carried London, they could conceivably carry the vote. Press Secretary Martin Hutchens, who had been on the phone for the better part of an hour, entered the room to announce, "It's in the bag, gents."

"What have you got?" asked Sforza, tipping up his half-empty can.

"Latest exit poll stats." He waved a piece of paper. "You're going to love this. It's from *The Times*—they're showing a referendum victory by an eight-point margin."

"Are they printing that?" asked Dennis Arnold.

"Uh, no," replied Hutchens, "they're holding the presses until they get a few more returns. But it's great. We've done it!"

Waring sucked his teeth. "We'll see."

Another hour passed, and the returns as posted on the BBC map did appear to bear out *The Times'* prediction. The blue was spreading outward now to include portions of the Midlands. True, there were some tiny purple bits showing—mostly in the sparsely populated areas of northern Scotland. Nevertheless, as Arnold pointed out, "Hell, we can give away *all* Scotland, and it won't make a blind bit of difference."

Sforza left a short while later, declaring himself satisfied that the trend would hold and that the referendum would carry by a narrow but sufficient margin. When Peter Bancroft predicted that the southwestern Cardiff-London corridor would go solid blue, Dennis Arnold departed. "Congratulations, Tom," he said. "I'll see you tomorrow and we can begin concentrating our full attention on our reelection campaign."

Waring returned from seeing Arnold out, and settled into his chair once more. "Want a drink or anything, Hutch?" he asked, feeling expansive for the first time in many days. "I've got some good single malt—twenty-four-year-old Springbank. What do you say?"

"Sure, why not?" Hutch agreed. "We've dodged the bullet. Let's celebrate."

The two sat and sipped their Scotch and watched as the BBC map of Scotland gradually turned purple. This did not alarm Waring unduly. "Arnie's right," he mused, "we can afford to give up the whole of Scotland and never miss it."

"Yeah, sure," said Hutch. "Whatever you say."

"Ever been to Scotland?" asked Waring.

"No."

"Never?"

"Never had a reason to go."

"You should. Fresh air, sea, sky. It's nice—apart from the midges."

"Well, I'm more of a city man, you know?"

They chatted like this for a while, and watched the purple stain spread down through the glens and seep southward. When it crossed Hadrian's Wall and started bleeding into the North Country, Waring grew irritated. When it claimed Yorkshire and the Lake District, the Prime Minister grew agitated. By the time the royal purple tide had swept down the west coast and into North Wales, Waring was anxiously pacing the floor in front of the TV, and Hutchens was on the phone to the pollsters, demanding to know what was happening.

BBC political commentator Peter Bancroft leapt around his little set like an overactive elf, excitedly pointing to this, that, or the other amazing development. Meanwhile, Newcastle, Sunderland, and Middlesbrough fell beneath the advancing purple flood. Once into the old industrial heartland of Britain, there was no stopping it. Sheffield, Leeds, Manchester, and Liverpool blushed bright purple, and were followed in quick succession by Nottingham, Birmingham, Leicester. The rout continued as the rural provinces around Coventry, Northampton, and Peterborough fell beneath the purple onslaught. Cornwall and Devon, long-time royal haunts, were swept away, followed by Somerset, Dorset, and Wiltshire.

The Prime Minister sank back in his leather chair and stared at the screen in abject disbelief. He felt sick to his stomach; his head ached and his eyes felt like dead embers in his head. "How?" he asked, his voice cracking with fatigue and defeat.

Martin Hutchens, morose and ashamed to meet his boss's eye, shrugged. "Who knows?"

"It was in the bag, you said. We had an eight-point lead, you said. We couldn't lose. For Chrissakes! Everybody was so sure we couldn't bloody lose!" The enormity of his loss was just beginning to strike home. The years of work, years of his *life* . . . gone.

"What can I say?" Hutchens bent his head and shook it slowly. "Exit polls are notoriously fickle. People lie."

"Do they now!" growled Waring. "Bloody hell!"

"They say what they think the survey taker wants to hear.

They lie to keep their ballot secret. They lie just to confound the polls. Nobody tells a pollster the truth."

"Eight points . . . bloody hell!" It would be a long, lonely night. "Eight bloody damned points."

"I know. It sucks. What can I say?" He shook his head again, yawned, and stood. "I'm going home."

He walked to the apartment door. Waring glared after him as if he were the cause of all human misery. "It's not the end of the world, you know," Hutchens volunteered. "I'll see you tomorrow."

Waring sat in his chair for a long time after his spin doctor had gone. "Tomorrow belongs to the victor," he moaned to himself. "For losers, there *is* no tomorrow."

The referendum coverage descended into nightmare. The home counties offered token resistance; here and there, pockets of blue stood out like island refuges in a surging violet sea. Lincolnshire, Cambridgeshire, Norfolk, and Suffolk were almost completely conquered by the royal purple of the monarchy. Oxford, that hotbed of political anarchy, joined the purple rebellion at first opportunity, while the rest of the county remained blue for a long while—until finally succumbing to the purple tide along with Gloucestershire, and Hereford and Worcester; Shropshire and the rest of Wales from St. David's to Llandudno pledged themselves to the purple, thus completing the patchwork map.

Waring poured his Scotch freely and drank deeply to ease the hollow pain throbbing in the space where his heart had been. As the dull alcohol mist rose in his exhausted brain, he sat in bleary-eyed agony staring at a political map tinted almost completely royal purple—save for the tattered swatch of blue that was greater metropolitan London.

Jonathan Trent, looking surprisingly alert and well rested, reappeared just before the telecast ended. With evident relish, the cheerful presenter pronounced the fateful words, "Judging from the returns of ninety-seven percent of the precincts, the referendum to abolish the monarchy has failed. I repeat, the referendum has failed. The monarchy of Britain has survived and will continue." Grinning widely, he

wished everyone a good night and a pleasant tomorrow. The
broadcast concluded for the night with a film montage of
Great Britain over a stirring rendition of "God Save the
King."

Waring sat long in the void that followed, gazing vacantly
at the blank screen, listening to the muted howl of the empty
airways.

※

# Forty-six

Holyrood Palace appeared much as it must have looked the day the last Scottish king had been crowned in Edinburgh. Less palace than prison, it began life as a guesthouse for dignitaries visiting the then important Holyrood Abbey next door—the site of the final resting place of the True Cross, so legend maintains.

Now it was a guesthouse once more, for the palace had been given over to the use of the royal party, which numbered well over a hundred and, with the coronation only scant hours away, increased with every passing minute. Friends and relations of the monarch, well-wishing subjects, and official representatives of churches, charities, and foreign governments arrived at the palace in an endless train. Those who did not attend in person sent cards, telegrams, faxes, and couriered greetings and congratulations—along with a mountain of fruit, flowers, gifts, and commemorative souvenirs.

Edinburgh has been in the kingmaking business every bit as long as London or York, and it was at Embries' insistence—with James' wholehearted approval—that the coronation of the first Scottish king in half a millennium should be held there.

The evening before the ceremony, Embries took James up

to Arthur's Seat—the city's most often remarked-upon ancient landmark. The rocky core of a long-extinct volcano, it rises majestically above Auld Reekie, giving anyone who endures the climb magnificent views over Scotland's capital city.

The Palace of Holyroodhouse sits directly beneath Arthur's Seat; owing to security precautions for the coronation, the hill and park environs had been closed to the public until after the ceremony. Thus, James and Embries had the entire place to themselves, and hiked up to the top of the hill for a little exercise after supper. Embries said the air would clear their heads, but, as James guessed, there was more to it than that.

They trudged up the empty pathways, Embries silent, lost in thought, and James in a reflective mood. The cold, wet winter had given way to a spectacular spring: bright, shower-dazzled days and exceptionally warm nights. The entire country had been enjoying the best planting season in living memory, and already by the end of April, the northern days were growing longer, the gentle twilights lingering for hours.

James' adventure in Glen Beag had been kept out of the press until the referendum was decided; he wanted no sympathy votes and the journalists, for their part, agreed to delay reports of the incident while the polls were open. After that, however, the papers and television broadcasts were awash with accounts of the newly confirmed monarch's derring-do, not to mention his surprise wedding to the woman who had captured the hearts of her people.

Having received a ringing endorsement from the nation's voters, James had decided on a May Day coronation, in keeping with an ancient tradition. The last few weeks had been taken up with planning the gala event, and now, on the eve of the big day, everything was in place. They walked to Arthur's Seat and stood to look out upon a city bathed in the rich honeyed light of a fine Scottish evening.

After a while, Embries said, "It is the time-between-times, a holy time, when the veil that separates this world's-realm from the next grows thin, and mortals are allowed a glimpse into the Otherworld." Glancing sideways at James, he said, "What do you see?"

Gazing out across the land, James saw the strong arm of the Firth of Forth, glimmering in the evening light like molten gold as it curled into the deep, blue-green fold of the hills beyond the city. "I see . . ." he began, and instantly the modern conurbation dissolved before his eyes.

Houses, buildings, streets, traffic—all gone; whole suburbs and districts disappeared as if they had been nothing more than smoke on the wind. He looked across to see Edinburgh Castle perched upon its rocky roost, but it was a smaller, far more primitive version of itself: a timber and thatch settlement sheltered in the shadow of Caer Edin's rock; the lower slopes and flats contained new-plowed fields. Instead of traffic noises, he heard the lowing of oxen being led to the cattle enclosure and the cackling of rooks as they settled in their high nests for the night.

Away in the east, the first stars were shining like splinters of burning diamonds. A new moon was rising pale and ghostly above the forested hills across the firth. The air smelled of peat smoke and sea salt; James drew it deep into his lungs and was overcome by the almost heartbreaking sensation that he had experienced it all before, an unutterably long time ago.

Into his mind flashed the image of two boys—one light, one dark—nine or ten summers old, barefoot and shirtless, wearing loose yellow-and-brown-checked trousers. They were running up the hillside through the long grass, the sun warm on their shoulders, larksong pouring from a high, bright sky. As they crested the hill, a vast encampment came into sight: clusters of tents, wicker huts, and leafy-branched bowers, surrounded by long lines of horse pickets, occupied the plain from end to end.

"The Gathering," he whispered, as an ache of longing pierced him through the heart.

"Yes," murmured Embries close beside him.

And James thought, *Surely, he has always stood beside me; it has always been this way.*

"What else do you see?"

Turning his eyes to the path by which they had come up the hillside, he saw a long string of lights flickering in the twilight—a torchlight procession. In the front of the parade were men with spears across their shoulders; upon the spears they bore a heavy round oaken shield, and upon the shield they carried a man, a prince of their people.

They brought the man to the clefted rock and placed him on it. The warriors gathered around and, at the Chief Bard's command, each came before the prince. Laying their weapons at his feet, they stretched themselves out upon the ground and placed the nobleman's foot upon their necks, whereupon he raised them up, embraced them, and returned their weapons. The Chief Bard then came forward and placed a golden torc around the lord's throat; he raised his staff over the prince's head and sained him with strong runes. This simple ritual observed, the war host rose up and acclaimed their King. They lifted him high, placed him on the shield, and carried him down the hill once more, singing as they went.

The scene blurred before James' eyes, blending into the evening mist rising in the valley below. The echo of the warriors' voices rang out across the lowlands.

"I have been here before," he said softly.

Embries nodded, watching him.

"I was made King here in this place. This is where I began my reign."

"King once, and King again," remarked Embries. "Tomorrow is Beltane, the ancient festival of fire. Always a good day for a kingmaking, I think."

James stared at his Wise Counselor, and he seemed to shed the burden of age. Whether a trick of the light, or of his own, James could not tell, but the lines of his face softened, his pale eyes deepened in color, and the woad-blue *fhain* mark reappeared lightly on his cheek—just for a moment—and then it was gone.

"Remember when you took me to Caer Lial?" James said. "I asked you how this was possible. I didn't get an answer, so I'm asking again. How, Myrddin? How is it possible?"

"I have often asked myself the same question," replied Embries quietly.

"And?"

"I really don't know."

"You must have some idea, some explanation."

Embries pursed his lips in thought, and they began walking back. "The human soul is that unique point in the universe where spirit and matter meet—so the Druid bards believed. They revered many such meeting places: like the time-between-times, which is neither wholly night nor wholly day, but a dynamic, creative blend of the two. The soul is the forceful expression of its contributing parts. And if we believe that each human life is given for a purpose, I see no reason why a soul cannot be given renewed expression when its original purpose remains unfulfilled."

"And in Britain's greatest hour of need, Arthur will return to lead his people to Avalon . . ." murmured James.

"A strange belief when you think about it—the notion of a return, I mean. Yet it persists. Only a very few people in history are longed for in this way. Arthur is one."

"As much as I like the name," James said, "as much as I feel that it fits me, the plain fact of the matter is that my name isn't Arthur. Not really."

Embries chuckled gently. "I'll tell you a secret: it wasn't your name the first time, either."

At ten o'clock the next morning, the royal party assembled in the graveled yard of Holyrood Palace to begin the procession. Eschewing the newfangled royal penchant for horse-drawn carriages, James had elected to walk. Surrounded by his friends, with his Queen at his side, he would stroll up the Royal Mile to the castle parade ground where the crown-taking ceremony would be held.

The weather, in typical Scottish fashion, refused to cooperate. A damp, drizzly morning followed a rainy dawn; mist obscured Arthur's Seat, and clouds hung low over Edinburgh Castle. Cal thought the poor weather could be a good thing, all in all, as it might help in crowd control along the procession route.

That was pure wishful thinking. People had been pouring into the city for days by plane, train, coach, and car—and it would take more than a few raindrops to prevent them from witnessing the restoration and renewal of the British monarchy. The route, virtually a straight line along a single street from palace to castle, was barricaded and lined with police, a uniformed constable stationed every few yards. For those who could not attend the ceremonies in person, the coronation would be broadcast worldwide, from the massed banks of TV cameras placed at every strategic location.

"Ready, my love?" he asked Jennifer as they took their places at the head of the procession. She had chosen a simple black dress and a black jacket edged in gold. Her black hair was swept back and held in place with a pair of gold combs. "You look ravishing."

"And you look . . . regal," she replied, brushing a piece of lint from his sleeve and smoothing the lapel of his black suit.

"Cal, are you ready for this?" he called over his shoulder.

"It's only a wee ramble up the street," Cal observed, joining them. "I don't know what everyone's getting so worked up about." He gave James a pat on the back. "Relax and enjoy it, Jimmy. You worked hard enough to get here."

The comment caused James to reflect on just how much had happened in the past few months to make this day possible: from the actual suicide of a failed monarch, to the political suicide of a would-be president. Even poor King Edward's demise, dismal as it was, possessed infinitely more dignity than former Prime Minister Waring's ignominious departure from public life. The British Republic Party's spectacularly acrimonious implosion in the wake of the Unified Alliance's solid election victory appalled even their staunchest supporters. Following the defeat of the fifth and final referendum, the most powerful party in British political history seemed to go into freefall. One pundit likened it to watching a kamikaze squadron take a flaming nosedive from a great height.

The new Prime Minister, Huw Griffith, had made it a priority of his government's first legislation to reinstate a few of the royal perquisites abolished under the previous administration; not all of the privileges were restored, to be sure, but enough, for example, to grant James adequate security when traveling around the country.

Part of this newfound governmental largesse could be seen in the regiment of King's Own Highlanders which had been requisitioned for the royal procession. Together with the famed Scots Guards detailed to bring up the rear, these traditional regiments had been returned to royal duty with the King as commander in chief. Where past monarchs had favored cavalry regiments, James was an infantry soldier at heart. The only horses in his parade belonged to the mounted police assigned to crowd control.

The honor of leading the procession fell to the pipe and drum band, directed by Pipe Major Alexander McTavitt, who went before them in fine Highland tradition. As kings of old marched into battle behind their pipers, and heralded each royal occasion with the pipes, so James would proceed to his crown-taking.

Thus, as the gatehouse clock struck ten, he signaled Pipe Major McTavitt, who promptly puffed up his bagpipe and, with measured, stately steps, led them out through the palace gate. They entered Canongate Street, the pipes in full cry, and the people burst into ecstatic applause.

From the first glimpse of the royal procession, the crowds went berserk, screaming, crying, waving banners and flags, signs and pennants. Pressed ten, fifteen, and twenty-deep on the street between the barricades and the buildings, they cheered and clapped and whistled. They hung out from the upper windows of every building, and leaned out from every roof—by the hundreds, by the thousands. They filled the air with whoops of delight and crown-shaped confetti. They reached out to touch the royal couple, to shake their hands, and to offer keepsakes and flowers.

Those who could not reach them threw bouquets instead, lofting them high over the heads of the throng, so that the King and Queen moved in a blizzard of flower petals and multicolored confetti. Buffeted by wave upon wave of applause, the procession marched slowly up the street, the roar of the crowd all but drowning out the skirl of the pipes.

Canongate became High Street, and the parade moved slowly on, arriving at St. Giles Cathedral—also decorated with flags and banners and colorful streamers on poles. The multitude in the square outside the kirk thundered their applause when, as the King and Queen paused before the war memorial to pay homage to the valiant dead, a little girl in a kilt and white socks darted out from the barricade to present Jennifer with a bouquet of daisies. The child received a kiss from the Queen, and James thought he would be deafened by the crowd's roar.

The girl was escorted back to her beaming parents, and the royal train moved on. High Street became Castlehill, and James could see the broad Esplanade with the castle brooding on its rock beyond. A platform had been erected in the middle of the Esplanade where the actual ceremony would take place.

They made the long slow climb up Castlehill and, as the procession entered the Esplanade, the band fell silent. The drums gave out a long, low, rumbling roll, and the pipes launched into "Scotland the Brave." The strains of that gallant song sent a thrill of pride through James, and he found himself singing the words under his breath. "Land of my high endeavor, land of the shining river," he sang, "land of my heart forever . . . Scotland the brave. . . ."

The Highlanders marched to the foot of the platform and surrounded it on all sides, facing the crowds. Jenny and James, Cal, and Embries mounted the platform steps to join the rest of the royal party already waiting there. Along with Archbishop Rippon, and an ecclesiastical contingent representing other denominations, there were ambassadors from virtually all of the former Commonwealth nations, the European Union, and a handful of officials representing government and the armed forces, including the Prime Minister, Huw Griffith, and James' old commanding officer, Field Marshal William Dawes.

An altar had been set up in the center of the platform and, before it, an antique throne; the clergymen and official witnesses were arranged in a half circle around the throne and altar. Before the throne, however, was a roughly rectangular block of yellowish rock: the Stone of Scone, known and revered by the Celts as the Stone of Destiny, on which the kings of Scotland have been crowned for ages past remembering.

James took his place before the Stone of Destiny, and the Prime Minister, looking earnest and dignified, stepped forward to read the proclamation. "Whereas it has pleased Almighty God to call to his mercy our late Sovereign Lord Edward the Ninth"—James could not help noticing he left out the phrase "of blessed and glorious memory"— "by whose decease the Crown is solely and rightfully come to the High and Mighty Lord James Arthur Stuart."

The Prime Minister stole a fleeting glance at his King, took a deep breath, and plunged on. "We, therefore, the Lords Spiritual and Temporal of this realm, being here assisted by these good hearts and true, with representatives of Great Britain's several States, and other Principal Ladies and Gentlemen of Quality, together with the citizens and subjects of this land, do hereby and with one voice and consent of heart and tongue publish and proclaim that the man standing here before us is our only lawful king, by the Grace of God, King of Britain and of its constituent realm and territories, Defender of the Faith, to whom his subjects do acknowledge all loyalty and constant obedience with hearty and humble affection, beseeching the Heavenly Father by whom earthly sovereigns do reign, to bless the Royal King, and his Lady Queen, with long and happy years to reign over us."

Raising his head, he smiled and then bellowed in solid Welsh tones, "God save the King!"

At this the multitude gathered on the Esplanade gave out a tremendous cheer, echoing the proclamation with the cry, "God save the King!"

When the uproar had died down, the ceremony continued with the enthronement. Turning to the assembled clergymen and officials, Prime Minister Griffith said, "I present to you King James Arthur Stuart, by Divine Right, Sovereign of Britain."

At this, those gathered on the platform bowed low before the King. Next, the Archbishop of Canterbury and Field Marshal Dawes, bearing the Sword of State, came before him. Archbishop Rippon proceeded to administer the Royal Oath, by which James affirmed that he would govern his people according to the laws of the land, and maintain the Laws of God, and uphold the Holy Church. The Field Marshal turned and, bearing the sword, blade upright, led him to the altar where he kissed the Holy Bible and signed the oath.

Next, he was led to the throne and sat down upon it. Rhys and Cal stepped forward and, removing James' tie, unbuttoned the King's shirt and bared his chest. The Archbishop then came before the King and, taking the Royal Ampulla and Spoon, poured out some holy oil with which he signed James with the cross; dipping his fingertips into the bowl of the spoon, he anointed the sovereign's forehead, his chest, and the palms of both hands. He then said a prayer, invoking God's wisdom, mercy, leading, and protection on James' behalf.

Field Marshal Dawes then removed the scabbard from the weapon in his hand, and presented James with the Sword of State. "With this sword do justice, halt the growth of iniquity, protect the sanctity of God and his servants in this land, and deal righteously with all your people," he said, laying the naked blade across James' outstretched palms.

Then the King stood and, still holding the sword across his palms, stepped up onto the Stone of Destiny. Embries, carrying his venerable old staff and wearing the cloak he'd worn the night James had first met him, stepped up to the stone. Raising his staff, he delivered a long oration in Old Gaelic, and then translated it, saying, "Great of Might, High King of Heaven, Lord of all that is and is to come, Maker, Redeemer, and Friend of Mankind, bless your King on Earth." To James, he said, "Kneel before the Lord of All, and swear fealty to the High King you will serve."

James knelt down on the stone, and Embries took the sword, turned the blade and offered it to him hilt upward so it now formed a cross. Grasping the naked blade, James held it at arm's length. "As you kneel before God, and in the sight of this multitude of witnesses," Embries said, "what is your vow?"

"By the power of God's might, and through his will, I vow to hold myself obedient to my Lord Christ, to be used of him to do his work in this worlds-realm. By the power of God's might, and through his will, I vow to lead my kingdom through all things whatsoever shall befall me, with courage, with dignity, with faith in Christ who guides me, to worship him freely, to honor him gladly, to revere him nobly, to hold with him the truest faith and greatest love all the days of my life."

"Do you," Embries said, "pledge to uphold justice, grant mercy, and seek truth, dealing with your people in compassion and charity?"

"I do so pledge," James replied, "to uphold justice, grant mercy, and seek truth, dealing with my people in compassion and charity even as I am dealt with by God."

After receiving the King's vows, Embries turned and retrieved from the Archbishop's hand a golden torc of the kind worn by the Celtic kings of old. Spreading the ends apart, he slipped the ancient ornament around James' neck, and then closed the ends once more. He took a slender golden circlet, also very old, and placed it on his brow.

Stepping back, he raised his hands palm outwards and commanded, "Rise, Sovereign Lord, and go forth to all righteousness and good works; rule justly and live honorably; be to your people a ready light and sure guide through all things whatsoever shall befall you in this worlds-realm!"

James rose to his feet once more, and the Field Marshal buckled the sword belt and scabbard around his waist. Embries turned then and, raising his staff over the gathered multitude, proclaimed, "People of Britain! Here is your High King! I charge you to love him, honor him, serve him, follow him, and pledge your lives to him even as he has pledged his life to the High King of Heaven."

At this the crowd gave a great shout of acclamation. James held out his hand to Jenny, and she stepped to his side, and together they stood before the watching world and received the adoration of their subjects. Standing on the

edge of the platform, gazing out across the crowds and the
city, it seemed to James as if he stood on the very pinnacle
of the world. He looked at all those people, almost delirious
with delight, and his heart went out to them. They were his
people, and he was their King—bound by ties as strong as
civilization itself, and just as old.

The drums began beating time, and the pipers played the
hymn "Be Thou My Vision." From the castle crag behind
them, seven cannons began firing volley after volley from
the high ramparts.

As the last cannon blast echoed out across the firth, the
low clouds parted and, as if on cue, dazzling sunlight
streamed down upon the King. From somewhere in the
crowd came the shout: "Arthur!"

The shout was immediately taken up as a chant, and soon
the entire assembly was crying, "Arthur! . . . Arthur!"

The cry coursed back along the Royal Mile and the streets
now filled with people, and all of them chanting: Arthur!
Arthur! Arthur!

As the King stood in the blazing light, receiving the homage of his people, he felt the platform quiver beneath his
feet. At first he thought it must be the vibration from all the
shouting. But it grew in strength, and he figured it was the
castle cannons firing again and the explosions were shaking
the stones.

An earthquake off the Cornish coast—the tremors of
which could be felt as far away as Kirkwall in Orkney, and
Bilbao in Spain—had shaken the entire British mainland.
The ensuing tidal wave had sent water surging up the estu-
aries, thereby briefly reversing the course of the Thames
and several other rivers. Long asleep beneath the waves,
Llyonesse had shaken off her slumber and risen from the
sea.

## ❋

## Forty-seven

Rhys brought the Tempest in low over the water so his passengers could appreciate the dramatic tilting slope of the gigantic new landmass off the Cornish coast. Like everyone else, Embries, James, and Jenny had seen the pictures in the newspapers and on TV; they had also been provided with a specially prepared previsit briefing. But none of what they'd seen or read captured even a fraction of the excitement of actually seeing Llyonesse jutting from the sea.

At first sight, Jenny thought it looked like the leading edge of an extremely large black paving stone rising at an oblique angle from the waves. Or, perhaps, a gigantic wedge-shaped slab of lumpy clay half sunk in a millpond. The thing that surprised her the most, besides the size—nearly four miles end to end and more than two miles wide, according to the info kit—was the amount of activity.

There were tents and pavilions of several sizes and colors scattered over the surface of the sloping landmass, two helicopter platforms had been erected, and there was a makeshift marina with room for fifty or more boats. Clusters of small igloo-shaped tents formed bivouac areas on the leeward side of the island and, nearby, a congregation of temporary huts surrounding a radio and microwave tower constituted the administrative center. While score upon score of workers—their blue or yellow overalls making them look like competing colonies of swarming insects—toiled at digging and scraping away centuries of sediment, a fleet of seagoing vessels of various sorts worked the waters round about. Some of the boats displayed the green-and-blue flag of the British Oceanographic Trust, the body controlling and funding the research; most, however, were co-opted fishing boats and small charter-cruise ships full of curious tourists. In among the divers and sight-seers, Special Branch police cruisers trawled the crowded waters, trying to maintain security for the royal visit.

*How amazing!* thought Jenny as Rhys dropped the helicopter onto the landing pad. *How absolutely astonishing!*

The chopper bounced down, and Embries smiled. "Welcome to Llyonesse," he said, grinning with pleasure. The royal visitors stepped out onto the platform, and looked back towards the Cornish coast—hazy in the distance—to see the scattering of tiny islets like stepping stones between the new island and the mainland, the tops of mountains yet submerged.

Then, alighting from the platform, they touched the surface of the new island. To Jenny it was like setting foot on the moon. She felt a strange, inexplicable exhilaration—as if she were in some way connecting with a power long dormant inside her, a primeval force she had suppressed all her life but which responded to this place. The feeling both thrilled and frightened. She looked to James, and he seemed equally dumbfounded.

"Good morning, Your Royal Highnesses. I'm pleased to meet you. I'm Dr. Fuller," said the woman waiting just beyond reach of the whirling helicopter blades. Christine Fuller, the coordinator of the multidiscipline research project and director of the oceanographic unit, was accompanied by two assistants—a slightly older man and a slim, brown-haired young woman. She said, "Claudia, my personal assistant, and Nicholas, our site manager, have prepared a little presentation at site headquarters; I thought we might start there before showing you around. If you would like to follow me."

They moved off towards a cluster of prefab huts, around which a group of Special Branch security agents in dark suits was maintaining discreet yet vigilant presence, complementing on land the police in the boats. Dr. Fuller led her guests past four large, diesel-fired generators and a half dozen portable toilets. The whirring whine of the generators drowned out all other sound and set the ground vibrating underfoot; the huge engines filled the air with a fine blue haze of diesel smoke and fumes.

The largest of the huts was a portable building anchored with ropes and covered by a canopy constructed of scaffolding poles and nylon-reinforced plastic sheeting to keep off the sun and rain. The interior looked like a jumble sale for used computer gear and office equipment. Monitor screens and consoles were heaped on every available surface; cords and wires snaked off in all directions. Members of the research team moved among the stacks of equipment, shouting above the din of the generators outside, checking the monitors, and making notations on charts and clipboards.

The pale blue interior was lit by halogen lamps centered over a large table covered with a white sheet. A space had been cleared around the table, and four folding chairs lined up on one side. At the director's invitation, the four visitors took their seats and, while Claudia nervously served coffee and biscuits, Nicholas led them through a printout which explained the technical aspects of the geologic dynamics at work in the area—all about plate tectonics, pressure zones, and sonar mapping. Then Claudia took over; using a prepared flip chart, she outlined the corresponding geophysical relationship of Llyonesse with the mainland and explained the topographical profile of the region.

Thanking her colleagues, Dr. Fuller continued, detailing the last, dramatic few weeks. "Having established the mean rise ratio over the entire site," she explained, "we fed the sonar data into our computers at Bristol University and were able to produce a virtual model of the active area. The computer model was used to create this. . . ."

She nodded to her assistants, who stepped to the table and lifted off the sheet to reveal a large-scale physical model of

Llyonesse as it had been in ages past and, by all calculations, would be once again—complete with white-capped waves and tiny boats all around. The new island was an elongated mass that looked like a slightly splayed inverted footprint, the heel of which was separated from Cornwall by a narrow channel, and the toes of which were formed by what had been the Isles of Scilly. The center of the island was dominated by a rising plateau—the tabletop, so to speak, part of which was all that protruded from the sea at present.

"The model you see before you," Dr. Fuller proclaimed, "is how we believe the restored landmass will appear. And this"—she indicated a smaller, less detailed model set into a corner of the table—"is how it appears now."

"How quickly is the island rising?" Embries asked, genuine excitement lending an edge to his voice Jenny had never heard before. "How long, that is, until the entire landmass is fully visible?"

"The rate of rise has accelerated since the primary quake to an average of nearly three centimeters per day," Nicholas answered. "Naturally, some areas are rising faster than others; the submerged region"—he pointed to the model, indicating the portion still beneath the surface—"is rising almost twice as fast as the area where we are now, which is rising very little." He held his hand out flat and tilted it to show how one part could rise more swiftly than another.

"As I say, three centimeters is the average over the entire region. That's a lot, and should the seabed continue to ascend at that rate, Llyonesse will appear as indicated by our model in approximately thirty-eight months—assuming the tectonic shift continues to follow its present course. We cannot predict that another cataclysm won't suck it back into the sea. I would point out, however, that the island rose almost eighteen meters as a result of the quake eight weeks ago."

"The Coronation Quake," James said, referring to the media tag which had attached itself to the phenomenon. "Might another quake produce equally dramatic results?"

"Certainly, Your Majesty," replied Dr. Fuller. "In fact, the entire region between Land's End and Scilly Isles is undergoing an almost continual series of tremors—three in one day last week. We have been fortunate so far in that most of the subsequent quake damage has been limited to the southernmost portions of the mainland. Again, our prediction skills are extremely rudimentary; it's difficult to say at this point how long the process will take. Nevertheless, I believe Llyonesse will one day appear as indicated by the model."

"What is this bit, here?" asked Jenny, running her fingertips across an unnatural line of bumps that ran roughly parallel to the edge of the plateau. "It seems unusually symmetrical."

Dr. Fuller smiled mysteriously and gestured towards Claudia, who said, "One of the first features to draw our attention was that very ridge system." She stepped to the model and pointed to several places where there was a ridge, or hump, running alongside the cliff formed by the plateau; one, perpendicular to the first, disappeared over the edge.

"Preliminary excavations—performed mostly underwater, although we soon hope to be able to carry them out on dry land—indicate that what we are looking at is, in fact, the remains of a sophisticated wall system, or perhaps a road."

"Walls," Jenny repeated. "The information we received said nothing about walls or roads of any sort."

"Indeed, Your Highness," agreed Dr. Fuller. "In order to discourage amateur treasure-hunting, which unfortunately has already occurred, we have ceased reporting our more sensational discoveries." She nodded to her assistant.

"My specialty is underwater mapping," explained Claudia, "and from what I've seen so far, I think I can say with a high degree of certainty that Llyonesse was extensively populated at some time in the past, and we are in fact standing on a site of ancient habitation. Unfortunately, the most comprehensive patterning is still underwater at the present time. Until we can begin excavations, we cannot say precisely what we're looking at."

"Nevertheless," said Dr. Fuller, "we have good reason to be hopeful." She bent down and retrieved a large wooden box from beneath the table. Handing the box to Nicholas, she reached inside. "One of the exploratory trenches turned up this fragment."

She brought out a slender, curved bit of reddish stone.

"Incredible!" enthused Jenny. "May I?" She took the bit of pottery in her hands and turned it over reverently. "Hand turned—and look: there is still some decoration along the rim. Oh, this is wonderful."

"There is more where that came from," announced Nicholas. "We found five more pieces just this morning. They are still *in situ* and we will be bringing them up shortly."

Jenny cradled the smooth fragment in the palm of her hand; being a potter herself, she could almost feel the way the clay had been worked by the hand that had shaped it long ago. It formed for her a strong connection with the past: she saw in her mind's eye a large, low-sided bowl decorated with dolphins and fish. "Where did you say you found them?"

"Just here." Nicholas pointed at the model, indicating the cliff face roughly halfway down the sheer slope where Llyonesse met the sea. "We have to rappel down there, so it's not easy work—but I can tell you it's pretty darn exciting. I was working down there earlier today, and—"

That clenched it for Jenny. "Could I see it, please?"

"You mean take you there, Ma'am?" Nicholas hesitated and looked to his superior.

"It is a fairly strenuous descent, as Dr. Wiles has indicated," began Dr. Fuller.

"I've done plenty of rock climbing," Jenny assured them. "If you wouldn't mind showing me, I'd love to see it."

"But of course, Your Majesty," answered Dr. Fuller. "We'd be honored to show you—if you don't mind getting dirty. It's pretty muddy down there, and the surface is fairly rough."

James added his endorsement of Jenny's climbing skills, and it was settled. The necessary gear was quickly assembled—a dry suit and inflatable life vest, climbing boots, and a bag of tools—and the royal party was conducted out across the compound and up the long, rising slope to the edge of the escarpment.

"This is why we use harnesses," Dr. Fuller explained as they approached the steeply angled slope. She introduced them to a bearded young man in a faded black tee shirt, identifying him as the excavation supervisor, who began explaining the system of winches and cables used for the dig.

A number of iron bars had been driven into crevices in the rock to anchor a crude stanchion of scaffolding pipe; more scaffolding was erected in a configuration which projected out over the edge of the cliff like two great fishing poles— an image aided by the fact that positioned at the bottom of each pole was an electric winch with nylon climbing rope. Three smaller hand winches held other ropes which passed through a plate with a roller bar and disappeared over the cliff side.

Jenny stepped forward and looked over the edge to see a sharply inclined plane, about the angle of a fast ski jump, slanting away to the water washing restlessly around the heaps of broken rock slicing up out of the sea perhaps a hundred and fifty feet or so below. The cliff face itself, mostly rock and hardened sediment, was crisscrossed with the low humps of buried walls.

James stepped beside her, taking her arm as she gazed over the edge. "Are you sure you want to go down there?" he asked. "It's a long, rough slide to the bottom."

"It'll be a doddle," she said. "All the same, I'll wait for the harness, thanks."

Retreating from the edge, they stepped back and rejoined Embries, Rhys, and Dr. Fuller, who were talking to the excavation supervisor. Two Special Branch agents kept a close but respectful distance; one of them was speaking softly into a tiny microphone attached to his lapel.

"Eventually, of course, the entire site will be thoroughly excavated," the supervisor was saying. "For now, a few exploratory trenches is about all we can manage because of the difficulty in reaching the area. Still, the fact that we're finding artifacts already indicates an exceptionally rich field for study."

"We may soon be able to establish a date from the samples found so far," Dr. Fuller added. "I hope to have a preliminary estimate by the end of the summer."

Nicholas arrived with a blue jumpsuit and the necessary harness—identical to the one he was now wearing: an all-body affair made of heavy nylon strapping and titanium fasteners much the same as hang gliders and sky divers used. As Rhys examined the harness, one of the security agents stepped forward and said, "Begging your pardon, Your Majesty, but you aren't thinking of going down there, are you?"

"I am," replied Jenny, shoving her arms into the sleeves of the blue coverall.

"The risk, Your Highness. I'll have to ask you to reconsider," began the agent.

Jenny stopped him. "We've had this conversation before, haven't we, Richard?"

"Yes, Ma'am."

"Fine," the Queen replied, zipping up the jumpsuit. "If you'll excuse me, I'll put on my harness now."

As Jennifer shrugged into the nylon straps of the harness, the Special Branch agent appealed to the King. "Your concern is duly noted," James told him, a small amused smile touching his lips. "Believe me, the Queen is fully able to take care of herself."

At a nod from Jenny, Nicholas took the rope from the winch at the base of the second pole. "If you would allow me, Ma'am," he said, and attached the titanium spring clip on the end of the rope to the ring on the chest strap of the harness.

Rhys expertly tightened the various straps, and double-checked the fasteners before giving her the all clear. He settled himself at the controls of the winch. "Ready when you are, Your Majesty," he called.

Jenny, eager to begin, stepped quickly to the edge and leaned backward. The rope tightened. "Lower away!"

Rhys eased back the red-handled lever on the winch; the motor engaged and the rope began sliding smoothly through the pulley, and Jenny started walking backward down the face of the cliff.

Behind them, Embries and Dr. Fuller, deep in conversation, moved off with Claudia to see a new excavation begun just that morning. Rhys, operating the winch, let the rope unwind slowly, allowing Jenny to abseil down the sheer rock face.

"Ready," announced Nicholas. He stepped to the edge, turned, and called, "Lower away." The excavation supervisor settled at the controls of the second winch, pulled the red lever back, and Nicholas disappeared over the edge.

James knelt to watch as the two walked backward down the steep incline of the slope. He gazed down at the restless wash of the water on the rocks far far below. Gulls circled and dived, working the rocks for small fish. Further out, two boats chuntered slowly by—one of them a police launch—and a third, obviously anchored a little way from the cliff, bobbed in the swell. The keening cry of the ever-wheeling gulls, the low groan of the winches, the far-off burbling of the boat engines, and the drone of the generators in the compound filled the air with a drowsy sound.

The sun was hot, and he was beginning to get a headache from the glare of the sun off the water, and wishing he'd brought some dark glasses.

The boat engines dwindled, and James watched as a diver emerged from the cabin of the anchored boat, threw out the anchor, and began arranging something on the deck. Due to the angle and distance, he could not see what was happening, but guessed the fellow was preparing for a dive.

Jenny and Nicholas had reached the excavation site, a trenchlike pit dug into the cliff face. The place was marked with a number of red-and-white beams—grid sticks, used for measurement in photographs; some of them had white flags attached to help give some indication of the wind's force and direction.

Reaching the excavation area, Jenny waved and called for Rhys to stop the winch. James relayed the message and watched as she dropped into the trench and unclipped the line. Nicholas likewise called for the winch to stop and eased himself into the excavation trench beside the Queen.

The two pulled tools from the bags at their belts.

James looked away and called to the supervisor, "You haven't got a spare hat, have you?"

"No problem, Your Majesty," replied the archaeologist. "I'll be right back."

When James turned back, Jenny and Nicholas were hunkered down in the trench. He could only see the backs of their heads and shoulders as they began scraping away the impacted sediment with trowels. Out on the sea below them, the boat rocked in the waves; the lone skipper was nowhere to be seen.

The supervisor returned with the hat, and James joined him and Rhys at the winch rig. As they began to talk, James felt the back of his neck begin to tingle as the *fiosachd* quickened. He looked around, trying to find the source. He saw Embries and Dr. Fuller near one of the huts, talking to a group of researchers. Moving to the edge of the cliff, he looked down.

"Something wrong, sir?" asked Rhys.

At first James saw nothing unusual—Jenny and Nicholas were still in the trench, digging away; the boat still rocked in the waves a little way off—but as his eye swept back towards the dig site, he noticed a shape in the water. It was difficult to see; the sun's fierce glare on the surface of the water had obscured it the first time. But as he looked, the shape resolved into human form as the diver rose from the depths and swam to the near rocks.

When the diver climbed up out of the water and began ascending the steeply angled slope, the *fiosachd* sent a shock of recognition through him. . .

He spun around and shouted for Rhys. "It's Moira!" he hollered. "She's going for Jenny!"

"Who?" wondered the dig supervisor, ambling nearer.

"I'm going down there," James shouted, taking hold of the nearest rope as Rhys came flying to the cliff top. "Try to get their attention."

Seizing the loose rope, the King began walking backward down the steeply angled slope. His shoes were slick, and he slipped, banging his knee hard; righting himself, he pushed away from the slope, and kept going.

Rhys shouted to alert the security men, then grabbed the second rope and started down. Jenny, in the excavation trench far below, was enraptured. Under Nicholas' expert direction, she had succeeded in freeing two more fragments of ancient pottery from the layer of soil under excavation. Scraping carefully with the edge of her trowel, she was tracing the outline of a third piece, larger than any retrieved so far, when she heard a cry from the slope above and glanced up to see James dangling on a rope partway down the cliff face, with Rhys right behind him.

Above them, the faces of two Special Agents, fierce with concentration, appeared over the cliff top. The security men were shouting and pointing.

*What on earth?* she wondered. As she straightened for a better look, a shadow passed over her, and she heard a grating footstep on the rock. She turned instinctively towards the sound and saw the silver shimmer of a metal object arcing through the air. In the same instant, Nicholas groaned and collapsed at her feet in the trench, the top of his head peeled back, showing bloody bone beneath a loose-flapping scalp.

Jenny sensed a movement above and behind her and dropped to her knees. The silver object sliced the air just inches from her head—accompanied this time by a grunt of effort that ended in a shriek as her unseen assailant leaped upon her.

Jenny felt hands on her throat, and her head was driven down against the side of the trench. Doubled over, her attacker on her back, she felt her chest compressed and she could not breathe. The hands tightened on her throat, and her lungs began to burn. She could not speak or cry out.

Blood-red mist gathered before her eyes. She knew she was just seconds away from blacking out.

Forcing her hands under her chest, Jenny got her feet under her, gave out a groan, and pushed away from the side of the trench. She landed on top of her attacker, and felt the hands loosen their grip. She rolled, squirming onto her stomach, and came face-to-face with the woman she had last seen on the Glenshee road the night of her wedding.

The left side of her face and neck was shriveled, the

scarred skin mottled and slick, bearing the livid bloom of a savage burn. Her hair was darker now, and cut mannishly short, and she was wearing a black wet suit, but Jenny would have recognized her anywhere.

"You!" she gasped. She saw again the snow-covered ravine lit by the flames of the burning wreck, and any fear she felt was swiftly engulfed by the surge of anger at what the woman had tried to do to James.

Moira loosed a wild scream and drove her hands into Jenny's face.

Jenny kicked free, landed on her back, half on top of the unconscious Nicholas. Moira, spitting mad, shouted something and leaped at her once more. Jenny managed to get a foot up and drove her heel into Moira's knee, pushing the leg back. She crashed down on her elbow and came up swinging. She was bleeding from a cut to her forehead, but the silver object was in her hand again. This time Jenny saw it clearly—it was a stainless steel diving knife with a wicked, serrated edge. The blade glinted hard in the light, and Jenny scrambled backwards over Nicholas' inert body.

Moira, triumph in her eyes, dived forward with the knife. Jenny lashed out with her foot and connected solidly with Moira's chin. Her jaw snapped shut with a teeth-shattering crack, and she pitched sideways against the back of the trench. Somehow, she held on to the knife. Gathering her feet beneath her, Moira scrambled closer, the knife glinting in her hand.

There came a shout from the slope above the trench. Moira glanced up to see James and Rhys on ropes above her, half sliding, half skidding down the sheer cliff face. Above them, the two security men, guns in their hands, were shouting for Moira to throw down her weapon and move away.

Jenny saw her attacker look away, and rolled to her feet. As she made to stand, her hand closed on the trowel Nicholas had been using. As Moira's eyes swung back to her prey, Jenny lunged forward, swinging the trowel with all her might.

The sharp-edged tool caught Moira under the arm and gouged a ragged hole in her wet suit up across one breast to her collarbone. Blood gushed crimson from the wound and she staggered back. Jenny seized the advantage and drove in on her. Moira tried to fend her off with the knife, but Jenny knocked it aside with the trowel, nearly severing Moira's fingers with it.

The knife went spinning from Moira's grasp. It flew up out of the trench and Moira lunged after it, throwing herself half out of the excavation trench as the blade went skittering down the slope just out of reach.

Jenny saw Moira's body arch away, and dived for her assailant. Stiffening her arms, she struck Moira in the small of the back. Unbalanced, Moira flipped up over the edge of the trench. She slid forward on her stomach and snatched up the knife; gathering her feet under her, she turned toward Jenny once more.

This time, Jenny was ready. As Moira turned and stood, she pulled one of the metal grid sticks from the soft earth and swung it with all her might, sweeping Moira's feet from under her.

"No!" she screamed. Tumbling backward, she struck the sharply angled slope, slewed sideways, and started to slide. She tried to flatten herself to the rock to slow her descent. *"Exis gorim fortis!"* she cried, scrabbling for a handhold.

Her hands flailed, fingernails scratching. But the bare stone did not yield and the angle dropped away beneath her. Sliding faster, gaining momentum, she struck a rocky outcrop and was pitched into the air.

Moira screamed again—a hissing, spitting sound like that of an enraged cat—and Jenny watched her sail out in a graceful arc as she plunged down and down onto the wave-washed rocks far below.

James was there beside her as the echo of Moira's final, defiant scream faded into the startled cry of the frightened gulls. "It's over," he said, gathering her into his arms. "She's gone."

Embries stood at the summit, surveying the scene below. He and Dr. Fuller had been alerted by the shouts of security personnel, who were now swarming all around the scene, alternately chattering into their microphones, listening to their earpieces, and desperately assuring the royal couple that everything was now under control once more.

Within moments a police cruiser had reached the rocks, and Embries watched in stony silence as Moira's battered body was dragged limp and lifeless onto the boat. As the launch bobbed on the ocean swells, Embries raised a hand to his eyes as if to shield them from the sun and whispered, "Good-bye, Morgian."

## ❋
# Epilogue

As James extended his hand to pull her up beside him on the cliff top, Jenny heard him say her name, and the world seemed to take a peculiar sideways lurch. In that instant, everything was changed. She saw her husband not as the man she knew but as a stranger dressed in a leather cuirass studded with tiny iron rings. His hair was long, and bleached by long hours on horseback in the sun; he wore it in a gold-clasped braid at the side of his head. A whitewashed shield was slung over his shoulder, and a well-used sword hung at his hip. He was leaning on the haft of the longest spear she had ever seen.

A wide band in the shape of a serpentine, tail-swallowing dragon gleamed on his upper arm, and a thick golden torc encircled his throat. His cloak was purple, the color of the emperors of old, and it was folded on his shoulder and secured with a brooch shaped like a winged dragon. He was watching her, his lips curved in a smile of pride and admiration.

Rhys stood a little way off, resting his arms on the iron rim of a large oval shield which had been whitewashed and painted with the sign of the cross. A great hunting horn hung from a strap across his chest, and the blade of his spear was whetted to a keen brilliance.

She heard a rustling of wings beside her, and Embries was there—a young man now, with a wild mane of long dark hair and a cloak made from the wing and tail feathers of ravens and crows. Sunlight glistened on the black feathers in darkly iridescent rainbows, and flecked his pale eyes with fiery gold. He carried a staff of oak topped with a curl of ram's horn inlaid with a delicate silver tracery of ancient Celtic design. His shirt was midnight blue woven with threads of silver which glinted like stars. On his feet were boots of soft leather, and he wore a wide leather belt on which hung a feathered pouch.

"Behold," he said, his voice resonant with an authority she imagined even the wind might obey.

She looked down at herself, and saw that she was dressed in the garb of a warrior queen. Her cloak was scarlet, and bordered with red-gold key work; her shirt was white linen, over which she wore a mail shirt of tiny silver rings. A small shield rimmed with iron hung on her shoulder, and her sword was slender, long, and sharp. Her hair was braided, the plaits bound and held by a silver boar's-head brooch. Her boots were soft white leather, and her belt was woven leather decorated with overlapping shells.

Raising his staff, the Wise Emrys stretched out his hand. "Behold!" he said again. Tilting his face towards a radiant sky, he said, "Lo! In Myrddin's hand she comes through the quickening glow, joining her noble husband, who stands to look upon his realm and ponder thus: is the King made for his kingdom, or kingdom made for King?

"While beleaguered and downcast the Britons sang, doom in shocks split the burning gloom. Lo! God's holy fire revives, the flame of life bestirs itself from ashes not yet spent. The Singer at the Dawn of the Age, the Bard at the Gate of Time, rouses, rises, and shortly wakes! The spark of Avalon glows, fades, and glows again. Lo! The Summer Realm's ancient throne knows once more her master and her lord."

And as the Wise Emrys spoke, she saw that the island of bare, blasted rock miraculously changed. All around her, like a sunstruck emerald aflame in a silver setting, was a

land green and blooming with the first blush of summer—
the fairest of Britain's seven isles, surrounded by a gleaming
silver sea. It was Avalon as it had been once long ago . . . and
would be again.